THEY HAD PROMISES TO KEEP . . .

KATIE—She pledged her body and heart to one man, but believed the promises of wealth and fame another whispered.

MICHAEL—Stripped of everything he had once held dear, he vowed to fight for justice in America and so made a promise that could destroy him and the woman he loved.

KEELY—She struggled to stay alive against the odds, sustained by a single promise—that Katie and Michael would be together again.

TULLY—He needed beautiful Katie for his acting troupe and wanted her for his bed. The promises he made were the lies every man tells.

Also by Sharon Salvato

BITTER EDEN
THE FIRES OF JULY
THE DRUMS OF DECEMBER

Donovan's Daughter

Sharon Salvato

A DELL BOOK

Published by
Dell Publishing Co., Inc.
1 Dag Hammarskjold Plaza
New York, New York 10017

To Raymond Zettler, Jeffrey Zettler, and Thomas Cappadona, three strong men who know how to love their daughters

Dell ® TM 681510, Dell Publishing Co., Inc.

ISBN: 0-440-12118-3

Printed in the United States of America

February 1987

10 9 8 7 6 5 4 3 2 1

WFH

1

MICHAEL Donovan leaned against the open doorway of his cottage. He had the glassy-eyed look of a man stunned beyond coherent thought. Within the space of a few months, he had gone from being an orderly, easygoing man to one for whom nothing made sense. Confused fragments of remembered talk and thought reeled about in his mind like so many bouncing echoes. He couldn't sort out the sense of these any better than he could sort out the twisted fears of his nightmares.

As he stared across the fields, his mind projected an image of his beloved Aislinn running toward him. He could see her brown hair whipping in the wind, her blue eyes sparkling with love for him, her pretty mouth curved with laughter. Then, as suddenly as it had come to taunt him, the vision vanished. With the quickness of a bursting bubble, his lean body slumped against the doorjamb, letting it carry his body's weight and the far heavier weight of his sorrow as he vainly battled the demons of doubt and remorse that had returned. His whole body shuddered feverlike. Unable to shake free of his haunting guilt, Michael kept searching himself for an answer, wondering if there was something he might have done differently to ward off the present circumstances.

He shook his head and rubbed the back of his hands across his eyes trying to clear away the scrambled images of memory. It was too late now. It was all over and nothing could change the past. Even if now he could find an answer, Aislinn was gone; his wife was dead. His family was gone, and tomorrow his home would be gone. No matter how many answers there were, no matter how many reasons he could dream up now, nothing would change.

His attempt to grasp the reality of his situation lasted only a moment, and then he went back to his quest for the magical answer that was not to be found. Surely, he thought, he must have committed a grievous sin to have brought this fate down upon himself. Yet, as hard as he tried, he failed to understand his offense, and that was the most frightening aspect of all. This hideous retribution might continue to devastate him and those he loved if he could not see the error of his ways and do right by God, or the Little People, or whoever it was he had offended. He had put his muscle, sweat, and heart into the Irish soil trying to bring forth a healthy crop, but that hadn't been enough. Nothing had been enough—only he hadn't known that until it was too late. Just at the moment he thought there was hope for himself, for his family, his people, the final shattering blow had come. His whole world had splintered into millions of fragments that could never be put back together again.

He gazed out at the moon-washed landscape. Fields of dark rich earth stretched before him. He knew every grain of soil, as had his father and his grandfather before him. He remembered so well how his father had taken him up and down the rows of potatoes when he was just barely able to toddle, talking about the land and the Faery People who guarded its fertility. Those had been wonderful green days filled with promises. Tonight, however, this land, this rich Irish soil that had always nourished him and had been as familiar to him as his own hands, was alien and filled with rot. He had the awful, cringing sense of shame a child feels when he has tried to do right only to find himself being punished for wrongdoing. Michael longed for some ultimate authority, some almighty judge with whom he could plead and win favor. Like so many other things in his life of late, this belief had become confused and distracted as well. Michael no longer knew who he should turn to for solace—the Christian God with whom he had been raised or to the Little People of his childhood who had never completely lost their power to influence him. Superstition and religious faith had melted and melded into a tangled mass of the pagan of old and the Christian of today. He cringed as he remembered how he had begged Clem Ryan for an answer but had gotten nothing. Yet, there had to be an answer or he couldn't survive.

He had said to Clem, "How have I sinned? I turned the soil. I didn't despair when the 'taties turned bad. I planted again. I thought we had survived the famine. Who was to know it would go on year after year? I never missed paying my rent. I watched my wife and babies die, but I didn't miss my rent. Isn't that enough? Why is he taking my home away from me? Fairmont knows me . . . my family. Why won't he give me time . . . just one more season? What have I done so wrong?"

Even now his face blazed with hot shame as he remembered the tears that had spurted from his eyes without warning. No man should be rendered so helpless that all he had left to him were tears.

Behind him, inside the cottage, he heard the weak mewlings of his daughter. He squeezed his eyes shut, relieved that she had cried. He hadn't realized how tensely he had been waiting to hear some sign of life from her cradle or how frightened he was to go to her without that lively signal. This time he could go to her crib and know that they had been granted one more time together. Once he had taken all his tomorrows for granted, never doubting that those he loved would rise with the sun, smiling and ready for the day. His eyes cast to the edge of the cottage garden. His parents' graves were in a plot beyond the garden to the east of the cottage. Four of his beautiful children and his lovely, laughing Aislinn lay buried in graves not far from those of the elder Donovans. It was a miracle that his little Keely had lived this long, and he was grateful for every moment he had with her. Again he was reminded of his conversation with Clem Ryan. Clem had screwed up his thin, expressive face into a horror mask of bitter disgust as he said, "The damned English don't know what they want. We're slaves for them. No more—just slaves. But then, their hatred of us is so big and awful they'd rather see us dead than in the fields plantin' their 'taties for them." He had looked squarely at Michael, his deep blue eyes almost black with pain as he said again, softly, "It's the Lord's truth, Michael Donovan—they'd rather see us all dead an' in our graves than put a bite of food in our mouths."

"To what end? It makes no sense. There's no reason, Clem!"

"Hatred has always been its own reason, Michael. It needs no other. You may be the lucky one, boyo. Fairmont will knock down your house. He will run you out of here. He will even force you to live in exile. But you will be alive —and without some damned Brit wishin' you weren't."

Michael swung round and through the door, nearly running into Keely's crib. He snatched the child up against his chest as though he would fend off the British then and there. No one, nothing could take this child from him. If he had nothing else, he had this daughter. For the first time that night Michael felt something decent. It was not the flood tide of bitter sorrow that still gathered, but an embattled protectiveness born out of a deep love for his two-year-old Keely. Given a tiny crack in the wall of despair that had encased him, Michael poured all his hopes, dreams, and desires through it and into the starving child.

Keely did not in any way look or behave like a normal two-year-old. She could not walk or talk coherently. Most days she hadn't the strength to sit up unassisted. The famine had robbed her as it was robbing all the children of Ireland. Even before Aislinn's death, the women of the village had been trying to prepare Michael for the loss of his youngest daughter. No one believed that Keely could continue to hang on to her slender thread of life. But Michael hadn't listened to any of their warnings. He couldn't bear to hear them. Keely had to survive, and there was something about the child that made him believe she would. He would look deep into Keely's dark, shiny eyes, and in their depths he was certain he could see her promising that she would live. He saw life and he trusted.

He took the child into the special West Room, the room to which his father and mother had moved when Michael had married and become head of the household. It was the room of the setting sun, the room to which the old people went to live, basking in the golden light of sunset until they entered the eternal night. A warm peat fire burned steadily on the West Room's hearth. Michael brought the child close to the fire and sat down on the hearth rug with her. Holding her close against him, he began to sing to her, warming her with the heat of his own body. With all his being Michael wanted to bind his life force with Keely's. Here in the West Room, a room traditionally designated as belonging to the Little People, Michael felt more powerful, more able to infuse Keely with his strength, his vitality. Here he felt closer to the old gods and the new.

The child's mewling cries quickly subsided and she found comfort in the sound and feeling of her father's resonant voice. She snuggled close against him, her tiny fingers closing over the fold of his shirt. She turned her head toward him until she could look adoringly into his eyes. A smile eased the strain on Michael's face. Keely's dark blue eyes were the one feature the famine had not been able to distort with starvation. He touched the tip of her nose. "You have deep-water eyes, Keely darlin', the deepest and the clearest on God's earth."

She made a low murmuring sound of pleasure as he began to sing again. The low sound of his singing was the melody of life for her. There was a melancholy in it that had no meaning for her except that she had felt it in those around her, and she knew that somehow it was a part of life.

Michael glanced down at her from time to time, and always he would smile, easing the line of his mouth, but it did not ease the pain that shone from his hazel eyes. He was thinking of the morning of Keely's birth. Aislinn, her dark hair damp and curling from her efforts, had smiled up at him. Her cheeks had been too rosy in her pale face, but she had been more beautiful that morning than he had ever seen her before—so beautiful that the sight of her had made Michael's chest hurt with fear that he was losing her. Aislinn had said, "She is a dawn baby, Michael. She is a morning star born as the night is banished. She is our beautiful one . . . Keely. May we name her Keely, Michael? Do you like that name . . . the beautiful one . . . a sign from Our Lady?"

"We'll name her whatever you like, my own beautiful one," Michael had replied, but he had been interested only in kissing Aislinn.

But Aislinn had been insistent that he listen to her and understand what she believed about her newborn daughter. She grabbed his groping hands and clasped them tight against her chest, her large eyes imploring him to be serious for just a moment. When she finally had his attention, she said, "Michael, Keely is special. All of our children have been, I know, but Keely is different. I can feel it." She had looked at him then, and already he could see exhaustion creeping up on her, but she had said, "You'll see, Michael . . . there'll come a time . . . when Keely will mean more to you than any . . ." She had fallen into an exhausted sleep before she could complete what she wanted to say, but she had impressed Michael deeply. He wasn't certain how she knew or in what way she thought Keely was more special than the other children, but he had heard the urgency in her voice, and he believed in Aislinn. He had smiled at his sleeping wife, gently kissing each of her eyelids and then her lips before he left her side to see his special daughter for the first time.

Jennifer Ryan, who had attended her friend during the birth, had just finished swaddling the infant when Michael came from Aislinn.

"She is perfect," Jennifer said with a broad smile. She placed Keely in Michael's arms.

Michael was all smiles. Keely was all that Aislinn had claimed, and he thought he understood why his wife believed she was special. But he didn't—not yet. In his arms, however, lay a perfectly formed, dark-haired, pink-faced little beauty. Keely had opened her eyes, blinking rapidly and sticking her tiny pink tongue at him. Her tiny hands waved about. Michael's heart pounded. Holding Keely was like holding a miniature Aislinn, only different. For even from this first moment, Keely was herself. He had the feeling that this tiny mite of a child was extending her arms up to him, trying to tell him something. But when he mentioned it, Jennifer laughed, saying, "She is hungry, Michael —that is all. Let me take her to Aislinn."

Reluctantly Michael had given Keely to Jennifer, but he couldn't rid himself of the feeling that his daughter had knowingly reached out for him. After that moment he never doubted that Aislinn was correct; the child had been sent as a sign from the Blessed Virgin that their life would be better. Michael, however, was not a man given to looking far into the future. To him the future was no farther away than the harvest. He had planted his potatoes, and that year they seemed to grow well. There had been rejoicing in the Donovan house. But within a week the potatoes had begun to stink of the same rot that had made beggars of the Donovans and all their neighbors the year before. The blight that caused the potatoes to rot had as strong a grip on Ireland as ever, and this year the rot was farther spread than it had been in the past. In the beginning only certain sections of Ireland had been affected, but now the blight was everywhere.

Soon after the blight spread over the land, Michael's sons had begun to sicken and his eldest daughter died of famine fever. Michael had dug the first of the graves at the side of his garden. Clem Ryan had carved and brought a headstone to him and Aislinn. It hadn't eased the pain of losing Maura, but knowing one's friends cared deeply enough to carve a headstone and to share the grief helped make it bearable. After that the deaths in the village came at such a rate that no one could keep up with making the markers. Michael buried his parents and then his three sons. To this day the small mounds of his sons' graves were unmarked. No one but Michael would ever know which boy rested in which grave.

Clem Ryan had lost his oldest boy. The McElroys had lost twin girls. The Donahue children were orphans now living with Clem and Jennifer Ryan. And the list of homeless went on and on. It gave them no comfort to know that their village was not the only one to suffer. All Ireland was suffering, and the dying went on. The village road became a throughway for the homeless and the hungry. Any villager with a scrap of bread or a bit of broth opened his doors to the scores of wanderers who were to be found on the road at any time. Men, women, and children burrowed into the sides of hills to live like animals and, unless someone could feed them, to die like animals. Michael and Ais-

linn had done all they could for the dying Irish of the
roads. They had fed them as often as they were able, gave
what cloth or clothing they could spare, and Michael had
dug roadside graves so often that it had become a part of
his daily chores. Each night as they turned to each other to
seek warmth and comfort in lovemaking, they thanked
God that they were not so destitute as those who went past
their door. They clung to each other and to the hope that
tomorrow would be better. Even when their children died,
they held on to hope and reassured each other that there
was a reason for such seemingly unfair deaths. There
would be more children, and they still had Keely.

The memory of that hope he and Aislinn had held now
made Michael feel ill and filled with bitterness. At that
time he had still believed help would come. He believed the
landlords and the mighty English government would aid
the Irish peasantry through the famine. He could not believe that the Irish would be left to starve and keep on
starving. But no help came. A nation was dying, and still
no help was forthcoming. It seemed as though the entire
world were willing to watch the Irish starve to death, offering no more than bits of unpalatable Indian corn. With
deep bitterness, Michael could recall hearing Mr. Fairmont
talking with three of his well-heeled, well-fed friends about
how the peasants had brought poverty and death on themselves. One of Mr. Fairmont's friends had agreed, adding
that the famine might serve to curtail the population of the
peasants.

All that Michael had seen and heard in the last year and
a half had burned deep into his soul. But until now, this
night when it was all ended, he had never had time to
think about it. All of his time and energy had been needed
just to keep his family alive. There had not been a spare
moment for thought or resentment. He had never had time
to hate. But all of his dedication had come to naught, for
Aislinn had seemed to sicken and die overnight. He knew

that wasn't true, but it had seemed that way. His mind told him that she had never really recovered from Keely's birth and that she had been slowly starving to death over months. But his heart couldn't stand the idea that he had stood by and aided in her death by his helplessness. He still couldn't face that guilt, but neither could he rid himself of it. He ran his hand over the sparse down of Keely's hair. She was all he had left of Aislinn, and he would never let her go or be harmed.

Keely slept, and Michael was still staring into the fire as dawn broke in the east. He began to feel the skeletal fingers of helpless fear clutch at him again. Those hideous fingers rendered him powerless, left him bewildered and immobilized. He didn't know how to banish them. Like so many others, he had not been able to pay the rent on his cottage or his fields this year. But never before had Michael felt the power of his English landlord as he had the day he had asked for an extension of time in which to pay. He had gone to the big house confidently, never once expecting that Mr. Fairmont would doubt his ability to pay or refuse his request. Michael Donovan knew his own worth. He was one of the ablest farmers, one of the most reliable and steady men living on Fairmont ground. He was one of the best. But he had never even gotten to speak to Mr. Fairmont. He had been turned away at the back door, and then two days later Fairmont had called a meeting of his tenants. Without so much as a grimace of sympathy from their landlord, Michael and his fellow villagers had been informed that all tenants who were unable to pay would be given passage to America—or they could put foot to the road if they didn't choose to take the bounty Fairmont was offering. The cottages of the laggards would be knocked down by the end of the month. Michael had stared dumbfounded all the time Mr. Fairmont spoke, then he pushed his way to the front until he stood looking eye to eye with his landlord. Even then he found it nearly impossible to speak. Shaking his head, he finally managed to stammer, "You can't do this, Mr. Fairmont. We've been good tenants. This is my home. I don't want to go to America . . . or anywhere else. I belong here!"

Fairmont had not given him the courtesy of an answer, but with a look of scorn had turned to speak to a man standing beside Michael. Michael had remained glued to the spot where he stood, hat in hand, like a man who was simple and could not understand what was taking place. Had it not been for Liam Flynn taking him by the arm and leading him away, Michael might be standing there still, so shocked had he been.

"Boyo, talkin' to the man will get you naught. Take the tickets of passage while the takin's good. They may not be offered on the morrow," Liam had advised gently and wisely.

"But I don't want to . . . go. Liam, my home is here. Fairmont knows I will pay him. You know me . . . my family. Why is he doing this? I belong here! My family was on this land before Fairmont came. I am Ireland . . . Ireland is me!" Michael had cried.

In a voice so low that Michael almost missed it, Liam said, "There is nothing here for you, Michael. Go while you can."

In the following days Michael had tried to approach Mr. Fairmont many times, but nothing he said or did changed Mr. Fairmont's mind. Now he was watching the sunrise bring vivid color to the hills and fields for the last time. In less than two hours the workmen would arrive to begin knocking down his three-room cottage. By this time tomorrow morning nothing would be left of his home to say that the Donovans had tilled this land and lived on this site for generations.

So desperately was Michael trying to comprehend the unbelievable events that had led up to this morning that he did not hear the rap on the door. Jennifer Ryan walked through the kitchen and main room, then, not finding Michael, poked her head into the special West Room. "Michael? Michael, answer me—are you there?"

His knees protested with sharp pains as he rose from his cramped position by the warm hearth. "I am, Jennifer—come in."

Jennifer looked back over her shoulder, calling, "He's in here," then, with a smile, she entered the West Room, taking it all in. "Ahhh, Michael, have you sat up the whole night with her and the ghosties?"

Embarrassed as Megan Flynn and Maura O'Connor entered the room, he cleared his throat and stared at a point over Jennifer's head. "This is the warmest room in the house. It was cold last night," he murmured.

"Well, there's no need for you to trouble yourself with her any longer. I'm here. Give me the babe. I'll see to her."

Possessively, his square jaw set, Michael pulled Keely closer to him. "She's no bother to me, Jennifer. Keely will stay with me."

A hurt look marred Jennifer's face. She had meant no harm. She had always enjoyed a special friendship with Michael, a trust that went back to their own childhoods. It had been Michael more than anyone else who had been able to comfort her when her oldest boy had died of famine fever last year. There was a time, before she had fallen in love with Clem, and before Michael had met Aislinn, that the villagers had all assumed he and Jennifer would marry. Before she had a chance to speak again, her startled attention was drawn by a command voiced from the open doorway.

"Give the child into her care, Michael."

The three women and Michael all looked to Sheila Flynn, Megan's mother-in-law and undisputed matriarch of the village of Fairmont.

"I wish to speak to you while there is still time, Michael Donovan," Sheila said in a voice that offered no room for dissent. "Let the women see to the cottage and the child. You come with me. We will walk a bit and talk."

Michael hesitated for only a moment, then he gently placed Keely into Jennifer's arms. For a brief moment his gaze locked with hers, then he leaned over and brushed a kiss on Keely's cheek.

In the deep gray of his eyes Jennifer saw too much pain and fear. She lowered her head. She still cared enough for Michael that she could not bear to witness the turmoil within him now. Her heart ached to bring back the loving, laughing man he had been so short a while ago. She squeezed her eyes shut and pushed away the thoughts. "I'll keep her safe and warm, Michael. You know I will," she said in a voice thick with emotion. Then she dared to look into his face, a tremulous smile on her lips. "Now you go on and take a few minutes' fresh air."

His eyes told her what could happen in a few minutes' time. The world could alter irrevocably in a few minutes' time. Lives began and lives ended in minutes. Then he felt ashamed, for he knew that Jennifer knew that as well as he did. He patted the child's head, then touched Jennifer's cheek in a gesture of trusting affection before he walked across the room to take Sheila's arm.

The old woman and Michael, by mutual, unspoken consent, left the cottage and walked slowly along the worn path to Sheila's cottage. Sheila held her silence for so long that Michael began to wonder if she had wanted to talk with him at all, or if she had merely wanted to get him out of the cottage.

As she sensed his growing restlessness, Sheila put an aged but well-formed hand on his arm. "The dead are not easy this day. They are moving about, reminding, remembering." Her eyes scanned the horizon, taking in other cottages. Built of limestone and thatch, these houses had stood for generations.

"When I close my eyes these last few days, I am taken

back to my girlhood, and I can see this village in my mind. What a beautiful place this was, Michael. We owned the land then. The Flynns and the Donovans could call the sod their own. But even after that changed, the village did not. It has changed little over the years. And until this awful time, it was for me the most beautiful place on God's earth.

"Your grandmother and I used to stand beneath that very tree and wait for your grandfather to come home from the fields. Later, after we both married, we'd wait together for Mr. Flynn and him." She sighed, her hand patting his arm seeking comfort as well as giving it. "By tomorrow half the homes you see will be gone, and the people with them. The beauty, too—we'll never be the same here again." She looked up at the hazy sky, then at Michael, her lips pursed in genteel fury. "It's the Devil's work and make no mistake. And happy he must be! So many of these folks will be homeless and many of them will not be able to make their way as well as you will, Michael. Those of us left behind won't be able to help—the land will be changed, the village will be in mourning for those faces we'll never see again. But we'll not be able to do anything but grieve. And grieve we will, Michael, as deeply and as sorrowfully as those of you who will be cast out from here."

Michael sighed. "It is said that Fairmont wants the land for grazing." He fell silent for a moment, then looked at Sheila from the corner of his eye. "I know what you are asking of me, Sheila. You want me to promise you I will look after some of the less fortunate ones, the ones you see as less able than I, Sheila, and I have always done. You know a Donovan has never turned a wanting soul from his door."

Sheila nodded her head. "But that was before, and you had only to share the little supper you had, or to give a man a place to rest his weary head. No more was asked of you than any wretch is free to give. But I am thinking that perhaps the Blessed Lord has it in His mind to ask more of you now, Michael."

A deep sound, almost a cry of pain, erupted from deep inside Michael. He began to speak, then couldn't. He shook his head. "I'm too tired, Sheila. If the Lord is asking, He has chosen the wrong man. I am no Abraham, nor even a Moses. I don't know how to lead anyone, not even myself, to a new land. I have tried to see myself strong, as someone for the others to lean upon. I have tried to think of the lost ones, but . . ." He made an angry gesture. "It is not to be, Sheila. I am in my own skin and none other. All I feel is my own bloody anger and pain. I have become a useless man, Sheila Flynn, though I wish to God and His Holy Saints that I were not." He turned quickly, halting their progress as he said, vehemently, "But it is not to lead them away that I wish I had the strength! I wish . . ."

Sheila's own eyes held a fire that matched Michael's. "I know what you wish, Michael Donovan. Not a man, nor a woman, nor a babe in arms does not wish the same thing. We all wish to be granted the power to wipe the British from our lands. Any one of us would give his life, and perhaps more, to be able to say we are free! But the Lord has not granted us that. On this day it is not to be, and you must turn your eyes and your heart away from it. Look forward, Michael! Take yourself out of the past. Let those of us left behind cry for the past. Save yourself for the day to come—the day when you and others like you can free Ireland."

Again Michael emitted a great, soul-shuddering sigh. "You mean live to fight another day."

"Yes, I mean that. Make no mistake, Michael—the Irish will fight until they are free. We cannot live in bondage. We will fight and fight until the end of time. But there are others matters that must come first for you now. Your daughter needs you. And others need you. We cannot al-

low more Irish deaths at the hand of English indifference.
When you walk the road out of here, look at your people—
lambs to the slaughter, that's what many are. They are
unprepared for life in a new and alien land. They need you,
Michael Donovan. They need your strength. I heard you
cry to Liam. 'I am Ireland. Ireland is me!' you said. I heard
you say that, and I believe it is true. Your people need you,
Michael Donovan."

She stopped walking and looked into his face. She saw a
fine man. Wavy, dark chestnut hair framed a face perhaps
a bit longer in the jaw than beauty decreed. He had large,
clear gray eyes. And though they were darkened with pain
and doubt this day, Sheila knew how fervently and how
warmly Michael's eyes could glow. His nose was straight
and well formed. His forehead was broad, his eyebrows
were heavy, masculine slashes, emphasizing the depth and
beauty of his eyes. His mouth was pressed into a tense line
today, but on other days it was wont to curve up at the
ends, bringing the long smile lines in Michael's cheeks to
prominence. His was a strong face, a good face, a man's
face. She smiled, past and present mingling again. "Do not
ever forget that you are a Donovan, Michael. You come
from a good and fine line of men and women—a line of
leaders. Live up to your heritage."

A flash of hope sprang into his eyes, then died again. "I
don't know how," he said simply.

Sheila gazed at him. She was surrounded by ghosts. She
saw his grandfather Riobard's face rise up to overshadow
Michael's, and then the face of Padriac, his father, was
there. Sheila could feel years roll away from her for the
moment. She was young again and thinking as she had
before what a handsome man—men—she was looking at.
Michael had noticed the distracted look on her face. Sheila
smiled, for the rugged masculinity of his face was softened
by the sensitive look of caring that was the way of all the
Donovan men. No matter how much he claimed that he

was too tired to help, she knew him to be strong. Gaunt from the months of privation and worry and sorrow, he still vibrated with vitality. Sheila had great faith in a father's ability to bestow on his son the mettle required to bear the crosses God sent. Because she had known his father, and the father of his father, and because they had seemed to come to visit her today, Sheila believed she knew Michael in a way no other human ever would. "You'll find a way," she said firmly. "When the time comes and Ireland calls, you'll find a way."

"Ireland is always calling. Her whole existence is an anguished cry, Sheila," Michael said.

"Don't you argue with me, young man! I know of what I speak. The day will come when you will hear the call, and it will be your name. On that day you will answer, Michael Donovan."

For a moment a twinkling merriment lit up Michael's gray eyes, reminding Sheila what a lighthearted young man he had been. "Is that a command, Sheila Flynn?"

She chuckled. "You may consider it a message from an aged angel and the best bit of foresight this old harridan has to offer you."

Michael shuddered, and he said unsteadily, "I'll miss you, Sheila." Then, after an emotion-filled silence, he added, "Would you see to . . . to the graves for me after Keely and I leave? I wouldn't want Aislinn and the children to think I have forgotten them." He looked at her with a sudden, appalling thought. "Sure Fairmont will leave the graves in peace! When he has the cottages knocked down, he wouldn't permit the graves to be desecrated. Even Fairmont wouldn't do that, would he?" he asked, his eyes seeking the desired answer in Sheila's face.

"Michael, my darlin', no one and nothing can bring harm to your Aislinn or your children now. She and your children are in the arms of God, guarded by His holy angels. Let Fairmont do his worst and he cannot touch them.

Now, see to yourself. It is time we went back. When the men and the soldiers come, you don't want them thinkin' you can't bear to watch. Even if it is the truth, we'll not give them the satisfaction."

Michael took a deep breath, squared his broad shoulders, and stood a bit straighter. Sheila smiled, her raddled old face shining with a beauty she had possessed all her life and would probably retain to her dying day. She said with satisfaction, "Ayeee, you are a true Donovan through and through. I knew you were."

Michael returned her smile but said, "Don't be hasty. It is yet to be seen. I have not yet found my way, Sheila Flynn."

By the time they had walked back to the cottage, Michael could hear the sounds of the soldiers and the workmen approaching, though he could not see them. His eyes fixed on the crest of the hill, almost defying the first head to make itself seen on the road. Talking to Sheila had calmed him, restoring his inner strength and resolve. But the return to the cottage and the sounds of the approaching soldiers and workmen shattered all that. Once again Michael felt choked, unable to draw enough air into his lungs. He began to take great gulping breaths that sounded like sighs. With a shudder, he looked at his well-tended front yard and forced his mind to think logically. He still had things to do for the Donovans of Ireland. The moment had come and he didn't want a Donovan to be caught scurrying around his own house trying to gather up his belongings when the wreckers arrived. He wanted to be outside and waiting—in command of himself. As Sheila had said, he might have precious little to call his own, but he had himself. He refused to give any Englishman the satisfaction of seeing an Irishman behaving like a beaten cur.

He was pleasantly surprised to find that Jennifer, Megan, and Maura had completed the little packing there was left to be done. Most of the household furnishings he had given away days ago, keeping only those things to the last that he and Keely would need. All of his belongings, his clothing, a few books—the pride of the Donovan house since his grandfather's time—and Keely's clothing were tightly packed in one sack. In another was a precious cache of food that would see them through the first part of their journey into exile. A table, two chairs, a rocker, Keely's crib, and a bedstead had been pushed against the wall near the door along with miscellaneous crockery pots, jars, and cooking utensils.

Michael touched the back of the rocker. How often had he watched Aislinn rock one or another of their babies in this chair? How many nights had he and Aislinn sat up late by the fire, her in the rocker carding flax, himself reading aloud so they could both enjoy a story and he could practice his reading. He said, "Have you any use for this, Jennifer? I'd like to know you had it . . . and so would Aislinn. She always had a special warm place in her heart for you and Clem."

Shy color flooded into Jennifer's cheeks. With head down she said, "I thank you, Michael. I'll take the best care of Aislinn's things—as good as she would herself, God rest her soul." She was quiet for a moment, then, with a sudden burst of tears, she threw herself into Michael's arms. "There is no justice, Michael! You should not be torn from us, driven from your home and us who love you!"

Michael closed his eyes and crushed her to him, holding her there for a moment, drawing strength from her, then gently he pushed her from him, his large hands still grasping her shoulders. He looked deep into her eyes. "Pray to the Almighty that I find a way to right that wrong, Jenny. That is all we can do this black day."

At Megan Flynn's signal, Liam and Clem Ryan came in to carry out the furniture. Michael picked up the two packs of his personal belongings, slinging them over his shoulder to settle on his broad back. Then he took Keely from Maura's arms and walked out of his family home for the last time. He was standing straight-backed and proud at the side of the road when the wrecking crew with its guard of His Majesty's soldiers came to knock down the Donovan cottage and half a dozen others.

The clang of hammer and ball were heard almost immediately. Clouds of dust rose into the air to sting the onlookers' eyes and throats as centuries-old lime and rock crashed to the ground. It seemed to take so little time and effort to destroy a building that had represented home and happiness to generations of Donovans. The garden wall, built of fieldstone from his own land, lay broken. Rock was scattered in all directions, all order gone. Memories and dreams were made of stronger stuff than rock and mortar, Michael told himself, though the sight of his home reduced to a heap of broken stone was a most bitter reminder.

The soldiers were edgy and on guard, as if they anticipated trouble to come at any moment and from any quarter. With perverse amusement Michael speculated that Mr. Fairmont had informed the regiment leader of Michael's patriotic bent and of his affiliation with Young Ireland, a group that called for homeland freedom from British rule.

Michael had been a naive and hopeful follower of Daniel O'Connell until late in 1843. O'Connell had called for a "monster meeting" on the fields of Clontarf, near Dublin, where Brian Boru had driven the Norsemen from Ireland seven hundred years earlier. The Clontarf meeting had thrown the British government into a mindless spin. As if they expected a powerful armed insurrection, the British had sent troops and provisions to Dublin Castle. A regiment of infantrymen was kept in readiness to suppress a revolt that existed only in the British imagination, and all they were really to do was deal with a meeting called by a man who believed in and practiced peace. The British had forbidden the meeting at the last hour, and even then O'Connell had maintained peace and asked his multitude of people to end the "monster meeting" and go quietly home. The people, Michael among them, had done as they were asked.

The British had not been impressed with the sincerity of O'Connell's efforts and had him arrested. In so doing the British government clearly announced to Michael and other young men like him that they would never listen to a peaceful Irishman. After that dark day, he had joined the less peaceable Young Ireland and had taken no care to hide his politics.

The soldiers eyed the crowd apprehensively, seeking comfort in their numbers and weapons. The sight brought a bitter smile to Michael's lips. His gaze met and held that of the soldier nearest him. Every drop of hatred he harboured within himself he poured through the windows of his eyes. The feeling he got from watching the wariness in his adversary turn to fear was cold, but oddly satisfying. Before this terrible day he had never known that emotional satisfaction could come from cold hatred. The realization instantaneously changed him.

He barely saw the fieldstone of the cottages crashing to the ground. The dust rising as the stone rolled to the dirt road meant nothing. He no longer held any attachment to the now ruined roof that he had himself repaired and rethatched countless times. With a sharp, quick pang that cut through him, Michael Donovan realized that in the few minutes it had taken to destroy his lifelong home he had managed to detach himself, to retreat behind some secure barrier of safety. This was not his home they destroyed. This was not himself the soldiers saw standing in the road. All that he was would be carried hidden in his heart, his love of Ireland, and his hatred of all that was British.

Though he had thought to stay until the wrecking was

completed, it no longer seemed important. He turned to
Sheila, who had remained close by, and kissed her cheek.

"I'll be on my way now, Sheila. I am satisfied that there
is nothing left to keep me here. A quick good-bye while the
others' attention is caught is best. Thank you, and take
care of them. . . ." He gave a nod toward the seven
graves.

"You'll have my prayers with you wherever you go, Michael." Then, as an afterthought, for she did not believe
the wizened little girl Michael held so protectively could
survive the journey, she added, "As will our Keely. God go
with you, and the devil see only your back."

Michael's intention of stealing away while his friends
and neighbors were mesmerized by the felling of the
houses was not to be. Almost as if a signal was passed, they
turned to him as he took his first few steps along the road.
In hostile reaction the soldiers brought their bayonets
down and stepped into the crowd, shouting orders to dis-
band.

Angry as a banty rooster, Liam Flynn showed he was
truly his mother's son and hopped in front of the foremost
soldier. "Kill me if you will, you bloody coward, but say
good-bye to a good man I will!"

With a look of scorn, Michael stepped up and grabbed
Liam in an embrace, crushing him to himself and Keely.
"You're a good man, Liam Flynn. I'll miss you sorely,"
Michael said in a low voice.

Others crowded in close to Michael and Liam, placing
their bodies between the two men and the child and the
jittery, uncertain British infantrymen. The soldiers exchanged glances at each other, then looked to their captain. A step was taken back, then another. The empty
space they left was quickly filled by the villagers. Men
shook Michael's hand, wishing him the best, some embraced him and awkwardly pressed pennies hard come by

into his hand. "For the journey—you'll need it more than we."

Others pressed small packets of food into his hands. "For Keely. Take care, Michael, take care, and don't forget us."

"Never!" he vowed. "Never!"

2

BUOYED up by his vow of fidelity and the well wishes of his friends and neighbors, Michael walked briskly along the road to catch up with the groups of other evicted families. He moved speedily along the well-beaten, hard-packed path leading uphill and away from the valley that embraced Fairmont. As it had all morning, the sun broke through the haze, momentarily brightening the landscape, then faded back behind the persistent mists and clouds. When Michael reached the summit of the familiar farm road, he turned and looked down at what was left of the once orderly village in which he had been born. So many of the cottages were now piles of rubble, scarring the beauty of Fairmont. Billows of chalky dust hung low on the heavy air. Bits of thatch blew along the ground with each breathy gust of wind. Michael stared for a moment, then his eyes were irresistibly drawn to the Big House, and the sense of calm detachment he had been trying to cultivate dissolved. Though he hated all Englishmen in general, and Reginald Fairmont in particular, the Big House had been at the hub of his existence for his entire life. He had no idea how one led a life that was not tied to the stabilizing factor of the landlord's grand mansion at the center of existence. As he

looked back at the solid gray stone bulk of Fairmont, he
realized that, regardless of his wishes or efforts, there was a
part of himself that was being left here. An important part
of Michael Donovan was Fairmont, just as part of him
belonged to his ancestors. There was nothing to be done
about it; he would just have to go on with his life with that
part of him left behind.

Michael sighed, trying to shake himself free of this renewed hold his old home seemed to have on him. And in
the next moment he set his jaw hard and a glint came into
his eyes as he thought harshly that he had been no better
than a slave to Reginald Fairmont. He decided that no
Donovan would bend his back for such a man ever again.
With his emotions swinging wildly from buoyant defiance
to abject loneliness and longing for home, Michael didn't
hear Jennifer Ryan calling his name or see her puffing up
the hill to catch up with him.

"Michael! For the love of God, man, can't you hear me
calling?"

Michael murmured an apology and waited until she had
caught her breath.

Still puffing, she looked up at his face and laughed.
"They say beggars can't be choosers—I should be grateful
you stopped."

A puzzled look in his eyes, Michael smiled, then joined
her laughter. "And why would you be feeling like a beggar
to me, Jenny Ryan?"

Jennifer smiled, then frowned, uncertain how she should
begin and not at all certain how he would receive her request. She plunged directly to the heart of her problem.
"You know Clem's cousin, Katie?"

"Of course, I know Katie," Michael said, now truly puzzled.

"Well, Katie is filled with bitterness and all sorts of other
nonsense she has gotten from all those books she's always
reading. It's turned her against us, Michael. She's leavin'.

We've all tried to talk sense to her, but she'll have none of it."

"And she's leavin' home, Jenny?"

Jennifer shrugged. "We had some heated talkin', Michael . . . and Clem isn't patient . . . with Katie. She's somewhere on the road ahead of you. I've come to ask if you'd keep an eye on her," Jennifer said, then looked away from him. "I know I've no right to ask, and you've enough on your plate for two strong men, but could you . . ." She looked directly at him again and shrugged, not really knowing what she wanted Michael to do for Katie. "She's so young—and she knows so little of the world even if she thinks her books have taught her all. She says she wants to sing on a stage—the innocence of her!"

"I'll do what I can, Jenny, but you know Katie. If she were going to listen to anyone, it would be Clem, and still she is going. If her own people can't stop her, I can't promise she'll listen to me. All I can do is give my word that I will try."

Jennifer shook her head. "I'm not askin' you to try to keep her here. I'm not certain himself would allow her back in the house. It was not an easy time for any of us, but especially Clem. I'd just be grateful if you'd see her safely on the boat . . . and whatever else might happen along the way."

"You've got a soft heart, Jenny, and I give you my word I'll do my best for Fairmont's little firebrand." Giving her a last, quick, one-armed hug, Michael turned and set off once again to catch up with the others and to find Katie Ryan.

He came abreast of Sean Sweeney, his wife, and their two remaining children. Sweeney had once been one of the more prosperous of Fairmont's tenants. It was a sorry day to see him brought so low, Michael thought, then thought again that it had a comical side, for Sweeney might well have paid his rent and stayed on had his wife been willing to part with some of their possessions. As it was all four members of the family were loaded down with boxes, sacks, and cases like so many packhorses. Despite the coolness of the day, Sweeney, the most heavily loaded of all, was sweating profusely.

"Good day to you, Michael," Sean said. "Did you see that my two boys romped right across the fairy paths on Fairmont's west side this morning while the old man was about his dirty work on our house? It's a certainty he'll never see a peaceful old age!"

Michael grinned, wishing he had witnessed the trespass of the fairy paths. Had his own Tom lived, no doubt he would have been about the mischief with the Sweeney boys.

Pat Sweeney gave Michael an impish grin. "We have brought the worst of luck down upon him for many years, Father says."

"If it can be done, I am sure you have inspired the Little People to do him a bad turn," Michael said agreeably.

Sean stopped to catch his breath, carefully straightening his back and mopping his brow of sweat. "The beggar could at least have given us the use of the farm cart, seein' as how he's doin' his worst by sendin' us off bag and baggage into the unknown. Ah, but he is a beast of a man—no heart at all."

"I would help you, Sean, but I am loaded down myself," Michael said.

Sean made a face. "Ah, this is the least of it, Michael. We'll carry our belongings, but who is to know what will happen then? It will be a lucky day for us if there truly is such a vessel and if it is seaworthy. Who but a fool would take the word of a man who knocks down another man's house?" Sweeney had no sooner gotten the words out than Mrs. Sweeney had let out a keening that nearly shattered the ears of both men.

Sean laid his boxes and packs down on the road and

hurried to the aid of his distressed wife. Michael hurried
ahead, hoping that distance would lessen the piercing quality of Mrs. Sweeney's alarm and that, with good fortune,
the Sweeneys would not catch up with him again until they
were in Liverpool. He passed several tight little clusters of
people making their way. In none of these groups did he
see Katie Ryan. Nearly half an hour later, when he had
made his way to the head of the straggling caravan, he
found Katie swinging along the road as if she hadn't a care
in the world. He had to smile in appreciation. She was one
of the few who had chosen to travel as lightly as possible,
which Michael thought an admirable trait. He came
abreast of her to have her flashing green eyes meet his
gaze, as though she had been expecting him. Michael decided, while in the embrace of her bold glance, that there
was a great deal admirable about Katie Ryan. Then his
cheeks reddened, for he was still in the habit of thinking of
himself as a married man. Even his embarrassment, however, could not stop the smile that came to his lips, and for
a moment he looked like any roguishly handsome, carefree
young Irishman.

Katie gave him a strangely adult, knowing look, then
said gaily, "Good mornin' to you, Michael Donovan, and
you also, young Keely. Could we dare ask for a better day
than we have to set out on a new adventure?"

Michael laughed. Despite the lingering gray mist, Katie
made him feel good. At this moment it was difficult to
think of taking care of her, or to respect the consensus
opinion about this outspoken young woman. Most of the
villagers thought she was fast—and foolish beyond measure for breaking with her family and traveling halfway
across the world by herself. Michael had overheard several
discussions in which various versions of Katie's fate, as a
wrong-headed girl on her way to a bad end had been offered. But as he looked at her sunny face, she didn't seem
at all someone who was heading for a bad end. The fact

that virtually no one approved of her or what she was doing didn't appear to bother Katie at all. But Michael had to wonder.

Before long he was thinking of how worried Jennifer was for Katie's safety. He mused aloud, "You think of this as an adventure, do you, Katie?"

"I do, and so should you. What is there for any of us back there?" she asked, tossing her head vaguely in the direction of Fairmont. "In the best years we had little, and in the hard years we've had nothing. I know more dead people than I do living. I am tired of watching those I love die on a road or in a scalpeen." She paused for a minute, her sea-green eyes filled with anger and revulsion, then said, "No one cares. Do you know what will be done with the land those cottages stood on?" Before he could answer, she went on. "It will be turned into grazing land. And do you know why, Michael? I will tell you. It is because cows are more valuable and less trouble than the Irish people. That is what we are worth in our own homeland—less than the blades of grass a dumb animal eats!"

"You are an angry woman, Katie," Michael said quietly.

"I am, and I will stay angry until someone cares for me for who I am and does not hate me because I am an Irish peasant."

"That could take a long time."

"Then it will take a long time. But I will not settle for less—nor will I stop searching until I am dead or until someone important sees the woman and not the peasant." Then, almost as if she could throw away bad humor with the same ease she would toss away a scrap of paper, she turned to him and smiled brightly. "I know our ship is most likely to go to a Canadian port, but I am going to the United States—New York. That is a very big city with lots of work and many houses for everyone. It is much better there for the Irish. I have it on good authority."

"Good authority? And who might this good authority be?" Michael asked, amused at her smugness.

Katie's head whipped around and she gave him a look filled with green fire. "You're no different from the other ignorant sods in the village! You all think that if a book is read something must be wrong! Well, let me tell you, Michael Donovan, if a few more of our people were educated, we wouldn't be treated as dumb animals! You can just be about your own business, Michael. I prefer to walk alone!" She increased her speed, then slowed, her anger losing steam. "Did Clem send you after me . . . to talk sense to me?" She shook her head. "No, it wouldn't be Clem. His pride wouldn't permit it. It must have been Jennifer. That is why you are talking to me, isn't it?"

Michael chewed at his lower lip, his eyes fixed on Katie. The idea of saying something soothing but untrue entered his mind and vanished so swiftly he barely realized the thought was there. Katie Ryan would never accept anything but the truth, and he sensed that she would instantly know the difference. This girl, who couldn't be more than nineteen at most, had more true courage and a pure, clean anger than Michael had seen in a long time. He knew he didn't want to lose her friendship. "It's true, Katie, to a point. Jenny asked me to look after you, and I sought you among the people walking. But I have not remained by your side talking for Jenny's sake. I am here now for my own sake. I like talking with you."

Slightly mollified, but still suspicious, Katie nodded her head once, and Michael knew he had won another chance with her, but little more.

With the saucy impudence so typical of her, Katie looked at him from the corner of her eye. "I'm not just a fool with my head filled with ideas I got from books. And I didn't decide to leave quickly or easily, Michael. I'll be going to America to friends." She patted a squarish package and smiled. "Letters from those who have gone before us."

"I never called you a fool, Katie, nor do I think you one, but neither are you worldly wise or experienced. Did your friends tell you that the passage is nearly three times as much to the United States as it is to a British port? You don't think that old skinflint Fairmont is going to do the likes of us the favor of sending us to the United States, do you?"

Katie looked away, her mouth turned down at the corners. "I do not think Mr. Fairmont would do anything at all for us. I am sure we will be lucky if there really is a boat to take us. But once I have put my foot on American soil, Mr. Fairmont nor any other man can stop me from going where I please. They say America is a place of freedom for everyone. I will walk to New York if I have to! I am going to sing. They say Americans love the theater. I'll be famous."

Michael threw back his head and laughed.

"You're laughing at me! Making fun of me! Michael Donovan! I don't have to put up with the likes of you!" She pulled her arms in tight against her body, as if the gesture would magically rid her of Michael. Awkwardly, she ran a few steps before turning back to face him, her eyes blazing. "I will get there, Michael. I will walk or crawl if I must, but I will have my day in the sun! I will make something of myself—in New York."

Michael reached out with his free hand. "Don't run from me, Katie. I believe you, I do, girl. But even you must admit that it is a tall order you are asking of yourself."

She stared at him for a moment, deciding, then she shrugged, and the sun broke through the clouds with her smile. "Keely is getting restless. She doesn't like all this bickering and angry talk. Let's sit over there by the trees and I'll share my dinner with you."

Michael looked down at the child nestled in the crook of

his left arm, then back at Katie. "The others will get ahead of us, and we must get to Cork."

Katie shrugged. "Then walk on. Me—I'm going to eat, and then I will run and catch up with the old ones if that is what is in my mind to do."

Michael stood, awkwardly holding Keely in one arm, then with a nod of recognition to Katie and a grin, he walked over to the trees and sat down. He dug a blanket out of his pack and spread it out on the ground. Gently, he put Keely down on the blanket.

Katie returned his smile, then opened her bag. Fishing through it, she pulled out half a loaf of fresh bread and some cheese. "Aren't you glad you decided to stay? It looks good, doesn't it?"

"I am very glad I decided to stay. I thought I had a feast of my own. Sheila gave us some turnips." He handed his offering over to Katie's charge and she fixed portions for each of them, then took charge of Keely as well.

To Michael's surprise, he didn't mind Katie's high-handed ways with him. He sat back and began to enjoy a leisurely and delicious dinner, something he had not done in many a day.

Billowy white clouds pushed their way through the morning mists and chased rain and darkness from the sky. Katie Ryan is a witch, he thought fondly. He was relaxed on what might rank as one of the worst days of his life. For the first time in over a year, his stomach wasn't growling with hunger and he wasn't worried about his only remaining daughter. All this and more was due to the effect of a mere girl. One he was supposed to be helping. He chuckled, wondering if Jenny were wiser than he had thought.

"What are you finding so amusing?" Katie asked, looking up from the piece of bread and cheese both she and Keely had been nibbling.

"I was just wondering if Jenny asked me to see to your welfare because she thought you would see to mine. You seem to be doing all the looking after. You even brought the sun out."

Katie's eyes glowed green with pleasure. She smiled, then returned her attention to Keely.

Michael closed his eyes, his mind filled with a new vision of Katie Ryan in gloriously brilliant colors. Katie, he mused sleepily. She couldn't be more than nineteen years old—about the age Aislinn was when he had married her —yet there was a power in Katie he couldn't recall in any other woman—not even Aislinn. For the first time he saw Katie in a new light, looking beyond the image Jennifer, Clem, and Katie's grandmother had always presented to him. To them Katie was a headstrong girl headed for trouble. But at this moment, comfortable as it was, and under Katie's magical spell, he could see her only as a brave and courageous woman who wanted something better for herself and would stop at nothing until she had reached her goal. Indomitable—that was what Katie was, he decided. She was a creature rare and wonderful, someone to be admired and loved for what she was doing.

He hadn't realized he had been asleep until she was shaking his shoulder, saying, "If we don't move on, Michael, we really will have to run to catch up with the others."

Michael didn't move. He was transfixed by the remnants of his thoughts and her brilliant sea-green eyes. They were almost blue, but not quite. He was happy where he was. He didn't want to leave. Ever. "Katie," he murmured.

She gave him a wry and knowing smile, plus the toe of her boot in his hip. "Get up, man! You're a slow-moving creature to be sure."

As soon as they neared the body of the group, Michael knew something was wrong. Kevin Murphy raced past him and bolted across a field to a small village, purple in the distance. Katie and Michael exchanged curious glances, then Michael reached out and grabbed the arm of Lawrence McGinty as he ran after Kevin.

"What has happened? You're all running about like madmen."

" 'Tis old Mother Murphy. She keeled right over on the road, and it's a priest we're lookin' for. She hasn't had her last rites," he cried as he shook free of Michael's restraining hand and hurried off across the field.

"God bless her soul, the old cow," Katie murmured. She remembered the unkind words Mrs. Murphy had had for her before they had left the village but did not repeat them. Katie took a deep breath and looked over at Michael, expecting to see a scowl of reproach on his face, but he seemed to be in his own world of thought. It lightened Katie's heart to be spared his disapproval. For all her bravado, it hurt deeply and made her feel frightened deep within when all those who loved her and those she loved turned against her. Why hadn't anyone wished her well? Was there no one who could see, as she did, that there was no future for her or any young person in Ireland? Did she have to die on this godforsaken land to prove she was a good daughter?

Michael startled her out of her gloomy thoughts as he said, "This will keep us here for the night. By the time a priest is found and Mrs. Murphy properly put to her rest, no one will journey on tonight. We should find a good place for ourselves."

3

IT had taken all that night and half of the next day to see to the last rites and burial of Mrs. Murphy. A wake of sorts had been held, which delayed their leave-taking but improved the spirits and outlook of several of the Fairmont travelers. They did not arrive in Cork until the end of the week, and all the Fairmont people were curious and more than a little frightened to enter what they considered a big city.

The town of Cork had become a hive of activity and struggling humanity during the time of famine. John Duross, a constable of Cork, had the task of seeing the passengers who entered and exited the town safely on board steamers. Those comparatively few who entered the port presented no problem to him. Seldom were there so many that His Majesty's Passenger Acts were in any way violated. It also helped that those people entering Cork by steamship almost always had a destination in mind and were not likely to fall prey to the profiteers and pranksters that abounded on any dockside. The thousands of Irish peasants who streamed into the town were the main source of John's worries, presenting problems as complex as those of a Chinese puzzle. As many human puzzle parts had to be neatly squashed into as small and compact a space as possible and still form a neat and lawful package. The Passenger Acts counted two children as one adult, so that on occasion as many as eight hundred were crowded on the deck of one steamer bound for Liverpool. He had never suspected what a highly rigorous job his would be until the famine struck and all of Ireland, it seemed to him, was determined to funnel through his small port on their way to other more distant and prosperous places.

For Michael, Cork came as a relief and a surprise. Having done nothing but farm potatoes all his life, he had assumed that a city was going to cause him no end of trouble and discomfort. But as he looked about him and saw draymen delivering goods and dockmen loading heavy bales and boxes, he knew that he could do any of these tasks and perhaps enjoy them. The work, after all, was not so different from what he did on his patch. Didn't he load heavy bales of straw, or peat, or bags of potatoes? Hadn't he driven many a heavy farm cart, which was not so much smaller than or different from a dray? He felt relieved to discover that he liked the noise and smells of the city. Even the odors, he thought, were not so very different from the farm. His stride became a little firmer and his chin lifted as some of his pride and a feeling of potency returned. Without realizing it, Michael Donovan had begun to look ahead into his future rather than backward into his past.

For Katie, Cork was quite a different matter. Ostensibly the bolder of the two of them, she kept all her doubts hidden deep inside, safely concealed from those who claimed to love her and want only what was best for her. But actually, all Katie had to buoy herself was a great desire to live a better life and a terrible fear of making a disastrous mistake. These two forces propelled her into all manner of bravery and inspired deeds that she might not otherwise have attempted.

As soon as she, Michael, and Keely had entered Cork,

Katie had felt overwhelmed—physically and psychically assaulted. Until this day the largest crowd of people Katie had ever seen had been at her county fair. Half of those she could have greeted by name. Cork presented her with a sea of strange faces. She had not been aware that she was unprepared to live among strangers. Michael's words to her began to take on new meaning.

Unlike Michael, she found no affinity to the smells or noises in Cork. The cacophony in the town confused her and the mixture of smells assaulted her senses. Scents of freshly baked breads warred with odors of pine tar and hemp and flax and sweet odors she had no name for. She moved closer to Michael so that her arm touched his with each step. Not ready to admit her weakness to him, she still needed the reassuring security of his closeness. Michael's massive shoulders, the muscular wedge of his torso, and the fierce protectiveness she knew to be deeply ingrained in his nature made her feel better able to face this new threat of a place of strangers and strangeness. With Michael near her she would have the time and security to learn to make her own way. And, she thought comfortably, if she should have trouble, she could always count on him to help her.

As they moved closer to the heart of the town, Michael encountered a problem of his own for which he was quite unprepared. Contrary to what Katie thought, he did read books, and enjoyed doing so, but for the most part he did not read English, preferring the Gaelic of his ancestors. As they moved along, more and more of the signs and notices were written in English. While being able to make out words, Michael was very slow and not terribly certain of his accuracy. He turned to Katie, confessing his difficulty, and unwittingly he gave Katie's pride a great and sorely needed boost.

She walked at his side, quiet for the most part, only speaking when there was a sign to read. Each time her abilities were called upon she reassured herself with the knowledge that she was a better and faster reader than Michael. It wasn't much to hang her confidence on, but at least it was something, and to a small degree it told her that Michael needed her as much as she needed him. And now she was willing to admit that she did need him and that perhaps Jennifer loved her more than she thought.

The three of them made their way to the Dublin and Liverpool Steam Packet Company, where the agent emphasized several times that Mr. Fairmont, his dear friend, had paid the passage, which was the princely sum of ten shillings per person. The exiles of Fairmont who had crowded into the office and had been forced to wait until all were present were properly impressed. They gave their thanks and blessings to the man who was driving them from their homes and their homeland.

Listening, Michael, for the first time, looked upon Reginald Fairmont with something other than shock. Hearing these unfortunate, hardworking people praise Fairmont because he had taken ten shillings from his pocket to be rid of the burden their hunger imposed on him made him angry. The insides of him felt as though he had been reamed as he allowed Fairmont's insult to touch the deepest part of himself. Before he lost control and could say things he would later regret, and perhaps lose his own passage tickets, he whirled for the door, banging into the man next to him. He fled from the office with three passage tickets crushed in his right hand.

Katie followed silently after him, still too unsure of herself to express the indignation she felt. Her eyes darkened with the suddenness of a roiling bank of storm clouds. She was angry. She tugged on Michael's sleeve.

"Wait here for me, please, Michael. Don't go on without me! I'll be but a moment."

All Michael wanted was to put distance between himself and this place. He did not want to stand still or wait for anything—not even Katie. But before he could protest, she had darted back through the mob and into the steam packet office. She pushed her way to the counter and stuck her hand in front of the agent's face. "I'll be after the passage ticket for Mrs. Frank Murphy, if you please!"

Without questioning, the agent sorted through the list of names he had been given by Reginald Fairmont. "Would that be Josephine Murphy?"

"It would," said Katie.

He handed her the ticket with still another reminder of Mr. Fairmont's generosity.

She took the ticket from his hand, this time daring to let the anger in her eyes touch him, then Katie haughtily stalked out of the office.

With the spirit of anger still flying about her like a battle flag, she rejoined Michael. "Put out your hand," she demanded.

Puzzled, Michael outstretched his hand, a question poised on his lips.

Into his outstretched palm she slapped the ticket of passage. "Sell it! We'll be ten shillings richer with thanks owing to Mrs. Murphy and the 'great' generosity of Mr. Reginald Fairmont."

Michael laughed, hitched Keely up higher on his arm and showed her the ticket. "See that, Keely? We have a very shrewd woman with us to look after our interests."

"You're not angry, are you?" Katie asked, all her newfound daring disappearing along with her anger.

Michael put his free arm across her shoulders, drawing her close. "I wish I had thought of it myself."

The wharf was now a mad scene of shouting, pushing crowds. In cities like Cork an unscrupulous element made an occupation of preying on the unwary, stealing luggage and forcing people to pay to regain their belongings by patronizing certain rooming houses. These runners were in evidence wherever Michael looked. Michael had heard of

such people, but he found it almost impossible to believe
that they would victimize people as destitute as those who
now crowded the waterfront. But he was soon proven
wrong. With a new group of emigrants, the runners were a
busy crew, grabbing anything that wasn't nailed down.
Men raced frantically after their belongings, dodging other
runners and the police, who seemed callously on the side of
the wrongdoers.

Michael heard the unmistakable cries of Mrs. Sweeney
before he saw her. He pushed the crowd aside, clearing a
path to the wailing woman as Katie hurried after him. The
embattled woman stood keening in earsplitting tones as she
defended her family's possessions from two persistent runners. Mrs. Sweeney had a white-knuckled death grip on a
valise, her plump bottom firmly planted on and securing
the other belongings. One of the assailants had hold of the
other side of the valise in a tug-of-war.

Michael handed Keely to Katie. With one big hand, he
grabbed the runner by the scruff of his neck and whirled
him around.

"Where are your manners, boyo? Don't you hear that
the lady has refused your kind offer? Now be a good lad
and be off."

"Hands off me friend," shouted the other runner, his
fists clenched as he came at Michael.

Michael, with stiff arm, shoved the first man into the
path of the second. Before either man could regain his
balance, his elbows close to his body, Michael stepped forward, driving his fist into the diaphragm of the second
runner. The man doubled over, coughing and gasping for
air. Michael brought his right fist up under the man's chin,
then stood back, poised for the next blow. The man col-
lapsed with a grunt.

The first man's small eyes registered surprise, then a
cunning avarice. "That's Dan O'Connor you just floored,

boyo. He didn't even get in a single punch! Do you know of Dan O'Connor?"

"No, I don't know of Dan O'Connor—nor do I want to," Michael said gruffly. "Be off with you. Take his carcass and let us be."

"Dan O'Connor is the best saloon fighter in Cork. Until today he has never been defeated or even marked by another man," the runner persisted. "Have you done any fighting yourself?"

"I don't fight."

The man smirked. "You don't fight? You looked to me like you knew what you were about. Ol' Dan didn't get off a shot. He never even saw what hit him."

"Your friend is coming round. I've asked you, man to man, to leave us in peace, now . . ."

The man put his hands up and backed off two steps. "Think about the fighting, boyo. You don't look so prosperous that you couldn't stand having a few extra coins to jingle in your pockets." He paused long enough to see a spark of interest flare in Michael's expressive gray eyes. "Me name's Will Smith. For a small share of your winnings, I can hold the purse and see to it you get a fair match. I know me way around the fight game. If you decide it's the thing for you, ask for me, Will Smith, at McGinty's Tavern tonight. I'll be there."

Smith didn't wait for Michael's reply but hauled Dan O'Connor to his feet and marched him off. When he reached the edge of the ring of onlookers, he called back to Michael. "I'll pass the word that you and yours are to be left in peace. I can't say that all will listen, but I'll do my best for you. Remember Will Smith—McGinty's! Tonight!"

Michael and Katie exchanged glances, laughter in their eyes, before they turned their attention to Mrs. Sweeney. By now the poor woman had been frightened into silence and was sitting huddled atop her boxes while she grasped the handle of the valise to her ample bosom. As Katie soothed her, one by one the male members of her family began to straggle back.

Michael explained what had happened, then added, "But it is as much your fault as any, Sean. You cannot be leaving your wife alone to guard your possessions. The dock is alive with these vermin."

With the Sweeneys once more together with all their belongings intact, Katie and Michael and Keely started back toward the main body of the town. Using the small cache of money they had, they stopped at a street stall to purchase a potato pie for each of them. Keely ate hers by herself and managed to smear it all over her face. Michael's heart contracted with joy. It was so good to see her doing something on her own and enjoying it. So far the journey had done her no harm, and there were even some signs that it was doing her good.

Katie interrupted his thoughts. "Our ship doesn't leave until ten tomorrow morning," Katie said. "We'll have to do something with ourselves tonight."

"As soon as we finish eating, I'll see to selling Mrs. Murphy's passage. That should give us more than enough to pay for a place to sleep," Michael said between bites, then added, "I never knew what a pleasure it is to eat decent food."

Katie murmured agreement but wasn't to be turned away from her aim. "We are very poor, Michael. What will we do in Liverpool? I suppose I could try to get Mrs. Murphy's passage ticket there too, but . . ."

"We'll manage. We know how to live poor," Michael said complacently.

Too complacently for Katie's taste. She said, "You are a good fighter, Michael. Everybody in the village knows it."

"I don't fight," Michael said again.

"But you used to!" Katie said. "Before you joined the older men in their meetings you used to love fisticuffs."

"I was a young smart aleck then and knew no better than to use me fists and me mouth to prove what a man I was."

Katie scoffed. "And now you're such an old and decrepit creature that all that is left to you is wisdom?"

"I am thirty-one years old!" Michael bellowed.

Katie looked away from him. "Maybe you're right. Too old to be fighting in taverns, you are. You were probably just lucky to get in the first punch with Danny O'Connor. It's no wonder you have such a fear of starting out fresh in a new country."

"And what is that supposed to mean?"

"Not a thing! I am just seeing your point of view, Michael. It means nothing else. What could it mean?"

The following morning Michael joined the mad scramble to board the steamer with a blackened eye, a bruise on his jaw, two badly skinned fists, and a slight limp that came as a result of his last bout, when his desperate opponent kicked him in the thigh. But his bodily aches were considerably soothed by the feeling of nearly a pound sterling in his pocket. Katie carried Keely, walking behind Michael as he shoved people aside to let her pass. She was smiling brightly, her green eyes sparkling with pride and triumph.

The passage to Liverpool was little better than a nightmare. It took from twenty-two to thirty-six hours to cross, depending upon the weather, they had been told. Michael and Katie both were praying fervently for fair weather, for the deck was packed solid with people and there was no place aboard the steamer for the passengers to seek shelter. The entire trip would be taken right on deck in the open air. Even a short rain would leave them a sodden mass of misery, and Michael dared not even consider what a storm would bring. He tucked Keely securely under his coat against his chest and covered her as best he could. The three of them huddled near the ship's funnel for warmth, their teeth gritted against the sparks and ash that occasionally spewed forth. They waited for the very long, uncomfortable voyage to be over.

All Katie could think of was how terribly much longer the passage to America would be. "D'you suppose the ship to America will be like this one, Michael?"

"No. We won't be on deck the whole voyage. We'll have a place to sleep. Those ships are much bigger," he said, feigning a confidence he didn't feel. He had seen the big ships before, but he had no real knowledge of what it was like to travel on one. He had heard them called "coffin ships," but didn't quite know why. That was something he didn't dare let himself think on too much. He put his hand on Katie's shoulder and squeezed reassuringly. "We'll be all right, Katie. We'll find a way to make ourselves comfortable. Haven't we done all right so far? I've got more money in my pocket this moment than I have had at any other time in my life."

Katie looked up at him. "I believe you, Michael—we'll be fine. But you won't leave me, will you? I mean, we'll make the voyage together, won't we?"

His eyes shone with amusement. "Is this the very independent and very educated Miss Katie Ryan asking for my company?"

She blushed and answered softly, "It is."

Liverpool was an astounding sight for the emigrants. For country folk it was an enormous metropolis. The second largest city in England, it had a character all its own. Liverpool was prosperous, having first garnered its wealth through the slave trade and privateering, and later with the commerce of American cotton and emigration. The Manchester mills depended upon the trade that came from the southern states through Liverpool. A full two-thirds of the large waves of European emigrants passed through Liverpool. The city had been built on the ambitions of these traders and had the look of affluence. The streets of Liverpool were wider and the public buildings more massive than those found in any other English city. The Albert Docks alone were enough to strike awe and reverence into the hearts of the passengers on the incoming steamer. Liverpool, unlike other cities, was not a tangled mass of wooden piers and a sea of masts crowded together. The Albert Docks, opened by the Prince Consort in 1845, were gigantic. Its warehouses stretched out beyond the passengers' line of sight and sported enormous cast-iron Doric pillars. The docks themselves were vast walls of granite-rimmed stone.

Katie was shivering with excitement and apprehension. "It's like a fairy world, Michael. It'll swallow us up whole and we'll never come out. How will we ever know which ship is ours? What will happen to us if we board the wrong one?"

Michael chuckled as he put his arm around Katie's shoulders and pulled her against him. "You are stirring us a real witches' brew, aren't you, girl?"

"But it's true! Look around you, Michael. There's no end to it. And such buildings—one of them is as big as all of Fairmont! Mother Mary, I hope New York isn't like this."

Michael looked around him. Katie was right; it was big. And busy. It seemed there were no idle hands on the Liverpool docks. Steamers plied up and down the river Mersey, steam whistles blowing in warning or greeting to other ships. Tugs and smaller boats with their oiled sails moved gracefully among the larger craft. Pleasure boats and cargo ships that brought brimstone, cotton, timber, coffee, cocoa, ginger, turpentine, sugar, tar, tallow and tobacco, and dozens of other useful and exotic imports moved side by side in congenial confusion. American steamers of the Collins line rode at anchor. Cunard transatlantic steamboats with their distinctive red funnels encrusted with the white salt of ocean spray saluted their rivals with cannon. Michael smiled.

"Well, Katie, you just read the signs for us and I'll find our way through this maze of ships and buildings. That's all it is, you know, a maze, no more complicated than the hedges of Fairmont." The smile still on his face, Michael again looked all about him, letting the excitement of Liverpool's docks sink deep inside, then he turned to Katie, his face now serious. "But there is one thing that is not like Fairmont, Katie. I am going to need your help. I must learn to speak this English language better than I do. It was one thing to say those few things necessary to Mr. Fairmont, and another to make myself understood here. And Gaelic will get me nowhere when we get to America. Will you teach me to speak it well and read it as fast as you can?"

Katie beamed with pleasure. This was the first time in her life that someone had given her something other than criticism for her bookishness and her desire to learn. With her cheeks glowing rosy, Katie looked up at him. "I would love to teach you. You are the only one who has ever wanted to share the things I have learned. But you must also learn to write in English. That is important, too."

"And to write—agreed. Now, would you ask one of the constables where we might find the agents' offices?"

Katie felt very proud of herself as she marched up to the constable asking in clear English for the information she and Michael and all of the other Fairmont villagers needed. After she had gotten her directions, they headed north toward the Goree Piazza, which took its name from Goree Island off the coast of Senegal.

"The constable said that this was the place the slavers took their cargoes. All the slavers' offices were in the Goree Piazza." Katie's intelligent gaze took in everything around her. She was quiet for a while, then she said, "Now this is the place where they send us so that we, too, can be shipped off. Isn't it strange, Michael, that there always seems to be special places in the world where unwanted people are collected? It is as if we all slide down the world's slop trough and end up in one or another refuse heap. Why do you suppose that is? Do you think it is possible that there is something tainted about us that other people sense and instantly hate?"

"You talk nonsense, girl," Michael snapped with an overabundance of anger.

Katie didn't let it pass. "If you think it is nonsense, why does it make you so angry?"

"Because it *is* nonsense! Say something with some merit and I won't be angry."

"I think it is because you are afraid it might be true—or partly so. If it weren't, why would it happen so often? Why would we be going to the Goree Piazza, the same place used for slaves?"

"Perhaps the fault is not in the unfortunate ones whose lives are dictated but in those who think they have the power to do so."

"But why do they have the power?" Katie persisted.

"Because there are men of peace and men of war. The peacemakers keep the world a place worth living in and the warriors spread about a little bit of hell no matter where they go. For that they are the rulers, but they are never the victors."

As they moved away from the dock area, the city changed. Here were the narrow, dirty, infested streets that plagued all cities. They walked along Waterloo Street and saw all the city evils they had been warned of by their priest. Shipping agents' and brokers' offices were sprinkled in abundance on both sides of the street along with fifteen provision shops and sixteen public houses, which spilled from their doors drunken patrons along with the stale odors of all manner of spirits. Crimps, touts, man-catchers, runners by whatever name darted about the street, some burdened down with the luggage of the unfortunates.

"Hold Keely close, Michael. I don't like this place— there are evil men here. They might do anything."

Michael nodded, then handed her a scrap of paper he had been given with the name of the agent the Fairmont people were to seek out. "What does it say, Katie?"

"William Fitzhugh," she read.

"Do you see the name? Tell me what these signs say."

"That one is for a Mr. Tapscott. Michael! He sends ships to New York! It says so right on his sign."

"But he isn't Mr. Fitzhugh and he'll not be sending any Fairmont people anywhere without passage money. Do you see Fitzhugh's name?"

"No, not yet. There is a Mr. Saul, and there is a Hornden and Company . . . oh! There is Fitzhugh!"

Several doors down, they entered the narrow little office and identified themselves. Michael listened carefully to the man behind the desk as he spoke. The man spoke quick, clipped English, making no accommodation for his Gaelic-speaking customers. Michael did not catch all that he said and wondered what he would have done without Katie. Michael was of two minds regarding the man. He was either impatient or indifferent to their problem understanding the language. But he was giving them advice, and that said something positive about the man. And it said something good about Mr. Fairmont as well. Fairmont must have told Mr. Fitzhugh to inform his people as well as possible.

"You must beware," intoned Mr. Fitzhugh, "of men who tell you they will 'dollar' your money. They will tell you that English gold is not acceptable in America. You must not believe them for it is completely untrue. English gold is good everywhere! And whatever you do, do not accept a 'California piece.' Men ask a sovereign for such a piece and they are worth only the eighth part of a far-thing."

A gasp, then broken sobbing was heard from one of the many Fairmonters who had followed Katie and Michael into the office.

Fitzhugh looked down at his desk. "I see at least one of you has already fallen prey to our unscrupulous element. Well, let it be a lesson to the rest of you. The people in America have no desire to have their shores overburdened with the destitute. It is your responsibility to see that you do not arrive in such condition."

"And how are we supposed to avoid that?" called a man from the rear of the dark little office. "If we were not destitute we would not have left our homes in the first place."

Fitzhugh did not like such questions and comments directed to him. "I am sure a little honest labor and sobriety would work wonders. However, that is not my concern. Remember that none of you shall be permitted to board ship without a medical inspection. Be at the Doctor's Shop at ten o'clock sharp."

"When do we sail?" Kevin Murphy asked.

"In the next three to four days. But mind—you must always be alert for the ship that may come in early," said Fitzhugh.

"What do you mean?" Katie asked. "Have we no set time to sail?"

"We are not a steamship line, young woman. Your bene-factor, Mr. Fairmont, and I have chartered this ship at our own expense. It will sail when it has been fully booked and not a moment before that. Nor a moment after."

Several others asked questions, and with each answer Mr. Fitzhugh's replies became terser and terser. His earlier impatience became more evident.

Katie and Michael left the agent's office dispirited. "It's such a long journey," Katie sighed. "The distance in miles is a small part though, isn't it, Michael? I feel like I have become an old woman overnight. Do you feel that too?"

"Don't complain to me about it, Katie. I still feel like an earthworm from your last bit of observation and philosophy. I don't think I can stand another dose of it. I live in the pig trough of the world and now I am to become an old man overnight and am destined to a long journey whose length is not determined by its mileage. What has happened to my cheerful girl who was setting out on an adventure?"

Katie giggled. "You are right. I have turned sour and grim. I must be tired, and, well . . . I do have the right. Do you know, Michael, that neither of us has shut our eyes for more than a few minutes for two full days? Only Keely has slept. Aren't you tired?"

Michael stared at her as though he had heard a great revelation. He handed Keely into her arms, then marched back into Fitzhugh's office. When he returned he had instructions as to how to get to a decent lodging house and who to ask for when he got there. He also had a scribbled note of introduction from Fitzhugh stating that he was recommending Michael and Katie.

The charge for bed only at the house Fitzhugh had sent them to was four pence, and the beds were actually boards stretched across supports. No bedding was included in the price. However, neither Michael nor Katie complained. They had been in Liverpool for only a few hours, but already they had learned that this accommodation was as good, if not better, than anything else they might find. Hardly a man or a woman they had met since their arrival didn't have some story to tell of being cheated, abused, or robbed. They paid the sum asked and were glad to rest themselves on the bare boards. Minutes after they had fed Keely and tucked her comfortably in a nest of blankets, both Michael and Katie were sound asleep.

Katie awakened early the next morning. Everyone else

in the room was still asleep. How different an awakening this was from all her others at Fairmont, and how good it felt to Katie just to have a few moments in which to be alone. When she considered the many hours and days she had spent at Fairmont walking alone or sitting by the stream or lying awake at night in her own bed trying to decide if she should leave her home in search of something better, it seemed odd that now, when she had actually taken the irrevocable step of setting forth, she hadn't found a single moment in which to reflect upon her actions. Ever since her arrival in Cork there had been noise and confusion and fear to be faced minute to minute. All the strangeness seemed to carry with it a discordant sound that blotted out all her efforts at thought. She was thankful for this quiet moment to herself.

The sounds of men and women snoring, coughing, stirring on their hard beds was natural and normal and in its own way comforting to Katie. She looked at Michael. He was balanced precariously on the edge of the board. He had taken Keely from her blanket nest and she was now tucked securely in the crook of his arm, her small body occupying the greater portion of the board. Katie smiled in satisfaction as she looked at Keely's sleeping face. She and Michael had done well by the child on the journey thus far. Keely looked healthier now than she had the day they left Fairmont. With care, and the aid of old Mrs. Murphy's ticket money, and Michael's winnings at his fights, the child had eaten better than she had since her birth. Katie took that as a sign of blessing. Everyone had said the little girl would not survive for more than a week. Not only had she survived, but she was growing stronger.

With a sigh, however, Katie looked upon Keely in another way. Today Keely, Michael, and herself would have to present themselves to the doctors of Liverpool to be declared fit to board the ship. She was reasonably certain that she and Michael would have no difficulty, but would Keely pass their examination?

With a sudden burst of energy and determination, Katie reached for Michael's pack and fished through it until she found a clean outfit for Keely. Then, gently and without awakening Michael, she took the sleeping child from her father.

"Come on, my little princess, we are going to see what we can do toward making you look every bit the grand lady your Daddy and I know you are. We'll dazzle those doctors so much they won't think twice about letting you on board."

Katie went outside and began to hunt for a water source that was clean enough to use to bathe the child and herself. It had been a long time since any of them had had the opportunity to really clean themselves. Katie had never before known what a cruel punishment it was to be unable to wash whenever one wished. Behind the house next to the boardinghouse she saw a barrel filled with rainwater. With a smile and a stealthy step she headed right for it, admonishing Keely, "Not a peep out of you! I don't think we would be given the use of the water any more than we'd be given free passages to America. We will have to be as quiet and shrewd as the Little People."

With complete sensual pleasure, Katie scrubbed both of them, washing their hair and reveling in the cold water running down her shirt. It was a tedious process, with Katie having to wash one part of herself, then another, as she dared not undress. The tedium of the chore in no way altered her pleasure in being clean again. Even Keely waved her small, thin arms and smiled at Katie. The child made no noise, and Katie wondered if Keely had understood her warning to be quiet. Because Keely did not talk as other children her age did, it was assumed she didn't understand either. Katie wasn't so certain. She quickly decided that Keely had understood. She wanted her to understand, because she had come to love Keely in the time they had traveled together, and she knew that Michael loved the child more than his own life.

Feeling happy for the moment, she gathered Keely into her arms and rubbed her moist skin to warm her up. As soon as she was far enough away from the rain barrel she began to laugh. "Let's go wake your Daddy. I have a marvelous idea that this is going to be our lucky day. Nothing can go wrong with us today, Keely—absolutely nothing!"

The child said nothing, but her dark blue eyes followed Katie's every expression.

Undaunted by the silence, Katie kept on talking. She was fascinated by the beauty of Keely's eyes. They were so dark they were almost violet in tone, and a keen intelligence was there. Katie was certain of it. "You know, Keely, when I awakened this morning, I was thinking that I had made a terrible mistake in leaving home. I was thinking that nothing could be worse than the hateful people of Liverpool, and that even if I starved it would be better to die among people who are honorable than it would be to live with people who steal from each other and do terrible things to one another. But I was wrong. We are clean and we are going to pass the inspection by the doctors. I don't know what we'll find in America, but I know our journey will be blessed." She looked down at the child. "You don't understand a bit of what I am saying, do you, little girl? I talk too much and I talk too fast for you." Then smiling, she added, "But it doesn't matter. We will be together, you and me and Michael. We'll be all right."

Michael was awakening when they returned to the room. His eyes registered fright as he patted the spot that had grown cool in Keely's absence, then anger came quickly as he saw Katie walking toward him with Keely in her arms. "What do you mean taking her from me without my knowing?"

"Hold your temper, Michael Donovan, and take a good

look at your daughter. She is as clean as a new rose and she is dressed to please the eye of the most heartless doctor."

Only slightly mollified, and feeling threatened, he refused to admit his deep fright. He took Keely and inspected her as if she were an article he might purchase. Finally he eased and with a deep breath finally admitted, "You frightened me. I didn't know where either of you had gone. I kept thinking I was having a nightmare. The next time awaken me and let me go with you. It isn't safe for either of you to be going about without someone to protect you."

Katie looked at the ground. "You are right, of course, but I didn't think. I wanted to surprise you. Doesn't she look lovely?" she asked wistfully.

Michael swallowed hard, still battling with the strength of his emotions, moved forward, and pulled Katie into his embrace. He stood there for a moment, Keely between them, then he said, "You both look beautiful." He fell silent again, keeping Katie pressed against him and Keely. "Don't ever scare me like that again. I thought you were gone."

4

AT fifteen minutes till ten o'clock, Michael and Katie and Keely arrived at the Doctor's Shop.

"Oh, no!" Katie cried in dismay. "We should have come much earlier! Look at all the people, Michael. It will be hours before we get our turn."

Michael had never seen so many people queued up in a line, and they were the worst-looking, most rag-tag bunch he had ever set eyes on. Even Katie's worries about them not passing the inspection were quelled. Not one man or woman that she could see was clean. Many had obvious sores on their bodies and were scratching as if they had just risen from a bed of fleas.

Michael took Katie's arm and steered her to the rear of the line. "Perhaps the doctors will make short shrift of most of these. It is plain enough to see that many of these people cannot travel as they are. If there are doctors by the government's order, there must also be medical aid."

"Such a faith you have in the English," Katie said acidly.

Katie pulled inside herself. She kept her elbows tight against her body, not wanting to be any nearer the sick and filthy men and women standing beside her than she needed to be. But as she protected herself from these people's vermin and their illness, she seethed inwardly at the landlords and the English and the famine that had reduced these people to what they were now. All the anger that Michael's kindness and protectiveness had succeeded in easing came rushing back to her now.

Through overhearing bits and pieces of conversation, Katie learned that the Doctor's Shop was not open all day. She turned to Michael, saying, "The bell tower has just struck the hour of two and we must be at least fifty or more places away from the doctor's window, Michael. The shop closes at three o'clock and will not open again until tomorrow at ten o'clock. What will happen if we do not get inspected and they call for our ship to sail?"

The man standing in front of her answered before Michael had a chance to. "You don't get the medical inspection stamp on your ticket and you don't sail, lassie—that is what happens."

"But will another ship honor our passage tickets if we do not make our own ship?"

"What shipping line?" the man asked.

Katie turned worried green eyes on him. "It is not a shipping line—it is a chartered ship, taken especially for us by our landlord."

The man laughed bitterly. "You poor sods. It'll be a coffin ship—and not a chance of anyone else honoring such a passage. You better get your tickets stamped or be ready to live in Liverpool. No one else will want you."

"Oh, Michael . . . did you hear? What will we do?" Katie asked. The tears in her eyes mixed with and then melted away the anger that had made them so brilliant a green.

"Don't cry over it yet, Katie," Michael said gently. "We may still get to the front of the line before the window is closed, and wasn't it one Katie Ryan who assured me that today is going to be a lucky day for us? Have you no faith, girl? Or are you telling me that your faith is in the bad? The day isn't over yet, and if the Little People promised you luck, then luck you shall have."

"You know there was no promise," Katie said, sniffing. "I just felt good 'cause for once my hair was clean and I could feel the skin of my cheek without grime on it, an' Keely looked like a pretty little girl and I felt good and told you that. But it isn't true, Michael. It isn't true at all. No one cares about us—not the Little People or God or the Virgin or the angels or anyone!"

Michael's big hand came down on her shoulder. He shook her until her head bobbed and tears flew from her face. "I'll not have you talking that way ever again, Katie Ryan! I'll leave you here alone to the mercies of the devil if one more such word comes from your mouth. We will get through this line and we'll board our ship. That is my last word on it."

But Michael was wrong. They did not get through the line that day. With only three people ahead of them, the window on the Doctor's Shop was slammed shut for the day. To make matters worse, they received word that night that their ship would sail the next day at one o'clock.

"We know we cannot count on that being the correct time. It will sail when its turn on the Mersey comes, Michael. It might even sail at eight o'clock in the morning before the Doctor's Shop is even open. We'll never make it on board! I have jinxed all our good luck!" Katie dissolved into a miserable ball of tears and hopelessness. Michael put his arm around her and began to walk up and down the street in front of their lodgings. He chuckled softly as she turned her tearstained face up to him. "Are you going to leave me here to the devil's mercies?"

"Katie, Katie, do you not hear yourself? You are saying that you've jinxed the luck you said we never had. You are tired, my little Katie—just too tired and too lovely to have to put up with all this."

By mutual agreement they returned to the lodging house and settled back into the room they had left that morning. Michael made Keely comfortable. He emptied out one of his packs and took the time to fashion a hammock for Keely that could be strung securely between the two boards that made up his and Katie's beds. Soon he had his little daughter comfortable and secure.

As Michael worked to fashion the bed for Keely, Katie prepared a cold meal for them out of their supplies. She laid the repast out on the board of her bed and turned to him. "Will you forgive my silliness, Michael?"

Before he had time to think of Aislinn, or his lost happiness, he had crossed the space between them and had Katie Ryan in his arms and his lips on hers.

Katie melted against him. She had dreamed so often that Michael would take her in his arms just like this, but it had always been no more than a dream to her. She had always known that it could never happen, and yet—here she was in his arms, her face wet with tears and her heart pounding so hard he, too, must be able to feel it. She felt the easing of the muscles in his arm and the slight withdrawal of his desire and she grasped him, wrapping her arms fully around him, holding him near to her.

"Don't let me go, Michael. Hold me. I know I am foolish, and I should be on my knees begging your forgiveness for the nuisance I am to you, but, please, don't leave me here—and don't let go of me."

Michael ran the tips of his fingers along the side of her face, then took a strand of her dark auburn hair. Using the clean, fresh-smelling tendril as a feather, he caressed her neck and face. "You'll never need my forgiveness, Katie, love, for you could never do anything I would not love you for."

Love! Love me for! The words flew in Katie's heart like wildly colored butterflies in a field of flowers, but she dared not say them aloud for fear they might mean something other than what she wished, something special to Michael. She knew she was thinking nonsense, but he had said *love*. Was it possible that Michael might truly mean *love* in the same way she meant love? Could he, could Michael Donovan ever love Katie Ryan? How she wanted to ask, but no words would come from her smiling mouth.

Michael kissed each corner of her smile, then, as Keely cooed from her hammock, both Michael and Katie turned their attention to the child. The rest of the evening was spent in comfortable companionship, but no more mention of love was made. Nor were there any more tentative, tender kisses. Katie wrapped herself in the warmth of the memory of Michael's lips on hers and fell asleep full of wishes and wonderment.

They took no chances the following morning. Both Katie and Michael were awake before the birds had begun to scavenge in the dirty streets, and they were lined up in front of the Doctor's Shop before six o'clock that morning. Now, all they could hope was that their ship would not sail out of the Mersey docks before ten o'clock, when the Doctor's Shop opened its shutters.

"Even if it does sail without us, we still have a chance of getting aboard," Michael said. "An old man I met told me that a boat can be hired to go after the ship. It takes some time for the sailing ships to get to the open sea."

"Oh, yes, and we are so rich and well padded in the pockets that we can hire a boat whenever we wish!" Katie said heatedly. She was immediately remorseful of her sharp tongue. After last night she had vowed to be sweet and have nothing but the nicest things to say so that if there were any doubt in Michael's mind that she was worthy of being loved he would soon forget it. Here she was with her wicked tongue wagging about in her head, her vows so quickly forgotten. "I'm sorry," she said contritely, but not very convincingly.

He laughed. "It is still cheaper than trying to get the

money for more passage tickets, and a far cry better than trying to stay in Liverpool. Though it has some fair streets and some admirable buildings, I don't think Liverpool is the place for us. I'll be glad to see the back of it."

"The place for us?" Katie repeated, and looked up at him. "Do you mean that, Michael? When you are thinking of the place for you and Keely, do you think of me being there as well?"

Michael looked down at her eager, questioning face. His eyebrow raised, giving him a rakish look. "If I didn't know Katie Ryan to be a headstrong, independent young woman in need of the support or care of no man or woman, I'd think you were asking me about my intentions regarding you."

Katie blushed to the roots of her auburn hair. "Oh, no! Of course, I'd not do that! I was meanin'—just because we're traveling together. That's all . . . isn't that right?"

"What else?" Michael asked with a straight face, which he couldn't maintain. He burst out laughing.

Katie was insulted and wouldn't look at him. They stood in silence until the Doctor's Shop opened.

Two doctors took their positions behind the window and opened the shutters. One motioned to Katie, the other to Michael. The doctor who crooked his finger at Katie already looked bored, and he had already glanced at the clock on his desk twice. He was already eager for three o'clock to arrive.

"What is your name?" he asked.

"Kathleen Margaret Ryan," she replied.

"Are you quite well?"

"Indeed, I am!" Katie said staunchly with her best smile, trying to show all of her very white, even teeth.

He made a face. He had seen a lot of teeth. "Show your tongue."

She opened her mouth wide, and stuck out her tongue as far as she could.

He stamped her passage ticket.

Katie stood staring at the ticket, stunned. "That's all? I'm free to go?"

"Next," he said. "Hurry along now, I've a lot of tongues to see."

"Michael!" she cried. "I am free to board the ship! I am healthy!"

Boarding ship was an experience none of the passengers was prepared for. It was true that all of them had heard stories of what had happened to others during such a boarding, but the reality far exceeded the imaginings that came with the tales of woe. As many as sixteen ships left the docks in a day, and the American liners carried one thousand passengers each. The dock area was a bedlam, a steaming swell of men, women, and children frantically trying to grapple with a foreign tongue and find the proper place in the proper line for the proper ship to the proper destination. This was complicated further for most of the emigrants understood little of what was shouted to them, partly due to the language barrier, but also because of the unrelenting confusion. Chaos was made worse by the runners who were still milling about stealing luggage or changing good money to worthless and ship's captains who would not permit passengers to board until all the cargo was stowed.

Michael with his heavily laden backpack swinging awkwardly, held Keely tightly in one arm and grabbed Katie's hand with his free hand. He was desperately tense and fearful that he would lose his grip on one or the other of them. "Hold fast to me," he warned Katie. "You could be trampled here."

His fears were fed by the many passengers making a frantic attempt to board the ship in the loading slip at the time. Men, women, and children were being shoved along a narrow gangplank, while others were clambering up the side of the ship like spider-legged monkeys. With a piercing scream a man plunged down into the muddy water of the Mersey. Three men on the dock reached for the floundering man.

"Holy Jesus," Michael breathed. "Hold fast, Katie, love, or I'll be fishin' you out of the filthy water. It's worth our lives just to get aboard."

"Which one is our ship?" Katie asked. Her hand was bloodless and numb from Michael's grip, but she didn't complain, for she was as frightened as he. Her other hand had nearly as tight a grasp on his coat.

"Katie, could you manage Keely with one arm?"

"I could," she said.

"Take her from me and hold fast to my coat. For the love of God, Katie, no matter what happens or what I do, don't let go!"

"I won't, Michael! I won't let go for anything."

Katie took Keely from Michael, telling the little girl to wrap her arms around her neck and not let go. Michael watched as Katie secured Keely in her arms. Though Keely cooperated and was holding fast to Katie, her small hands entwined around Katie's neck, Michael wasn't satisfied. He took off his backpack and fished through it until he came up with a rope belt. He fastened the belt around Keely and Katie.

"Michael, it is too tight! We can hardly draw breath!" Katie complained with pleading eyes.

"It will only be until we are safely aboard. Be my good girl, Katie, and hold tight to me." Michael set his jaw and moved forward like a battering ram. With only the slightest twinge of guilt did he recall his promise to Sheila to look after the other Fairmonters. Right now he felt no loyalty or obligation to anyone but himself and his two little women. With both hands clenched in tight fists and his big shoulders shoving aside any who were in his way, he made for the gangplank. The press of the crowd tested every ounce of strength he had. Always he was aware of

Katie's grip on his coat. Twice he felt it falter, and with a mighty heave he shoved, knocking from the plank one man and felling another. He did not even look back to see if either man was all right. Not until he had the three of them safely on deck did he look to see if any of the others needed help.

The boarding was a nightmare. As soon as passengers reached the deck, they clustered together in frightened, shocked huddles, not moving, not knowing where to go or what to do. Among them hawkers pranced, trying to talk them into buying wares. The ship's captain and the crew were not interested in steerage passengers. Their hands were full with the duties of getting a ship ready to sail. The hauling of blocks and ropes and the shouted orders were all that occupied their minds and hands. Terrified passengers made the orders nearly impossible to hear, and quickly the officers were hoarse and irritable. Katie's eyes were wide with fear and wonder as the huge sheets of sail went up. It was like looking at a sky of canvas. Already the motion of the rocking ship was making her queasy, and they hadn't even left the dock.

"Deaide! Deaide!" a child cried in Gaelic. Michael recognized the voice as one of the Sweeney boys, but could not see him. Then, with a quick rush to the rail, he realized that the sound was coming from over the side of the ship. He raced to Sean Sweeney's side, leaning as far over the rail as he dared. Others hanging over the edge of the gangplank pulled the dripping-wet boy along until Michael's hand closed over the boy's slender wrist. Together Sean and Michael pulled the child aboard. Sean went down on his knees, hugging the boy to him. "My son, we thought we'd lost you! Oh, thank God!" Tears streamed down Sweeney's face as he rose to thank Michael. "Twice now you have saved one of my family, Michael. What would have come of us if you hadn't been there? I don't like to think—and I don't want to believe a time will come when

you won't be there. Bless you, Michael Donovan, and all those you love."

Michael put his hand on the other man's shoulder. "Go on with you now, Sean. Take your boy to his mother. I must see to Keely."

The ship began to move out of the slip into the river, but they had only gone a short distance when the anchor was once again dropped. Officers shouted orders in such rapid staccato that even Katie could not catch all of what was said. She and Michael stood on the deck, holding on to each other, trying to understand what was happening. Several of the seamen began taking hold of people and pushing them toward the rail. Below was a rowboat waiting, and other men were shouting in harsh tones. Katie saw one man who had tried to sell her jelly tarts and finally she understood what was happening. "These people boarded the ship to sell their wares. There is a ribbon woman—see her basket—and that man tried to sell me tarts. I guess they are being sent back to Liverpool."

"Are you certain they are sending back only the hawkers?" Michael asked.

"No, I don't know." She looked up at him. "They can't put us off the ship now, can they, Michael? We have our tickets of passage . . . and we've passed the medical inspection. They are honor bound to take us to America. Michael?"

"Hush, Katie. We will have to wait. I have no answers. Just wait. No one I know has been taken off yet." He clenched his fist, his jaw set hard in frustrated anger. "It is the devil's language! If I could just understand!"

"We'll learn. We'll practice every day. It is just that they are talking so fast. We'd understand if they'd talk just a wee bit slower. I know we would, Michael," Katie said desperately, then burst into tears. She buried her face in Keely's neck. "Oh, I am sorry. I just can't seem to stop."

As Michael comforted Katie, cap merchants, gingerbread girls, mirror hawkers, and a variety of others were taken off the ship. Michael watched intently and listened to every word spoken, trying to learn in a few seconds everything that would allow him to understand the next set of confusing events. He realized all too quickly that the mysteries and dialects of a foreign language were not to be plumbed so easily. As soon as the hawkers were off the ship, the mate stepped forward with a sheaf of papers and began what sounded to Michael like a chant. For several minutes, and until the mate was losing patience, none of the steerage passengers responded. They all stood mutely around the deck, staring. Finally one man recognized his name and stepped forward.

"Will'am Jones, show your bones, Jackie Doyle, perch on the coil, Mary Sweeney, sail'd the good ship Queenie," and the singsong list went on. Slowly all the men and women of Erin began to understand that this was a roll call to weed out stowaways.

As soon as the roll call was finished, having turned up only one poor soul who had tried to take free passage, the mate pointed to four men, motioning them to follow him. Michael handed Keely back to Katie and stepped forward. One of the crew who had also been selected handed Michael a long stick.

The man spat over the side of the ship, then said, "Just do as you see me do, mate." Seeming to understand the intensity with which Michael listened, he spoke slowly, and though his London accent was difficult for Michael, he understood. The man gave Michael a quick smile and a friendly thump on the back.

The men spread out, poking at dark corners, occasionally breaking open suspicious crates and barrels. The seaman with Michael nudged him and said softly, "Watch this." He turned his pole. On the end of it was a sharp nail. Quickly he jabbed the sharp pointed instrument into a dark space between several loosely stowed barrels. A shrill

cry startled Michael. The crewman pushed harder with the
spiked pole, shaking it viciously into the space. A barrel
overturned and a small man shoved his way into the open
holding his bloodied hand.

The man begged mercy as he tried to climb over the
fallen barrels. His eyes on the spiked pole, he stumbled and
fell with the rolling barrels. The crewman laughed and
moved in closer, jabbing at the man's legs and back as he
tried to regain his footing. Each jab drew blood, and the
man had several wounds in his legs and buttocks and a
jagged tear along one sunken cheek.

Michael yelled above the man's screams for the crewman to stop, but the crewman understood his Gaelic no
better than Michael understood English. He gave another
vicious jab at the man, driving the nail deep into the man's
side. Michael leaped forward and grabbed the crewman's
wrist, wresting the pole from his grasp.

"No!" Michael shouted, finally managing to string a
couple of English words together. "No more! Leave it!"

The man released the pole, giving recognition to the raw
strength of an angry man. "Y'damn paddies are all alike.
Stick together. I tried to do you a good turn, but throw it
in my face you do. A'right, y'have y'ere way, mate, but
you'll pay for it, Paddy, you'll pay. Y'ere kind allus does."

By the time Michael got back to Katie she had secured a
berth for them, but she was looking a bit shamefaced. "I
lied to the captain, Michael. I told him we'd married in
Liverpool so that I could stay with you and Keely. Are
you angry?"

Upset as Michael was, Katie's "sin" meant little to him.
He shook his head and sank down on the small wooden
square that was called a berth, his head in his hands.

"I've done a stupid thing, Katie. I've made a bad enemy
for us."

Katie's heart thumped painfully against her chest. Michael would not say such a thing if it weren't true. "What

happened?" she finally managed to ask in a choked voice. By the time he answered her she was trembling.

Michael told her about taking the pole from the crewman and trying to help the stowaway. "But it was all for naught. I did not really help him. They might even have been kinder were it not for my interference. My God, Katie, they took the poor sod and threw him over the side of the ship. They took no more care of him than they would when throwing a cask of slops out. And with all that, the seaman I stopped from poking the poor soul with his stick has a hatred of me that I am certain to feel the whole of the voyage."

Katie's eyes were wide. "What can he do to us, Michael?"

Michael's head was so low his voice sounded muffled. "I don't know, Katie. Dear God, I don't know that nor any else."

Katie said nothing. She looked at him, her eyes big with fear and sorrow. She remained quiet for a long time as did Michael. Neither of them knew what to say, nor did they have much energy left to talk. She sank to her knees beside him. Finally Katie asked, "What happened to the man?"

Michael looked up, shrugged, then shook his head. "I don't know. There was so much foam in the water I couldn't see, and then the men—they pushed me from the railing, threatening to see that I would follow him if I didn't go below decks." He rubbed his hand across his face. "What difference does it make? Oh, God, Katie, I am tired. I thought I was doing the decent thing. Maybe I wasn't. I don't know. I know nothing these days. Nothing."

Katie fought back tears. She got up off her knees, placed her hands on Michael's shoulders, and gently pushed him down on the berth. "You are tired in mind and spirit. Sleep for a while. Let it all fall away from you, Michael. We will talk again when you awaken. I will take care of Keely. We're safe here."

Michael did not resist her, but he gave her a bitter smile. "We're not safe anywhere, Katie."

Katie watched as he stared at her for a time, then he closed his eyes. Katie sat there for several minutes longer. She didn't know if he had fallen asleep or not. She thought not, but she was glad his eyes were closed. She didn't want to talk now, and she didn't want to see the haunted look on his face. She didn't like to hear that they were not safe anywhere. Any man or woman born Irish knew that, but it was quite another thing to live your life thinking about it. She knew it and ignored the knowledge, preserving a space of illusion that allowed her to think that someday, perhaps tomorrow, she would find that place of safety. Michael denied himself that illusion, and she could not understand how he survived without it.

Katie got up and busied herself, finding a reasonably safe place to store their provisions. Not a single steerage passenger was well provisioned, and all of them had known hunger for a long time. How well Katie knew that a hungry man will sell his soul for a piece of bread to ease his pangs. She would have to be careful and vigilant of the little bit she and Michael had.

The aisles between the berths were very narrow and all the belongings of the passengers had to be stored there. She squeezed her eyes shut. Michael's words continued to press in upon her. She had been told that a voyage would take as little as twenty-nine days. That was what she had to keep thinking about. She could survive for twenty-nine days. She would think about that and blot all else out. Twenty-nine days and she would be free! She would be in a new land with a new chance at life. The stinking, crowded berth would be behind her, the queasiness in her stomach would be gone. She would have fresh air again and a whole new world to explore. She had been told that America was very large, so if she encountered men like Reginald Fairmont in one place, she would go to another. There had to be someplace in the world where such men did not live.

Michael might be correct in what he said, but he was wrong in dwelling on it. Of that Katie was certain with all her heart. Sometimes reality could not be borne, and the only way to change it was to create a new reality. It could be done, and that is exactly what Katie pledged herself to do. To fortify her resolve, she began to sing, her voice soft and low so as not to awaken Michael if he were really asleep or to disturb the other people who were so close she could hear their breathing and feel their fear.

*"A Mhairin de Barra, do mharaigh tu m'intinn,
do chuir tu beo i dtalamh me i gan fhios dom
   mhuintir,"*

Katie stopped singing, her brows knitted in concentration. Hesitantly, she began to sing again.

*"Oh, Mairin de Barra, you have murdered my thinking,
and
flooded the deep cup of pain for my drinking,"*

" 'Tis beautiful," a voice said from somewhere nearby. Katie peered into the murky gloom of the hold, but all she could see was bobbing heads and innumerable packs and bags.

With a smile and a shrug, she said, "I cannot see you, but I thank you all the same."

There was no answer and Katie returned to making herself busy. She took a bit of their food and headed topside to try her hand at cooking some of the Indian corn, which had been the cheapest and most abundant provisions they could buy. When Katie returned to their bunks and awakened Keely and Michael to eat, she was harried and exhausted. Michael didn't seem to notice and she said nothing about it then. She didn't want to hear any more of his dreary warnings tonight. She was too tired to withstand them. But she would think about this first day aboard ship as soon as she could close her eyes and gain that especially private place of inner darkness. She was close to impatient, as Michael and Keely were unusually slow eating. She had been able to make the Indian corn into nothing more palatable than a kind of pudding. It was bad enough and would have been worse if the lady next to her had not been willing to trade some of the pudding for some onions and turnips. At least the vegetables had given it some flavor. Keely never complained about what she was given to eat, being too happy to have anything at all in her stomach, but Michael was also reticent. Most times he would have been quick to excuse Katie, laying no blame on her for their poor meal, but nonetheless commenting on what a sin it was to put such swill down his throat. Tonight, however, he remained quiet, saying nothing but his thanks for his food.

When finally everyone settled in for the night, Katie closed her eyes and began to worry over her two newest problems. Throughout the voyage, she now knew, cooking was going to be a problem. Though cookstoves had been provided for the steerage passengers, there were not nearly enough of them. It was rather like standing in line for the Doctor's Shop. One could not do without the stove, but it meant waiting in a long line for a very long time. And the time was short. Too many people had to prepare their supper in far too short a time. Their food was never going to be cooked properly. Perhaps Michael already knew this and that was why he had not complained about the hard little knots of uncooked corn floating in the midst of his pudding. Mentally, Katie shrugged, and returned to worrying her problem. Tonight had been bad enough, but if she did not find a solution, it would only get worse. Even on this first night, when everyone was a bit apprehensive and diffident, there had been fights over the cookstoves. Many harsh words had been exchanged, and two women had gone so far as to knock each other down. It was a terrible sight seeing them roll about the deck like two street urchins. Katie lay quietly, her eyes closed but her mind working furiously for a long time before she decided she would seek out half a dozen other women and see if they could pool their time and cook supper in one pot. The only difficulty she could foresee was that it was not terribly likely that any one of them would have so large a pot. Then she thought of Mrs. Sweeney. Twice Michael had come to their rescue. Mrs. Sweeney had brought all her belongings along. Perhaps she would have a decent-sized pot.

Satisfied that she had an answer to her first problem, Katie moved on to the next and potentially the more serious one. The water was not being measured fairly. Katie knew that each passenger was to be given a full gallon of water per day. Indeed, each of them had been given a bucket of water, but it was by no means a gallon. Katie guessed it to be about three quarters of what they should have had. Her desire to work out solutions for her problems exceeded her endurance. She fell sound asleep thinking that she would ask Michael what he felt they should do about it.

Almost the first words out of her mouth when they awakened were, "Is there nothing we can do about getting our proper allotment of water, Michael? We have less than a gallon a day to drink and cook with, and if there is any left we can wash."

Michael blinked at her, unsure where this tirade had come from so early in the day. He stretched, trying to iron out the stiffness and cramps that had come from sleeping on the uncomfortable berth that was far too small for his large frame. He glanced back at Katie, who stood waiting for her answer. "I'll try. Perhaps if I hadn't helped that man—the stowaway—I would have a better chance of changing the water measurement."

Katie's patience was short this morning and he had exhausted it in one sentence. She snapped. "Will you stop going on about that man! We need water, not penance over something that is past!"

"I'm sorry, Katie."

"Och! Stop apologizing! Saints preserve me, Michael, what is wrong with you? You were the pillar of our strength taking us through everything, and now you are a whining apologist unable to cope with the simplest of things."

"Then the simple truth is that I cannot get us more water," he said coldly. He turned his back on her and again curled up on his short berth.

Katie was too angry to speak to him for the rest of the day, and they spent it and the following day in cold silence, or reserved unpleasant courtesy when speech was necessary. Both Michael and Katie were miserably lonely without the company of the other, but neither would give in. By the third day, Katie was not only miserable, she realized how unproductive this behavior was and how much they needed each other for practical, as well as emotional support.

Every moment, the voyage was becoming more difficult. When Katie remembered how worried she had been that the doctors might not find her fit, she almost had to laugh. Some of the people they had passed as well would never see another shore, she was certain. It didn't take a doctor's eye to spot it. Death was written on the faces of several of these people, and they were not yet a week at sea. Each day that passed, more and more of the passengers were coughing, vomiting, and falling victim to dysentery. Some of the difficulties were seasickness, but most were not. The area where the steerage passengers spent most of their day and all of their nights was becoming a filthy pit.

The horrible odor and the filth of the area more than anything else made her want to break the icy silence between herself and Michael. Each day she had waited expectantly for someone to come to clean their quarters. Each day she waited in vain. It was as if the captain and the crew forgot their existence as long as they were safely closed below decks. She now knew that there would be no cleaning. She needed Michael. Together they would have to work to try to keep themselves clean, and fed, and to get as much fresh air as possible. Katie felt a terrible threat to them, and she knew they could not afford petty bickering. Already she had found that some of the extra food supplies they had brought would be worthless. They had spent some of their precious money in Liverpool on rice. Now she realized she hadn't enough water to cook it in, and they could not bear the thirst that would come after. She would keep it, but use it only if and when they became desperate for food. She no longer doubted that time would come. Just as the captain was not going to measure water for them accurately, nor clean their quarters, she believed he would not see that they got the fair amount of provisions they were promised with the passage. To the captain they were cargo of little importance, and everyone knew that a certain amount of the cargo in any voyage got damaged or lost.

Even though she and Michael were barely talking, she had noticed that he was eating almost nothing. What little he had, he gave to Keely. On at least one occasion Katie had said nastily, "I don't know what good you think you are doing her. She will not be helped by having a dead daddy when she arrives in America."

"I won't die," he replied curtly, and, as had become his habit, he turned his back on her.

Now she approached Michael with mixed feelings. She

knew they had to help each other, and yet it galled her to have to give in to him and be the first to ask for a cease to their hostilities. He was a pigheaded beast, she thought, and it was he, not she, who should be begging to be granted her cooperation. He wouldn't. She knew that. He would die first. She would. She knew that too. She went up to him, trying her best to look meek, and keep her angry thoughts and words well hidden. "Michael," she said sweetly.

He turned to her. "Michael," he mocked just as sweetly, then suddenly he grinned as though there had never been a cross word between them. "I wondered how long it would take you to come to your senses and ask my forgiveness."

"Swine! You miserable, arrogant swine!" she screamed. "I wouldn't ask your forgiveness on my deathbed!"

"Temper, Katie, temper."

She tried to hit him with her cooking pot.

"Now that you are in your natural high-spirited state, I ask your forgiveness, Katie Ryan."

She swung wildly at him again, not having heard a word he said.

"Katie! I'm askin' your forgiveness!" Michael repeated, and ducked. He grabbed her wrist on her next swing. The pot went flying and Michael pulled her toward him onto the berth.

"Let me go!" she screamed, her auburn hair flying wildly around her head and into her eyes as she tried to claw him.

They wrestled a squirming mass of arms and legs until Michael got both her arms pinned to her sides and his weight on top of her so that she couldn't kick him. He said breathlessly, and quietly, "I thought you were going to apologize."

"I hate you! I will never apologize, you uncouth lout!"

"You love me," he said.

"Arrogant pig fart!" she hissed.

He made a face. "That was a cruel thing to say, Katie Ryan. Now tell me you love me. Come now, be a good girl. Say, Michael Donovan, I love you."

She pressed her full lips tightly closed, her green eyes blazing.

He leaned over and kissed her cheek, then he looked at her and smiled. He kissed the corner of each of her eyes. He whispered, "Say it, Katie. Tell me you love me." He kissed the edges of her mouth and the hard set point of her chin. "Tell me."

"You're stubborn and cruel," she said.

"I am, but you love me. Tell me, Katie."

"You love Aislinn."

"I did love Aislinn. She is dead. Tell me, Katie."

"You don't love me."

"I love only you, Katie Ryan. Now tell me. Tell me you love me, Katie. You lied to the mate so we could be together. You said you were my wife—be my wife."

"Marry? Here? On board ship?" Katie's breath was coming in ragged gasps.

"Between us and God it will be here, but we will not have this captain say the words over us. He does not care if we live or die. For the words we will wait until we can stand before a priest of God—but only if you love me. Do you, Katie?"

She looked up at him, her eyes pleading. "Why are you doing this, Michael? Why can't you just let me be?"

Michael shifted his weight so that she could escape if she wanted. "I think that is answer enough, Katie. You have my apology. I have misunderstood your caring and attention to Keely and me."

Katie lay where she was. "You are not making fun of me?"

"Did I sound as if I were making fun?" he asked.

"No, but I thought . . . I mean, I have made calf eyes at you ever since we had our lunch on the hill outside of

Fairmont. I thought . . . I mean I . . . you loved Aislinn so much and I am just . . . you would never have
sought me out had it not been for Jennifer asking you. No
one ever takes me seriously, Michael. Everyone thinks I
am nothing but a willful, wrongheaded girl who will come
to a bad end. 'Help poor Katie in spite of herself.' That is
all I have ever heard."

He sat up straight, his head touching the top of the next
berth. "And you thought I was no different. Is that what
you are telling me, Katie? After all the time we have spent
together and the things we have done together, you still
think that I treat you as no more than a wrongheaded girl
I must help in spite of herself?"

"No! Oh, no, Michael, you never have! I don't know
what I mean."

"Maybe you had better figure out what you mean," Michael said in a far less understanding voice.

"Please, don't leave me, Michael. Come back! Tell me
again and I will answer you now."

"Tell you what?" he grumbled.

"That you love me! Tell me, tell me, Michael. Free my
stupid tongue—I have so much to say to you!"

Michael hesitated, remaining where he sat, looking at
her. Katie sat up, put her arms around his neck, and began
pulling him back toward her on the berth.

She kissed his ear, whispering, "Tell me, Michael, and I
will tell you that I have dreamed about sleeping in your
arms every night, and that I have wished and wished that
you would look at me just once the way you do in my
dreams. I will tell you that when you sleep I watch you
and imagine what it would be like to fill the dark space of
your sleep with visions of me. I will tell you that when I
prepare your meals I am making love to you in my heart."

Michael buried his face against her neck. Katie put her
arms around his broad back and arched against him until

their bodies fit perfectly against each other except for the bulkiness of their clothing.

Michael's hand moved restlessly over the mound of her breast, then down her side to her hips. The more excited he became and the greater his need for her, the more frustrated he was with the impeding clothing. Suddenly he became aware of the many people only a few feet away.

Michael rolled off of her onto his side and gave a shuddering sigh.

"Michael?" Katie whispered uncertainly. "What is wrong? What did I do?"

"My love, you have done nothing wrong. I am regretting all those days and nights in the countryside when we could so easily have found a wood or a cave and been together. I threw those days away as if there would never be an end to them."

Katie looked around at the other people. Some looked away, trying to give her and Michael the privacy of avoidance. Others were staring with avid curiosity and appreciation. They had little in their own lives, and Katie and Michael were a blessing to them. Still others were gawking, lascivious leers on their faces. Katie blushed, and inched closer to Michael. "How do others . . . I mean, I know . . . I have heard . . ." She choked on her last admission, her face scarlet.

Michael didn't smile. "I know. I have heard, too, Katie, but it makes no difference. Many of these people have gotten used to living like animals. But I have not and neither have you. Nor will we ever. This is not for you and it is not for Keely. We will wait," Michael said harshly and bitterly.

"I don't want to wait," Katie whispered. "Something might happen. I can only trust that we will have today. If we don't take it, Michael, maybe we will never be together."

"We will be together. We should have no more than two or two and a half weeks left to the voyage." He turned her toward him, then brought her close so that she rested against his chest. His lips were soft and gentle on hers. "And then, my love, the minute we place our feet on American soil, I will hie you off to the nearest clump of trees and we will lie together in the sunlight and know each other."

Katie wrapped her arms around him and held on for dear life. "Oh, Michael, promise me that will happen. Promise me you will let nothing prevent us from that day. You are my dream. I couldn't bear to lose you now."

"I promise you," Michael said. "And you, Katie? Do you also promise?"

THE Atlantic Ocean was kind to the emigrants. No hellish storms rose to meet them, no icy winds froze them, and no maddening calms plagued them. But the Atlantic stood alone in her kindness, for the men and women in steerage found all other aspects of their journey hard and cruel. They had boarded the *Mary Grace* starved and ill, already the victims of unkindness. Twenty days out to sea, the illnesses they had carried with them from Ireland began to take their toll in the steerage quarters of the ship. With the dawning of the twentieth day out, the fourteenth man had died, and Michael and Katie stood silently and sadly as Sean Sweeney was sent to a watery grave. Thirty other passengers were desperately ill with what was sometimes called famine fever and at other times called ship's fever, or typhus.

Fear was the constant companion of every person on board. At night the continual coughing and vomiting of the ill was heard without stop. Each day brought with it the uncertainty of another day of health for those still unaffected. Lack of fresh water, poor and inadequate food, and, above all, filthy conditions in steerage rendered every day a game of chance for each person.

Katie hoarded their supply of water like a well-practiced miser. She doled it out in small, infrequent measures so that they never felt terribly thirsty, though never really satisfied. With every bit she could save by doing this, she washed Keely every day. It had become an obsession with Katie that the three of them should keep as clean as it was possible under such hampering conditions. Several times she sent Michael to the mate begging for vinegar so that she could clean their area. But word of Michael's interference in the matter of the stowaway had spread, and true to his word, the crewman was making life miserable for Michael every chance he got. Michael had become the least likely person on board to be granted any special favor. On all occasions he returned to Katie angry and empty-handed. "All the bastard would say is that before we enter port a thorough cleaning will be given."

"For the love of God, Michael, we may all be dead by then! Do they not see what is happening to us? Can't that bloody fool of a captain see that his passengers are dying every day? Is it that he wants to enter port with an empty ship and a full pocket?"

Michael did not know what to say. There were so many questions, but never an answer to be had. It always came to the same nagging question—did anyone care, or had Katie been correct when she said that they were to be sent down the slop trough and that was all there was for people like them.

Katie was on her knees scrubbing their berths. She had already thrown away the filthy, bug-infested bedding they had been using, and she had swept up and tossed overboard the straw they had been given to cover the floor. Angrily, she threw the rag she had been using to clean the floor. Once that rag had been a pretty red scarf she wore round her head. Those days seemed much farther away from her than three weeks. She wanted to cry, but she wouldn't. "What's the use!" she shouted to anyone within hearing. "No one cares! Why should I? Why don't any of you help yourselves? Why?"

Michael got to his knees beside her and took her in his arms. "Some do care, Katie, love. Don't trouble your head with those that don't. You'll make yourself sick with the worry of it. You've kept us all well, and that's a great thing you've done. Think of that. Think of how few the days until we land in America, and think of how many days your care has already taken us through. Those are behind us. We've nearly made it to America, Katie. A bit more than a week and we'll be there. That's not so bad, is it?"

She raised her lips to his to be kissed, then she smiled. "It isn't so bad. I used to tell myself I could survive twenty-nine days of anything. Now I will tell myself I have to survive seven days of the devil's worst. Just keep reminding me that there are so many days behind and so few ahead of us until we get there, Michael. It gives me heart and makes me feel like smiling."

"Then I'll tell you hourly. I would do anything to keep you smiling. Give me the rag, and I'll finish the scrubbing."

"I'll do no such thing, Michael Donovan!"

"You will, and then you will take Keely and go above to the deck and smell the fresh sea air."

"They'll just chase us below decks again."

"But not before we've filled our lungs full of good air and taken a bit of a look around."

"You're coming with us?"

Michael grinned, then, giving a shrug, he said, "If you'll wait for me to finish me swabbin', mum."

"Oh, do be quiet!" Katie giggled. But the merriment died in her eyes quickly and her eyes were troubled again. "It's an awful world we live in, Michael, when one man can keep another from smelling the good air the Lord God gave to us all."

Michael gave her an impish look. "But we will be like

water, Katie, and seep through the cracks. Just when they
think we are under their thumb, a trickle of the Irish who
have never given up will have seeped out and they'll be
smelling the good air. The conqueror is always the cuck-
old. He can never have enough eyes to see, or ears to hear,
or hands to hold his vanquished. It is only the man who
has nothing left to lose who always has everything to gain.
That's us, Katie."

"Och! All that means is that as long as we live we have
everything to gain, because we are always on the bloody
bottom of the heap!" Suddenly Katie plunked herself down
on the floor beside him, stilling the wash rag. She fixed him
with a piercing green stare. "Michael! Why is it, Michael
Padriac Donovan, that every time I am feeling cross with
the world, you are the great optimist? But when I speak of
the good things that might come our way, you always say
that there is always going to be someone to keep us from
gaining our place in the world?"

"I think it is my natural contrariness—or mayhap it is
my great ability to see all sides of a question," Michael said
gravely.

Katie snatched the scrub rag from his hand and tossed it
into the bucket. She stood up. "Let's go take a look at the
sea. You get rid of this pest-ridden water and I'll get Keely
ready."

It took Katie ten minutes to get Keely sufficiently bundled up to go out into the brisk Atlantic wind, and not
more than five minutes after they had reached the deck
they were chased below by the mate. It seemed that the
very sight of them was offensive to the first-class passengers.

Katie and Michael stuck out their tongues and ran from
the seaman, skittering past the first companionway, causing the irate man to give chase. They disappeared down the
next ladder they came to. The mate shouted after them but
did not follow. They returned to their berths laughing and

rosy cheeked from the biting wind. With Keely between them they embraced, their noses touching and their breath mingling as they continued to chuckle, enjoying the memory of their stolen moments.

"Did you see his face when we ran past the companionway he pointed to?" Katie gasped. "It was as red as my scarf."

"And tomorrow he will do his best to make us pay for it. Mark my words—he will be on guard at the cookstove and you'll never get near the thing."

Katie laughed merrily. "Let's give him fits then. We still have some dried fish. We'll eat that and he'll think we slipped right past him."

But the next day neither the mate nor Katie or Michael were thinking about cookstoves or outfoxing anyone. Two more people died during the night, and three others were on their deathbeds. Still at least eight days out of port, the *Mary Grace* was beginning to earn the name "coffin ship." Katie overheard the captain talking to the mate about the possibility that they would be forbidden entry if many more cases of typhus were found.

Katie immediately went to Michael to report on what she had learned. "The only good thing is that the captain has ordered that we all be given more time on deck to see if that will slow the spreading of the fever," she said, but couldn't keep her lips from quivering. She moved closer to him. "Michael, hold me. I am so afraid we will never reach America and we'll never be together. Make me believe that all our promises will be kept. Please, Michael, talk to me, make me believe."

"They'll be kept, Katie, love." He put his arms around her and drew her against him. One of his hands cradled her head, tilting it at the best angle for his lips to meet hers. His other hand spanned her back and pressed her hips against his. He kissed her hungrily, tasting of her, wanting all of her. His mind was a fire storm of visions. As he had so often before, he transported himself and Katie to a sun-soaked glade, made private by a curtain of leaves and flowers. He ran his hand across her back, and instead of the coarse texture of her dress, he could feel the silkiness of her soft, bare skin. Her hair blazed with healthy highlights in his imagined sun, scented with the rain-cleansed air. He stood holding her and dreaming of a time yet to come for several minutes. His breath was ragged and his heart was beating fiercely.

Katie turned her face up to his. With her lips against his, she asked, "Must we wait?"

"I will not have the others staring at you. You are for my eyes alone, my love, as I am for you."

"And if they could not see?"

He kissed her quickly, thankful she was talking and giving him a chance to remove himself from his most satisfying dream slowly. "But they can," he answered, hardly giving thought to what she was saying.

Katie's eyes sparkled. "But what is can be changed!"

Katie was afire with ideas of how to close off their tiny area in the steerage so that they would have some privacy. Then suddenly she felt ashamed. She was on deck because two people had died and were to be lowered into an anonymous grave in the ocean. She had turned to Michael for comfort in facing their grief, and now all she could think of was stealing a dead person's blanket so that she and Michael could lie together—and they were not even married. She tried to think of Michael's words—that they would pledge themselves to each other in the eyes of God. But Katie did not—could not—bring herself to think that any priest would ever approve that.

She shook her head and wondered if ever before she could have thought of such callous things as stealing a dead man's blanket or if there had ever been a time before when she would have done such a thing. What she did know was that she was going to do it now. Whatever the cost to her life later—or even to her soul. By one means or another she was going to find a way to be with Michael Donovan. For all his brave talk of what would be for them in the future, Katie wanted whatever happiness she could take hold of now. With the splash she now heard, she was reminded of what happened to some people who counted on tomorrow. Tomorrows were for dreamers and for saints. She was neither.

Katie was too late to get the blanket from the man who had died. Someone had beaten her to it. When she approached the berth of the dead man, another woman was already there going through his possessions.

"It's mine for the taking," the woman said with a hiss. "He told me I could have it all—anything I wanted." She waved Katie away. "I took care of him in his last moments on earth. I get the reward."

"All but the blanket. That is mine! I fed him," Katie lied as easily as she knew the woman was.

The woman grabbed the blanket and hugged it to her bosom.

Katie stood tall and put out her hand. "Give it to me. I'll leave all the rest to you. I won't take another thing. All I want is the blanket."

"What's he hidden in it? Eh?"

"Nothing," Katie said in exasperation. "It's just a blanket—a dirty one at that."

The woman was frantically running her fingers all over the rough cloth, trying to see if something had been sewn into it. She batted at Katie's outstretched hand. "Y'dirty little tramp! It's mine what you're tryin' to steal from me. The devil himself will visit your dreams for tryin' to make a liar out of a dead man, God rest his soul. He gave me all his things. He did!"

Katie took a deep breath, then lunged forward. She gave a mighty tug and pulled blanket and woman off the berth. The woman landed on the floor with a painful thud, but she did not relinquish her hold on the blanket. Several other men and women gathered round to see the excitement, knowing that a fight was about to erupt. Katie gave the blanket another mighty tug, and still the woman hung on. With a howl of pain as the woman's shoe jambed against her shin, Katie was brought to the floor. The two women were wound up in the blanket. The woman grabbed a fistful of Katie's thick, long hair and pulled for all she was worth. Now furious, Katie became a screaming, scratching banshee. She beat at the woman with both fists. The woman began to scream and then to whine. "Take your blanket," she mewled. "Take it and leave me be. You're hurting me."

Quick as a cat, Katie regained her feet, took hold of the blanket, and ran. "Ha! You old witch! You probably put a pillow over the poor soul's face! See who it is the devil visits!" Katie bellowed triumphantly from a safe distance as she walked off with her prize.

Before Michael could see her, Katie straightened herself and set her hair to rights, then set to work on their hideaway. Bright-eyed, Keely sat in her basket watching Katie's every move. She had waved her small arms as Katie made her triumphal return walk down the row of berths. It was almost as if Keely understood what had taken place. Katie could hardly contain herself. She smiled broadly at Keely.

"I've got it, Keely!" she cried as if she were talking to a contemporary. In a strange way Katie often felt that Keely understood far more than her two and a half years and retarded development would indicate. The brilliance of the little girl's eyes alone gave testimony to what Katie was certain was a lively intelligence wanting only to be given proper food and care to bring it out. In the past couple of weeks of the voyage, when Katie and Michael had had so much time to give to Keely, she had even begun to speak a few words. Keely alone of all the passengers aboard had not decreased in health but gained. Of that feat Katie was very proud. She would always be able to look back upon this time and know that against inhumane odds she had managed to provide enough cleanliness and sufficient food for the frail child.

Holding the blanket far from the child, Katie displayed her prize. "This is not for the likes of your precious skin, my love—not until I have had a chance to clean it through and through." She bent down and planted a kiss on the tip of Keely's nose. "You be a good girl for a few minutes while I go above."

Katie was getting to be an expert at sneaking on deck when no one was looking so that she and Keely could get fresh air or just have a moment to themselves from time to time. She and Michael had also learned of several spots where they could be together of a night, but there was always the risk of being caught, and neither of them was comfortable. The blanket, she hoped, would end their infrequent and unsatisfactory attempts at lovemaking.

With a plank of wood and the blanket being secured over the rail, Katie accomplished her task just as one of the crewmen rounded the corner and shouted that she was in an area forbidden to the steerage passengers. With an impish smile she curtsied, saying, "Pardon me, sir." With a flip of her heavy skirts, she spun on her heel and quickly headed down the companionway, once again feeling proud of herself and triumphant. This was her day! Nothing could go wrong. Her head was full of fantasies of the night she and Michael would spend together hidden behind the protecting blanket.

Michael was aware of Katie's adventures and misadventures that day, but he had studiously absented himself. He had awakened that morning with an uncustomary bout of seasickness, which both dismayed him and worried him. All through the voyage he had been relatively free of the queasy and nauseous feelings that had repeatedly attacked other passengers. Now all of a sudden he was ill, and he could only hope that it was no more than seasickness. He also hoped that he would feel better by the time evening came, for above all else he did not want to disappoint Katie. Katie was always worrying that something would keep them apart and now, if that turned out to be true just when she thought she had found a solution for them, Michael would never convince her that nothing would prevent them from being together.

When Aislinn had died, he thought never again to be with a woman he cared about as he had once cared about his wife. Now there was Katie, a green-eyed enchantress and an answer to all his prayers. She wasn't at all like Aislinn except in how she made him feel. He was complete with Katie as he had been with Aislinn. Dreams that had seemed to die with the death of his family now had begun to revive. He found himself thinking of the house he and Katie and Keely might live in together. He pictured her as a mother to Keely, and all too often ideas of other children crept in—his and Katie's children. He could not imagine being without the warm loving way she had that made him feel she was all his. Even when she was at her most head-strong and most disapproving of him, she was still his, and every fiber of his being told him so. Tonight he didn't want to disappoint her. He could not.

Katie took pains to be certain the three of them had as good a meal as she could manage, and because of this she regaled Michael with the tale of what she hoped was her last battle of the day. With her mouth full of smoked fish and rice, she got up to demonstrate her fight to get and keep the cookstove for as long as she needed to get the rice fully cooked. With arms akimbo and her cheeks puffed out, Katie waddled toward Michael.

"Here she came, Mrs. Duffy, big old sow that she is, and with her fists doubled up and looking for all the world like two big ham hocks. 'Step aside!' she says to me, and I did.

One step nearer to the stove I took. I was so close I all but steamed the tip of my nose in the rice pot." Katie's eyes gleamed with the memory of it and she chuckled, parading a bit for Michael's pleasure. "Well, and didn't that send her into a rage? 'Step aside!' she screams at me again."

Michael began to chuckle. Shaking his head, he said, "I wouldn't dare ask and I don't think I want to know what you did next."

Katie made a face at him, dipped quickly, and planted a kiss on his cheek. "But just like you were thinking, I am going to tell you what I did to her. I stepped aside like she asked me to do. She has bunions, you see—great big ugly things on the sides of her feet. And in steppin' aside like she asked, it just happened that my foot landed ever so accidently right on a bunion. Such a howl the devil himself has never heard in the depths of hell! You would have thought that the giant Culcullen had come back to get Finn MacCool, she made such a racket."

Michael reached for her and pulled her down onto his lap. With a graceful swoop she draped herself around him. "Katie, Katie, what am I to do with you? You are going to get yourself into awful trouble."

She smiled and nuzzled her face against his. "You will come rescue me, won't you, Michael?"

"Then we will both be in the most awful of troubles."

She giggled contentedly. "Then you will have to keep me captive and under your constant and vigilant protection. Keep me flat on my back like any contented woman would wish to be kept and I will cause no trouble at all."

Michael had entertained thoughts of putting her off tonight, but he knew now, as he had always known, that he could not. As soon as they had finished eating and Keely was already nodding sleepily, he whispered, "Hang your blanket, woman."

Katie made certain Keely was secure in her basket in the upper berth and then hung the blanket. Katie was even more pleased with her ingenuity when she saw that it was large enough to enclose Keely above and them below. Both Michael and Katie kissed the sleepy child good night and then sat with her as Michael told her what he called a bedtime story and Katie called a horror story of the terrible lives they had led in Ireland.

When Keely was nearly asleep, and Michael and Katie had climbed down from the upper bunk, Katie said, "If you must be telling her stories, they could be cheerful. You'll be giving her nightmares. And you might remember that we are leaving the old country behind. Ireland didn't want us, and there's no reason you should be teaching your daughter to pine after it. Tell her the glories of the new land we'll be coming to. That's where our future is—and everything that is important."

"I don't know any stories of the new places we'll be going to," Michael replied sensibly. "I don't even know where it is we'll settle. Maybe I won't like the stories of that place."

Katie wrinkled up her nose. "You'll use anything for an excuse to keep on telling your stories about the Irish ghoulies." With a spritely hop, Katie stepped on the bottom berth and poked her head close to Keely's again. Softly, she said, "You listen to Katie, my pretty little lovely. I'll sing you a song of the fairies. They are pretty little creatures like you and not at all your daddy's beasties all covered with mud and dung from the tatie beds and the stables." Keely was nearly asleep, and it was to Michael Katie was really speaking as well he knew. She looked down at him with a quick, caustic glance, and then turned all her attention on the half asleep Keely. In a lovely, clear voice she sang a song of Queen Mab.

When she finished, Michael climbed up beside her. He leaned over and kissed Keely's forehead. From the corner of his eyes he looked at Katie as he whispered. "She is filling your head with things of no substance. Listen to your *deaide*, Keely."

Keely was already asleep, but somehow her mouth made a crooked little smile that could have meant anything or nothing. Michael swore to Katie it meant that Keely had heard, understood, and agreed with him.

Once more Katie and Michael climbed down into the lower berth. With the blanket in place the already cramped quarters were next to impossible. Katie looked at Michael with laughing eyes.

"We are two crazy people, aren't we, Michael?" Katie began to giggle and then to laugh hard as Michael tried to sort himself out of the tangle of blanket and assorted belongings that were stowed at the side of the berth. Michael began to laugh and Katie tried to shush him, then laughed all the harder herself. She couldn't stop now. She felt silly and very nervous.

"No one can see a thing," she said proudly between bursts of laughter.

"Including us," Michael answered and put his arms around her, for there was no place else to put them—and because he wanted to. "We are going to smother in here."

Katie burst into giggles again. "Don't think about it— maybe it won't bother us if we don't think."

Michael took in a great rush of air, puffed out his cheeks and held it for several seconds, then let it out with a great *"Paugh!"* "It doesn't work."

"Just think, Michael, this is our first home," Katie said.

Michael let out another expulsion of air in a guffaw.

Katie giggled and smacked playfully at him. "Come closer and let me undress you. I have a surprise for you."

"Another?" Michael asked, being totally uncooperative and kissing her as she tried to unfasten his shirt. To add to her difficulties, and her giggles, he began to unfasten her clothing as well, doing as much tickling as he was unfastening.

Quickly they became a hopeless tangle of hands, arms, sleeves, and shirttails. With the blanket hanging in place, it was so dark in the crowded little cubicle, neither Michael nor Katie could see anything.

"Where did you go?" Michael asked, perplexed as he grabbed what he thought would be her wrist, but was her ankle.

Katie was lying on the berth, her head hanging over the edge as she fished in the dark for her surprise, which she had hidden under the berth. "Don't move, Michael, or you will spoil everything."

"What are you doing?"

With a cry of success, Katie scrambled upright again. Carefully, she balanced a pot of liquid.

"What do I smell?" Michael asked. "What are you up to, Katie Ryan?"

"It's lime you smell. And it is for us. I am going to bathe you and you are going to bathe me in this sweet fragrance."

"Where did you come by a lime? We had no such thing."

Katie's tinkling laugh floated musically in the dark cubicle. "The seamen won't miss one or two, and we have a greater need than they. One lime is for Keely to keep the fever away. It does that, you know. I heard the captain talking, and as soon as I heard I knew that we would need some of those limes."

"You stole them! My God, Katie, but it is true you have a liking for danger and a great larceny in your heart."

"I did and I do," Katie said happily. With unerring accuracy, she placed her hand against his chest and pushed him to the bed. "Lie back, my love, and let me cool your skin and bring the lovely scents of the outdoors into our small world."

Michael lay back and turned himself body and soul over to Katie's ministrations. Katie shivered as she placed her hands for the first time on Michael's naked flesh. Gently she soothed along the length and breadth of his torso.

Michael breathed deeply with pleasure. Her hands were like magic wings that were carrying him out of the cramped confines of the ship to a place of beauty and comfort he hadn't known before.

Too often Katie had been aware that Michael had been happily married and had loved his wife deeply, and always in her mind she suffered when comparing herself to Aislinn. Tonight she fought away any thoughts of Aislinn, concentrating on what she wished for Michael and herself. She spoke softly of the trees and the heavenly sky above that would one day be theirs. She spoke of a running stream, the scent of flowers, and fresh grass, and all manner of growing things.

Michael sighed contentment, murmuring, *"Ta se ina shamhradh."*

"Yes," Katie crooned, "summer has arrived. For us it will always be summer, Michael. Always the warm sun will shine upon us, and we will cool ourselves in the clear waters of a stream. Wherever we are, Michael, there will always be sunshine and clear water."

"Lie down, Katie, and let me do for you. I am cooled and soothed and mad to touch you, my love, my summer love."

Gently, but without Katie's delicate patience, Michael bathed her as she had bathed him. His hands moved easily along her arms, his lips following the path of the lime scent as he kissed every part of her, lingering on her breasts. Katie moaned her pleasure under him, and his breathing became ragged as he struggled to complete his bathing of her. The cubicle smelled fresh and sweetly of lime water, and Michael was dizzy with the heady scents of man, woman, and nature that flooded the small space. He parted her thighs; his fingers met the moist warmth of her. His indrawn breath was loud in the space.

Katie put her arms on his shoulders and wrapped her legs around him, drawing him to her. Michael stretched out the length of her, his cooled, moist flesh touching the length of hers. His lips closed hungrily over hers, his tongue probing deep and lovingly into the warmth of her mouth. His hands roved the silky curves of her body. For a long time they explored each other, getting to know the sanctums of the other's passion. Then Michael shifted his weight, and knowing, Katie raised her hips to receive him.

"Ta se ina shamhradh," she murmured, and allowed herself to be transported to the same verdant, heated place of summer that she had created for Michael earlier.

Michael moved in an easy, gentle motion, bringing both of them to a breathless peak of pleasure. Trembling, he held himself in control as he raised his chest off her so that he could look into her eyes. "Katie Ryan, I love you. I want you as my wife, my friend, my love, my life." He kissed her first gently, then with unleashed passion as they exploded in a burst of mutual desire.

"Hold me, Michael. I don't want you to leave me—ever. I always want to be one with you, never separated, never without you. I would be so lost without you—always keep me safe, please."

"You needn't worry, my love. Fate has brought us together. We will keep ourselves together. It is our pledge."

6

For the next several days Katie walked around in a haze of happiness. She and Michael spent playful and passionate nights behind the protective covering of their blanket. During the day, Katie spent all her energies and concentration on preparing their food and stealing enough water to keep them clean. In only three more days, it was said, the ship would be coming into the Saint Lawrence, barring late-season ice. Though the air was chill, Katie detected air frigid enough to indicate the river would still be clogged with ice from the last of the spring thaw.

"Ah, Michael, love, it is going to be a rushing, golden river coming right out to meet us and welcome us to America."

Michael chuckled at her language. "Is that a river of gold, Katie, or one choked with yellow mud?"

"Hush, you awful man! It will be golden, for the sun will shine and make it so."

Michael pulled her over to his side of the berth, burying his face in the apron of her skirt, then he peeked up at her, smiling like a young boy. "Then it will indeed be a golden river for you."

"And you," she said complacently, disentangling herself

from his embrace. "I am going to take Keely up on deck. Will you come?"

He started to say yes, then stopped himself, remembering how often of late he had been feeling light-headed and nauseous when he stood or moved around too much. He could hardly bear the thought of looking down into the moving, churning waters of the ocean. "No, I think I'll stay here and take a little nap. You wear me out," he said, and reached for her again.

Katie easily sidestepped him and, laughing softly, went to fetch Keely to bundle her up for their clandestine trip to the upper deck. Keely seemed to understand and enjoy almost as much as Katie their game of cat and mouse with the crewmen who would chase them below decks.

Michael, however, lay back on his berth as soon as Katie was out of sight. He had said nothing to her, and aside from a few comments about how thin he was, Katie seemed to notice nothing peculiar in his behavior or his health. That, more than anything else, gave him hope that perhaps he was not really ill but merely suffering from a general shipboard malaise. But even that hope was of little comfort to him now when his head was throbbing so painfully he thought it would crack open. He was cold, but his body was bathed in sweat. The terrible memories of wiping down the overheated bodies of his sons, his daughter, and Aislinn haunted him. It was all he could do to tell himself that this was not the same and that he could not compare every sweat he had to those of his departed family. He was grateful that Katie had chosen this time to take Keely on deck. He did not think he would have been able to hide his discomfort from her this time. Never before had the spasms of pain in his head and stomach been so severe— nor had he ever before sweat as profusely as he was sweating now. Weak as a newborn, he rolled to his side, willing the pain to subside. He had to look and act normal when Katie and Keely returned.

Katie had one of her successful days at evading the eyes of the watchful crewmen. It was nearly half an hour later when she came back below decks laughing with Keely. Both of them had cherry-red cheeks and sparkly eyes from their adventure in the chill, brisk air. "Oh, look at him, Keely. Your daddy is sound asleep." She touched the little girl affectionately on the tip of her nose, saying, "And that, my little lovely, is where you should be. So, I shall get you ready for your nap and then sing you to the land of Nod where you shall spend a happy hour chasing the rainbows of the Little People. Perhaps you can bring back a whole pot of gold with you when you awaken. Wouldn't that be a wondrous thing, if we could really do that, Keely? Just think what fun we could have with a pot of gold!"

Katie took off Keely's outdoor clothing, chattering the whole time. "Wouldn't it be wonderful if we could but close our eyes and go to the land of the Little People anytime we wanted. We could chase after their treasures whenever we wished. Now that would really be an adventure, Keely—and so much more fun than dodging the crewmen . . ."

"You talk too much, girl," said old Mrs. Dunn, who had the berth two down from theirs.

Katie peeked out from behind the blanket. "I may not be able to make wishes come true, but at least my dreamin' and talkin' makes it seem like they might."

"And might be with all that talkin' and dreamin' you don't see what's right under your nose," said the old woman.

"And what might that be?"

"Look carefully at that man of yours. He's sick, he is."

"Michael?" Katie said with disbelief. "He's thin as a rail, but fit."

"He's not fit. He's sick. You got your head so full of nonsense you can't see, but I'm tellin' you, he is sick. Some of us got no dreams to dream and we see what is before us."

Katie stared at the woman for several seconds, her tongue itching to make a smart comment, but something in the older woman's eyes arrested her. With a sudden clutch of fear grasping her throat, she whispered, "Thank you for telling me, Mrs. Dunn. Michael never would have." And she ducked back behind the blanket. She finished putting Keely down for her nap, then sat on the edge of Michael's berth. She placed her hand on his forehead and immediately drew it back. "You're burning up!" she said to herself.

Michael opened his eyes and took her hand in his. "The old woman has too big a mouth and too big a yen for other people's business. I am not feeling so good today, but I am all right."

"You are not all right!" Katie said in a panic. "You're too hot, and your skin is dry as powder. And this isn't the first time this has happened, is it? You've been hiding it from me, haven't you? All those times when you didn't feel like going on deck with us . . . you were hiding your illness. Why, Michael? Why would you hide it from me when you know how hard I've tried to keep us all healthy?"

"That is why I hid it from you, Katie. You've been working yourself to the bone. There is nothing you can do."

"I could, and I can!" Katie said, her small jaw set in determination. "You should have told me."

Michael sighed, lacking the energy to fight against her seemingly endless reservoir of vitality. He closed his eyes. "I wasn't certain I didn't have a touch of seasickness until a couple of days ago. I still am not sure."

Katie's face crumpled, and she put her hands up to cover it. She cried brokenly. "Oh, God, Michael, you can't be sick. I am so afraid without you. You have to get better. We are almost there."

"I will, Katie, don't you worry. *Is Eireannach me.*"

Katie sniffed and looked at him. "What has being an Irishman to do with your getting better?"

Michael's eyes glowed with feverish intensity. "It has all to do with it. You can't kill an Irishman."

"That's not funny!" Katie said with some heat. "After the dead we've left behind, there is not a bit of humor in that—or truth!"

"Is Eireannach me," he repeated. "I am an Irishman. That is all the truth there is. I will get well, Katie."

"Oh, God, you're delirious! You're not making sense," Katie wailed. "What am I going to do?"

"For one thing, quit your caterwauling, girl. You've got water. I've seen you stealin' it and hoardin' it all these days," Mrs. Dunn said as she intruded into the tented berth. "Get your water and wash him down. Break the fever, and then see if you can steal a few more of those limes."

"How did you . . ."

"I may be an old woman, girl, but parts of me still work just fine. I can smell as well as the next fellow."

"Oh, I didn't realize that the scent was so strong."

"There you go chattering again, and him still in the grip of his fever. We've work to do if you don't want a corpse to land in America. Folks have been dying off like flies these last few days. It's a wonder that skinny little wisp of a girl hasn't caught ill as well."

"She's fine! Keely isn't sick!" Katie said in a fright.

"I can see that," Mrs. Dunn said waspishly. "I still say it's a miracle. Now, are you going to strip the clothes from him, or am I?"

"I'll tend to Michael," Katie said, then began crying again. "I don't know why I am acting so terrible to you.

You are only trying to help me, and I don't know what I would do without you. I am so frightened."

"And you are angry that I told you what you didn't want to hear or know. Don't make so much of it." Mrs. Dunn, her back bent with arthritis, stooped to the bucket of water Katie kept hidden and covered under the berth. Slowly she sponged Michael off. "When the fever breaks, it will be important to keep him warm. But the first thing is to break the fever. Without that happening, there is no hope. I've sat through many a long night with my man and my son waiting for a fever to break."

"Did they live?" Katie asked in a breathy voice.

"Would I be alone on this ship if they had?" Mrs. Dunn asked. "But it wasn't the fever killed my man—t'was a runaway horse. Now, my son was a different matter. The fever took him. He was just too weak to fight any longer, poor little soul."

"I'm sorry." Katie looked away from the woman. "I guess I'm not a very nice person. I don't know what terrible things have happened to other people down here with us, because I didn't want to know. You are right. I dream too much. And sometimes my reasons for those dreams are not very good."

"No, girl, I've watched you. You've a lot of love in you, and you've taken good care of these two. Neither of them would likely have lived through the voyage if it weren't for you and all your washin' and stealin' limes and the like. You're a good girl."

"My name is Katie . . . Katie Ryan . . . I mean Donovan."

"I know your name, girl." Mrs. Dunn handed Katie a wet cloth. "Before you start takin' all I say to heart and get for yourself a big head, start spongin' the man down."

"Can we make him live?"

"You know better than to ask a question like that of me,

girl. His life or death is between himself and his Maker. We can sponge him down."

Michael stirred. "Will you two old crows stop talking about me as if I were in my grave? I am not that sick. I'll be fine as soon as I rest a bit."

Mrs. Dunn smiled and chuckled. "He's probably tellin' us the Lord's own truth."

"I am," Michael said firmly.

Katie and Mrs. Dunn worked tirelessly throughout the night and the next day. Michael seemed to get no better, but then, as Mrs. Dunn pointed out hopefully, he was no worse.

"It can't be long now before we reach land," Mrs. Dunn said. "They will have doctors there." Then she shrugged. "Doctors aren't worth much, they aren't, but they will have a bed for him to lie in and some decent food."

Katie was tired and depressed. "I have been thinking for the last three days that we would be coming to land. The fact is that none of us knows when we will land. We could all die down here, every last one of us, and still they would tell us nothing."

Katie was almost correct, but not quite. Though they were not told in words that they were coming into port, the actions of the crew confirmed their guesses. The morning after Katie's complaint, a work crew invaded the steerage quarters with mops, buckets, and many casks of vinegar. The moldy, vermin-infested straw that had served as their bedding and a covering for the floor, unchanged throughout the voyage, was swept up and tossed over the side of the ship. The steerage passengers had more time on deck this day than at any other time during the voyage.

Katie was nearly sick herself as she looked down into the Saint Lawrence River and saw the filthy straw, rank bedding, casks of refuse, old rags, and bits of tattered clothing floating on the surface as far as she could see. It seemed every ship that came up the river followed the same procedure at this point in the voyage. The sun was shining, and Katie wanted to cry for the ruination of the golden sunstruck river she had told Michael would greet them.

Michael could barely stand, but he had been determined that he would make it up on deck by his own power. He was deathly afraid that if he appeared incapacitated the doctors would not permit him to land. If they could prevent him from boarding a ship in Liverpool, he saw no reason to believe they could not prevent him from leaving a ship in Quebec or Montreal. The one thing he could not bear to think of or allow to happen was for him to be separated from Keely and Katie. He had been told by several people what a vast land it was that he was coming to. It was like hundreds of Irelands. If he was separated from them now, he feared, he'd never find them again. He had to look well enough to pass the simple medical examination the doctors gave. Michael took heart when he saw how many ships were lined up in the river. Surely with so many the doctors would not be too careful, and then he could recover his strength with Katie's care.

Michael's assessment was essentially correct, but he had no way of knowing the magnitude of the problem thrust upon Dr. Douglas, the medical officer in charge of the quarantine station at Grosse Isle. Stories of fever raging in Ireland and of the huge number of emigrants who would be coming to Canada had been heard and noted. Dr. Douglas, hoping to be ready for an unusual number of ill passengers, asked his government for three thousand pounds to finance the quarantine hospital. He was allotted slightly less than three hundred pounds and allowed one steamer, the *Saint George,* to ply between Grosse Isle and Quebec. He was granted permission to hire an additional sailing vessel on the condition that such vessel could be had for no more than fifty pounds. Dr. Douglas was appalled but got nowhere in his requests for a more reasonable sum to handle the emigrants. The citizens of Quebec were equally alarmed and begged the Canadian government to take action. Petitions were filed with Earl Grey, the secretary of state for the colonies, for aid with the deluge of Irish emigrants, all of whom they claimed were poor and destitute. The *Montreal Gazette* joined its voice to the pleas for action to be taken to meet the coming crisis, pointing out that Quebec was only the port where the Irish would stop for a few hours before boarding another ship and going elsewhere, mainly Montreal. Montreal, it claimed, would take the brunt of the problem.

The Emigration Committee of Montreal called a meeting of Montreal citizens on May 10, 1847, to consider the problem. However, the meeting was so poorly attended, it was adjourned that same evening. Everyone recognized that a tragedy was in the making, but no one seemed inclined to take the necessary actions that might prevent it.

Alexander Carlisle Buchanan, chief emigration officer, was a powerful man and might have saved the people of Canada and the arriving Irish a good deal of anguish had he spoken out on the subject. Buchanan was a highly respected man whose reports were studied and attended to. He might have been the one person who could have made known to the right people the enormity of the problem that was in the process of growing as the number of emigration ships in the Saint Lawrence increased. But Alexander Buchanan said nothing in any of his reports about the emigration problems Dr. Douglas faced because, he said, the subject of emigration problems was not under the control of his department.

When the Saint Lawrence opened late in the year of 1847, the first vessel to enter was the *Syria,* on May 17. She was carrying eighty-four cases of fever aboard out of a total of 241 passengers. In Dr. Douglas's opinion at least an additional two dozen passengers would sicken with the fever soon after landing. There was little he could do, how-

ever, for his hospital was built to accommodate 150 people
and could be forced to handle as many as 200. With the
Syria the first ship to enter port and filling 84 beds, Douglas knew it was hopeless to think he would even come close
to being able to care for the others that would follow.

Dr. Douglas went to the government again, this time
telling them that he had reliable information that ten thousand emigrants had left Britain for Quebec since April. He
told them that hundreds of these would have to be hospi-
talized and asked for an additional one hundred and fifty
pounds to build another hospital. He had given up asking
for the amount he really needed. Even with his small request, he only received one hundred and five pounds.

Four days after the *Syria* came up the Saint Lawrence to
Grosse Isle, eight more ships arrived carrying an additional 430 cases of fever. Two hundred and five were taken
ashore, which dangerously overcrowded the small, inade-
quately sized and staffed hospital. The remaining 216 cases
of fever had to be left aboard their ships and the ships left
in the river.

Three days later, seventeen more vessels arrived to ride
at anchor in the crowded river. Every ship carried fever
victims, and the Saint Lawrence was clogged with infested
debris. The air above it rang with the cries of the ill and the
dying. Dr. Douglas turned a shed normally used for quar-
antined passengers into a hospital and brought as many of
the ill ashore as he could. He managed to house 695 of
them. One hundred sixty-four were still on board one or
another of the ships. While contemplating what he could
do, Dr. Douglas was given the message that another twelve
ships, all carrying fever, had arrived.

By May 26, thirty vessels with ten thousand emigrants
aboard were waiting at Grosse Isle. One of those ships, the
Mary Grace, carried Michael and Keely Donovan and Katie Ryan. Five days later the number of waiting vessels had
jumped to forty. Word had reached Dr. Douglas that an

additional forty-five thousand emigrants were now expected. In less than a week the problem Dr. Douglas had tried to forestall had become a raging tragedy that no one could stop.

Katie and Michael stood at the rail of the ship listlessly watching as a boat approached to remove the dead from the ship. So often did the dead boat make its rounds along the two-mile line of ships in the Saint Lawrence that the surviving passengers had no emotion left to give to the dead or to the remaining living relatives, even when the deceased had been their friends. With dull eyes Michael, Katie, and Mrs. Dunn watched as another member of the once raucous Sweeney family was brought from below decks wrapped in a canvas bag. Only young Pat Sweeney had survived the voyage, and he looked as though it were only a matter of time until he joined his mother, father, and brother. Michael thought about the impish grins the Sweeney boys had given him as they were leaving Fairmont and Pat had told him about crossing all Reginald Fairmont's fairy paths to bring him bad luck. How long ago that seemed, and though Michael would always recall it as one of the worst times of his life, right now all he could think of was that Pat Sweeney had been smiling. Sean Sweeney had been alive and proud of the boy. His mother had been there keening over her possessions. The sun had been shining. It had been a long time ago, more than a month that translated into a lifetime. He looked away from the men and their canvas-wrapped cargo. Those *things* that were taken off the ship were not Michael's friends. He didn't know what they were, but somehow, somewhere between Fairmont and this place in the Saint Lawrence River, they had ceased to be people. He stared morosely at the debris in the river.

Even Katie was having a difficult time keeping her spirits up. She had lost all the bright spots in her world. Even her dreaming didn't help. Michael had continued to manage to keep on his feet, but he looked like a death's head. His skin was sallow and old-looking. He no longer could walk straight-backed, and she could tell that he was in pain more often than not. She fully expected him to keel over one day and just not get up again. She had seen it happen before to other people and knew that it was possible. Because he tried to remain silent about how ill he was, Katie did not talk to him about it either. He was surviving on sheer willpower. She didn't understand how he kept doing it, but she thanked God that he did.

Katie stared bleakly ahead of her, her sight unclear for the unshed tears. Slowly Katie took a deep breath, and then another. She began to think. She kept on breathing deeply and slowly, and then tried to find something that was better today than it had been yesterday. They were trapped on this ship of disease and death, that was true, but, on the other hand, Dr. Douglas had issued orders that the bow and stern hatches had to be opened so that fresh air flowed freely through the hold at all times. The stench in their quarters was nearly gone and the ship was now kept spotlessly clean even in the steerage section. And the steerage passengers could be on deck as much as they wished. Michael still had the yellowish look of a sick man, but even he looked better than he had that first day they had anchored in the river. And there was Grosse Isle, a quarantine island but nonetheless a promise of what lay beyond. It was a first step to freedom, and a rather attractive step at that.

Grosse Isle was a beautiful island in the middle of the Saint Lawrence River covered so densely with trees and shrubs that grew so near the water that it appeared to float on the surface of the river. When the sun set in the evening and turned the river to liquid fire, Grosse Isle was an almost black oasis of coolness and invitation. Katie couldn't look at it without remembering how often Michael had said that as soon as they set their foot on the shore and he could find a wood, he was going to take her there and make love to her in the privacy that only nature could give. She smiled. The isle was such a pretty place to be used for a quarantine island. It deserved better, she thought, and then realized that for the first time the steerage passengers were being provided with something special. This was not a slave mart or a place that was undesirable and therefore good enough for them, the chaff of the world. Grosse Isle was beautiful. So many little rocky bays cut into its shape, each one almost begged for a rowboat and a lazy afternoon spent in fishing or lovemaking. On a hill nearer to the center of the island sat a white church, its delicate steeple dominating everything around it, a constant reminder that there once had been an Eden—and a God who benevolently watched over the inhabitants. Katie shivered with renewed hope.

"It's almost over, Michael. Just a little while longer and we'll be off this ship," Katie reminded him.

Lost in his own thoughts, Michael barely grunted in response, his glassy eyes staring blankly out at the river.

Katie told herself it was the fever that had brought on Michael's cold, withdrawn mood. Yet, as she hugged Keely closer for warmth, she knew that was only part of the truth. Whatever the reasons for it, Michael's periodic melancholy bothered her. She didn't know exactly what it meant. His moods touched off something in her that made her resentful and unhappy. At least that part she understood. Michael insisted on emphasizing his Irishness. He would let no one, including her, forget it for a moment. He wrapped it about himself like a battle flag, never allowing others to know him without knowing of his heritage. The fact that Katie was Irish was something she didn't want to think about now or ever. All too often, Katie thought, people failed to look beyond her nationality and see her true worth. Everyone hated the Irish, made fun of them, called them names, believed that they deserved no more than poverty and ignorance and that they wanted no more, except, of course, their drink. All Irish meant to Katie was hunger and degradation. It was something she could do without very well. Michael wanted to rub the world's nose in his ancestry, and for Katie the future meant losing her origins in the mists of a new existence. When the dark moods were upon Michael, she couldn't forget anything, and she didn't like it.

Michael reached over and covered her hand with his. Wordlessly, his gaze met hers. Katie smiled in relief. Michael's moody storm was over for the time being. Her resentment and resistance to him vanished. She put her hand to his forehead. It was still too warm, and his eyes maintained the glassy look that told her he still carried a fever.

"Do you want to go below to rest for a bit?" she asked.

"No, I don't want to be down there when they are taking out the dead."

"The doctors are finished with all that for today," Katie said.

"I don't want to be down there," Michael said.

The doctors were not finished. They returned later that day to remove another man who had died that afternoon, and now the decision had been made to remove any person from the ship they suspected of having fever. When Katie told him what was being said, Michael's eyes were wide with fear. His greatest dread was to be separated from Katie and Keely. Several times he had awakened in the night in a cold sweat from a dream in which he had lost them and could not find either one of them. In his dream he had been wandering alone, searching for his daughter and for Katie. If he had to jump overboard and swim for shore, he was not going to allow the doctors to remove him from the ship until Katie and Keely went too.

Too well, Michael knew the early symptoms of typhoid fever, and he hurried below to see if he could rid himself of some of the outward signs before the doctors examined him.

"Katie, help me," he said, pulling her along. "Where have you hidden the wash water? I know you have some."

"But if you hide your illness, Michael, no one can help you. The doctors do have medicine. Michael, please, let the doctors take care of you. I have tried but I don't know what else to do."

"You've done well by me, Katie. I'm not nearly so sick as some of the others. I have no rash."

Katie stared at him for a moment, then admitted that was so, saying, "But is that because you are getting better?"

"Of course," Michael said firmly. "Now, help me cool my face so the flush doesn't show. How are my eyes? Are they glassy?"

They were glassy. Katie didn't know what to say. She wasn't sure what she wanted to happen. She was scared, and she didn't know if Michael was really getting better or if it was just a matter of time before he was covered with a rash and vomiting as the others in the hold had done. She wasn't even sure how much she really knew about his illness, because he hid it so well. She knew he had had several nosebleeds, yet not once had he told her about it. She had found out by herself and by accident. Now he was sticking his tongue out at her.

"Look," he said. "If I wash it, I think it will pass for normal, or as normal as anyone else on board. I don't think the doctors will take the time to look carefully at any of us. They are too harried and there are too many sick."

Katie shook her head at him, then began to cry.

Michael's embrace was quick and gentle. "Don't cry, Katie, love, it will be all right. I will be all right. All we need is each other, and that is all I'm asking of you, darling. Help me to keep the three of us together." He kissed her cheek, then bent down, placing soft and breathy kisses along her neck. "Help me, Katie, love."

"All right, Michael, I will. And I pray to God that you are doing right. If you bring me grief with your stubborn ways, I'll never forgive you. Do you hear, Michael Donovan? I mean what I say, I'll never forgive you."

Michael was moving as well as a man in pain with a debilitating disease can manage when the doctors called all the passengers on deck. Both Michael and the doctors knew that many—too many—men and women would be passed along as healthy when they were not. All that Michael prayed for was that he be one of those passed over. The doctors were praying that they might catch the worst of the victims and that none who slipped through their fingers would move on to cause a tragic epidemic elsewhere. By the time Dr. Douglas's staff of exhausted, overworked doctors saw Michael, they had gone without sleep for days and had seen so many faces of illness they hardly knew a healthy one when they saw one. After a while it was difficult to tell who merely had dysentery that might kill them, and who had rickets, and who had typhoid, and who was just starving to death, or who might have hepatitis. There were not enough hospital beds, there was not enough medicine, or time to diagnose, and not enough nurses or doctors, many of whom were now as ill as the patients they treated. With the miles-long line of ships anchored in the huge river carrying their cargoes of the sick and dying people, no matter where the doctors were, they were aware they were needed elsewhere. As had been the case at the port of exit in Britain, the physical examination was reduced to what a doctor's eye could see when a person stood before him and stuck out his or her tongue. If the fever was advanced enough to be obvious, the emigrant might be put into the hospital. If it was not advanced enough, or if it was merely missed, the man or woman was free to go on, perhaps to infect others or die in some other place.

Michael dressed in the cleanest clothes he had and used the remaining water Katie had to scrub his face until his cheeks were so rosy that Katie said, "You look more like you have a fever now than you did before, Michael."

"Lord, do I?" Michael asked, too nervous to joke about anything.

Katie tried to laugh, but her sense of humor was flagging also, and to make matters worse, she thought he did look like he had a fever. "Keep bathing your temples," she suggested. "It might take some of the heat out of your skin."

Michael shut his eyes and swayed dangerously from the vertigo of the fever. "They will never let me go ashore with you and Keely." Then he opened his eyes and stared hard at her. "I'll jump overboard. I'll swim to the shore." He began to talk faster, his hands clamped on Katie's shoulders. "You can meet me. They'll let you take Keely if you tell them you're her mother, and then you can come ashore and I'll find you. We'll go on from there. We'll find a place where . . ."

"Michael! Michael, stop it! Say no more! You are raving like a madman. Hush, now."

Michael clasped her to him, holding her so close she could barely breathe. "I can't let them take you away from me, Katie. If I go to that hospital, I know I'll never see you and Keely again. I'll die there."

"No, my love, no, never. You aren't going to die. Don't even think the thought, for you might give the devil ideas. Come now, it is time. I can hear them calling the passengers to the doctor's table."

"I could hide. They'd never know I was aboard."

"Michael! Come on now, man. There's no help for it. The sooner it's gotten over with the better."

Trembling like a frightened child, Michael made his way up the companionway and took his place in the line of passengers to be given their quick examination by the doctors. Already there was a huddled group of people standing to the side, looking as though they had just had the death sentence passed upon them. At the sight he began to shiver uncontrollably. His skin was clammy with a thin sheet of sickly moisture.

Katie, in line behind him and holding Keely in her arms, touched his sleeve, whispering, "Michael, you look as if you'll fall over at any minute. Are you all right? Shall I get you help?"

Michael didn't answer. He couldn't speak. His mind was as frozen as the chill of his skin. Shuddering, he took a deep breath, and with it came a ray of hope. Perhaps this was good. Perhaps for a moment at least the fever had broken and that was why he felt so clammy. He turned, still shaky, but with a smile on his face. "Kiss me, Katie darlin', and tell me what you feel."

Katie gave him a strange, questioning look, but she stood on tiptoe, leaning toward him.

"No! Not on my lips—on my forehead."

She kissed his forehead, then went down on her heels with a surprised thump. "You're cool! Michael! There's no fever."

He laughed aloud. "My God!" he cried in thanks. "They'll pass by me, Katie. I know it. We won't be separated."

7

KATIE, Michael, and Keely found themselves on Grosse Isle in the company of thousands of other emaciated, sick, bewildered, and penniless emigrants who had finally been discharged from the ships. Katie had never seen such an awful sight. The starving and fever stricken were in such condition that one had to wonder if they would live to board the steamer that would take them to Montreal. The laments for the dead and dying were never ending. Both the day and night were pierced by the high-pitched, inconsolable sounds of grief.

Katie huddled close to Michael and kept Keely pressed warm and safe against her breast. Though exhausted, she kept talking throughout the night, for somehow it seemed a dangerous thing to sleep. Katie was certain that an evil sprite would creep up on them as they slept and afflict them with some awful disease. So in a soft voice she talked and talked to Michael, even when he dozed off and had no idea of what she said.

"I think when we finally find the right place for us, Michael, it should not be a pretty place. Pretty places seem to be the favorite of the devil, I'm thinking. We were born on the most beautiful piece of land in all the world. God didn't make a place any lovelier than Ireland, and look what has happened to all the poor souls who called it their home. And now, here we are on this lovely island, floating like a cloud on one of God's most beautiful rivers, and there's death and pestilence all about us. I cannot bring myself to believe that is an accident. I think that the Lord is telling us something, Michael. We must not deserve all this loveliness, for otherwise so many would not be dying and in such pain here." Katie paused, waiting for Michael to say something. When he didn't, she nudged him. "Michael, are you awake? Did you hear what I said?"

Michael stirred, shifted his arm behind her to restore his circulation. "I dozed off, Katie . . . I'm not sure . . ."

"We will go to a place where no one will notice us. If there are so many people about that you cannot tell an Irishman from anyone else, perhaps the evil ones will not be able to find us and we will be able to live like other people."

Michael chuckled. "Katie, my love, my lovely Katie, you are an optimist. There is no spot on this green earth that one man will not look up and recognize an Irishman for the poor forgotten, misbegotten creature that he is."

"No!" Katie said fiercely. "No. There must be a time for everyone . . . a time of good, a time of peace and plenty."

"Every dog has its day," Michael murmured.

"And why not?"

"No reason, Katie, love—no good reason anyway." Michael yawned. "Go to sleep for a bit, Katie. Nothing is going to get you here. We'll be safe till morning."

"I think I'll just say my prayers, if you don't mind, Michael."

He smiled in the dark, knowing that this was her way of saying she would go to sleep without having to actually admit it to him. She would begin counting off her prayers on her fingers to be certain she slighted no saint or person of the trinity, and at some point the counting would end and Katie would be asleep in his arms. Michael counted himself as a lucky man. He had managed to slip past the doctors and he was here with his daughter and his love. He could not ignore that he was very ill, but he would get better. It hadn't killed him yet, and he wouldn't allow it to. He remembered Aislinn, and how fevered she had been. He had known then that if he could have broken her fever she would have lived. He had decided that several times a day, while they awaited their turn on the steamer, he would immerse himself in the river and thus take the heat from his body. He was certain this would cure him. Surely the fever would be broken and stay away.

When they awakened the next morning, the steamer *John Munn*, which plied between Grosse Isle and Montreal, had already taken on a full load of passengers. The other steamer, *Queen*, would come in soon. For a brief moment Katie held the hope that they would board *Queen*. All too quickly she had to admit that it was unlikely they would. There were too many people waiting. She reconciled herself to another wait and turned her attentions to other things.

"Michael, what are we to do for food? I've enough left for one more meal and that is all."

"I'll go to the sheds and see if they haven't something to spare," he said.

"You'll do no such thing! They'll take one look at you and realize their mistake. Quicker than you can blink your eye they'll have you into the hospital. I'll go if you think you're strong enough to watch after Keely."

Katie walked up the hill to the hospital area. Grosse Isle was a beautiful place to be, she thought. The sun kissed the Saint Lawrence and the trees that covered the island swayed gracefully in the softest of breezes. Katie breathed deeply, her stride lengthening and becoming brisker as she moved over the swells of the hills. It was a shock and an insult to her senses when she came upon the place where

Dr. Douglas had built his hospital. There were tents and sheds and blankets laid on the ground with the sick lying about like the forgotten, ruined toys of a careless child.

"Ochh," she said aloud. "Dear God, but I would smother him with my own hands before I'd let them bring Michael to this horrible place of Satan!"

A ragged skeleton of a woman heard her and raised her bony arm to Katie, pleading for something in a voice so dry and cracked from thirst that Katie could not understand her.

Katie walked into the first building and gagged at the hideous stench that permeated the room. She hurried up to the first person she saw wearing a stained white apron, guessing he was a doctor or perhaps a priest come to help out.

"Please, sir," she said. "I've a small child, and we'll starve if we don't have food. Can you tell me where I might go to get provisions?"

"Can't you see I'm busy tending to those who are in greater need than you?" the man snapped, and walked away from her.

Katie tried twice more and got the same kind of response. To the last man, she shouted, "And is it that you're wanting me and my family flat on our backs and dying so that you can feel charitable for helping us pass on into the next world? Can you not find it in your hearts to keep us alive and well in this one? Hypocrites!" she shrieked. "All of you! Hypocrites! You don't care a bit that we die!"

A black garbed priest hurried across the room, weaving his way among the beds. "My child, calm yourself. Sit down, please. You are overwrought and don't realize what you are saying. And who can blame you. But surely you can see these good doctors are doing all they can. There are so many to be cared for and so few resources to do it with and so few able people. We are not hypocrites, my dear. You must know that. We are merely mortals doing the best we are able."

Katie had listened patiently, but now her eyes flashed green fire. "And willin' to let me starve. Didn't you hear me say that I have a child? Will you stand here and say you haven't a crust of bread and a bit of cheese to spare her?"

"I will, for it is true. My child, you still have your health. You can work for that bread and cheese. These poor ones in here cannot move from their beds of pain. They cannot help themselves at all. All that we have must go to the helpless. 'What you do for the least of my brethren, so you do . . .'"

"Suffer the little children, and let the dead bury their dead!" Katie snapped. "I am alive, and I want to stay alive. It is I and my family who are the least of your brethren!"

"Blasphemous talk, young woman. You must . . ."

"Life is a blasphemy, Father!" Katie said, and walked away from him. She was glad to be outside that room again. But she hadn't given up yet.

Systematically, Katie poked her nose into every tent and building she saw until she found the supply tent. Her conscience barely pricked her at all. From it she took as much food as she could stuff into her sleeves and the pockets of her dress. She took clean clothing and some powder for Keely, a bar of soap for all of them to enjoy, and a bucket, which she filled with food but would later use to haul water from the river. Bold as brass, defying anyone to question or stop her, she walked through the compound swinging the loaded bucket as if it was rightfully her own. She was singing by the time she returned to Michael.

The only thing that worried her was that never in her life had she spoken so insolently to a priest. Katie wasn't at all certain that God would like what she had done or forgive her for it. All of a sudden, Katie had a deep, sickening, sinking feeling that somehow He was going to punish her for what she had said to that priest. She didn't tell Michael about that part of her morning's venture. As far as he knew the good doctors had given her permission to take all the food and supplies she needed out of the kindness of their hearts.

It was two more days before Michael and Katie boarded *Queen* for the journey to Montreal. Michael was not getting better. To Katie he insisted he was, but she couldn't believe him, and she was exhausted. Much of the time he was so fevered he was talking nonsense. It was made all the more difficult because Michael didn't realize it. When he wasn't delirious, he insisted upon taking the frigid baths in the river. Michael thought it would cure him. Katie feared it would kill him. Nightly she prayed that they would be among the next to board one of the steamers to take them to Montreal. She was certain that if they could just reach Montreal they would be all right. She would find a position there as a housekeeper until Michael was well enough to travel, and then they would be on their way to New York. She held on to her plans as though they were a life raft.

The journey to Montreal was a nightmare, the steamer captains boarding as many as could be jambed on deck. It was a repeat of the crowded, unprotected journey from Cork to Liverpool, only this time none of them were as well or as able to withstand the trials of the voyage as they had been then.

They had barely left Grosse Isle before Michael was violently ill, nausea racking his body in violent waves. Katie cringed in fear. She couldn't help him and he didn't seem able to help himself. She was sure that he was going to die before they reached Montreal. It didn't seem possible that he could go on as he was now. Much of the time he was delirious now, not even recognizing her when she approached him. He alternated between heated sweats and bone-shaking chills that shook him nearly as violently as did the vomiting. Katie was frantic, for she didn't know what to do and there would be no help from the captain of the ship. All he wanted to do was unload his unsavory human cargo and return to Grosse Isle for the next load.

She was also fearful for herself and Keely. For so long she had been proud of her good care of them, but she was no longer so cocky. She didn't know what was keeping them well. As she watched Michael suffering, she could not restrain a deep horror and fear that she might soon suffer the same way, and Michael would not be there to help her. The idea of Keely going through such an illness horrified her. As always when she was frightened and cornered, Katie gritted her teeth, took a firmer hold on Keely, and repeated over and over to herself, "We'll be all right. We'll be all right." Then she prayed that it was so. It was a desperate faith she clung to, riddled with doubts, but it was all she had right now. She hoped God understood.

In his own private hell, Michael spent his days and nights in a haze of delirium and pain. He no longer knew when he was lucid and when he was not. He could not even bear Katie's touch. The thought of food revolted him, yet some strand of rationality told him he had to eat and drink or he would surely die.

When the steamship finally came into Montreal, neither Katie nor Michael was looking for a miracle. They just wanted some small oasis of relief, if even for a short time. Neither had the endurance to keep going without hope— or so they thought.

Montreal was experiencing its own nightmare, because of the lack of preparation for the emigrants; no one had foreseen or anticipated the extent or burden that the Irish famine would bring to them. By the first of June, Montreal was being deluged with emigrants, many of them ill, at a rate of 2,304 in a twenty-four hour period. The city was awash with the sick, homeless and destitute masses. Hordes of children roamed the streets with no place to go and nothing to eat. Petty thievery in the shops was rampant. Until the fifth of June, Montreal did not even have a board of health to deal with the problem, and even then it was quickly apparent that the situation was moving at so swift a pace and was of such proportions that no plan was going to protect the city from the aftermath of the emigrants' arrival.

The newly formed Board of Health immediately issued several directives. First it barred the emigrants from using the harbor in the center of the city. All emigrants should be landed at Windmill Point, a place outside the city above the Lachine Canal. They went on to close down the lodging houses catering to the emigrants, declaring these places to be hotbeds of infection. It further ordered that more hospital beds be made available and the city be cleaned, which ordinarily happened only when the heavy winter snows were shoveled. Unfortunately, none of the orders was heeded. The Board of Health had been created but not financed. None of its recommendations could be carried out.

Mr. Brown, the secretary of the Board of Health was a concerned man and a compassionate one for his concern extended beyond the peril of Montreal to the emigrants themselves. Never had he seen such misery as he did when the Irish were literally dumped on his wharf. The beautiful, historic stone wharves of Montreal could barely be seen for the numbers of people on them. Many of the passengers the *John Munn* and *Queen* brought in could no longer walk. Mr. Brown stood aside, watching men and women crawling along the wharf without strength to stand. Dying people lay where they fell; others inched their way along looking for some cool spot out of the sun.

As Michael landed, he knew that it was only a matter of time before he was one of those who could no longer keep to his feet. He was nearly at the point that he didn't care. He would take oblivion for a time at least. Just drawing breath was an exhausting effort. His bathing in the river had accomplished little but to give him a cold. He was feverish so much of the time, a spinning, uncertain footing was becoming the usual for him.

Katie left him as soon as they had set foot on the wharf, knowing she had to find shelter for them right away. As she set out to find out about the lodging houses with Keely in tow, Michael was left to his own devices on the wharf with no more onerous responsibility than to find himself a place to sit until Katie returned for him. Michael managed to reach the wharf standing up, thanks to Katie's help, but once she was gone, he knew he would lose his balance the moment someone or something was not nearby for him to hold on to. Rather aimlessly and in a heated haze, he shuffled about the wharf area. People were everywhere. Those who had already given up and were lying on the ground where they fell were being stepped on and over by those still ambulatory. Michael looked up and saw a tree near the outer edge of the area. With one thought only in his mind and his eyes fixed on the tree, he moved in that direction.

Mr. Brown was horrified at the chaotic scene he found at the wharves. The Board of Health might not have any money to carry out their plans, he thought, but it did have some authority. He looked for an able-bodied man and said, "Bring my cart over here. We'll get as many of these poor wretched people into the hospital as we can. While you're at it, send out a call for carts. We'll need as many as possible. Be quick!"

While he waited for the man to carry out his instructions, Mr. Brown made a circuit of the wharf. He checked the area called the long shed and found dozens of others lying there. Many who were not desperately ill were simply too tired and emaciated to help themselves. Mr. Brown realized that by morning most of these would have gathered their strength and gone on. He did not worry so much about them when others' needs were so great.

As soon as his man returned leading a caravan of several carts, Mr. Brown began to direct the work, pointing to people needing hospitalization. There was no need to check a man or woman's tongue now. The fever was so advanced there was no doubt as to who was ill.

Michael had found his place in the shade and sunk down gratefully at the foot of the tree. Within seconds he was sound asleep. Even as he was drifting off, he was thinking of what a pleasure sleep was. When Mr. Brown gently prodded him with the toe of his shoe the first time, Michael did not react. A toe pressed into his ribs was hardly discomfort after the knees, elbows, and bodies he had been pressed against throughout the voyage. But the toe of Mr. Brown's shoe was persistent. Mr. Brown kept prodding and finally Michael opened his eyes to stare directly into the bright sun. Mr. Brown looked like the black looming specter of death from one of Michael's confused delirium dreams. Michael edged away from the now offensive prodding, but Mr. Brown managed to stay right in the glare of the sun. Too tired and wearied to fight the simplest of threats, Michael closed his eyes and surrendered himself to the specter.

Mr. Brown waved his arm at the cart man. "Get this one to the hospital as quickly as can be. He'll never last the day out here."

With little ceremony, Michael was piled onto the cart with several others and taken to the already overcrowded hospital in Montreal.

Having filled all his carts and the known hospital beds, Mr. Brown returned to his office. What could possibly be done in the next several days he wondered, when two or three thousand emigrants would again be deposited on the wharves. Mr. Brown was feeling put upon, threatened by forces beyond his abilities and slightly panicked. He wasn't at all certain that his best efforts would have any effect on the problem at all. The enormity was staggering.

Katie returned to the wharf not more than a half hour after Mr. Brown had taken the sick away. With Keely braced on one hip she made a quick circuit of the area, expecting to find Michael easily. She scanned the crowd, noting that there were fewer now than when she had left. She kept looking for the friendly wave that would be Michael. For a few minutes she stood in place, shifting Keely to her other hip. The child weighed little, but Katie had been carrying her for a long time, and she was hot and tired. After it was apparent that Michael was not going to come forward, Katie started out around the wharf again, this time asking if anyone had seen him. For the most part she got vacant stares or muttered answers that meant nothing to her except that they had nothing to do with Michael. She was getting angry thinking that he had probably not listened to her and had gone into the city on his own, looking for her.

She said to Keely, "Your daddy can make me very angry sometimes. We'll probably spend the rest of the day passing each other on different streets."

'A voice nearby said, "They come and took your man."

Katie turned and saw an old man sitting cross-legged against a piling. "Are you speaking to me, sir?"

"If you're looking for that tall, skinny Irishman you're always with I am talking to you," he said, his fingers never stopping as he shredded hemp and placed it in a basket beside him.

"Where was he taken?" Katie asked, then quickly added, "Who took him?"

"Mr. Brown . . . with the Board of Health took him. I can't say where. Maybe to bury, maybe to the hospital. He's gone."

"But where!?" Katie cried, fear rising. "I must find him. When did they take him? How long ago?"

The man kept working at his pile of hemp.

"How long ago? Isn't there anything else you can tell me?"

"I'm thinking on it," the man said. "I believe it must have been half an hour, maybe a bit more. But there's no point in you running off to look for him. Wherever they took him, they won't be letting you take him away. He belongs to them now. There's no room in those places for able bodies. They won't let you in."

Katie's face screwed up. She blinked hard, but couldn't hold back the tears. "They have to. I must find Michael. We're going to America."

The man was uncomfortable. She wasn't the ordinary emigrant—he could see that—and he could tell she was a bit smarter than the usual, and nicer too. "Don't cry, lass," he said as soothingly as his gravelly voice allowed. "Maybe your man isn't so sick as he looked. Maybe . . ."

"Michael looked worse than before?" Katie said in alarm. "What do you mean? What happened?" Katie had terrible visions of Michael having another attack of the awful nausea right here on the wharf.

The man shrugged.

"Tell me! Please, I must know."

Again the man shrugged. "Well, he was lying over there on the ground—by that tree. Half dead, he was. The man —Mr. Brown—came by pokin' his toe at him, then, after a bit, he had him hauled away in the cart."

"Michael wasn't walking?" Katie asked breathlessly. A steel band seemed to have been wound tightly around her chest making breathing difficult. She dreaded to hear what the man would say.

The man didn't actually say anything, his eyes merely holding Katie's told her the answer.

"I have to find him," she said distractedly, and began to walk away. After a few paces she turned back. "You're sure we are talking about the same man. Michael is . . ."

"I know who you are talking about, lass. I've seen the two of you. I was watching. I'm sorry for you, that I am."

Katie nodded, then softly said good-bye. She would take Keely back to the lodging house she had found for them to stay in, feed her, and try to figure out what she was going to do. She supposed there must be a way to find people in the hospital who had been picked up off the wharf. She shuddered again, for if Michael hadn't been walking—and she was sure now that the old man was correct, for Michael would never have ridden in the sick cart if he had had a choice—what would she do with him after she found him? As ill as he must be, she would not be able to nurse him and go out and find work at the same time. How would she ever feed them? And pay for their lodging? Suddenly she wished the doctors at Grosse Isle had recognized how sick Michael was and put him in the hospital there. At least she would have known where he was, and they could have made arrangements to be with each other when he was cured.

Her wearied mind returned to the beginning, the basic problem for her. She had to find Michael. She had to have him with her. Then the tormenting questions circled through her brain again. Would the authorities permit him to leave the hospital? From her own experience with authorities, Katie had little faith, and from what she had heard since she arrived, she didn't think the Canadians liked the Irish any better than the English. Katie smiled wanly. One thing that Michael had never gotten confused, even when he was out of his head with fever, was that he was an Irishman. How tragically humorous it was, she mused, that one set of people had no regard for an Irishman and another had greater regard for Irishness than life itself. The world was a strange place, she decided, but not very nice. She hoped there was a heaven, but for all she knew that might not be very nice either.

"Oh, Keely, listen to me," she said aloud. "I am thinking that I am very tired. Not even my thoughts make sense anymore. We'd just better eat and both of us take a nap. At least we have a bed—for a while—and we can wash." Again Katie's overworked mind went to work on her worries. She had most of the money Michael had gotten from his saloon fights in Cork. That seemed an age ago, and it seemed impossible that the emaciated, sick man she had left at the wharf was the same man who a little over a month ago had been fighting with the best boxer Cork had to offer—and winning. "Glory be, Keely Donovan, what are we to do about your father? We need him so, and he cannot even fend for himself."

"Da!" Keely cooed. "Da!"

Tears came to Katie's eyes again. "Ooch, my love, what a cruel place this world is. Will you ever be catching up with yourself?" She hugged Keely, the pretty, petite little gamin who behaved as if she were ten months old and weighed no more than an infant when she was well on her way toward her third year. Then, with a start, Katie realized that Keely was three years old. She had had her third birthday on board ship, and they had all been so concerned about Michael, it had passed unnoticed. She hugged Keely close again. "Will it ever come right for you?"

After they had eaten, Katie sat down with Keely in a chair near the window of the lodging house. The house she had chosen wasn't so bad as some of the others, but it was more expensive. Katie knew the little money they had was not going to last long. She had counted on Michael being with them. She had thought he would stay here, get well while she worked for the first couple of weeks, and then he would be out making money so that they could continue their journey. Now he was gone and everything changed. There were so many things to consider, she didn't know where to begin. She had no idea of what to do about Michael now. She did know that Keely needed the attention of a mother and good food and care in order to grow up normally. Even with such luxuries, Katie wasn't certain that Keely hadn't been deprived for too long already. How was she to care for Keely and work too? Yet if she didn't find a position soon they would both starve. Katie, hugging Keely, sat in the chair staring out the window, rocking and thinking and crying.

It was dark when Katie finally marshalled her strength and felt able to face what must be done immediately. She changed Keely, washed out her napkin, and dressed her in fresh clothing. Katie had always been particular about cleanliness, but since she had started on the voyage over here, she had become fanatical. She was always scrubbing herself and the child until their skin shone, and their clothes constantly smelled of soap. If they needed one bar of soap, Katie stole two—just in case. She had a horror of having to do without it. She would go without food before she would go without soap.

Satisfied that neither she nor Keely looked like or smelled like emigrants, Katie picked up Keely and headed for the lodging house kitchen. Mrs. Holmes, the plump, cheerful landlady, was sitting at the kitchen table, sipping tea and reading the newspaper.

"Good evening to you, Mrs. Donovan," she said. "You're a bit late for supper, aren't you? The others have eaten and gone."

Katie's instinct was to apologize, but she didn't. She smiled sweetly, reminding herself that she was *not* a poor emigrant but the respectable wife of an ordinary man. That was how she had to act. "I'm afraid I fell asleep while I was rocking Keely. We are both hungry now. I suppose that it's all to the good. We'll be sure to enjoy our food."

Mrs. Holmes looked at her, saying a bit waspishly, "I've already cleaned the kitchen after the other boarders."

"You needn't worry. I'll clean up after myself," Katie said.

The woman settled back to her newspaper. After a moment, she said, "Well, don't bother to make tea for yourself. I've plenty and would be pleased if you'd join me in a cup—or will your husband be coming down? You did say he'd be coming this afternoon, didn't you?"

Katie's heart nearly stopped. Unable to gather her thoughts, she looked down at the floor. "Yes, I did say that, but—he—I received bad news today. He—he's been detained—business. He won't be joining us as soon as I had hoped. I—I got a message that he must travel to—to a —city north of here."

Mrs. Holmes gave her an inquisitive look. "Would that be Ottawa, or could you mean Quebec?" she asked.

Katie's head whirled. She had never heard of Ottawa—wasn't even certain there was such a place—but she had heard of Quebec. "I do, yes, I do mean Quebec," Katie said too fast, but with a smile. "I was woolgathering and couldn't think of the name, but it was Quebec. Yes, Quebec."

Katie sensed Mrs. Holmes watching her every move for the next several seconds, but then the uncomfortable moment passed, and Mrs. Holmes continued to read her paper while Katie prepared her dinner.

Katie shared the cup of tea with Mrs. Holmes, fed herself and Keely, and managed to keep up a pleasant conversation with her landlady, never once mentioning her voyage or the fact that she was fresh from Ireland, just let off a coffin ship. For Katie it was as important that people not know her origins as it was for Michael to be known for them.

That night when Katie went to bed, it was not to sleep for a very long time—until it was nearly dawn and her wicked mind would do nothing but mull over and over all the things she had to do. The first was to find Michael. The second was to find a way of supporting them all until Michael was well enough to work. Light was creeping in through the curtains when Katie shut her eyes to dream of ways to find Michael, then take him home.

8

KATIE was frantic and exhausted after several days of fruitlessly searching for Michael. She had haunted the emigrants' hospital but had not been able to gain entrance. Every time she was stalled at the door. Each time she tried to find a new face, someone who had not spoken to her before. But each time she had told one of the doctors or priests or nuns that she was looking for a particular person, she was kindly, gently, and firmly told to return to her quarters in the shed.

"But I don't live here! I am not waiting for one of the barges. I live in town. Please! You aren't hearing what I am saying. I must find my husband. I know he is in your hospital."

The nun to whom Katie was talking this time was not without sympathy, and she understood that Katie must be having a terrible time understanding why they did not know who was in their hospital. But so few had carried identification when they entered, the records were sparse and terribly incomplete. She said, "My dear, we have no one named Michael Donovan here. There is no such name on our records. You must be aware that there are many who are too ill to give their names. We do not know who they are."

Katie felt very frustrated, but she forced calm into her voice. "I do know that. But don't you see, Sister, that is why I need just a few minutes in the hospital. If I could just walk past the beds, I know I could find him. Please."

The nun remained firm. If she allowed one distraught woman to enter the hospital, there would soon be others. "We cannot do that, my dear, and well you know it. This is a place of pain. All caution and care must be given to those within. We cannot make a sideshow of them for all to gawk upon. We have a difficult task. We have not enough hands now to care properly for the sick and dying."

"But . . ." Katie began.

"No! I cannot allow you to wander about the hospital. If your Michael is here, he will join you when he can. You must trust that the Lord will look after him—and you."

Katie lost all control, and her voice grew loud and harsh. "I must find him! I *will* find him!" Katie blushed, aware that she had lost her temper and her perspective. She knew she must look like a wild woman to the nun, and why should she allow a wild woman entrance to the hospital.

"I'm sorry," the nun said, and folded her hands in front of her habit, her body blocking the entrance. "I am not able to help you, my dear, and I must return to my duties. There are so many ill to be seen to, and so few of us left to do the task. Pray for your Michael as I will pray for you."

Katie lowered her eyes. She was mildly ashamed at the time she was taking from this nun. She knew that what Sister Maria Annunciata said was true. So many different religious orders had been sent to Montreal to help with the deluge of sick that Katie did not recognize half the habits. Even the cloistered sisters of St. Joseph had been given dispensation to leave their contemplative life in order to meet the emergency. But Katie did not feel sufficient shame to give up.

She asked, "Is there no one else in authority I could talk to? Surely there must be someone here who can help me. I may not be dying of the fever, but I need help."

The nun put her hand on Katie's. "Pray for strength. It will be granted to you. And you might wish to talk with Father Richards. If anyone can help you, he can, and we'd all be grateful if you could stop his labors, if for only a moment." Sister Maria Annunciata smiled, and Katie could see a rare beauty and the drawn look of deep fatigue warring in her face. "You will find Father Richards in that wing of the building."

Katie had no difficulty identifying the priest everyone loved, though she had never met him before. Father Richards was a small man, well past retirement age. He moved gracefully along the crowded rows of hastily built wooden beds that looked like coffins to Katie. The old man's face shone with love. Katie had heard of such a phenomenon, but she had never seen it until today. She knew he had to be exhausted, but in no way did he show it. She stood at the end of the last row of beds, patiently waiting for him to complete his rounds. She did not feel the brash impulse to run through the rows seeking Michael as she expected she would after being granted entrance to the room. Her eyes remained on the priest the whole time. A strange and beautiful peace emanated from him, and Katie basked like a sun-starved flower in the grace that flowed from him to her. It had been a long time since she had felt this particularly restful love, and she knew she would lose the feeling as soon as she left the man's presence. The kind of love he had came from within, from God. Katie realized she had lost that long ago—sometime around the time she had taken her First Communion, she thought. She sighed, regretting the absence of that sweet innocence, then moved forward to meet Father Richards before he busied himself with some other self-appointed errand of mercy.

"Father, may I speak with you, please. I am in grave need of help," Katie said.

Father Richards's deep-set eyes turned full focus upon her. He had the capacity, even in the midst of turmoil, to fully concentrate on one thing or one person at a time.

The words Katie had been going to utter died in her throat. She had intended to tell him that she was looking for her husband, but she could not bring herself to lie to this man. She told him the truth—everything that had happened since they had left Fairmont until this moment. She confessed all her hatreds, her resentments, her thefts, fights, disappointments, hopes and dreams, and her love for Michael and Keely.

"We do keep records as best we can," the old priest said hopefully, then his eyes clouded as he added, "Of course, so many can't give their names, we do not know who they are." He took her hand in both of his thin, dry hands. A shiver ran up Katie's spine. She knew what he was thinking.

"I have already been to the dead house," she said. "I have gone there every day since he was taken from the wharf. He is not there. I know he isn't. He is alive." She bit her lip and looked away before adding, "He is in here, Father. I am certain he is among the ill, but no one will permit me to see. If I could just . . ."

"If it were so simple as merely giving permission, you must know that I would give it to you," he said. "It isn't that simple. Even now you are exposing yourself to grievous danger, and you said you have a child who needs you. This is a terrible disease. It strikes with violence. I should not be allowing you to remain in here. Please, walk outside with me. Sister Annunciata should not have told you to wait for me inside."

"But how did you know . . ."

"I saw you come in," he said with a sweet smile. "And I think you asked of her the same things you are asking of me. She probably sent you to me, because she thought I needed a rest."

Katie didn't smile with him. "I am sure she did, Father, and I appreciate that all of you working here do so under great strain, but I am not just a woman with an imaginary problem to be used to rest other people. Do none of you listen? Do you not understand?"

"You must have patience . . ."

"I can't *eat* patience, Father!" Katie snapped. Once again, Katie was beyond all ability to control herself. She screamed out her frustration and fear to the old priest. "I've got his daughter to feed and care for! What would you have me do? I can't work and leave the child alone. Would you have me take to the streets? Would you, Father? I could manage that—you could pray over my soul after I've become a fallen woman. Would that make it easier for you, Father? Is that easier than letting me look through the beds for a man, an honorable man who will marry me and care for me and his daughter?"

The old man raised his hands and made the sign of the cross over her.

Katie's eyes widened in horror at what she had done. Her eyes filled with tears, and she fell to her knees, taking the priest's hand and pressing it to her lips. "I'm sorry," she sobbed. "Oh, Father, forgive me, I am so sorry."

"Ask God's forgiveness, young woman, not mine. Ask Him for help. You are at your wit's end and need succoring. Now get up off your knees. Go to the church—please, go there and pray." He reached inside his cassock and brought out a small amount of money. "This is not much, but it may help a bit. Take it. But go to the Church, for that is where the Lord will give you real help. He is always there, waiting for you."

Katie shook her head, pushing his hand with the money

away from her. "I can't. I can't take that, Father." She looked into his eyes. "I will go to Saint Patrick's. I've been there before."

"Good. Good. You will find peace there," he said, smiling. "But you take this as well. If you don't wish to use it for yourself, then for the child. You said Michael has a child?"

"Yes, Father," she said, and allowed him to drop the coins into her hand. Her eyes looked to the door to the hospital again in hopes that she might see or hear Michael —something. But nothing happened, and Katie gave up.

As she walked out of the compound of hospital sheds, a man sauntered up to her. He wore good clothing, though loud, and he smelled of expensive cologne. She had seen him standing near the hospital sheds before and wondered why he always seemed to be there.

"You come here a lot," he said to her.

Katie glanced at him, but didn't answer. She walked faster, moving slightly to the side to avoid his path.

"Can't you speak English?" he asked, keeping pace with her.

He was Irish. She could tell that. He had black hair and unmistakably Irish blue eyes. He might be handsome. She wasn't certain, and it didn't matter, because she didn't like him. His face was too narrow and he was too bold by half. There was a deviltry in his eyes she didn't trust. She reasoned that she knew his kind—a silver tongue—all kindness and good nature until he got what he wanted. But he was also making her angry. She knew he assumed she was Irish too.

In her best English, she said curtly, "I can speak English. Now, will you go on your way and let me be? I don't want to talk to you or walk with you."

"I'm Tyrone Tully, lately of Cill Ala. Ever hear of me?"

"No."

"But you have heard of the Tully Girls, haven't you? Everybody has heard of them."

"Well, I'm not everybody, and I haven't, nor do I want to. Will you please leave me alone, sir. I will be forced to find a constable and ask him to make you stop bothering me."

His walk became jauntier than ever. He threw back his head and laughed. His eyes crinkled in amusement. "You wouldn't want to be doing that, little Erin girl. No one here wants to do with a colleen fresh off the boat."

"I'm not . . ."

"Oh, yes, you are. It shows all over you. Look at your clothes . . . the way you walk. Your family must have been 'tatie growers. I can tell." He paused and gave her an assessing look. "But it is not in the way you talk. That is different. How did you manage that?"

"It's none of your business. And why should I tell you? You have an answer for everything, don't you?"

"I might have an answer for you," he said.

Katie laughed. "That will be the day the sun does not shine. You have nothing that interests me."

"Those are big words for a little girl who just took a handout from the old priest. I know Father Richards, as does anyone in Montreal. No finer man ever lived, but he does not give his pennies to ladies of wealth. He has too precious few of them."

Katie stopped walking. She turned to face him. She stamped her foot. "Oh, will you go! Leave me be! I have important business to see to."

"Oh-oh-oh! I have important business to see to . . ." he mocked. Then he came toward her, his eyes hard. "You put on too many airs, and stupidly so. You haven't a penny to your name, and you have a pocket filled with trouble, and you are trying my patience. You are a pretty lass, but there are others as pretty, and a lot more cooperative. I'm givin' you one more chance, little girl, and that is all. Can you dance? Or sing?"

Katie was taken aback. She blurted without thinking, "I like to sing."

"Sing," he commanded.

"S-sing?" she stammered. "Now? Here? What . . . what . . ." Katie looked around her like a frightened deer. "I—I can't . . . I can't sing here in the street. You're a madman!" she cried, and ran away from him down the street.

Tyrone Tully, lately of Cill Ala, veteran showman, stood with his hands deep within his green plaid trouser pockets, his feet planted in a wide stance, his head back, his eyes shadowed as they watched Katie with admiration. Suddenly he moved, calling after her, "Tomorrow, little girl! Sure and you'll sing like a bird for me tomorrow."

Whistling, he walked down the street in the other direction, thinking of how her voice was likely to sound. Not that it mattered much. Dressed in the right way, that little Irish girl could sound like a choked crow and it wouldn't really matter. She would fill a stage and delight the eyes of every man in the saloon.

Once Katie had begun to run, she couldn't stop. Feeling like the madman she had called Tully, and probably looking worse, she raced up one street and down another trying to remember how to get to St. Patrick's Church. She felt as though she had met the devil himself and now had to cleanse herself. When she finally stumbled through the church doors there were a dozen or more poor people scattered throughout, praying or trying to find solace or a place to sleep. St. Patrick's was never empty, but somehow Katie had expected to be all alone here with God. She had been thinking that maybe for once He would have time just for her. Someone had to have time for her. Tully did. The thought frightened her.

She genuflected and slipped into a pew. She knelt on the

hard kneeling board, her head bowed low. Eyes closed, her
lips moved with silent words as she prayed the Our Father,
the Hail Mary, and Glory Be in rapid succession, the
words running together in a soundless jumble. Her mind
was racing so fast and was so filled with awful and fearful
thoughts, she could grasp nothing. She couldn't seem to
slow down. She sat back on the seat, giving up her pose of
piety. Now she was just tired. Tyrone Tully no longer
seemed like the devil, and she no longer had such an urge
to cleanse herself. He was just a man. And now she realized she had been so frightened and so upset with not being
able to find Michael, she had not listened to what the man
had said. She couldn't remember a thing he had said except that he had asked her to sing right there in the street
in front of the dead house. It had horrified her then. Now,
in church, where she should be solemn, it struck her as
funny. She thought of herself with Tyrone Tully. She saw
herself through his eyes. She began to giggle. Clapping her
hands over her mouth, she quickly knelt again, her eyes
merrily peeking and tearing over the top of her hand to see
if anyone had noticed she was irreverently laughing in
church.

Katie left St. Patrick's feeling much better. Tyrone Tully
had managed to put a little cheer back into her life. She
was feeling buoyant and optimistic again. It was still early,
and she decided she would try to find a position as a housemaid. People were always looking for good Catholic Irish
girls to scrub their floors and clean their houses. That she
had a child to care for was something she would deal with
after she was accepted for a position. If she impressed her
new employers sufficiently, Katie thought, perhaps they
would allow her to bring Keely with her. Keely was no
trouble whatsoever and would stay where Katie put her.
Katie imagined Keely spending the day in a warm kitchen.
It would work out wonderfully.

Katie walked up and down the streets until she thought

her legs would drop off, but she was hunting for a certain section of town. She would know it when she saw it, for in any village or town they were always the same. There would be big houses, and shiny carriages, signs of bounty and indications that lots of servants were needed. If she was going to hire herself out, it was going to be to someone who could pay her and give her decent accommodations.

She finally turned down a tree-lined street graced with several large, imposing brick homes. The houses had extensive grounds and intricate, well-kept gardens. Katie stood still for a time just gazing at the gardens. She noted that the houses had freshly painted trim. Most of the stables that she could see were large. This was definitely the street she had been looking for. Now she had to decide which house to try. Since she had Fairmont as the main point of comparison, it was a difficult task for her to choose among so many.

Being practical, Katie chose the house in front of where she stood. Straightening her skirt and short jacket, adjusting the small straw hat she wore, she marched straight-backed to the rear door of the house. She knocked and, while she waited, tried to assemble her face in an expression denoting dignity and maturity. In her head she repeated, "I am very experienced and have many references."

A heavyset woman came to the door and opened it wide. Katie's nostrils flared at the marvelous odor of beef cooking that wafted out from the kitchen.

"Yes," said the woman. "State your business, miss. How can I help you?"

"My name is Katie Ryan. I am looking for a posit . . ."

"Get off with you!" the woman all but screamed. "Irish death peddlers! You'll kill us all!" The door slammed firmly in Katie's shocked face.

At first Katie's breath was taken away. Then she was

angry. She kicked the door. "Y'ol' cow! I'm wishin' a pox
on you an' all your children!"

Shaking with anger and reaction to having a door
slammed in her face, Katie marched back to the street.
Pulling the waist of her jacket down, she headed for the
house on the other side of the street. By the time she had
gone to that house, and two others, she had a firm grasp on
the fact that no one in Montreal wanted to be within one
hundred miles of an Irishman. To the people of Montreal
all the Irish carried the plague and would bring evil and
misfortune into the house just as they had to the city.

Katie's cheerful demeanor shrank away, and she walked
the long distance back to Mrs. Holmes's lodging house
slump shouldered and defeated. Even the thought of Keely
did not lift her spirits as it usually did. Tonight Katie just
didn't know what she was going to do. She had never
dreamed that she would not be able to find a position as a
servant. All along she had been thinking that she would
not become a housemaid, because of her own pride. How
dreadful it was to find that no one even wanted her for the
most menial of tasks. They wouldn't even allow her inside
their houses—or their stables. What was she going to do?
Oh, God, how she needed Michael.

Most nights when Katie arrived back at the lodging
house, Mrs. Holmes was busy preparing her own supper
and had plans for the evening. With a quick exchange of
pleasantries, Keely was pressed into Katie's arms and that
was that. However, as fate would have it, on this night that
Katie wanted only to shrink inside herself while she healed
from the blows the day had dealt her, Mrs. Holmes greeted
her with a smile and a wave to enter her apartment. The
woman hurried to her kitchen, her tiny feet carrying her
with amazing speed. Katie came through the door of the
well-lit, warm kitchen as Mrs. Holmes turned around, her
hands on Keely's small shoulders. There in the kitchen

stood a smiling Keely sporting a new pink dress and tiny kid slippers on her white-stockinged feet.

"She's growing!" Mrs. Holmes announced proudly, and the tone of her voice denoted that she was taking credit for it. "And look at her! She still looks younger than what she is, but she is walking like any three-year-old, and look! Her teeth! Come here, darlin'," Mrs. Holmes demanded of Keely. "Show Katie your pretty teeth."

Katie obligingly bent over to see Keely's swollen gums, and the tiniest bits of white had broken through next to the front teeth she already had. She forced herself to say something admiring and glad, but her heart sank. She couldn't afford to get Keely clothing to replace those things she was outgrowing. Even good news on this day was turning against her. All that Katie could think of was that soon, when the last of her money ran out, Mrs. Holmes was going to have to put them out. She and Keely would have no place to go. How would she feed them without work? She stood up and put her hand to her head as she realized that Mrs. Holmes was looking strangely at her.

"I'm sorry," Katie said. "I am truly delighted to see Keely looking so lovely—and her teeth are wonderful. We are so grateful for all you've done, Mrs. Holmes . . ."

"Then why are you looking like a cloud full of dark waters?"

"I—I have a headache," Katie said, and again rubbed her forehead. It wasn't a lie exactly. She did have a headache now.

"You aren't falling ill?" Mrs. Holmes asked, a look of alarm on her bland features.

"No, no. I'm fine, really. It has been a long day, and I expected to have a position by this evening—now I won't know for several days," she improvised. "The man of the house is away on business. It is a terrible annoyance," she ended lamely, feeling as if she would be sick at her stomach if she couldn't get out of the warm, odor-heavy kitchen immediately. "I'll be fit as soon as I lie down for a few minutes."

"Shall I keep Keely for you a bit longer? I do enjoy her company," she confessed.

Katie started to protest, then thought better of it. "That would be nice," she said with a forced smile. "I'll just take a nice wash and lie down for half an hour."

The steps to her third-floor room seemed unusually steep and long tonight. Katie felt like an old woman drained of all energy and strength. She had a thumping headache now and wondered if she wasn't going to be sick to her stomach before she reached her room. She managed to get the door open and enter, pulling her hat from her head and throwing it on the chair—a rash act for Katie, who usually took good care of the few decent garments and accessories she owned. Her forehead clammy and pounding, she fell on the bed and didn't move even to make herself more comfortable.

She remained that way until the pulse stopped throbbing at her neck and temples and she could breathe normally. Slowly the headache receded to bearable proportions, but still it lurked behind her eyes, waiting to do her evil when given the chance. She knew it had been longer than half an hour since she came up and that she should be putting Keely to bed at this time, but she didn't care. She just hadn't the energy to move. Finally Mrs. Holmes brought Keely up, knocking sharply on the door. Out of breath and in ill spirits, Mrs. Holmes had a choice word to say about mothers who neglected their daughters. She handed the child over and haughtily walked back toward the stairs.

Katie felt a stab of guilt and started after her landlady. The woman had been more than kind to her, and Katie didn't know what she would do if Mrs. Holmes refused to watch Keely while she went out to find Michael or to find employment. Then lethargy took over again and she closed the door. If Mrs. Holmes was going to take care of Keely, she'd find out tomorrow. Tonight all she wanted was to sleep.

It wasn't until morning that Katie truly appreciated what Mrs. Holmes had been so proud to show her the night before. She dressed Keely again in the outfit Mrs. Holmes had spent hours sewing and in the light of a new day Katie could see how fine Keely looked. Tears brimmed in her eyes as the little girl held the edges of her skirt out to show off. How she wished Michael were here. His heart would burst with pride for Keely, and he'd be so relieved to see that finally she was doing well. Mrs. Holmes had been right. Keely was beginning to look like a normal little girl. Still thin and small, she had lost the wizened look that had made her seem more like a sickly infant than a toddler. And her hair was beginning to grow. She was a beautiful child! "Oh, Michael, where are you?" wailed Katie aloud.

"Da!" cried Keely, clapping her hands. "Wan' Da!"

Katie sat down on the floor and cried.

As it had the night before, the good news of Keely's progress brought a slew of troubles to Katie's mind. Bitterly, she cursed everyone and everything that made it so that a woman and child had to think of food and clothing and shelter as impossible problems. In a civilized world it should not be that the helpless could not count on living. Katie fumed inwardly, drawing newfound energy from her anger and indignation. She might be Irish, and she might be an unwanted emigrant, but she had a right to live. To put bread in her mouth she might be forced to live below stairs, but they had no right to deprive her of life itself. That much she had a right to depend on.

She took Keely to Mrs. Holmes's apartment, made profuse apologies for her behavior the night before, and finally made amends. As she left, she kissed Keely, then with a jaunty wave she promised, "I'll bring back something delicious for our dessert tonight."

She was no sooner out the door than she was cursing herself for a fool. Why had she promised such a stupid thing? She didn't have enough money left to pay their rent next week, let alone spend any of it on frivolities.

Angry with herself, she began to walk without thinking where she was going. As a matter of habit, she stopped in a cafe, ordered tea, and looked at all the seats until she found the object of her search—a newspaper left behind. As soon as they learned she was Irish and newly arrived, all the placement agencies had refused to help her find a position, so Katie was dependent upon the newspapers. They weren't of much help, but at least she could identify those families with enough money and a large enough household to be wanting a staff of servants. It wasn't much, but it was something. It gave her the illusion that she was making progress.

Katie finished her tea and stuffed her pockets with the little crackers the cafe placed on the tables. These would be her lunch. Then, with her mind in its usual whirl of angry thoughts and vague plans about extracting herself from this terrible situation, her feet guided her along the path she always followed. Before she knew it, she was standing out in front of the white emigration sheds. And so was Tyrone Tully.

"Right on time," he said, as if they had had an appointment. He walked up to her, his manner familiar, that of an old friend.

Katie watched him, uncertain of what to do or say. In a strange way he did seem like an old friend.

His eyes crinkled as he smiled. "What will it be today? Another sparring match—or will you sing for me?"

"No, sir, I will not. I do not sing on street corners, nor do I wish to talk to the kind of men who stand on street corners. So, Mr. . . . Tully, I'd appreciate it if you'd let me pass with no more said about it."

His smile broadened into a grin. "Och! I knew I was

right about you. You can put on quite an act when you're a mind to." He stepped closer to her. "Now listen to me—please, just for a minute. If you've no interest after I've finished, I'll leave you alone." With eyebrows raised and an innocent look on his face, he studied her, waiting for her response. "I promise," he added as insurance.

With a sigh, Katie said, "I must be touched by the pixies to believe the word of a man like you, but say what's on your mind."

"Yesterday I saw you take money from the old priest—Father Richards. I know what straits you must be in for him to give you money and for you to take it. Well, I have a problem too, but it isn't money—not at the moment anyway. I need girls—special kinds of girls—ones who can sing and dance and, well, look nice. I am putting together a traveling show. It isn't so much right now, but my shows are well received, and none of us starves. That is all there is to it. I mean you no harm. But my instinct tells me you are a natural actress, and maybe you can sing. I can always teach you to dance."

"You asked me to sing," Katie commented, not knowing whether to believe him or not.

"I did, and you never sang for me, nor did you answer me. Can you sing, Miss . . . ?" he asked, his eyes sparkling as he watched to see if she would give him her name. When she didn't answer immediately, he went on. "When the show is put together, we'll travel all through lower Canada, and then we are going to New York. I am hoping we can find a permanent home for the troupe there. New Yorkers always like to see a good show."

"New York," Katie said softly, a thread of her old dream wavering through her mind.

Tully's eyes lit up as he recognized the longing in her voice. "You want to go to New York?"

Katie could barely hold back tears. "I did . . . once. But that was a long time ago. Once I planned to go there

. . . and I even wanted to try to be a singer. But I don't think I'll ever get there now."

"But you will!" His excitement bristled around them, charging the air with electricity. "I can get you there! You haven't been listening! Och, girl, our meeting was fated! You are just what I have been needing for my show. You are everything I've been looking for—a woman who is beautiful and can act. I know you can act—it stands out in everything you do—the way you walk, even the way you talk. If you only knew how long I've haunted the emigration docks for one of my own countrywomen who was educated and beautiful! I never really thought I'd find her, but here you are! What is your name? Please, tell me."

In spite of her response to Tully's excitement, Katie was feeling low again. Here was her dream, tantalizingly close, and it was going to slip right past her. She raised her eyes to his. "What difference does my name make? You're better off not knowing. I am not the woman you are looking for. I cannot go to New York or anywhere else, Mr. Tully. I am not Miss Anybody, I am Mrs., and I have a small daughter to care for and a husband I can't find."

Tully's expressive face showed his disappointment. "The reason for your frequent visits here," he asked. "Did he have the fever?"

"Yes. I left him at the docks when we landed while I went to find lodging. When I returned he had been taken away by the carts. His name is not in the records, and no one seems to know anything about him."

"There are more names off that record book than there are on it," Tully said. "They are doin' the best they can, poor sods, but it's gone way beyond them. But surely they've told you that many hundreds have died and been buried without a name. How long has it been?"

"A little more than three weeks," Katie said, her throat so constricted the words came out hoarse.

Tully tried to assess Katie's need for her husband

against the longing he sensed she had to go to New York. "Maybe it is time to face . . ."

She shook her head violently. "He's alive! I know he is here . . . somewhere. He must be!"

"He wouldn't have left you alone, knowing full well you might starve. No decent man would do that, and I am certain your man is a good one, so you have to think that he can't be here, isn't that right, Mrs."

The tears would not be held back any longer. They streamed down Katie's face. "I don't know. I don't know anything."

"Then think of what I can offer you. Even with the child, I'll accept you as part of the troupe. You'll have food and a place to sleep every night, and some money in your pocket that doesn't come from the charity of the old priest. That's a great bit more than you have now. I told you, and I believe it in my heart—we were fated to meet."

Katie stared hard at him. "And my husband?"

Tully shrugged. "I am betting that the good man is dead and buried. You could be spending your whole life waiting for a dead man. If he comes before the troupe is ready to leave, then I've made a mistake. I lose. I'll beg your pardon and let you be on your way." He tipped his hat and began to slowly take one step away from her, then he backed away another step. He stopped, a perplexed expression of caring on his face. "Let me buy you a meal. I owe you that. After all, you have told me you aren't interested in what I have to offer, and you haven't refused to think on it. I've taken your time and patience. Let me repay you. Please?" he asked engagingly.

Katie hesitated, but the truth was that she wanted to go with him. He didn't seem half so threatening today as he had yesterday. She wanted company and a sympathetic ear; Tyrone Tully offered both in abundance. And though she wasn't ready to come out and admit it, she didn't want him to leave taking with him all his fine promises of the

stage and New York City. There was a hunger in Katie for
all of that, and she wanted to hear him talk about it even if
she couldn't have it now. Someday, she promised herself,
she would. She couldn't quite make herself accept him, so
she smiled slightly and gave a nearly imperceptible nod.

Tully returned her smile, but his eyes were speculative
and showed puzzlement. His sixth sense was twitching.
Something about this young woman did not add up properly. She claimed to have a husband, but she didn't seem
like a married matron. He would have bet money that she
had never borne a child, yet she said she had a daughter.
He wondered but could think of no reason why she should
lie now. Whatever she might be, she was fascinating—and
very beautiful. He stepped forward and gallantly took her
arm. It had been the right thing to do, he noted right away.
She was pleased. Another puzzle. Supposedly, she was just
a little country girl fresh off the boat, yet she spoke as if
she had been educated and she knew the rules of proper
behavior like no other country girl he had ever met.

He took her to a small tearoom not too far from the
docks. It wasn't large or fancy, and it wasn't expensive, but
it was the nicest place Katie had ever eaten in. Her eyes
shone with pleasure.

Tully sat across from her, his eyes never leaving her face,
a look of amusement dancing in his eyes and around the
edges of his mouth.

Katie finally acknowledged he was staring at her. "What
is it you find so amusing about me, Mr. Tully?"

"Before I tell you, do you think you could trust me
enough to know your name now? I don't fancy calling you
Mrs." He grinned at her. "Make one up if you like, but
give me something decent to call you or I will make something up myself."

It was Katie's turn to be amused. She cocked her head
prettily to one side. "And what name would you make up
for me, Mr. Tully?"

He thought, making a show by pursing his lips and studying her carefully. "Sheila—no, no, Sheila hasn't the grace you need, or the playfulness. Jenny—maybe—or Kathleen—no, it would be Katie."

Katie's eyes widened and her mouth worked, but Tully already had another amendment to make. "No! I know what I'd call you! I would call you Kitty. Yes, that is it— Kitty, my pretty Irish kitten."

Katie had recovered and now gave him a hard eye. "You talked to Father Richards. He told you my name."

Tully chuckled. "He would have, but you neglected to give him your name—or perhaps he forgot it. In any case he didn't know it." Then he sat back. "But you have told me by your reactions. Your name is Katie, is it? And do you have a last name?"

"Ryan," she said hastily, then corrected. "I mean Donovan."

He chuckled again. "Ryan-I-mean-Donovan. A strange name for such a pretty puzzle as you are."

Katie frowned. "Och! Do stop teasing me. I shouldn't have come here with you at all. I'm going to leave if you don't stop."

"But not before you've eaten," Tully said, tempting fate.

Tully watched the flare of temper rise along Katie's fair skin and flash in her brilliant green eyes. What a witch she would be on stage! With her coloring she was a gorgeous woman, he thought—and what she didn't have naturally, he could teach her. If she could really sing, he could make a fortune with Kitty Ryan. But there was more. He had never spent so much time trying to convince other young girls they should be a part of his show. Some of them had been as pretty as Katie, and some of them had had voices that would have melted the hearts of angels, but none had inspired him to pursue them so relentlessly. Tully knew too well that there was always another girl coming on another boat, eager and needing a start. He did not need to waste his time cajoling and coaxing. So why was he here with Katie Ryan?

He laughed aloud, causing Katie to look curiously at him as he admitted to himself that he wanted her for more than a show. He did not want her lost husband found. He hoped the man was dead and in his grave. Tully wanted her for himself. He leaned forward in his chair, bringing his face nearer to hers. He decided then that he wasn't going to give up on Katie. He wanted her and he would have her. One way or another, she was coming to New York with him.

He began to talk earnestly to her about the great American city to the south, and Katie's eyes sparkled. At the end of the meal, Tully knew that he had her interest and her desire to go but not her willingness. Her husband still stood between them. He had another idea.

"I am having a little party tonight—at my apartment. Most of the girls of the chorus line will be there—and some other friends. I'd like you to come. You'd enjoy yourself. Even if you can't go to New York now, you can meet some people who will be there when you finally face up to the fact that you are alone and come later. It never hurts to have friends."

Katie wanted to go, but she could see how Tully was dressed. His clothing was loud, but it was of good quality and a nice cut. It didn't take much imagination to guess what she would look like at the party in her country dress alongside all the pretty women he would have invited. She would make a good brunt of any joke. She shook her head. "I am sorry, but I can't. I would be like a fish out of water and I have nothing to wear."

Tully said nothing. He helped Katie from her seat, paid the bill, and walked with her out onto the street.

Katie expected him to bid her farewell as she had him, but he didn't leave. He continued to walk at her side. Not knowing what to do, she walked aimlessly. She was not going knocking on doors asking for the position of a scullery maid with Tully grinning at her side. And she wasn't going to humiliate herself by telling him what she was going to do and get rid of him that way, so she walked.

"Where are we going?" he asked.

Flustered, Katie stammered a moment, then blurted out, "I don't know where you are going, but I am going home."

"Good!" Tully said triumphantly. "I'll walk you there."

Katie protested, but with little strength. He walked her home, did not tease her anymore, and made a courteous bow when he left her at the door to Mrs. Holmes's rooming house.

Katie waited in her room until she was certain Tully was no longer lurking around the house or neighborhood. The man was as persistent as an itch. She just wished she knew for certain why that should be. To her regret, she had made it clear that she would not become a part of his show, and she felt certain that he now believed her. Yet he had taken her to lunch, and he was unusually generous. Right before he left he had pressed money into her hand and with a smile told her to buy something pretty for herself and for Keely. Either he had a whole different idea of a "bit of change" than she did, or he knew exactly what he was doing. The amount he had given her would pay her rent the following week with enough left over to buy something for herself and Keely.

Katie had a terrible time searching for someone to hire her and a wonderful time going through shops to select the best possible dress for her money for Keely. When she arrived home late that afternoon, her spirits were in far better shape than they had been the day before. The only thing that bothered her a bit was that all her good moods and all the good things that had happened to her lately had happened with or because of Tyrone Tully. Then Katie shrugged it off. She wasn't going to question it now.

Mrs. Holmes had been waiting for her to get home. As

soon as Katie opened the front hall door, Mrs. Holmes poked her head out the door of her flat and motioned to her.

"Come in," Mrs. Holmes said, her eyes bright as she gestured for Katie to hurry. As soon as they were in the flat, Mrs. Holmes pointed to a large box. "This came for you by special messenger not an hour ago. What is it? That's a very exclusive shop, that is."

Katie began to shake inside. She said, "I don't . . . I'm not sure."

"Well? Open it!" Mrs. Holmes said, fairly hopping with curiosity.

Katie moved toward the ornate box. It smelled of perfume—expensive perfume. She had the quivering, anxious feeling that she knew what was inside the box. As she and Tully had walked home, they had passed many stores and window-shopped in each one. Katie had seen an expensive white satin gown in this shop and admired it. It was not something she would ever have occasion to wear, but in her relaxed mood, she had let herself dream aloud to Tully. Even now she could hear her own voice saying to him, "If I were really on a stage, I would always wear white. Never another color—just white. Everyone would know me because of my beautiful white gowns." With trembling hands she took hold of the string that held the box closed. She could hardly breathe as she opened it. The gorgeous white satin gown with tiny rosettes embroidered down the front panel and at the hem rested on a bed of tissue paper.

Mrs. Holmes drew in her breath. "Oh, my!" she exhaled. "It must have cost a fortune! What a lovely gown."

"There is . . . I am . . ." Katie couldn't get control of her voice. She tried again. "I am going to a party tonight—that is, if you can watch Keely."

"A party? In a gown like this?" Mrs. Holmes asked suspiciously. "I thought you were a settled married woman."

"I am!" Katie said quickly. "My—my husband, as you

know, has been detained—on business. I am to represent him. Important people will be there, but if you are busy tonight . . ." She shrugged sadly. "Well, I'll just send Mr. Donovan's and my apologies."

Mrs. Holmes hesitated, but basically she was kind—and there was something about Katie she liked. She wasn't certain she believed everything Katie told her, but so far nothing untoward had happened. She had never brought a man to her room, and most nights she was in the house at night, so Mrs. Holmes said, "I'll be glad to watch the little one. We'll try on her new finery, and perhaps I can begin to make another outfit for her from that piece of material you bought. She'll be the finest young lady hereabouts. She may even rival her pretty mother."

Katie beamed with pleasure and pride. She gave Mrs. Holmes an unexpected and hearty hug. "Oh, thank you!"

Once upstairs in her own room, Katie was appalled at what she had done. She had committed herself to Tully's party. And that carried with it a series of problems to be dealt with. Nothing was ever so simple as it seemed or should be. She could hardly arrive at a gala on foot. She would have to hire a cab, and that cost money. Since she had spent the extra money Tully had given her on Keely, all she had left was her rent and a small amount set aside for food. If she hired the cab, she and Keely could go without food, or without housing. Katie stamped her foot in exasperation. Somehow life always seemed to be a series of little annoyances, and she was heartily sick of them. Tyrone Tully didn't seem to have all these little hitches in his life. When he wanted a cab and a good meal in the same day—even the same week—he could have them.

She washed carefully and took time putting her hair in an elaborate swirling twist atop her head, letting a few curling tendrils caress the nape of her neck and soften the frame of her face. She had only a small mirror Mrs. Holmes had provided, but it was enough for Katie to see that she looked her best. The dress fit as if it had been made for her, and she wondered what kind of a wizard Tyrone Tully was to have known her size so well. Pleased with herself, she went downstairs to show off her gown and to use Mrs. Holmes's larger mirror. Tonight Katie took great pleasure in looking at herself. Perhaps she *could* be on the stage. Dressed like this, it did not seem so much a daydream as it did a possibility. She took one last look at her face in the small mirror, making herself look sultry, then surprised, happy, sad, and angry. Finally she flashed a brilliant smile of self-appreciation. She felt like singing and did. All the way down the stairs, Katie sang. Doors opened with people gawking in surprise at seeing the white-gowned woman with the voice of an angel floating gracefully in the hall of their boardinghouse. Still singing, she opened the door to Mrs. Holmes's flat, swirled through the door, down the hall into the parlor, and with a deep curtsy presented herself to Keely and Mrs. Holmes.

"Why, my land!" Mrs. Holmes said, blinking. "You look like you just walked out of a painting. Why, Katie Donovan, I never knew you were such a beauty."

Katie curtsied gracefully. "I thank you, Mrs. Holmes—I didn't either. Isn't it wonderful what a beautiful dress can do for a woman?"

"Oh, yes, the dress." But Mrs. Holmes hadn't taken her eyes off Katie herself. Katie was excited. The color was high in her cheeks and her green eyes shone with happiness. Her figure looked slender and lithe in the gown, no longer gaunt as it did in her ill-fitting country clothes. Tears came to Mrs. Holmes's eyes. Katie was magnificent. She wished her boarder a good evening and stood watching the door close as Katie left the lodging house to go to her party. Mrs. Holmes wiped her eyes, but more tears came.

Along with the happiness she felt for Katie, Mrs. Holmes had a cold lump that wouldn't leave her chest. Tonight was a turning point for Katie Donovan, she knew, and she wasn't at all sure it would make Katie happy for long.

9

Kᴀᴛɪᴇ was floating on a cloud heightened by the compliments and the admiring looks she had received from Mrs. Holmes and Keely when she had stepped outside the house onto the street. Instantly, she was greeted by the harsher realities. Even though she had decided to use what little money she had to take a cab to Tully's house, it was quickly brought to her attention that in this neighborhood few cabs traveled. It was not worth their time, for the inhabitants hadn't the money to be taking cabs. The people who lived here walked.

Moments after this realization hit her, she realized that she was cold. Tully had provided her with a gown, gloves, stockings, and slippers, but he had not thought of a wrap, and Katie could not bear to wear her coarsely woven shawl over the gorgeous white satin gown. So now she stood on the corner of the street without a wrap and with no means to get to Tully's but walk. Tears began to form in her eyes, and she was fast sinking into her old melancholic ways of believing that for people like her there was never an end to misfortune. Even the best of things were empty promises.

Defeated, Katie turned slowly and walked back to the front stoop of the lodging house. Her hand on the rail and her foot on the first step, her head whipped around as a shiny black C-spring coach careened around the corner. The grinning driver, dressed from head to foot in bright green and, looking like a leprechaun, pulled his snorting, blowing horses to an instant halt in front of the lodging house. The man jumped from the driver's box to land lightly on his feet at the curb. With a grandiose, sweeping bow, he announced himself as Katie's driver, compliments of Mr. Tyrone Tully. At first Katie was aghast. The man was posturing and talking like no driver she had ever seen. He was larger than life—someone she would expect to see only on a stage—and then she understood; he most likely was one of Tully's performers. She began to laugh, and graciously, and in as exaggerated fashion as he was using, she played the grand dame and allowed him to seat her in the coach. Inside, folded on the seat, was a white velvet cape with a note pinned to it.

"Please forgive my forgetfulness and accept this cloak in the spirit in which it is given." It was signed, "Your most enamored admirer, Tyrone Tully."

Katie didn't even hesitate. She unfolded the soft, beautiful cloak and put her face into it, luxuriating in the feel of it. Then she put it around her shoulders, feeling completely pampered. It was a different sensation for her, and she liked it. She felt an uncomfortable twinge of guilt as she pushed away a quick thought that it was unlikely that Michael ever could or would provide her with a night such as this or that she would ever go anywhere with him dressed in such a gown or a cloak. She did not dwell on the thought, however, for this was one night probably never to be repeated, and she wanted it all for herself. Tyrone Tully would soon leave, and once again she would be plain Katie Ryan who no one wanted even for a scullery maid.

Tully's house was not particularly impressive from the outside, but Katie instantly realized that this was a street she had walked along when she was looking for a position.

Quickly she tried to recall whether she had approached
any of these people and just as quickly wondered if Tully
himself had seen her wandering up and down, going from
door to door, searching for someone who would hire her.
Flaming heat scorched her cheeks, then she settled back. It
was too late to be embarrassed now if that had happened.

The coachman held the door for her and dropped the
side steps on the coach. Then, just as though she really
were a very special person, he helped her alight from the
carriage. Katie's head was swimming. She felt as though
she were in the midst of one of her very best dreams. All of
this couldn't possibly be real. She walked up to the front
door and, before she even had a chance to knock, it was
opened to her. A man also dressed in green livery opened
the door, escorted her in, and took her wrap for her. She
waited for only a moment, her eyes filled with the wonder
of the entry hall. An enormous crystal chandelier with
hundreds of candles glowed with a bright warmth, lending
all the furnishings and woods in the hall a golden hue. The
floors were highly polished dark wood. On them were expensive multihued handwoven carpets. The vibrant colors
and the warmth of the house took Katie's breath away. She
still could not get over the idea that she was here in this
house as a guest and not as a maid. Even in her most
fanciful dreams she had never elevated herself to such
grandeur. On her left and right the hall opened to a dining
room and to a parlor, respectively. The dining room was a
blaze of candles, silver, and crisp white linens. The parlor,
to which the butler was taking her, was an enormous room
in which all the furniture had been moved to the sides. The
entire middle of the room was barren of everything, including carpets. It was a gay confusion of sound and people,
with innumerable musical instruments lying about or in
the hands of some of the men and women. The clothing
worn by these very attractive people made a rainbow of
vivid reds and greens, purples, lavenders, blues and golds.

Katie was overwhelmed. The butler announced her, but she did not even hear him speak her name.

Tully, in formal black garb but sporting a brilliant green vest and cravat, was sitting at an enormous piano. Surrounding one side of the piano, four women, their attention fully focused on him, sang. Their voices filled the room, and Katie was mesmerized. She was light-headed with the unreality of it. Then, suddenly, the piano stopped playing and the women stopped singing. All eyes were focused on her, and she realized what the butler was saying.

Joe Dawson, fondly known as "Jeeves" because he played a butler so well, stepped fully into the parlor and announced, "I present Miss Kitty Ryan, the Irish kitten of Manhattan!"

Once Katie awakened to what was being said, her immediate reaction was to shrink away, but then she stepped forward, her hand outstretched to greet Tully as he hurried across the room to her side. Tonight, in this place of lights and vivid color, she wasn't Katie—she really was Kitty Ryan. She smiled happily as Tully bent from the waist and kissed her hand.

Katie noticed that one of the women who had been singing and was still standing by the piano did not look especially happy to see her, but nonetheless she allowed Tully to tuck her arm in his and possessively take command of her. This was her dream, and Katie had no intention of allowing anyone to rudely awaken her with something as mundane as jealousy.

In rapid succession Tully introduced her to the most unusual assortment of people with the most outlandish of names she could imagine. She wondered if there was one person in the room who was using the name with which he was born. And then she realized that even she was using a made-up name tonight. It was close to her own name, but before tonight she had never been Kitty Ryan, and tonight, in this company, that is who she was.

Katie once more met the man who had been her coachman. His name was Maxwell Phipps, and he was now
amusing everyone by balancing trays of filled champagne
glasses, prancing about, swooping down just long enough
for someone to grab a glass off the tray and be gone again.

"Maxwell is a master of anything acrobatic. He can jug-
gle, dance, tumble, and even drive coaches on occasion. He
even has a passable baritone. We couldn't get along without him. He is also the company clown and manages to
keep us in good spirits most of the time," Tully said as
Katie stared in delighted amazement at Max's antics.

As soon as everyone had a glass of champagne in his
hand, Max put down his tray and motioned to two women
who had been standing near the fireplace talking. In a
wink, Lawrence Dill, serious-looking and thin as a whip,
was seated at the piano, and Angela Parks, Daisy Marshall, and Max were in the middle of the floor dancing.

Katie put her hand up to her face, shaking her head.
"Does this go on . . . I mean, is the way you live, Tully?"

He laughed. "Most of the time, but we only dress like
this when we're on stage or giving a party or trying to
convince a beautiful colleen she should join us."

"I think one of your group would disagree with you,"
Katie said, and glanced in the direction of the one singer
who was standing with a thundercloud expression on her
face by the piano.

Tully raised an eyebrow. "Oh, Margaret," he said off-
handedly. "She is always in a huff over something or
other." With a deft move, he steered her across to the
other side of the room. "I want you to meet our most
serious member. He takes care of the books, so he is always
worried and mostly despondent."

Slumped into a chair, off in a corner by himself with
only his champagne glass to keep him company, was the
saddest man Katie had ever seen. He had the long, wrinkled face of a bloodhound, and she almost laughed, be-

cause like everyone else in this room he was so exaggerated it was difficult to believe he was a real person.

"Katie, I'd like you to meet Amory Wilson Peabody, our wizard of numbers and player of all parts requiring sobriety and elderly dignity," Tully said with a twinkle, and Katie couldn't help herself and burst into a fit of giggles.

Slowly turning his large, droopy eyes to Tully, Amory said, "What is this, Tully? You have found a new and diabolical way to make my existence unbearable? To bring a beautiful woman to laugh at my poor meager demeanor is the cruelest cut of all!"

Katie tried, but she couldn't stop laughing. Tears were forming in her eyes. She put her hand out and rested it on his forearm. Amory rolled his enormous doggy eyes in ecstacy. "I'm sorry, Mr. Wilson," said Katie. "I mean no disrespect. I am having a wonderful time and am overwhelmed by it."

"Oh, Tully," Amory cooed. "She is very well spoken. You have caught yourself a gem, I think. And you, my dear, may make fun of me whenever you wish. I am transported by your touch."

Tully laughed and waved him back to his seat. "Enough of your emoting, Amory. I want Kitty to meet Angela and Phoebe."

Obediently, Amory sank back into his chair and resumed his melodramatic, brooding pose.

Angela was a healthy, well-endowed soprano and Phoebe was a tall rawboned woman with the voice of a tug whistle. Katie was enamored of all of them.

As the evening continued, more and more people wandered into the house, the formality of her entrance long ago forgotten. Tully introduced her to so many people, the names were lost before she ever really knew them. Some were musicians and others were dancers or actors or a combination of everything, which seemed to be the more common rule. There was little space in Tully's kind of theater for someone who could manage only one job. Donald Whitney, Phoebe's brother, as handsome a man as his sister was plain and ungainly, was the set designer. He proudly complained, "I do not own a stitch of clothing that hasn't paint on it! You can imagine how terrible it is for the leading man to be wearing stained garments. I am constantly in need of a whole new wardrobe—isn't that so, Tully? It is the bane of my life!"

"And mine," Amory intoned morosely from his corner.

"Amory has no sense of reality," Donald said confidentially into Katie's ear. "You must take everything he says very lightly or ignore it entirely or he will cause in you a great blue funk."

Shortly after this, Lawrence Dill, a stovepipe of a man, complained, "Tully, why are you always trying to starve us? Are we never going to eat dinner? Did you even think of dinner?"

As if on cue Max Phipps, now in his waiter's guise, shouted from the hallway, "Dinner is served, Mr. Dill."

The midnight supper was as raucous and disorienting as the rest of the evening. Though the table was set formally, that was where formality began and ended abruptly. The jugglers were far more likely to spin or toss the assorted dishes, dinner rolls, salt and pepper shakers as not.

Throughout the dinner Katie smiled and laughed as she had never done before and drank champagne. She was enchanted and deliciously happy in the company of these strange, unreal, and irrepressible people. To her impressionable and unknowledgeable eyes, it seemed that they must always be like this—always happy, always extravagant, always outgoing and filled with merriment. She had no idea that Tully had given each of them strict and specific instructions regarding his desire to lure Katie into their midst.

As Tully watched Katie, he was more committed than

ever to having her as part of his troupe and as his woman. Her color was high from the excitement and the champagne. He had never seen a more beautiful woman. In all, he was very pleased with the way the evening was going thus far. He was equally thankful that she would see none of them tomorrow, when the bills had to be paid and the hangovers dealt with and all the ill tempers that come of too many nights spent in too many strange cities and rooms came to the fore. This group that looked so cohesive and fun-loving was, in fact, a bunch of overworked, underpaid, rootless, loveless wanderers. Most of them had played parts for so long and so often they no longer knew who they were—nor cared. All that mattered was the next creation they would bring to life on a stage. That was when they were alive. In Katie, however, he thought he had found a woman who could perform without losing herself. He hoped so, for he longed for something solid and warm and real in his life to balance out all the greasepaint and cardboard rooms and cardboard people.

After dinner they all returned to the parlor, and within minutes the room was filled with music, juggling, and dancing just as it had been before the supper. Katie was beginning to wonder if these people ever slept or tired. It seemed that they did not. Tully sat at the piano and accompanied Maria Della Nova as she sang, then he looked at Katie.

"You still have not sung for me. Will you sing tonight?"

She hesitated, but she was tempted. He could see it in her eyes. Patiently, Tully waited, and when she continued to stand silent and undecided, he said,

"Give me one song as a gift, please. I will never forget this night if you will bring it alive with one song."

Katie was deluged with thoughts of all the things Tully had given her and the things he had done for her. She wasn't certain that everyone wouldn't laugh at her, but secretly she thought she could sing much better than Maria Della Nova, who had probably been born Agnes Smith. With a shy smile that made her all the prettier, she said, "I do not know the songs you sing. I know only those from home—is that all right?"

Tully was so excited he was shaking. With a thick voice, he said, "My darling, you sing anything you wish, and I will follow." Tully almost fell off his chair, because with a start he realized that he was blushing. He couldn't remember having blushed since he was eight years old and had been caught by his mother with his hands in his cousin's drillies. He cleared his throat and made a grandiose roll on the piano.

Katie stood quietly and amazingly poised, trying to think of what she should sing. All these people were so sophisticated and sang the popular songs of their day. All she knew were the country songs she had heard for years as she was growing up. She also was trying to think of something she could sing in English. Without thinking of what other meaning it might have for Tully, she sang the second verse of "Shule Aroon."

In a clear, melodic voice, Katie sang:

> "His hair was black, his eye was blue,
>   His arm was stout, his word was true.
>   I wish in my heart I was with you,
>   Is go-dhe-thu, Avourneen slawn?
>   Shule, shule, shule, A-roon . . ."

Katie's voice had barely died away in the hushed room and Tully was off the piano stool and around the front of the piano to where she stood. With a groan of deep gratitude, he clasped her to him. He kissed her on either cheek, and before either of them thought about what was happening, his arms were around her and he was kissing her deeply and passionately.

Like a frozen bird being warmed by the fire, Katie trembled in Tully's embrace. She had not known just how desperately lonely she had been since she had lost Michael until she was returning Tully's kiss with the same hungry eagerness he had brought to her.

Only the applause and humorously lewd comments shouted by the others broke them apart. Katie stood in blinking wonder at what she had done and what Tully had made her feel as she stood accepting the compliments of the others as if it were her due and this a nightly occasion.

By the time Tully returned her to Mrs. Holmes's lodging house it was four o'clock in the morning. The champagne and the fevered excitement were beginning to wear off, and Katie was a whirlwind of conflicting feelings and thoughts. Tully was not helping her. He was in love with her. She knew it. But there was Michael. Where was Michael? Was there a man named Michael Donovan left for her or had he died, as Tully insisted?

Tully was holding her hand and kissing each of her fingers. "I have no secrets left, Kitty. My heart is yours and it always will be. I want you to come with us . . . I want you for my wife . . . I want you with all my heart."

"Tully, I . . ."

He put his finger gently on her lips. "Don't say anything —not yet—just listen to me. We must move on from here. There is no more work for us in Montreal. Two days from now we start our journey south. We'll perform in every sizeable town on the way to New York. Come with us, Kitty—please come with us."

"Tully, you must underst . . ."

Again he put his finger to her lips. "Don't say no. Think about it. I know you are going to tell me about your husband, but you cannot throw your life away waiting for a man who may never come back, Kitty. I once told you our meeting was fate. I believe that. We are magic together."

Katie wanted the life he seemed to offer so much she could taste it, but she drew up all her courage and said quickly, before he could stop her, "Tully, I love Michael Donovan."

Tully sat back against the carriage seat, deflated. He said nothing for a long time, his eyes fixed on the darkness outside the window. He did not look at her when he spoke, and his voice was harsh and ugly. "Michael Donovan is dead." Then he turned to face her and took her by the arms, holding her tight so that she could not move away from him. His face was only inches from hers and every word was punctuated by a gust of his breath hitting her face. "You are alive, Kitty Ryan. You are going to throw your life away if you don't wake up to your situation as it really is. You have no money and no one will hire you. Mrs. Holmes will have you out of that lodging house one week after you can't pay your rent. You're going to be on the streets and Michael Donovan will not be there to help you. Neither will Tyrone Tully. Think about it, Kitty, and think hard. You are a born actress. You belong on a stage, not in a gutter. Even your Michael would tell you the same."

"Tully . . ."

"No! Don't say anything. I'm deadly serious, Kitty. You think on this hard and long, because what you decide is going to change your life for good or ill." He got out of the carriage and held his hand out to help her. He gave her a chaste peck on the cheek. "I'll see you the day before the troupe leaves. You can tell me what you've decided to do then." Without a backward glance he climbed up to the box of the carriage beside Max and the two men drove off.

For a moment Kitty Ryan, the Irish kitten of Manhattan, stood on the roadside watching after the carriage. The carriage turned the corner and disappeared from sight, as did Kitty. Katie turned toward the lodging house, a little headachy from too much champagne and as confused as ever.

KATIE walked into the quiet, sleeping house. For a moment, she stood in the entry hall debating whether she should go to Mrs. Holmes's apartment and get Keely or just go to her room alone. She knew Mrs. Holmes must have expected her long ago. Turning away from the landlady's door, she started up the long flights of stairs to her room.

After Tully's bright house, her room seemed dingy and crowded. One month ago, the day they had landed in Montreal and Katie had found this room for herself, Michael, and Keely, she had been proud and pleased that they would be in such comfortable surroundings. But Tully had opened a door for her on a whole new world, a world Katie had dreamed of but never really believed she would ever enter.

She lit just one candle and began to undress by its thin, pale light. Slowly, almost regretfully, she removed her dress. With great care she folded it and put it back in the box. Katie looked down at it lying in its bed of tissue paper. It looked as if it had never been worn. Katie's mouth twisted into a wry, bitter smile. She mused, maybe it never had been worn. It might be that she had dreamed this whole night and all the people she had met. Perhaps none of it was real and tomorrow, when she awakened, the night, the gown—everything—would have vanished like a will-o'-the-wisp. She put the lid on the box and carefully tucked it under her bed.

With her mind blank, Katie began to move through her nightly ritual. She poured water into her basin and washed carefully, and for so long her skin felt taut and shiny. She reached for her threadbare nightgown and pulled it over her head. As she turned to empty her wash water, her eye caught her image in the mirror. In the reflection she caught a glimpse of Kitty, and yet it was Katie standing before the small looking glass. She put her hands to her cheeks. She didn't know who she was anymore. She didn't know who she wanted to be.

She took a step back and her eyes fell on Keely's empty crib. Katie was shaking as if she faced a frost-driven wind. She grabbed her hair, wanting to scream, but she dared not. Her frantic mind would grasp little more than names for her, and she kept screaming inside her head, "Keely!" "Michael!" She felt as though both of them had been torn away from her and she could do nothing to stop what was happening. Unable to stand it anymore, she threw herself on the bed with a cry and buried her face in her pillow.

Once the floodgates of her emotions had opened, Katie could not hold back the torrent of tears that poured forth. She thought of the villagers in Fairmont and the many who had died so cruelly and needlessly. Her heart constricted as she saw again the road people, wandering homeless and hungry, digging hollows in the sides of hills because they had no place to go.

She cried for the people on the ship and all those who had not survived the voyage. She thought of Michael and the times they had spent in the tented berth that seemed golden to her. She writhed on her bed and pressed her pillow to her mouth to still the howls of pain that wanted to burst forth, for once she began to think of Michael she couldn't stop. Michael had awakened in her something beautiful and good, something too new and tender to die. But it couldn't live without him. Katie mourned the death of that wonderfully special part of herself that was Michael as she mourned her loss of Michael himself.

At dawn she fell asleep still crying, because her body had no strength left to keep her awake and because her soul was gentler and would allow her to suffer no more that night.

When Katie wakened the next morning, she knew she could not go on any longer as she had been. She dressed carefully, then went downstairs to Mrs. Holmes's apartment. Without giving explanation about her late arrival home or why she hadn't fetched Keely, Katie somberly asked Mrs. Holmes to watch Keely for the day.

"I know I owe you an explanation for many things, Mrs. Holmes, but I beg your indulgence. When I return this evening I will explain everything. Will you please watch her for me?"

Mrs. Holmes felt very put out, and last night she had thought up many biting criticisms to level at Katie, but this morning none of it seemed very important. She didn't know what was happening, but she could recognize that Katie was immersed in deep troubles and doing the best she could. "I will be glad to watch her, Katie, but we must talk when you return. I think it is time you were a bit more honest with me about certain things."

Katie looked down at her feet. "I know, Mrs. Holmes, and I will be, but please give me today. There are some things I must do before I say anything to you."

Mrs. Holmes did something that surprised her. She walked over to Katie and hugged her. "I trust you, Katie. You'll do what is right."

Katie was filled with a sense of determination when she walked out of the lodging house. With a brisk step she walked to St. Patrick's Church. She entered into the cool dimness of the interior. It had the special smell that houses of God have. Incense from the Benediction of the night before hovered in the still air and mingled with the scents of beeswax candles and Holy Water that rested quietly in deep stone founts. As the heavy door closed slowly behind her, a narrowing shaft of brilliant sunlight cut across her path on the floor, and then all was quiet and shadowed and peaceful. With the closing of the door, the world was shut out and Katie was alone with her Maker.

She moved up the main aisle, her eyes on the altar. She slipped into the first pew and knelt down. She didn't bother going through her usual prayers. She had only one thing on her mind and she asked it right away. "Father, on this last day I will look for Michael. Guide my feet. And if I should not find him, Heavenly Father, show me where I should go."

Having said what she wanted, she got up, made the Sign of the Cross, and left St. Patrick's. As she dipped her hand into the Holy Water on the way out, she thought that this would be the last time she ever did this if she did not find Michael. She was frightened, but she felt better for having made a decision.

She left the church and turned in the direction of Point St. Charles. With every step she took to the new and distant location of the hospital, Katie cursed the people who decreed such things.

On July 10, the citizens of Montreal had held an indignation meeting in the Bonsecours Market demanding that the immigration sheds be moved. There wasn't a citizen left in the city who wasn't terrified of the emigrants, and the horrible diseases they had brought with them. The people's choice of location for the hospital, and the sheds had been Boucherville Island where the Board of Health, and the Emigration Society had found good water, plenty of shade, and several buildings almost in a state of readiness for occupation as well as a number of caves suitable for some of the emigrants to live in.

Fortunately for Katie, the medical commission had vetoed the locations, stating that Boucherville Island was too inconvenient and every supply needed would have to be brought from Montreal by steamer. Katie would never have been able to get to Boucherville Island, because she would not have had the money for the fare even if she had been able to get permission to visit there.

Nearly a mile above the Lachine Canal, Point St. Charles was a very long walk from the lodging house, but Katie was determined to get there. She walked doggedly, her mind focused on finding Michael and nothing else. That alone took willpower, for Montreal was experiencing a very hot summer. The temperatures often were climbing into the nineties, and if anyone had asked Katie about the temperature this day, she would have sworn it was well over one hundred. She felt like a steamed onion, all layers of sweat and heat.

It was midmorning when Katie entered the hospital compound at Point St. Charles. The hospital buildings were situated so they formed a large square with a court in the center. It might have been attractive, Katie thought, but someone had chosen to use the court as the place to stack the coffins. Katie considered that people here would not want to be so constantly reminded of death, but it seemed both doctors and patients were past caring. Some of the coffins were empty, gaping wooden rectangles waiting to be filled. Others awaited the next free burial crew.

Katie looked away from the grisly crates. She entered the nearest building and spoke to the first nun she saw. She had asked about Michael so often, she now had set questions to ask in a set order. Though she could anticipate almost every answer, even to the kind of language it would be delivered in, she asked her questions anyway and listened patiently to all the answers.

She left the first building and entered the next. She ignored the exhortations for her to leave as though they had not been spoken and asked her questions, insistent until she had again been told that there was no record of Michael Donovan. He might be there, but if he was, he was with those who had remained nameless and very ill. No, she would not be granted permission to walk through the hospital checking the occupants of the beds—both for her own safety and that of the patients.

Katie continued her mission until she had entered and exited every building in the compound and received essentially the same answer every time.

She left the compound to begin the long walk back to the city with several possibilities in her mind: Michael was ill in one of the hospitals, a nameless man. He had never been taken to the hospital, but instead had been loaded onto one of the barges that took emigrants farther inland to Kingston and Toronto. He had voluntarily boarded one of the barges, leaving herself and Keely behind. This possibility was difficult for Katie to consider, but it was easier for her to think he had abandoned them than to think of the last possibility and the most likely. Michael was dead.

Katie had been told so often and by so many people that this was the likelihood, she now had to test its veracity on herself. Always before this day she had refused to even consider the idea. It was abhorrent to her, and she never permitted herself to linger upon the thought. The old man who had first told her Michael had been hauled off in the cart had suggested that Michael was dead. That had been weeks ago. Father Richards had gently hinted at the possibility, and though she had not even given him an answer at the time, or indicated she understood what he meant, she had. Sister Maria Annunciata had been more blunt, and Tully had simply said it plainly several times. No one but her thought Michael could possibly be alive. Maybe it was time she faced the fact that their conclusion was correct.

She tried the idea out. Softly and to herself, but aloud, she said, "Michael is dead. He died the day we reached Montreal." Tears slid down her cheeks, but she had no argument to counteract her conclusion. "Michael is dead," she repeated.

While Katie was facing the hard facts she could no longer avoid, Tully was having problems of his own. He, too, was being forced to face facts. His chief tormentor was Amory Wilson Peabody. While Amory was their mainstay comedian and often the brunt of their jokes, no one in the troupe disputed his position as the ultimate authority when it came to finances.

"We are broke!" he intoned, his long face expressing his melancholy. "We are worse than broke. We are deeply in debt, and if we do not hie ourselves out of Montreal in the next few hours we can expect all of our creditors, and perhaps several constables, to pay us a nasty, unwelcome visit."

"Well, it was fun while it lasted," Max said cheerfully. "When do we leave, and by what means? Since we owe the livery a great deal for the coach, do you suppose they would consider us any more criminal if we borrowed it a bit longer? It would be nice to ride in as we make our midnight escape."

Tully frowned. "Surely we have something left, Amory," Tully said. "We can't have spent everything so quickly."

"How poorly you count, Tully. But you are nearly correct. We would not have spent it all if you had not insisted on chasing after that very attractive girl. Kitty, pretty Kitty. But her gown cost us several months' rent. Her cloak cheated the livery stables out of their payment. That lovely supper show we put on for her did all of the grocers out of their due. Shall I go on?"

"No," Tully said ungraciously. "And you can stop acting as though it wasn't worth it. She will come with us—I will stake my fortune on it."

"You already have, my dear," Amory said morosely. "And ours as well."

"I am going to see her tomorrow. I am positive she will come with us."

"Not if she finds out that we are not exactly leaving by choice," Joe "Jeeves" Dawson said. "You have painted a very rosy picture for her. What do you think she is going to say when she sees that we occasionally sing on street corners just to get coins for dinner?"

"Are you saying you don't want her to join the troupe?" Tully asked crossly.

"No!" they all cried in unison.

Then Angela said, "We all want her, Tully. We're not fools. Every one of us knows that she'll help the troupe. She's completely untrained and she had us all captivated the night of the party. We're a tough audience. No, she's going to become a favorite—that's certain. We want her, but what have we got to offer her?"

Tully knew what he wished he could answer, but Kitty had made it plain on more than one occasion that she loved Michael Donovan. He couldn't bring himself to say anything to Angela. He got up out of his chair and walked outside.

Angela looked over at Amory. "I think our Tully has a bruised heart to go along with his broken pocketbook."

Amory grunted assent.

Katie returned to the lodging house late in the afternoon. With some of the money she had left, she bought sweet buns and entered Mrs. Holmes's flat bearing the gift. With a smile, she said, "If you will make tea, I will set these out and we can talk, Mrs. Holmes."

"You look different, Katie. What happened?"

"I think I am different, Mrs. Holmes. I'll tell you all

about it, but first let's enjoy this little tea." She reached down and picked up Keely, placing her on her lap. As Mrs. Holmes bustled about the kitchen, Katie said every nursery rhyme and played every nursery game that she knew with Keely.

Keely laughed in glee, and when Katie's voice died away, she demanded more. Katie listened open-mouthed, then realized that for the last few weeks she had been so preoccupied and busy with trying to find a position, she had paid very little attention to Keely. She had bathed her and dressed her and fed her, but she had done little real listening to the child. Keely had changed considerably, and it had slipped right past Katie's notice. Keely was sitting in her lap talking to her, making her wants known, and Katie had not assessed what that meant until this very moment. Neither had she realized how much Mrs. Holmes had done for the child.

She kissed Keely's cheek and hugged her. Then she said to Mrs. Holmes, "You have done so well by Keely. She is a different child since you've been caring for her during the day. Anything I say will be inadequate, but I am so grateful to you, Mrs. Holmes."

Mrs. Holmes smiled with real pleasure. She couldn't have been prouder of Keely if she had been her own granddaughter. Her reply to Katie, however, did not convey her deep feelings. "It was time for Keely, my dear. All of God's creatures have their season. Keely is just beginning to catch up with herself. She will be fine now, I am sure. Good food and regular meals do wonders for little ones like her. You're very fortunate that she was so young when the famine came. She will recover. She must have been very strong to have lived through her first year. That is always a good sign."

Katie just looked at Mrs. Holmes, not certain what all she was saying, but knowing it was more than it appeared to be.

Mrs. Holmes met her curious gaze. "This is our day for truth, is it not, Katie? I am thinking perhaps I will place the first bit of it out on the table. I have known from the start that you and Keely were fresh off the boat. I am not certain what prompted me to allow you to stay here, knowing as I did about the fever, but I did, and I have never been sorry. Perhaps the good Lord knew that Keely and I had something to do together that needed doing. I've come to love her, you know." Mrs. Holmes turned away, suddenly shy. Then she said, "The only thing I was never certain was the truth was what you said about the man. Is there a husband, Katie?"

Katie was instantly at war with herself as to how she should answer that question. She said truthfully, "I am not sure how to answer that, Mrs. Holmes. In my heart there is a husband, and to be sure Michael Donovan is a real man. Keely is his daughter, not mine." Katie looked down at Keely and fell silent for a bit. This was the first time she would have to speak aloud the hard answers she had come to this morning.

She began with Fairmont and briefly told Mrs. Holmes what had happened. Then she said, "Michael was taken from the wharf while I came here to get lodging. Since then I have looked for him every day, but no one seems to know anything about him. Except for a few people who were on the wharf that first day, no one even knows who I am talking about. I don't know if he left us, or if he died, or if perhaps he was sent on to Toronto by one of the barges while he was still so sick he didn't know what was happening."

Mrs. Holmes listened, but didn't interrupt. She waited for Katie to gather her strength to go on.

Katie began to tell her about Tyrone Tully and the troupe he led and wanted her to join. "Once, before I met Michael, this was my dream. Even with Michael, I didn't entirely give it up. I love to sing . . . and I like the idea of being someone special. I am so tired of always being turned away, Mrs. Holmes. As soon as it was known that I was Irish, no one would have me even for a scullery maid. With Tully I could be someone people respected."

Mrs. Holmes thought of the way her friends thought of show people and wondered if Katie could truly be that innocent and decided she could. How would she know how the Tyrone Tully's were looked upon or what kind of life they led. Truth be told, Mrs. Holmes didn't know either. She just knew that it was not a nice kind of life. Everyone said so. She said, "I am guessing that you have no more money and no hope of any coming in unless you get a position. Am I correct?"

"Yes, but that is not all of it. Even if I manage the money, who is to care for Keely? I can't always ask this of you."

"Well, perhaps you can't, but I can offer, and that is what I am doing. The high feelings against the Irish will end, Katie. The river will be closed soon. Ice forms early on the Saint Lawrence, and when that happens no more ships will come in until next spring. The fever will die out. From what I've been hearing, it already is. Mr. John Mills, our mayor, said just the other day that the deaths at Point St. Charles have dropped to about twenty-two a day. That is a terrible tragedy, but not nearly so many as before."

Katie's face was white. "Twenty-two every day," she repeated in a thin voice. "Any one of those on any day might be Michael."

Mrs. Holmes did not know what to say.

Katie looked up, her eyes too large in her ghostly pale face. "I don't want to live here if Michael is dead. I could never stop looking for him. Everywhere I went, every face I saw, I would be wondering and hoping that it would be him, Mrs. Holmes. I must leave—I just must."

"But perhaps not with Mr. Tully," Mrs. Holmes said gently.

"And how else?" Katie asked, a tinge of bitterness creeping into her tone. Then she changed her tone and her attitude. "And he isn't a bad man, Mrs. Holmes—truly. He is kind and he can help me go on the stage."

"And Keely? What does he think about having the child with you? Or have you not told him about Keely?"

"I have told him. Of course, Keely will go with me. I would not think of having it any other way."

"And what of Michael? If he was sent to Toronto or Kingston, or if he is in one of the hospitals ill, what do you think he will do when he comes back here and finds you and his daughter gone?"

Tears formed in Katie's eyes, and still again she was crying for Michael. "We have been here over three months. If he was coming back, he would have come by now, Mrs. Holmes. It has taken me all this time to be able to say that even to myself. I want him to come back. I want him to walk through that door right now and take me and Keely in his arms. If he were here everything would be all right, but . . . but he isn't going to come back to me, Mrs. Holmes . . . ever."

Mrs. Holmes took a deep breath. "So you are going to New York with Mr. Tully."

"He is going to meet me tomorrow. I will tell him then."

Mrs. Holmes's eyes were on Keely. "I will miss you both." She put her arms out, and Keely hopped down from Katie's lap and raced to Mrs. Holmes. "But especially her. She is my own special little girl." She looked up at Katie. "You will write to me?"

"Of course I will. Keely and I will miss you too." Katie looked away, fighting tears again. "You have been very good to both of us."

Katie didn't hunt for a position that day. She and Mrs. Holmes and Keely spent a pleasant last day together. Katie felt freer about spending the last of their money, since Tully would be providing for them after tomorrow. The three of them ate in a tearoom and went shopping afterward. Katie bought some ribbons for Keely's hair, and Mrs. Holmes added a pair of stockings and little kid shoes to her wardrobe. It was getting dark when they returned to the lodging house to prepare their dinner. They ate together and spent the evening in Mrs. Holmes's parlor. Neither woman wanted this last day to end and they stayed up far into the night.

Katie left the house the next day at noon to meet Tully in front of the Bonsecours Market. Tully, in his usual brilliant green garb, was waiting for her. Idly, and a bit down at the mouth, Katie thought, he was swinging a silver-tipped ebony walking stick. Katie walked up to him and was quite close before he noticed her. It gave her a moment's discomfort. Perhaps he had lost all interest in her and no longer wanted her to join the troupe.

That wasn't the case. Tully was just preoccupied and impatient. He came right to the point. "Well, have you decided? Are you coming with us?"

Katie was a bit disturbed by the curtness and wondered about the cause, but she answered with as much economy. "I'll go if I have your word that Keely will always be with us and you'll never let her go without. You will promise to take food from your own mouth before Keely ever goes without one meal."

Of all the things she might have said, he hadn't expected this. He couldn't help his curiosity, so he said, "And if I refuse to give my word?"

There was not so much a flicker of doubt in Katie's big green eyes. "Then I won't go with you," she said.

Tully's curiosity deepened and had a disturbing quality to it. How had she changed so radically in two days? He had left her on the street corner the night of the party a frightened and vulnerable girl, little more than a child. But this was no woman-child he faced now. This was a woman through and through, and she had almost overnight acquired a toughness he hadn't suspected was in Kitty. He said, "I'll give you my word. I told you once before I have no objection to the child."

"Then I will go with you," Katie said, but she didn't smile.

Tully frowned slightly. She didn't seem particularly happy about her decision. She was determined, but not happy. It was almost as if she were taking a bitter medicine she knew necessary but very distasteful. From the first time he had seen her he had thought of her as Kitty, the Irish kitten of Manhattan. Now he was thinking his kitten was more cat. "We leave at five o'clock this evening. Be ready. The coach will stop by the house for you and your luggage. Only one trunk allowed per person." With that said, Tully turned and walked away from her.

Katie watched after him for a minute. He hadn't been very friendly. Then, she thought, perhaps it was better this way.

FOR Michael, the month following the May day he had been taken from the Montreal wharf had been a nightmare of pain and dreadful darkness. He remembered little that made sense and had not even known where he was until the weather had turned warm and the deerflies hummed happily around him. The first indication he had of how ill he was came when a young nun walked by, almost off-handedly checking the pulse of the patients in the section of the hospital where Michael had been put. Without looking at his face, she had reached down and taken his wrist. Her eyes on her watch, she had not noticed that he was watching her until she released his hand and it did not fall limply back to the sheet. Her eyes had widened as they met his, and she had turned, scurrying off down the aisle calling for a doctor.

Even for a miracle, there was not a doctor available, but the Right Reverend Hudson, vicar general to the Catholic bishop of Montreal, happened to be at the hospital on one of his mercy visits. Over a month before, shortly after Michael had been brought in, Right Reverend Hudson had given Michael the sacrament of Extreme Unction. Now, on this May morning, the priest smiled. He took Michael's hand and sat on the edge of the hard wooden bed. "The good Lord must have work for you. All of the doctors thought you could not survive."

Michael tried to answer him, but he hadn't the strength, and his mouth was so dry he would not have been able to speak in any case.

The priest got up and within minutes was back with a gourd of cold, clean water. He lifted Michael's head and placed the gourd to his lips. Michael could not remember anything that had tasted better or any action that was kinder. He tried to smile, but the simple act of aiding the priest in lifting his head had exhausted him, and he fell asleep again.

It was a full two days before he awakened again, and from the talk he heard around him he learned that the priest who had given him the water was ill with the fever. Michael had tried to remain awake that day and he had again tried to talk, but his chest hurt, and his throat would not cooperate. But he also learned that he was in a section of the hospital where those who were not expected to survive were placed. During the next two weeks in his moments of lucidity, which were coming with greater frequency, he noticed that several times a day the beds in this part of the room were checked and many people were taken away. Almost as quickly as a bed was emptied and fresh straw laid, a new body was placed in the bed. He also noticed that the doctors, nuns, priests, and nurses who worked at the hospital were consistently vigilant, but overworked and extremely tired. Michael thought some of them looked sicker than the patients they cared for. It was not until mid-August and the hospitals had been moved from Montreal to Point St. Charles that Michael was really beginning to recover from the pneumonia that had nearly killed him. He was finally able to sit up. And now all that was ever on his mind was Katie and Keely. At first he had been too ill to notice or even care that Katie was never among the memories he had of people who flitted in and out of his fevered dreams and moments of consciousness. Now her absence made her notable.

It was due to his questioning about Katie that he discovered another startling and very upsetting piece of information. No one knew his name—not the doctors who cared for him nor any of the priests or nuns. He was a nameless Irishman. He quickly realized that, had Katie come looking for him, no one in the hospital would have been able to tell her he was here. No one knew who he was.

From the moment Michael realized that, he told everyone who would listen what his name was, and he was determined to get well and strong again. Day by day, he sat up longer and constantly tried to walk. He could not believe a grown man known for his physical prowess could be as weak as he had become. Even standing was a trial. His legs shook and waving fits of dizzying nausea assaulted him when he tried to take even one step. But he wouldn't give up and soon became noted for his raw determination. He was also known for his constant, endless questions. When her name wasn't known, Michael insisted, "But you must remember Katie—she would have had a child with her—a very pretty little girl."

Because his pride in them and his concern for them was so great, no one lost patience with him, but he received unhelpful answers such as: "Oh, Mr. Donovan, nearly every Irish woman has a child. There are more children running about loose than cats and dogs. I'm sorry I can't be of more help to you, Mr. Donovan, but I wouldn't worry too much. I am certain your wife and daughter will turn up. They can't have gone far."

As far as Michael was concerned, they could very well have gone to the moon. It was almost the end of August before he was strong enough or well enough to leave the hospital for any length of time. But at least he had a little more freedom and could talk to people who visited from

Montreal. The only thing of which he was certain was that neither Katie nor Keely occupied any of the hospital beds. Unlike Katie, he had been able to check and recheck every bed in the entire compound. He had also gone over every record that had been kept of the people who had passed through the hospital and were known by name.

What Michael feared most was that Katie and Keely had been transported on one of the barges that plied into the interior of Canada. The hospital compound in which he had recovered was only one set of buildings at Point St. Charles, and it had been the same when he was in Montreal; the other buildings were called emigration sheds, where the destitute were housed until they could be sent elsewhere. He knew Katie would have fought against being sent anywhere, but what frightened him was that he could not see how she would have had enough money to keep herself and Keely. He was certain that by now she would have used all the money they had brought from Ireland with them. She might have had to go wherever the authorities told her to go. Canada was so vast and its population so widespread, the idea of trying to find his wife and daughter seemed a terrifyingly enormous task—especially when he was not yet able to walk as far as Montreal without collapsing from exhaustion.

Finally Michael got to talk to the very busy Mr. Brown, the man he had learned had been responsible for bringing him to the hospital in the first place. Brown listened carefully to Michael's story, but he had no real answers.

"My God, man, you've had a time of it," Brown had sighed as Michael finished talking. "I suppose if I talked to anyone of these people I'd hear a similar story or worse. It's a terrible thing."

"It is, it is, but can you help me find my wife and child? I remember nothing after seeing that delusion."

"Well, I can clear that up for you. I was the specter in the sun. I don't know why I remember you, Donovan, but

I do. I thought you were dead when I first came upon you. Sorry, old man—I didn't realize you had seen me at all. I didn't mean to frighten you. But I can also tell you that no one else was around you. There was no woman or small child."

"You must have found me before she returned from the village."

"Village?" Brown asked. "What village had she traveled to?"

"Why, Montreal," Michael said perplexed. "Are there other villages nearby?"

Brown smiled a bit. "No, no—it is just that it is strange to hear Montreal called a village. We are all very proud of our growth and size, but since it is Montreal you meant, I can tell you that she would have been sent back right away."

"She went to find lodging for us, and if I know my Katie, she took the time to find a position for herself."

Brown was shaking his head adamantly. "Not in Montreal, my friend. It is a sorry situation to be certain, but she would have been chased out of Montreal. Folks there are frightened to death of you Irish—won't let you in home or shop. That's how terrified they are of catching the fever. She would have been back in a twinkling. Of course, she might have fallen ill like you did. Have you inquired at the hospital?"

"I have," Michael said, then asked, "Mr. Brown, is there nothing you can do to help me? Is there no means of finding lost people?"

"I'm afraid not. A few organizations have tried, but with the numbers coming in . . ." he shrugged. "We've had our hands full trying to keep you people alive—and ourselves. Every one of our nuns has fallen ill at some time, and we are still burying thirty people a day." Mr. Brown hesitated, then added, "I know this is something no one wants to face, but did you hear what I said? We are burying thirty a day. Could it be . . ."

"No!" Michael snapped. "I would know. Katie has not been in the hospital—and neither has Keely. They are alive and well somewhere. I will find them."

Mr. Brown looked sympathetically at him. "I would do the same in your place. I truly am sorry that I can't help you, Donovan. Wait a minute! Perhaps we can help each other. You have not yet recovered enough to travel far or do a full day's work, but you could do a service. Do you have money?"

Michael rolled his eyes to the brilliant blue sky. "You know I have not," he said.

"We desperately need men to haul carts of water to the sick. Surely you, of all people, know the terrible thirst. Haul water for us, Donovan. You look like you were a strong, stout fellow before your illness. You could be of great help. I can't pay you much, but I could give you something. If you are to find your family you are going to need money to keep you fed and traveling, and we desperately need the help. You've already had the fever, so there is no danger to you. What do you say?"

Michael thought for a moment. He knew that what Mr. Brown said was true, and yet any delay in searching for Katie and Keely seemed intolerable.

Before he could answer, Mr. Brown said, "If she is still around here, isn't it likely that she would look for you here?"

"I don't know. I was told that even as short a time ago as two weeks ago a woman had come here inquiring about me. But no one thought to ask her name or where she lived." Again Michael looked up at the sky. "I don't understand. No one seems to remember anything!"

"Those were—and still are—desperate days, Donovan. One woman seeking her man hardly makes an impression when hundreds are lost or sick or dying. I hope to God that none of us ever has to live through a thing like this again. The streets of hell will be crowded with those who will have to pay for letting this happen."

Michael stood looking at the man as he spoke. Brown was a conscientious, good man and the conditions at Montreal would have been far worse without him, yet Michael could not help feeling resentment as he looked at Brown's clean, neatly pressed clothing. The man was wearing a suit that still had a crease in the trousers. His shirt was unstained and louse free, and he was probably wearing underwear that had recently been washed. Here in the sheds there wasn't enough water to drink, let alone wash in. Michael knew that it wouldn't be long before people were saying that the Irish didn't care for bathing or cleanliness.

Michael sighed. Mr. Brown was a good man, but he could not stop what was happening now. He wouldn't be able to change the ideas people would get as a result of this tragedy. And Mr. Brown would not be able to do anything to change the misconceptions that would continue. Good people like Mr. Brown were charitable, but they did not and never would really understand what the Irish suffered. For that he would have to have lived through the last several years. Or maybe it was centuries.

As Brown continued to talk about the difficulties he and the Order of Grey Nuns faced in trying to handle the ill, Michael panned the area. Along the fences of the compound people were thronged. Every day the sightseers from Montreal came to stand by the fence and gape at the inmates. Michael had been told that this had been written about in the *Montreal Gazette*. The newspaper had reported that four to five o'clock in the afternoon was the favored time for sightseers to promenade near the immigration sheds. For his life, Michael could not comprehend how such abject suffering as was to be seen in the compound could be looked upon as an afternoon's entertainment. But then, Michael remembered that Canada was under British rule, and to his mind the British could find entertainment in the most brutish of ways.

Michael pushed down the familiar rage that came when he gave even passing thought to anything British. He had to remember that for the most part he liked these Canadians. He said, "I'll haul water for a time, Mr. Brown. I cannot promise for how long."

"That is wonderful!" Brown said gratefully. "Any time you can give us is more than we have now. You will be such a welcome aid when you are well enough to begin."

"I am well enough now," Michael said.

Michael saw no point in waiting until tomorrow to bring some relief to those still in bed unable to help themselves. How well he remembered lying in his bed hour after hour wanting water but unable to get it for himself and even lacking the strength to cry out for it. He found the cart and loaded empty casks onto it, then started off on his first trip. The task required only his muscle, not his mind. That was left free to contemplate what Katie would have done in the circumstances she had found herself in. Regardless of what Mr. Brown had said, Michael was certain Katie would have found a place for them to live. Mr. Brown may have been correct about the Irish being unwelcome, but it was obvious that Mr. Brown didn't know Katie. Michael chuckled and repeated to himself that Mr. Brown did not know Katie Ryan.

12

MICHAEL pushed the water cart tirelessly. Not only was he doing it as a much needed service to the ill and repaying those who had cared for him, he was also building his own strength and stamina. As Michael's strength began to return, so did his hope. The oppressive feelings of being unable to cope with his world were receding. He was once more beginning to feel capable and powerful within himself. Having been fed decent if uninspired food had helped.

Michael swam in crystal-clear streams, basked on the grassy green banks, and ran through fields that returned to him some of the lightheartedness that had nearly been crushed by the famine and its aftermath.

Shortly he was making frequent trips into Montreal. He asked about Katie constantly, not hesitating for a moment to approach total strangers. He didn't mind the peculiar looks he got or the seemingly endless stream of negative responses. He was going to find Katie if he had to knock on the door of every house in the city.

He tried to make himself think as he believed Katie would have and tried to assess the problems she would have had. He walked through the same neighborhoods she had walked, looking at the big houses with the same eye to wealth and need for servants. At each one he knocked and asked if Katie Ryan or Katie Donovan worked there. Over and over he was told that no such person worked in any of the houses—nor had she ever. Though he didn't find Katie, he did find out something about her in a backhanded sort of way. He now knew that it was highly unlikely that Katie had found a position for herself in Montreal. And he realized what a terrible time she must have had with the attitudes of the people. In this Mr. Brown had been accurate. The citizens of the city were terrified of the Irish and their diseases. Even Katie would have found this rock-solid terror an insurmountable barrier. But he didn't give up. He knew that Katie wouldn't have.

Early in September he found the tearoom where Katie had gone every morning for a cup of tea and to filch a newspaper left by another patron. The cheerful, rotund proprietor chuckled with the pleasant memories evoked as he told Michael how he had looked forward to Katie's morning visit. "I think it was for the discarded newspaper she came. The tea cost less than the paper and she was always looking for a position. She was a cheerful, kindly lass—always certain that the day would be her lucky one." He had frowned a bit when he said that, then added somberly, "I don't know as she ever got her lucky day."

Michael fortunately did not hear the last as he was having a terrible moment in which he thought he was having a recurrence of the fever. He was light-headed and his legs were like water. His heart was pounding and his pulse was throbbing, giving him a headache. He could barely draw breath as this genial man was speaking about Katie. It was almost as if she had become unreal for Michael until this man verified her existence.

When he was able to speak again, Michael asked, "Did she have a little girl with her?"

The man thought and shook his head. "I don't think so

—no, I am certain she never brought a little girl in here with her. I would have remembered."

"And you don't know where she lived?" Michael asked without any expectation of receiving an answer.

As he had anticipated, the man said he did not know where she had lived, but he added, "But she probably lived near here. We're not a fancy place, you know. Most of the people who come in here live nearby. Seldom do we get strangers—unless they've just moved into the neighborhood and then they are not strangers for long."

Michael thanked the man and left the tearoom with renewed hope. Finally he had met someone who actually knew Katie here in Montreal. That was all the encouragement he needed. He would find her now. He left the tearoom and stood in the street for a moment. He had grown used to being patient in the hospital, so now he realized the value of taking time to plan. He decided to move methodically from one house to another in the five-block radius of the tearoom. Buoyed up by having heard news of Katie, he knocked on every door asking about her. He was sent round back to the servant's entrance by some and received curt answers and slammed doors at other houses. Occasionally, he would be greeted by a friendly person wanting to help, but they didn't have the information he wanted. Finally, he arrived at a tidy little house with a stoop several steps off street level. He liked this house and knew Katie would, too, had she seen it. His spirits grew as he walked up to the house and knocked.

Mrs. Holmes was feeling lonely and not very friendly today. Already she missed Katie and Keely and she wasn't at all certain that Katie's decision to leave Montreal had been a good one. The last thing she wanted to face now was a salesman on her doorstep, or even someone who wanted to rent Katie's newly vacant room. She was not yet ready to have that third floor room occupied by anyone other than Katie and Keely. She opened her door with a jerky motion. "If you are here to sell me something . . ."

The man's eyes were filled with warmth and the bright light of hope. "No, ma'am, I have nothing to sell."

Before he could say more, Mrs. Holmes said, "I've no room to rent now. You can try next week." She could see by the expression on his face that it wasn't a room he wanted. "You aren't looking for a place?" she asked, her heart suddenly beating faster.

"No, ma'am," he said with a broad, engaging smile. "Me name is Michael Donovan. I've come to ask about . . ."

Mrs. Holmes didn't hear the rest of what he said—she didn't need to. She knew. She clung to the door as if she'd fall if it didn't support her. Her mind screamed, "It's him, Oh, dear Jesus, have mercy. It's him, Katie's man!" Mrs. Holmes couldn't speak. She wanted to reach out and touch him. For Katie's sake, she wished with all her heart that she was the young woman for this one moment. She wanted to take Michael in her arms and say for Katie all the things she knew that Katie had been feeling. She wanted to pour out for her all the longing that had filled the lonely nights for Katie. She wanted to tell him of all the tears that had flowed and the anguish that would never again be told about. That was the difference between man and his God. God could give all the good things for a man to take to himself. But once a man had lost his moment of grace, he had lost it forever. Katie's moment had been lost, and Mrs. Holmes wanted to snatch it from the jaws of fate and return it to both her and Michael. Her longing was so intense, the sun darkened and all was blackness for a moment.

Michael stopped talking. He didn't know what was happening to this woman, but whatever it was was eliciting feeling from him for which he had no explanation. He could see that she was being overpowered by emotion. But she was frightening him, for she had turned ashen except for two highly colored spots on either of her cheeks.

He stepped forward and held her upright as her knees sagged, his huge hands under her elbows. "You are not looking so well, ma'am," he said. "Let me help you to a chair."

Reality slid away from her again. The sound of his voice was like music in her ear. She gasped and the darkness sparkled with her own tears. Oh, how she understood Katie now.

Mrs. Holmes let him lead her into her parlor. With his help she sank gratefully into a chair. He was concerned and would be patient with her so she took advantage of the few moments this gave her. She leaned back and closed her eyes. She didn't know why the dear Lord had chosen to allow her to be granted such painful insight into the lives of Michael and Katie as she had been, but she knew that somehow she was going to have to be strong. It was Michael who needed her support, or he would when he knew what had happened. She gave momentary vent to cowardice and thought about lying to him. In a way it seemed as if it would be kinder just to say that Katie had never lived there. But she knew he would go on searching until he found Katie, and Mrs. Holmes couldn't lie to him anyway. She'd tell him the truth. She prayed that it wouldn't kill them both.

She opened her eyes and managed a wan smile. "I am all right, really. I must have given you quite a scare. I know I have startled myself."

"Is there anything I can be doing for you, ma'am?" Michael asked.

"Let me sit for a moment, then you and I will go to my kitchen, Michael Donovan. If it wouldn't be offending you, you can make tea for us, and then we'll have a long chat. You have come to the right door."

"You know Katie," he said.

"I know Katie," she answered. "And I know your daughter Keely." She paused for a moment, then added, "I love them both very much."

Michael was overcome. He turned away so she wouldn't see the tears in his eyes. He didn't even know this woman's name, and here he was crying like a new babe in her parlor.

Mrs. Holmes said gently, "Don't turn away, Michael. These will not be the last tears we shed this day." He looked at her in alarm, and she said, "All in good time. I don't think I am able to begin yet. My name is Margaret Holmes. My friends mostly call me Maggie. I think that is what you should call me. I feel as if I know you very well."

When she was ready, he accompanied Maggie Holmes into her kitchen, and while she sat at the scarred wood table wondering how she could tell him all that had happened these last months, he puttered about her kitchen, finding odds and ends to make a proper tea for them.

He served their repast, then sat down opposite her. "I understand you want to tell what is on your mind in your own good time and way, but I must know. Katie and Keely—they are not dead?"

"Oh, no! No, my dear. The last I saw them they were very well. Keely was making wonderful progress. She was like any other child a bit small for her age, but she was catching up with herself. And, my, what a pretty child. She has stolen my heart."

Michael smiled, his blue eyes shining. "I do know how you must suffer, for she stole my heart the moment she was born. I am like never to have it back again."

They drank their tea and ate the biscuits Michael had found, and Mrs. Holmes knew she couldn't put it off any longer. Slowly, carefully, and in great detail she told Michael everything she could remember from the first day Katie had arrived on her doorstep to the day she left. When she was finished, a deep, flat silence fell in the room.

Emotions trembled in the air around them and died unexpressed. The silence remained.

Finally Mrs. Holmes said tearfully, "She had to make a choice. It could not go on . . ."

He looked up at her, and she had never seen such pain in a man's eyes before. "But didn't she know I'd never leave her . . . I'd come for her . . ."

"Oh, Michael Donovan, how could she believe? How could she think you could rise from the dead to find her?"

"Yes, damn it—she should have believed. I would rise from the dead to find her. I did rise from the dead!" he shouted.

Mrs. Holmes let the tears pour from her eyes. Her voice was broken as was her heart. "I know, Michael, I know."

Michael stayed at the lodging house for the next two days. He was incapable of doing anything else. He stayed in the same room Katie had lived in, and the scent of her drove him to a frenzied madness. She was everywhere. The ghost of her voice remained in the room, her scent hung like hoar frost on the rich moist earth and screamed at him that she had taken another man.

Mrs. Holmes was terrified. She thought he was dying. He lay on the bed semiconscious for two days. He ate nothing, and he was bathed in a sheet of cold, clammy sweat. Even when he opened his eyes and stared madly at her, she knew he wasn't seeing her. He was in his own private hell, and she had no meaning for him.

What he saw was Katie with the man named Tully. What he saw was that she had told him the truth when they had first met and she had said she would do anything to get to New York and be on the stage. Anything included leaving him. Anything meant giving herself to the first man who promised her a place in the spotlight.

On the morning of the third day he awakened and could not bear to stay in the room a moment longer. The bed beneath him, the bed Katie had slept on, was loathsome.

He bathed from the same basin Katie had used so often. He dressed and went downstairs.

As soon as Mrs. Holmes heard his footsteps on the stairs, she came out of her flat into the hall. She knew immediately that the man who had ascended the stairs two nights ago was a different man from the one who descended them this morning. She felt a terrible sadness and loss as he turned his gaze on her. His eyes still blazed a glorious blue, but the fire was cold and hard and hurtful.

She said, "I was afraid you were dying."

He gave her a crooked, bitter smile. "Unfortunately, Mrs. Holmes, we do not die when our lives end. We die only when our usefulness ends."

"You're going to find her, aren't you?"

"She took Keely," he said simply with an air that claimed that was all there was to be said.

Mrs. Holmes looked away from him. She thought perhaps it was all there was left to say.

Michael returned to the hospital sheds. He dared not allow himself to think of Katie, for a rage so deep and bone-shaking struck him that it also shook his precarious health. Neither did he dare think of Keely, for fear and longing struck at him with equal force. His instinct told him to focus on something impersonal and absorbing while he worked to regain his full strength. The road before him was going to be hard and long. He would need every bit of stamina he had ever had.

Michael took up his water cart with a vengeance. When the muscles in his back, shoulders, and legs screamed in a fiery torment, he gloried in the pain and pushed himself all the harder. For once not a patient in the hospital was in want of water. Even the emigrants in the sheds waiting for transportation to the interior of Canada had plenty to drink and, on some days, even enough to wash in. Michael was deluged with tearful thanks, and he thought that it was a simple thing he was doing to warrant so much gratitude.

Mr. Brown was so impressed with Michael's tireless industry, he felt obligated to seek Michael out and commend him personally. Michael listened politely and thanked Mr. Brown for his kindness. Again the thought ran through his mind that all these thanks and excessive notice was over giving the sick water to drink—a thing that should have been taken for granted as common decency. He said nothing of this to Mr. Brown. He had no reason to be anything but courteous to the man, for at least he cared. And Michael did not doubt that the small salary he was being paid came from Mr. Brown's own pocket. Mr. Brown was a good man. And Mr. Brown was a man who needed a sympathetic ear. He talked, but Michael was suddenly hearing another voice. It was as if he had suddenly been visited by a ghost, for as clear as clear can be Michael was hearing the strong voice of Sheila Flynn.

The old matriarch was repeating in his head the same words she had said to him that last day at Fairmont. "We'll never be the same here again. It's the devil's work and make no mistake. And happy he must be! So many of these folks will be homeless and many of them will not be able to make their way as well as you will, Michael. Those of us left behind won't be able to help—the land will be changed, the village will be in mourning for those faces we will never see again. But we'll not be able to do anything but grieve. And we'll grieve, Michael, as deeply and sorrowfully as those of you who be cast out from here."

Innocent that he was, he had answered her, "You want me to promise you I will look after some of the less fortunate ones, the ones you see as less able than I, Sheila, and I have always done. You know a Donovan has never turned a wanting soul from his door."

Sheila had nodded her head. "But that was before, and you had only to share the little supper you had, or give a man a place to rest his weary head. . . . Perhaps the Blessed Lord has it in His mind to ask more of you now, Michael."

Michael had all he could do not to laugh aloud in bitterness while Mr. Brown finished talking about the problems and progress being made in the hospitals and with the Montreal Board of Health. All Michael could think about was how prophetic Sheila had been. He wondered if she had foreseen what was to come. He had seen much more of the devil's work since he had left Ireland, and, yes, the Lord was asking more and more of him.

Mr. Brown had finally wound down and bid Michael a good day. With a fond handshake, he was on his way. Michael, however, stood where he had been as if rooted. Sheila had said, "Your daughter needs you. And others need you. . . . When you walk the road out of here, look at your people—lambs to the slaughter. . . . They need you, Michael Donovan. . . . When the time comes and Ireland calls, you'll find a way."

Had Ireland called? Was that what he was hearing in the recalled voice and words of Sheila Flynn? Did all the pain and all the loss have a voice that was in truth Ireland calling?

13

SURPRISINGLY, the conclusions Michael reached the day Mr. Brown had come to talk to him did not spur him into a spate of frenzied activity. Instead he became very introspective and deliberate in all that he said and did. He talked endlessly to the people still waiting for transportation in the quarantine sheds and heard many stories appalling in their similarity. Almost to a man, every person he talked with expressed their loathing of the British and all that nation of brutes stood for. Michael made little comment but tucked away inside himself every scrap of information he gleaned. One of the conclusions he reached was that these people to whom he spoke were too fresh off the boat and still too stunned and weakened by their experiences to want to or be worthy to take up the battle against the British rulers. For those patriots he would have to go elsewhere. Elsewhere was New York, where he had been told there were thousands of hearty Irishmen and where he was certain Katie would have gone with Keely. In all ways a trek south suited his needs and desires.

But still he felt no urge to hurry, and he did not question the sudden deliberate slowness of his actions. September was cold—far colder than Michael imagined it would be, but he had never experienced a Canadian winter before. He looked with mesmerized amazement at the powerful St. Lawrence. Like an old man closing the door firmly on the west side of the house, the St. Lawrence clogged up with ice. Quickly the mighty river that had allowed miles of ships to sail freely up and down its huge body all spring and summer permitted no sailing vessel entry now. Michael watched the moody river shut everything out. He felt a strange, almost magical kinship.

On October 21, Montreal had its first snowfall. What the cold of September had not told him the snowfall did: If he didn't leave immediately, he was not going to be leaving until the following spring. The hospital had less than one hundred people left in it, and because no more ships would be coming from Britain, everyone knew the fever problem was over—at least for this year. Everyone also knew that never again would Quebec or Montreal ever be caught so totally unprepared or vulnerable to such a tragedy again. Michael's services as water carrier were no longer crucial, so he packed what few possessions he had and, as had so many before him, headed south. Michael was both tantalized and a bit taken aback as he set out. This new country he had come to was vast and it was beautiful. Its rivers were broad and deep and fast running, filled with fish and ripe for commerce. A man could walk for days between settlements and see only a house here and there, and yet almost everywhere there were signs of industry. Small communities of prosperous houses and businesses abounded. He was entranced by the contrasts, and those contrasts grew stronger when he walked over the Canadian border into the United States. On the one hand, a man could stand and look in any direction and see hills and trees and forests and rivers almost untouched, as fresh-looking as the day God had created them, and hours later come upon a construction crew building a canal or a railroad line.

Once he had awakened from his lethargic reluctance to begin his pursuit of Katie, he made the greatest haste he could. But he found it slow going for several reasons. The first one was the unexpected enormity of the new land. He was used to Ireland, and though it was a task, walking from one end of it to the other was nothing compared to how it was here. The second one was the ferocity of the winter. Again his ignorance of this new land had left him unprepared for a northern winter. And the last was his lack of money, the full effect of which he had not completely considered. He was not properly dressed and he had to stop in his travels frequently or detour to a place that was out of his direct route in order to work long enough to feed and clothe himself. Sometimes he was delayed for only a day or so; other times it was weeks before he was on his way again. His last major hindrance was his lack of knowledge. New York was a name to him, and most of what he knew had come from Katie and inquiries he had made along the way. Some of those he had met were knowledgeable, others had not been. He had once traveled fifty miles west because a man had given him very detailed and totally erroneous directions.

After that costly side trip, Michael made up his mind to head for the coast and never vary from it. Though it was a longer route, he knew he would eventually reach New York harbor that way. Traveling from one seaport town to another, he would have access to the docks, which were almost always in need of unskilled laborers.

Near the end of February, 1848, Michael had reached Boston, and there he got his first realistic taste of what life was going to be like for an Irishman in his new country. Boston had for many years been a port of entry for emigrants from Ireland as well as other countries. For the nine years previous to 1847, however, approximately five thousand emigrants had come to the city by legal or illegal means and had been absorbed into the population with grumblings but little notable disruption. This last year Boston had received over thirty-seven thousand emigrants coming into the city by one means or another. With a population of just over one hundred and fourteen thousand, the thousands of emigrants disrupted and caused problems throughout the city. Among those coming in, there were twenty-five hundred beggars flooding the streets with no income and no place to live. The outrage was immediate, and Boston authorities screamed that Massachusetts was being turned into "the moral cesspool of the civilized world." Moral Bostonians also developed a curious attitude. The Irish starving in Ireland were unfortunate victims, and all right-minded people were obligated and desirous of helping them with great generosity. However, the Irish who had managed to cross the Atlantic to starve on the streets of Boston were declared the scourings of Europe and an intolerable burden to the taxpayers of the city.

Michael first heard this expressed in a grog shop in a house on Hamilton Street where he had found refuge when he first came to Boston. Geographically Boston was not well set up to absorb the emigrants, so nearly all of them ended by crowding into the North End and the once prosperous Fort Hill section in the 8th Ward. The whole section had become a loud, odorous, overcrowded place. Over a thousand grog shops were open seven days a week, and most of them were owned and operated by foreigners— mainly the offensive Irish.

As far as Michael was concerned, the grog shop on Hamilton Street was a lifesaver. He had come into Boston cold, hungry, and feeling that he would never succeed in getting to New York. Only his longing for Keely kept him going. The nameless little groggery was tucked into a lower room in the large house that was inhabited by ten families and was open and warm. The round-bellied man who ran the shop was warm and friendly. Cormac, better known as

Corry, Maguire, nearly pulled Michael into the room. "Never in my life have I turned a good man away from my door. You look a good sort to me, if a little long in the face. What's your name?"

Michael stated his name, but before he could say anything else, Corry Maguire was off and running again. Michael would come to know that he was seldom at a loss for words. He was everybody's friend, but no one cheated him, for he could also be a terrible enemy—relentless until he had satisfied his own version of justice. At the moment he was determined to befriend Michael. "You look like you need a good friend, some food for your belly, some work, and a cup or two to warm your innards," he diagnosed.

Michael couldn't argue with any of that. Before he knew what had happened, he had an apron tied around his waist, a broom put in one hand, a wash rag in the other, and he was pushed in the direction of the barrel and crate chairs and tables Corry had set up for his customers. Spittoons had to be cleaned, and two or three unconscious bodies had to be removed every hour or two. Corry decided which were deserving of a warm place to sleep and which Michael should deposit outside the establishment to be left to the elements.

Out back of the house Corry had a pit, and he always seemed able to have a pig available to roast. When Michael wasn't cleaning or removing comatose patrons, he was usually to be found out back roasting the pig so that Corry could sell the hundreds of shredded pork sandwiches he counted on per day. Unlike many of the proprietors of the grog shops in the 8th Ward, Corry had an eye to his future, and one day soon, he hoped, he was going to have a real saloon with a mahogany bar, and paintings on the wall, and the best sandwiches and stews money could buy.

Michael was given a blanket and a place to sleep in a small storeroom, all the food he could eat, and fifty cents a day for helping Corry. He had only been there for three days when Corry discovered he liked talking to Michael Donovan. When the groggery was not too busy or crowded, he turned its running over to his two sons and came out back to sit with Michael while the pig was being prepared. He liked to cook and enjoyed these times more than any others. It was during one of these conversations that Corry had told Michael about the peculiar attitude Bostonians held about the Irish here versus the Irish in Ireland.

Corry leaned back on his bench. His broad shoulders were braced against the black gnarled trunk of an apple tree. He chuckled so hard that his round belly bobbed up and down. "It takes a lot of good living before a man can think like that, Donovan."

Michael started to say something, but as usual, before a single word was out of his mouth, Corry was on to his next thought.

"But I'll tell you, these folks are the same as people are the world over. They don't like their ways tampered with, don't take easily to new people comin' in—'specially those with foreign ways like us Irish. But if a man can show them he's got something to offer that they haven't got and would be wanting, they'll accept him quick as a flash." He sat up straight and extended his hands out to warm them at the pit fire. "That's why I run a clean house here. When the God-blessed snooty Committee of Internal Health comes nosing into this neighborhood, they never have a harsh word for Corry Maguire's place. No, they don't— and more than once one of them has gone out of here with pork juice running down his chin."

"How long have you had the shop?" Michael asked as his boss fell into an unusual silence.

"Two years come May. I figure to be here another year, maybe a bit longer, and then I'll be looking for my saloon." Again he fell silent, then he looked speculatively at Michael. "I don't know you too well, Donovan, but my gut tells me you're a man to be trusted, and a hard-working bastard to boot. My sons are still young—maybe too young to be saddled with their old man's saloon—and maybe they would be going to college. I might be persuaded to consider a partner if you could come up with some cash."

Michael was flattered and stunned. He stared at Corry for a moment, then got very busy turning the pig on the spit. "I wish I could say yes, Corry. It's a tempting offer."

"But . . . ?" Corry prompted.

"I am on my way to New York. I have some business I must take care of there. I can pledge my honor to nothing until that is taken care of."

The two men sat together and talked for another hour, Corry prodding and probing until he had extracted from Michael the whole story of Katie and Keely.

Corry's dark brown eyes shifted back and forth as he groped for a memory. He focused on Michael, his expression face alight with excitement and triumph. "I knew I had heard that name—Tully. Blessed saints, man, he and his troupe were here—right here in Boston—a few days after Christmas! Bejabbers! I saw her myself! I saw your Katie, only that's not what he called her. It was Kitty— Kitty Ryan, the Irish kitten. Holy saints, but she's got a voice that melts the wings off an angel's back! That's your Katie? Bejabbers!"

Corry barely paused long enough to draw breath, then chattered on, "That Tully, he's always turning up like a bad penny, always searching for the girl that'll make him his fortune."

Michael grabbed Corry's forearm to slow down the spate of words. "Did you see Keely? My daughter—did you see her?"

"No, I didn't, and it's thanking God you should be that I did not. I saw your Katie in a dingy place over on Ann Street. Tully is not fat in the pocket these days, and from what I'm told he has more creditors wantin' to see his pretty face than he has payin' customers. He left town just hours ahead of an angry pack of shop owners." Corry belatedly realized how tactless he had been. He looked down and said in a milder tone, "It's not a pretty life your Katie's taken for herself."

"Don't call her my Katie. She's Kitty Ryan, and I have no interest in her. It's my daughter I want and care about," Michael said.

Shortly after this, Corry was called back inside, and Michael was thankful. He enjoyed Corry's exuberant company very much, but this latest news had been a shock, and he wanted to be alone to sort out the uncomfortable and confusing feelings that were so strong in him.

That night seemed never to end. All the patrons of the grog shop had bottomless appetites and, apparently, the money to keep their cups filled. It was the small hours of the morning before Michael got back to his small cubbyhole to lie down on his blanket. Even then, tired as he was, he found sleep difficult. His dreams were restless and filled with tantalizing visions of Katie, which he could keep at bay during the daytime but had more difficulty warding off at night. At four in the morning, he got up, too restless to lie still and too irritated with his inability to control his longing to go back to sleep, so he went out into the tavern to get a cup of poteen.

Corry was there, sitting on a barrel, his feet up on top of a crate, his dark eyes glazed over and sad.

"What's the matter, Donovan? Can't sleep? Neither can I. Get yourself a cup and join me."

Michael fished in his pocket for coins. He never took anything from Corry that had not been promised in his wages.

Corry rocked forward, his feet coming down with a slam. "Put your money away. I owe you. Wanta know why I'm sitting down here working on giving myself a bad temper and an aching head in the morning?"

Michael filled his cup and watched Corry from the corner of his eye. He had never seen his friend like this before. Though Corry was very outgoing and seldom would be found without a glass in his hand, he actually drank rather sparingly, keeping the ever-filled glass more for show than anything else. Now he was well pickled and on his way to a great blue funk. "I couldn't begin to guess," Michael said with an attempt at cheerfulness.

"You're going to be leaving now. I can feel it—I can smell it in the air. I opened my big mouth when I should have kept it closed, and now I am going to lose a friend and a business partner."

"I've stayed longer than I intended already," Michael said quietly, not bothering to go through the formality of protesting that he wasn't leaving immediately. He knew as well as Corry did that it would be one day soon.

"How do you even know she'll be in New York?"

Michael shrugged. "She may not be there when I go, but I know Katie. Sooner or later she'll be in New York."

Corry sighed. "Ah, well, I've already opened my mouth too much, so I might as well tell you that you're right. All theater people end up in New York sooner or later." Corry leaned far back, nearly overbalancing himself as he downed the last swallow from his cup. "The curse of my life is my tongue. My wife always told me that."

Michael had accumulated enough possessions during his travels to warrant a backpack again. Slowly and with mixed feelings, he packed his belongings the next morning. He worked during the busiest part of the day and evening, then bade his friend good-bye. Except for Corry Maguire, Michael was not particularly unhappy to bid Boston good-bye. Though he did not expect to find conditions much better in New York, and some people had told him they were worse, Michael was sick of seeing his countrymen crammed into tenements and old houses eight, nine, and

ten families to a space that should have held no more than
eight or nine people all told. He was sick to see so many
turning to drink and fighting, because there was no decent
work for them, no decent place for them to live, and no
one who wanted them.

The winter set in for its last days of frigid cold. Michael
discovered what an unrelentingly dreary and frosty month
February can be. He bound his hands and feet in rags, and
wore every stitch of clothing he had to keep warm as he
walked through quaint villages. Occasionally he would get
lucky and be able to ride on a farm wagon going to market.
The farther south he moved, the less frightened of the Irish
he found the people to be. Though he was still not wel-
comed warmly, he was not feared as he had been in Montreal, nor had he been so looked down on as he had been in
Boston.

Michael arrived in Albany in late March, a city notable
to him for two reasons. The first one was that on a pole he
saw posted a notice that Miss Kitty Ryan had performed
at the Gormley Music Hall on the twenty-second and
twenty-third of March. Today was the twenty-fifth. Nonetheless, he found the music hall, and was assured that the
troupe had left Albany late the same night of their last
performance.

"Do you have word of their next stop?" Michael asked.

The man smiled. "I'll tell you what Tully told me, and
then you decide where they are headed next. He says to
me, 'We've letters so heavy, begging us to come West, we
need a trunk to carry them all.' Then he says, 'New York is
my home, and the best place in the world to perform. The
crowds will love her there.' He's probably going to some
little outpost for all his big talk."

Michael started to walk away, "Thank you, sir. Good
day to you . . ." He paused, then walked back to the man.
"She . . . I mean . . . you didn't happen to see a little
girl with her, did you?"

"Sure I did," the man said jovially. "She and Tully got into a donnybrook over that little girl. I've got a couple of apartments over the hall—rent 'em out sometimes when an act has enough money to pay good. Miss Kitty insisted her and the little girl was going to stay in one of those rooms. Tully's screaming like she stuck him with a hot poker. 'No!' he shrieks. 'You're drivin' me to the poorhouse!' She turns her back on him and says she won't sing. She gets the room for herself and the little girl."

"The little girl was . . . well?"

"Well? Sure she was. Pretty little thing. Tully wants her in the act, but Miss Kitty won't hear of it."

Michael thanked the man again. He felt a mix of relief and gratitude that Keely was well and deep anger that Tully would even think of putting his daughter on a stage like some sort of painted doll. It was bad enough that Katie had chosen to make a spectacle of herself, but it was abominable to even think of Keely standing in front of a gawking audience.

The second reason Albany was notable was that he had been able to secure passage on a boat. The travel was still not ideal, and there were places in the Hudson where the ice lingered, but it was much faster than walking and much warmer. He had worked as a stableboy for a week at a quaint village named Briarcliff Manor, then had continued his trip down to the island of Manhattan. New York City, he was told, was at the tip of this island.

Expecting a sizeable town in the midst of the same kind of rural villages he had been passing through, Michael was both pleased and shocked when he entered the raucous rough-and-tumble city that was New York. It was the strangest combination of decadence and beauty he had ever seen. He gawked as he walked, amazed by everything, wanting to miss nothing. Construction crews seemed to be everywhere. Some of the time Michael couldn't tell if they were tearing down or building up. Enormous foundations were being dug, huge mansions that bespoke great wealth stood side by side on tree-lined streets, and then no distance away at all Michael dodged a racing pack of pigs scavenging along the garbage-strewn, mud-rutted street.

When he had gotten over his shock, he threw back his head and howled with laughter. This was New York! He had barely gotten his boots muddied and already he loved it! Sound was everywhere. From somewhere out of eyesight he heard musicians playing. The inharmonious clank of picks on rock clanged nearby. Carriages swung past him on Third Avenue, and again he had to dodge the onslaught or be felled by the goings-on.

As he had come to make a habit, Michael headed for the dock area. Not only was he likely to find a congregation of emigrants near the waterfront, but also it was the most likely place for him to find work quickly. On his way, he passed tenements six and seven stories tall and marveled at the height of them, wondering what kept them from toppling over right into the streets. As he would learn later, occasionally they did topple over, and other times they simply burned to the ground.

Michael had found himself torn by conflicting emotion many times since he had left Fairmont, and this time was no different. New York excited him. There was something sophisticated about it, and it undoubtedly had great wealth, but still there was a certain rough pioneer feeling here as well. He thought a man could do very well for himself in this city. Yet, he looked around and saw children running like ragamuffins along the streets, and corn girls carrying baskets while singing their song.

> "Hot corn! Hot corn!
> Here's your lily white corn.
> All you that's got money
> Poor me that's got none—

> Buy me lily white corn
> And let me go home."

The sight made him wonder if the Irish or any poor man
was any better off here than he had been in Ireland. People
were obviously packed into the tall, narrow wooden buildings that reached to the sky. Laundry and people hung out
every window. Stoops were filled by the lounging idle, and
in the darkness he could see others sitting on the steps.
Women and men alike rummaged through trash, hunting
anything of value to use or sell. On the one hand, he could
see the enormous wealth, and on the other, the abject poverty—and somewhere in between, he knew, was the abode
of opportunity. The excited part of him said he was the
man to find that opportunity, and the dejected side said he
could walk right past it and, dumb emigrant that he was,
he would never know. He thought of Keely and bringing
her to one of the ugly rooms that must be behind the tenement walls. He would find the opportunity. He would have
to for his daughter, and he knew that somehow that opportunity would have something to do with Ireland herself—
his two women, Keely and Erin.

Michael had no difficulty finding the main center of sea-
faring trade. The noise alone would have led him to South
Street on the East River, but the dense forest of masts left
no doubt whatever. South Street was a whole street of
warehouses and merchants' stores. Flags of all nations
flapped sharply in the whipping breeze.

For a few moments, Michael simply stood and watched
the activity. He moved away from the main thoroughfare,
his back against a warehouse, for the cobblestoned street
was a writhing mass of movement. Draught horses pulled
heavy drays loaded with huge casks. Men looking no
larger than ants scurried under the bowsprits of the mam-
moth ships. Casks wobbled and clunked as they were
rolled down swaying gangplanks onto the piers. Boxes,

crates, and other cargo was stacked high along the lines of
ships. The iron rims of the dray wheels kept up a steady,
deafening din that was the thunderous background music
of South Street. Michael picked out several men he knew
to be runners. By this time he was familiar enough with
runners that he could spot them as fast as they could spot
an unsuspecting emigrant. His eye drifted away from the
runners to several well-dressed ladies and gentlemen
searching for their ship. He moved away from his protective wall and began to walk up past Coffee House Slip, the
Fulton Market, and James Slip to the foot of Pike Street.
His pace slowed, his eyes wide with wonder. He saw shipyard after shipyard—so many he could not count them,
nor imagine how far he would have to walk until he
reached the end. He could see they extended at least to a
bit of land that jutted out and he later learned was called
Corlears Hook. He didn't know if they continued beyond
that point, but he guessed so. He stood watching the work
for almost an hour, then he turned back walking toward
Fulton Market and Coffee House Slip. It was getting late,
and he realized belatedly that he had spent the whole day
gawking and hadn't a place to stay for the night.

As he neared the lower end of South Street, once again
the first people he saw were the always busy runners. He
had a mild flare of pride when he realized none had approached him. They could tell he was not newly arrived
and didn't bother with him. He chuckled to himself. They
probably thought he was one of them.

His easy amusement was shattered when he came near a
ship disgorging its steerage passengers into the waiting
arms of the runners. A young woman, her hair wild and
her face as pale as oatmeal was shrieking like a banshee
and kicking at the man who had hold of her satchel. Michael hesitated to interfere for at the moment it seemed as
if the young woman was on the verge of victory and would
need no help. Then the runner released her satchel, and

attacked her, pummeling her mercilessly until she was huddled on the pier. Michael sprinted over and hauled the man off the woman.

Accustomed to the mere sight of his size settling a good many arguments for him, Michael expected the same with this one, for the man was quite small. But the man was not frightened off by Michael's interference. Ferret faced and vicious, he spun round to face Michael. In a deep crouch, and a knife in his left hand, he darted in at Michael.

Michael backed away, cautious, and put his hands up, wanting this man to be on his way. "You've got plenty others to choose from. Be on your way—leave us to ourselves."

The man laughed deep and low in his throat, slowly circling Michael, his eyes never leaving Michael's.

On the periphery of his vision, Michael could see that the woman hadn't left. Without looking at her, he waved his hand at her, trying to make her run away.

The man chose that moment to lunge at Michael. At first he felt nothing, then a sharp pain jabbed through the base of his hand.

The man had darted back out of reach. He lunged again and with a slicing cut slashed across Michael's thigh.

Another leap forward on light feet and Michael had a long, though not deep cut along the muscle of his upper arm. The man was in control and playing with him. Compared to the small nimble-footed man, Michael was a graceless clod. He was either going to have to wade in and take his chances with the knife or run. With the man in control of the fight and dictating the rules, Michael was going to be in bloody tatters.

He watched the man's eyes carefully and with the next lunge managed to sidestep the thrust, but he wasn't quick enough to grab hold of the little man.

Both men whirled and faced each other again. As he spun into position, Michael caught a glimpse of the woman. She was still standing where he had left her. "Get out of here!" he yelled at her, his eyes intent on his assailant. Michael danced as did the man, shifting back and forth feinting motion, then sidling to the opposite direction. Finally, the man moved forward, his knife aimed at Michael's chest. Everything happened fast after that. The woman swung the satchel high over her head and brought it down with all her weight and might on the back of the man's neck. The man's momentum carried him forward, the lethal knife still in his hand. Michael jumped trying to get out of the way, tripped, and fell onto the man. Michael knew as he was going down that there was going to be damage done. The cracking of bone and the fierce expulsion of air verified it.

A large, heavyset man was now standing beside the woman. The woman ran forward and grabbed Michael by the collar of his jacket. "Get up! Hurry, Mister, get up before the police come by."

Michael scrambled to his feet. The man lay still, his head bent like that of a pigeon with a broken neck. Michael backed up, horrified at what he saw.

"Pick 'im up! Come on, now, do it—we haven't much time," the woman urged. Then she turned to the man with her. "Garry, help 'im. Hurry now! You know what to do."

"Take him by the arm. We'll drag him between us likes he's had a cup too much."

Michael moved like an automaton, but he did as he was told. Before the fog cleared from his mind, or he lost the electrification of adrenaline, he was racing down dark, narrow roads with Garry, the dead man hanging like a rag doll between them.

Garry hurried down James Street to Cherry Street and turned, nearly dragging Michael along. The woman was on his other side whispering words of encouragement.

"How much farther, Garry?" she asked.

"Just a bit," the man panted. Moments later he turned

into a long double row of tenements called Gotham Court, or more popularly known as Sweeney's Shambles. Pushing loungers in the hallway, Garry shoved his way down the stairs. Long before he could see it, Michael could hear water.

Under Gotham Court was an open sewer. Many a straggler who could not pay his rent had exited the world by this route, and with a heave from Garry, the knife fighter followed the same path. Without saying a word, Garry and the woman turned and started back up to the street. Michael followed. Again Garry hurried through the dark streets with the woman and Michael following until he turned down Maiden Lane and vanished alongside a narrow wooden building. Michael tripped over something solid but giving, and he guessed it was a sleeping vagrant. Behind the main building was a shack—a lean-to, really, tacked onto the main house. Already Garry had a candle lit and a small paneless window glowed golden.

Michael entered, and already Garry was on his knees pulling up the boards of the floor. He extracted a bottle. Getting up, he grinned at Michael. "Welcome, friend. Meet Eileen Brennan, my cousin fresh off the boat. I'm Garret O'Hea."

"Michael Donovan," Michael said tersely, his eyes on the bottle. His mouth felt like it was full of cotton, and now his arm and leg and hand were hurting.

Garry handed him the bottle. "Get him a stool, Eileen. You're not properly grateful to a man who just saved your skin." He shoved the three-legged stool toward Michael. "Sit, have a drink, and accept our thanks, Donovan."

Michael sat and drank with Garry, not protesting when the silent Eileen got water and a clean cloth and began to clean his wounds.

Eileen Brennan was as plain as a mud fence, but she had a spirit that danced in her eyes and Michael liked her. Or perhaps it was the very strong contents of Garry's bottle that made her seem so pleasant. He wasn't certain, because he had no time to even consider what had happened that night. Before he knew what hit him, he was curled up on the floor of Garry's shack sound asleep, thus ending his first day in New York City.

KATIE awakened to a cold, drizzly April morning. She lay in her bed and stared in the direction of the single window in the room. Beside her, Keely was curled into a ball, still sound asleep. This time last year, she and Michael and Keely were still trying to make their way to Montreal, and Keely's birthday had passed without anyone taking notice. This year they were in a strange town, and Katie had to think for a moment to recall that they were in Philadelphia. Tonight she would perform once again in some music hall, and then they would pack all the trunks and be gone with the light of the moon. Most likely Tully would not pay the hotel bill, and if they ever returned here, they would not be permitted to stay in this same place again.

But as Tully had told her so often, "They don't pay us enough, and by the time we come back there will be ten new hotels built and we will have our choice."

Katie had begun arguing with this kind of logic, but she had given that up months ago. She wasn't sure he wasn't correct, and most of the time she was too tired to care.

At least, she thought, she could take comfort in the knowledge that she was popular as a performer. Quickly,

as she allowed herself that moment's grace, she took it
back. Tully had only tried her on the entertainment-
starved folks along the frontier, and in the mining towns
. . . and the clay towns.

Vividly, she recalled such a town in southern Ohio.
Tully had announced they were going to make a circuit of
towns in southern Pennsylvania, Ohio, and Kentucky. Not
knowing what this meant, Katie set out with the troupe
enthusiastically. The towns on their "circuit" were little
more than temporary frame sheds placed along a well-
driven track that served as the main street. The opera
houses were saloons and the stages were no more than
rough platforms hastily nailed together because Tyrone
Tully was bringing Kitty Ryan, the Irish Kitten of Manhattan to them. If the men who labored on the railroads
and canals, the mines, and the clay works had not been so
pathetically grateful and appreciative of her talent, she
would have cringed with embarrassment. The Irish Kitten
of Manhattan had never stepped foot inside that city, and
she was beginning to wonder if she ever would.

When they entered the little town in Ohio just north of
Nelsonville, she noticed that there was a pinkish haze over
everything. The gentle mountains blended with patchy valleys and vast acres of dark forest lands, but it hadn't the
rich verdant look of Pennsylvania. This was a dusty, dry
place, swirling with pinkish dust. Katie instantly disliked
the place, and she cast an apprehensive glance at Max.

Max seemed oblivious to the strangeness of the place.
He was laughing, saying to Amory, "Don't forget, old man
—don't clap anyone on the back here."

Amory chuckled in his long-faced fashion. "Right—
clouds of red dust rising. It will certainly cramp Tully's
style."

Joe Dawson joined the laughter, saying, "Well, now,
Tully, and how are you going to backslap and sweet-talk us

into free lodging here without enveloping yourself in a cloud of dust?"

Tully tipped his hat. "I am going to wear my best pink suit and do my best," he said with a grin. "I can guarantee you, we will not only get a good box office, but free meals and lodging to boot."

Amory nodded slowly. "He's probably correct. These people have probably not seen a decent show since they came here."

"True!" Joe said. "Who but us would come?"

Katie's apprehension grew. Why had Tully brought them here? Wasn't she good enough to be popular with real theater audiences? She really had no experience by which she could measure her own ability. She had never been to hear many performers. All she knew was that she could sing better than anyone else in Tully's group, and the men in these little outback places loved her.

As Tully had anticipated, the house was packed that night. So many men, as well as a few women, were jambed into the frame building that Katie could have reached out and touched the whole front row of people. Worse, they could reach out and touch her. They were a loud, whiskey-soaked, foot-stomping crowd. Billows of red dust rose from the floor with each burst of wild acclaim that came from her audience. After her first song, which was interrupted twice by loud clapping and stomping and once because Katie was scooting away from a man determined to grab her ankles, Joe Dawson, Max, Lawrence Dill, Donald Whitney, and Amory stationed themselves onstage to act as a bodyguard and barrier. Knowing then she was safe, Katie relaxed and began to enjoy herself. She danced more freely, weaving her way in and out of her line of body-guards. She sang in a throatier voice than usual, partly because of the irritating dust and partly because a bawdier presentation seemed appropriate.

Her audience went wild for her, not wanting her to leave

the stage. They tossed coins and flowers, handkerchiefs, and hats onto the platform. She sang song after song, and still the rain of coins and tokens kept coming. Katie finally put her hand to her throat and, smiling prettily, begged release. "I cannot sing anymore!"

"The lady's tired!" A basso voice from the middle of the room shouted above the tumult. "Let her be!"

When they finally managed to clear the hall, Tully was ecstatic. They had nearly doubled their take. Katie was exhausted. The excitement of performing left in a rush, leaving her limp and drained. And when she had finally gotten a chance to look at herself in a mirror, she wondered why anyone would have wanted to look at her. Her face was streaked with perspiration and clay dust, and her beautiful white gown had a brick-red hem and a pinkish cast to the rest of it. It was ruined. She began to laugh in exhaustion and quickly the laughter turned to tears. She wondered how it was possible to look forward to the next performance, when tonight all she could feel was a deep, deep fatigue and nerves that had quivered and trembled into tearful release. But she would look forward to the next performance. Tomorrow night they would be on their way to Kentucky. She would not battle clay dust there—it would be the black dust of coal—but the men who came to see and hear her would be the same. They would pour out to her their affection and approval, and she would blossom again on stage as she had here tonight. Within a month and fifteen scheduled performances in as many small towns, Tully would take them back to Philadelphia and a different kind of audience.

Now she was in Philadelphia, and somehow it didn't seem like the relief she had thought it would be. Tears formed in Katie's eyes. As soon as she had awakened, she knew that it was not only a gray, drizzly day outside, but she was feeling sad and blue as well. Most of the time, she looked forward to when she would go to New York and she could count on singing nightly and living a fairly normal life, but occasionally that seemed as far away as it had been when she used to dream about it in Ireland. She had been in America for a year and in so many places she couldn't keep count, but she hadn't stepped foot in New York. Tully held it out in front of her nose like a carrot, and sometimes she accused him of having no intention of ever going there.

"New York is a tough town and it's a wonderful town, but we don't want to walk in there until we have some money in our pockets and a few handbills and newspaper items to show around. Don't worry, Katie, I'll get you there."

Katie had asked the same question of Amory.

"Oh, yes, we've been there many times, and most of them rest in my memory as very good times. I think you will like being there. It seems to me you are very well suited to it."

Katie was no longer as certain as she had once been. She asked quietly, "Don't you ever get tired of moving from one town to another? I lose all sense of where I am. It seems as if we belong noplace and everyplace, and we never know if we will have a penny in our pockets or not. We always leave at night. I never know if someone is on our heels or if that is just Tully's way."

Amory's hound-dog face arranged itself into a smile. "Sometimes someone is on our heels, but mostly it is just Tully's way. One of his best qualities is that he is never aware of whether he is rich or poor." Amory grew introspective. "My father was a rich man. I believe the main reason I am not is because he was. It was a very burdensome manner of living. He was always captive to his dollars."

"But isn't it just as bad to be captive to the lack of them?" Katie asked, remembering her time in Montreal.

Amory chuckled. "No, my dear—one simply leaves in

the dead of night and searches out another stage in another city."

Katie had smiled, and knew that for Amory there would always be an amusement in such activity. Amory lived his life in parts, without need for cohesiveness, but she needed that constant thread running through hers to make it satisfying.

Katie kept looking out of her window, bits and pieces of memory floating idly by, making her wonder about this past year and the people with whom she shared her life. Always near the edge of the thoughts she allowed to penetrate and become full memories was the longing for Michael. She wouldn't permit herself to think of him often or dwell on how much she missed him, for she was afraid that, once she gave in to the longing for him, she'd never be able to pull herself out of it. Days like this one, particularly because it was also Keely's fourth birthday, she had more than she could do to keep thoughts of Michael at bay.

The worst thing besides not being with him was the way she had lost him. She had been so unprepared to find him gone. She could still remember what she had been thinking and feeling that day when she had first walked into Montreal and found Mrs. Holmes's lodging house. She had not been as optimistic as she was sometimes, but she had felt practical and hopeful, for at least they had survived the ocean crossing. Now, at last, they could get Michael well and get on with their lives. But when she had returned to the wharf he was gone. She had felt so cheated. It was as if someone had walked into her life unseen and stolen the most important part of it without her knowing. She still felt that way, and she still had the helpless, frustrating feeling that Michael was somewhere—only she couldn't find him.

Tully had told her so many times she would simply have to accept that he was dead, she no longer mentioned his name to Tully. And she knew he was right. Even if Michael had been alive when she was hunting for him in Montreal, she had to accept that he was no longer. He would have found her by now if he were alive. He was not alive, and she could not keep living and loving and looking for a ghost.

Before she started crying in earnest and would not be able to stop herself, she rolled over and kissed Keely. Gently she patted the child's arm to awaken her.

Keely opened her eyes, and a quick, sleepy smile brightened her face.

Katie's heart contracted. Why was it that Michael had never gotten to see his daughter when she was well fed and healthy-looking? No one would ever know that Keely had been the emaciated little thing they had taken on the boat with them. She was still small for her age and probably always would be small, but other than that she was a beautiful, endearing child. Her teeth showed almost no damage from her poor beginnings and she was now well spoken and energetic. It didn't seem fair that he hadn't lived to know she would be well. Tears threatened again, but Katie forced a smile and asked, "Do you know what day this is, Keely?"

"My birthday!" Keely chirped, and sat up in the bed, her curly, dark hair flying in all directions.

"Yes. And you and I are going shopping for a very special dress, because tonight when I am singing, Uncle Amory is going to take you to dinner, and then he has promised to bring you backstage for a little bit."

"Is Uncle Max coming too?"

"I am not sure," Katie said doubtfully. "It is difficult to know what Uncle Max is likely to do."

"I wish Uncle Max was taking me," Keely said. "He is always much more fun than Uncle Amory."

Katie laughed. "You mean he will let you do anything you please. He is as much a child as you are." She got up and began to ready Keely's clothes, rang the bell for warm water to be brought up, and then sat on the edge of the bed, enjoying the sight of her little charge. "You really like Uncle Max, don't you, Keely?"

"He is always a lot of fun. He does very silly things. Sometimes when we take a walk I walk on my feet, but Uncle Max turns upside down and walks on his hands."

Katie put her hands over her face, but Keely could still see the smile peeking out of her eyes. With a sudden leap, Katie had grabbed Keely and entwined her, squealing and laughing, in all the bed covers. Keely fought back, batting at Katie with the pillow.

When the maid entered the room, leading the man carrying the tub water, the two of them were on the floor whooping with laughter, the room a wreck of thrown pillows, sheets, and blankets scattered everywhere.

The maid shook her head, but said nothing. She had seen them like this almost every day since they had arrived, and, after all, she was Miss Kitty Ryan.

Katie thanked the woman and gave her a coin as Tully had instructed her to do. He would cheerfully cheat any hotel out of its just due, but he was always generous, if not overgenerous, with anyone who served him.

The woman bobbed a curtsy and smiled. "You two have all the fun you want. We'll set it all to rights while you are out."

Katie and Keely had a pleasant afternoon shopping for Keely's dress and window-shopping for all the things they imagined a queen would wear. Late in the afternoon, Katie brought Keely clutching her new doll and her new dress back to the hotel for a nap before Uncle Amory would come to get her. For Keely her wonderful day had just begun, but for Katie it was over. As soon as Keely was asleep, Katie had to go to the music hall to rehearse.

All afternoon while they had been shopping, it had continued to be gray and overcast, raining off and on in a fine, steady spray, and Katie hadn't been aware of it at all. Now, as she had been in the morning, she was aware of the dank gloominess and felt sad and down again. She tucked the blanket gently around Keely, then began to prepare herself mentally and physically for the evening ahead.

Katie now understood that Tully wanted her to bolster up a sagging troupe. For the last ten months to a year, the Tully Girls had been more a figment of Tully's imagination than fact. Except for their stay in Montreal, they had been living pretty much hand to mouth. Tully was having little problem finding saloons and music halls for Katie to perform in, but he was not having the same luck with his other acts. As with everything else, the popularity of variety shows and those of single performers waxed and waned. Tully was aware of that; he had ridden through many such cycles, but this time he was having to deal with discontent within his troupe. His greatest worry was that Max Phipps would leave. Max was the most versatile of all of them, and he was always a morale booster, for Max was irrepressible. He was Keely's favorite "Uncle" and Katie's favorite leading man. But Max was restless, and he was young and thinking in the direction of a small town outside of Albany, where he had met a lovely young girl. Eugenia Davis's father had made it very clear that there would be no match between his daughter and traveling showman. However, he had offered Max a position in his own business, a stone quarry, with the promise of an eventual partnership. Max was torn between one kind of captivity and another. He had said to Katie, "I can be trapped inside Genie's world or I can be trapped outside of all that's stable and respectable if I stay with Tully."

Katie didn't want to see Max leave, but she was beginning to understand quite well what he meant. Tully's troupe could not even properly be called theater people. They fell somewhere between itinerant showmen and Tom show folk. Much of their terrible reputation came from men like Tully sneaking off in the middle of the night without paying his bills. There was also the gambling that supplemented their meager income. Too often that activity ended in a barroom brawl or a shooting, and then there would be yet another race through the darkness to the safety of another town.

Katie sighed. This was not an easy life, and she could never quite make up her mind if she liked it or not. She loved to sing, and she found that, within limits, she enjoyed the adulation she received for her performances and her appearance. But she suffered from the same temptations Max did. There was always the lure of living a "normal" life. She couldn't help but think how nice it would be to have a house or a room she could call her own. She would like a bit of respectability. She found it peculiar and more than a little strange that so many respectable and often wealthy men would wait for hours to ask her if she would have dinner with them, or accept a gift from them, but she was not herself, as a person respected. It was as if she had become the forbidden fruit that everyone wanted to taste but no one would admit to having anything to do with.

One part of Katie sided with Max when he was tempted to throw it all over and settle into the little rose-covered cottage with Eugenia. Another part of her sided with Tully as he tried to find more and more that Max could do with the troupe and funneled more and more of their funds to Max. Tonight Tully was going to try to have Max play a part on the stage while Katie sang. The music hall had wanted only a female singer, and for the first three nights of the engagement they had complied. Tonight and tomorrow night—if they didn't get hauled off the stage tonight—Max was going to appear with her.

She went back over to check on Keely. She was already sound asleep, twisted in the coverlet and sprawled sideways on the bed. Katie shook her head and laughed softly to herself. How many times had she complained to Keely that sleeping with her was worse punishment than sleeping with a new colt would be.

Katie turned at a tap on the door. She admitted Amory and his stack of ledger books and papers. He would stay in the room with Keely until she awakened, for Katie would not leave the child unattended. After many loud and heated arguments with Tully, she had gotten her way. Amory was delighted. He liked nothing better than to be Keely's nanny. It relieved him of the necessity to make himself busy and useful moving stage props and making certain costumes were in order and singers, dancers, and musicians were all ready to perform—together. And he particularly liked Keely. Where Mrs. Holmes and Katie left off with her education, Amory was finding that he delighted in taking over. He finally had someone who listened to his long, windy historic tales of England and Scotland and Wales—all the places he had lived before coming to this country. And he had no lack of tales to be told about America either. Keely even took a mild and rather awkward interest in figuring, and little by little Amory was teaching her her letters. His great ambition was to have her reading by the time she was five so that she could coach him when he had lines to learn. In all, Amory was very pleased with the change Keely had made in his life.

Tully felt quite differently. When Katie emerged from the hotel, he was waiting in their now rather badly beaten up coach. Many of the niceties he had once performed for her as a matter of fact were no longer forthcoming or done only because he might make a bad impression on others. He alit from the coach and held the door for Katie, helping her inside. She smiled, for she knew that if there had not been many people walking up and down the street in front of the hotel she would have had to manage the door and the steps and her skirts alone.

"It took you long enough to get out here," he said when

he got in and seated himself beside her. "You are going to make us late again. Max is waiting at the theater."

"I came down as soon as Amory arrived, Tully. If I am late, it is because you were late in bringing Amory here."

Tully steamed in a broth of his own making for a bit, then turned in the seat to look at her. "You've come a long way, haven't you, Kitty? You might remember from time to time, when you're giving all these orders, that when I found you you were starving. You didn't know where you were going to come by the next penny or bit of bread. You've acquired some fine airs. You might try to acquire a bit of gratitude as well."

Katie gave him a tired look. "What are you upset about today, Tully? Every time something goes wrong you throw that same old tired reminder up to me. Is Max talking about leaving again?"

"He is, and for good reason. Ever since you joined us, you have taken over this entire troupe. You have everyone jumping attendance on that little girl . . ."

"Her name is Keely," Katie said coldly.

"I don't give a damn what her name is—the truth remains the same! No one can move without consulting you first regarding that little girl."

Katie sighed deeply. "Tully, we've been over all this before. If you don't want Keely and me as part of this troupe, we will leave."

Tully laughed harshly. "That's what you want, isn't it? Even you are not so hard that you can turn your back on all that I've done for you, so you need to make it so uncomfortable that I will be the culprit and force you to leave." He fell silent for a moment, but then started up in great agitation once again. "Well, you are doing a fine job of it! I am not going to have a troupe if you keep riding roughshod over everyone. What do you think Amory feels about being made into a nanny?"

"I think Amory is perfectly happy watching after Keely. They get along very well."

"And who is to do his work backstage, while you are out there smiling and fawning to the audience?"

Katie smiled sweetly, a smile that did not reach her eyes. "Why, I suppose you will have to do Amory's job there, won't you, Tully."

"I run this troupe! I own it, by God, I am not a stage-hand!" he shouted, his face inches from hers.

Katie had had enough. Her deep auburn hair seemed to lighten to a fiery red and her green eyes blazed with the heat to melt glass. "All right, Tully. If you are spoiling for a fight, why don't we just fight about what you are really angry about. You can drop the concerned entrepreneur act now. All this is really about is that you want to be in my bed, Tully."

He was taken aback at her bluntness, but not enough to quiet him. "You are living like a queen up there with your little princess, and where do you think the rest of us are? We are jambed into two tiny rooms in a run-down lodging house!"

"But that's not what has your goat, is it, Tully? I didn't ask for a room in a hotel. Keely and I would have been quite comfortable in the lodging house as long as we had some privacy granted us. You got the hotel room, and it wasn't for Keely and me! It was for you! You thought you were going to be up there in that room with me."

"And what if I did? If anyone is housed grandly, why shouldn't it be me? I run this outfit. Without me you'd all be on the streets hunting for someone or someplace to show off your wares."

"If that's what you want, then take the hotel room," Katie said.

That did give Tully pause. He was speechless for almost a full minute. "Do you mean that? I can move in with you?"

Katie laughed. "Not quite, Tully. You move in, and Keely and I will occupy your room at the lodging house."

Tully folded his arms across his chest and slumped back into a dark sulk. "Bitch!" he muttered under his breath, then turned his head to look at her and said it aloud. "That's all you are, a greedy bitch!"

"Thank you, Tully," she said.

"I am a fool for putting up with you."

"I am sure you think you are, and you may be correct," Katie said, not unpleasantly. The heat of her anger had left her as quickly as it had come. Once again, she felt only tiredness and a little sad.

Tully fell silent too, his mood not too different from Katie's. "I've never met a woman like you, Kitty. Most of the time I am the one trying to get away from some overeager female, but you—you won't even give me a chance to be nice to you. Why? Don't even answer that. I don't want to hear about your precious Michael. I suppose you're going to tell me you are still mourning for him. He probably didn't die at all. He probably ran off and abandoned you and Keely. He probably couldn't take you any better than I can. Selfish bitch!"

The coach lurched to a stop and Tully jumped out and disappeared inside the music hall, leaving Katie to fend for herself. No one of importance was walking along this street.

Joe "Jeeves" Dawson had been driving, and now he climbed down from the box and offered her a hand. "Don't pay any mind to him, Kitty. He woke up this morning in a foul humor. He won't even remember he was yelling at you by tonight."

"He is worried about Max leaving," Katie said quietly.

"Sure—but he's always worried about something. It's his way—and don't let him tell you any different. We are all glad you are with us. We never had as many bookings as we've had since you came. That's the truth, Kitty—any one of us will tell you that."

"Thank you, Joe. I appreciate your telling me."

Gratefully she entered the dark music hall and let the door close behind her. She certainly hoped the rest of the evening would go better than this.

Katie and Max went through their stage directions and movements with Tully screaming at the top of his lungs at them. It was a difficult bit of work, for Tully was not at his artistic best when he was upset and he had not really given Max anything of substance to do while Katie sang. He was a moving, breathing stage prop and little more. It was difficult for him and distracting for Katie. No matter how hard they tried, Tully wasn't pleased. By the end of the so-called rehearsal both Katie and Max were exhausted and upset.

Katie was in tears when she ran offstage to the small, filthy room in which she and everybody else was to dress for the performance. "I wanted tonight to be good—special for Keely. It is going to be awful," she wailed.

Max felt murderous. All he wanted to do was find Tully and give him a piece of his mind—and maybe something else. The performance he had put them through was needless and humiliating, and it probably wouldn't be much better with the lights on and the theater packed with people. But he stayed by Katie's side and gingerly patted her back. "It will be fine tonight. Tully won't be out front howling his brains out. As soon as you see the lights and hear the people, you'll be fine, Kitty."

"But it's Keely's birthday, and I wanted it to be more than fine!"

"I know, and it will be," he said, but he was losing his ability to keep his voice calm. He wanted to find Tully.

"I'm all right, Max, really," Katie said, sensing his need to leave her. "I just want to sit here for a few minutes. And if you don't mind, I'd like to be alone—just for a while."

Katie lay down on a cot in the cluttered room that

smelled of greasy makeup, dirty clothes, and sweat. She closed her eyes and tried to sleep.

By the time the performance was to begin, she had gotten rid of her headache and she was composed, ready to make the best of the night. But she was no happier, and she knew she could not let this row between her and Tully go on. No one in the group could stand this much tension for long. Max was already livid and angry with Tully. He was more likely to leave because of his anger than he was for Eugenia. She washed her face yet again, let Angela dress her and do her hair. The last thing she did was check to see if Amory and Keely had arrived yet. They had, and Amory had Keely seated comfortably in a chair near the curtain where she would miss nothing. Katie felt better, but took Amory aside.

"Whatever you do, Amory, keep Tully away from Keely tonight. He is . . . he isn't in a good mood."

Amory gave her his hound-dog smile, which was really a twitching of his jowls. "I have heard. Don't fear—I shall defend the little princess with my life, if necessary. By the way, we have had a wonderful dinner, and she was regaled with the playing of violins at a little Slavic place I found. Wonderful! And so rare!"

Katie kissed his cheek. Three minutes later she was standing on the stage smiling brilliantly to an anticipatory audience. She blocked from her mind all thoughts of Tully and began to sing. Whenever she could, she stole a glance in the direction she knew Keely to be sitting. Somewhere in the middle of the performance she began to sing to Michael. She didn't know how it happened, nor did she plan it. It just happened—and with tears glistening in her green eyes, she sang of her love and longing for him.

It was the most triumphant night Katie had ever had. The audience thundered, stamping their feet and throwing coins and tattered flowers onto the stage. She hadn't even noticed until then that Max hadn't been on stage with her.

Only now did he come bounding out, tumbling, doing handsprings, feigning acrobatic adoration for her as he deftly scooped up coins and bills alike. Somehow he also managed to grab flowers and fashion them into a bouquet as he bowed low before her and presented them to her.

Katie was in a haze. It was almost as if she were awakening from a wonderful dream, and she wondered if she had hit upon the right solution for herself regarding her continued longing for Michael. She would sing to him, to his spirit. The intense emotion she felt pouring over the footlights from the audience to her was not so terribly different from what she had felt coming to her from Michael. There was a passion and a magic in that collective admiration that was very much like love. Maybe if she sang to Michael she would be able to retain and experience at least a bit of the passions they had known together.

She was nearly floating when she finally left the stage for the last time and returned to the communal dressing room. There, too, she was showered with congratulations and well wishes, and a surprise. Near her chair and table was the most enormous basket of golden yellow roses she had ever seen. The card was hanging in plain sight and she took it, feeling strangely elated and apprehensive as she opened it with everyone watching her.

There was but one line on it. "Forgive me." There was no signature, but none was needed. It was from Tully. Katie moved to the roses and pressed her face into them, breathing deeply of the exquisite fragrance. She turned, her cheeks still flushed from the excitement and her eyes bright. "Tully?" When he didn't answer, she looked around the room and asked, "Where is Tully? Isn't he here?"

Angela looked at Joe Dawson, then said, "He wasn't sure you'd want him here."

"If it's all right with you, Kitty, I am to get him," Joe said.

"Of course it is!" Then the thought of Tully wisped away as she saw Max and ran over to him to find out what had happened to the show they had rehearsed that afternoon.

Max hugged her and added his congratulations to the others, then he laughed, saying, "My God, Kitty, you were wonderful tonight. I wish Keely had a birthday every day if that's what it does to you. You were like a shining star in a night sky out there."

Katie blushed to the roots of her dark red hair, then recovered again to ask, "But what happened? Why weren't you doing the skit Tully choreographed this afternoon?"

Again Max laughed. "You didn't really think I was going to let Tully make a fool out of me—and you—with that piece of garbage, did you? I told you everything was going to be all right."

"But how did you talk him out of it?" she asked.

"I didn't. I just didn't show up. Since he didn't go over the routine with anyone else, there wasn't much he could do."

Katie began to giggle. "He must be hopping mad. But look, Max—look what he sent to me." She indicated the flowers, then handed him the card she still had clutched in her hand.

Max looked at it and handed it back to her. "He means it, you know. Tully really isn't a bad sort, Kitty."

"I know," she said softly. "I do know, Max, and maybe . . . maybe sometime . . ."

She stopped as Tully came through the door and Angela poked her arm to get her attention. Katie threw Angela a quick look of gratitude, then ran over to Tully. She took both his hands in hers and kissed his cheek. "Thank you for the roses. They are beautiful. And for this," she added in a lower voice, and indicated the card.

Tully smiled at her, but he had noticed that she had hold of his hands, and she had been in control of the chaste kiss on the cheek. She might be thanking him, he thought, but nothing had changed.

They all crowded into the room, Keely included. Joe Dawson disappeared with Daisy Marshall for a moment and returned bearing a very large, very chocolate birthday cake for Keely. In his best voice Donald Whitney followed Joe and Daisy, singing "Happy Birthday" in very dramatic fashion.

If Tully had had any real doubt that Keely was a favorite with everyone in the troupe but himself, he could not have it any longer. Every one of them had some little gift for Keely, and though this party was not nearly so raucous as others they had had and would produce no hangovers, everyone was having a good time. The room was filled with laughter and good feelings, and Keely, sitting beside Katie, was in the middle of it.

Tully watched for nearly an hour, then quietly left. No one noticed his leave-taking but Katie. For the first time his absence gave her a strange feeling that perhaps she had lost something important to her.

That night when she lay in bed, in those moments before she fell asleep, she went over the events of this whole day. It had been a strange and disturbing one, and Katie recognized it as being one of significance. For once Katie allowed herself to think freely about Michael. She felt the pleasure of the love he had had for her, and the pain for her of having lost it when he . . . She stopped in her musings and made herself face one of Tully's accusations. Could Michael still be alive, and could he have abandoned them in Montreal? She considered that for a long time, but the sweet, humming feeling inside of her said that Michael loved both her and Keely too much to have ever done that. If he was not with them it was because he was dead. Nothing but God himself would keep Michael Donovan from his daughter or his . . . wife.

Again Katie tested the thought and the feeling it

brought with it. Michael was dead. Michael was dead. This time it brought with it a feeling of comfort along with the sadness and loneliness. He had loved her—he hadn't left her. And tonight she had discovered a way she could keep alive that special feeling they had between them. Every man in her audience was Michael Donovan and every word she sang was to him.

She turned her thoughts to another part of her life and again did not allow herself to turn away from the direction her thoughts were taking. She and Tully could not go on as they were. She had never lied to Tully, and he certainly knew that she had loved Michael with her whole being— and still did in a way. Yet Tully still loved her and wanted her.

She brought back to mind different times she had been with Tully. For the most part he had been kind and patient with her. It was true he did not handle being thwarted well. Tully was a handsome man with a great deal of impish charm that appealed strongly to women. He had never been refused before and did not know what to do, so he got surly and sullen like a disappointed schoolboy. But if that was his worst, it wasn't so bad. Katie wasn't such an innocent that she didn't know that many men would have tried to force themselves on her and would have reacted in a far more brutal way than Tully had ever done. If she couldn't have Michael, she could do far worse than Tully—and so could Keely. Again Katie didn't fool herself that she was going to have a difficult, if not impossible, time raising Keely by herself. Tully's resentment of Keely would disappear fast enough if he had a place of his own in Katie's life.

She lay awake for a long time wondering why she didn't give in to Tully. He was a kind, good man, she decided, and in his way he really loved her a great deal. Things within the troupe would quiet down also if she would just give him the slightest sign that she cared for him and would be willing to let him win her . . . and sleep with her.

Katie couldn't go any farther with the thought. She rolled over, her eyes shut tight. She moved closer to Keely, letting the child's warmth warm her.

15

MICHAEL could not have fallen into the hands of a more knowledgeable or amoral man than Garret O'Hea. The only value Garry had that could be considered moral was a deep sense of obligation and loyalty to his family. Other than that he operated by the laws of expediency and gratification of self. He was a cheerful man and most of the time enjoyed his wayward life. But he was also a cautious man. He was grateful to Michael for having come to the rescue of his cousin but still suspicious. There were always men who might be out looking for Garry O'Hea, and he couldn't be certain that was not the reason Michael had been so quick to come to the rescue. After all, thought Garry, what other reason could he have? Eileen was no beauty, and there was no more virtuous a woman alive.

When Michael opened his eyes that next morning after their sordid venture, the sun streamed through the cracks in the little lean-to and sent a pain through his eyes that made him feel sick. Not only that—Garry was sitting on a barrel, elbows on knees, leaning over watching every move Michael made. The next move he made was fast. He got to his feet and ran out the door of the shack. He barely made it around to the back before he emptied out his stomach.

When he returned to the shack, he was weak-kneed and his head was pounding so hard he could hardly see. Whatever poison had been in that bottle Garry had shared with him last night was murderous. Michael could not understand how Garry could look so normal and unaffected while he felt as if he might die at any moment—and not one too soon.

Cheerfully Garry said, "Feeling better?"

Eileen was sitting primly and quietly in the darkest corner of the shack, watching everything and listening to every word.

Michael, head hanging, muttered, "No," and slumped to sit on the floor. "What was that stuff we drank?"

"Just a little poteen," Garry said.

"Not like any I've ever drunk before."

Garry shrugged. "All right now, Donovan, what is it you want? Did you know she was my cousin?"

"How could I have known? Was she wearing a sign?"

Garry frowned and glanced over at Eileen. "I asked you nicely, Donovan, and I got my reasons for wanting to know."

Michael's head lolled to the side so he could see Garry better. "I didn't know—I had just walked into the city a few hours before."

"Then what in God's name made you take on that dirty fellow?"

For the first time, Eileen spoke. "Some men are moved to decency without the need for profit, Garry."

Garry whirled on her, his face dark with anger. "This is men's business, woman—keep your mouth closed." He drew back his fist as if to hit her. Michael was on his feet in a flash and had hold of Garry's cocked right arm.

Garry let his arm go limp and turned openmouthed to face Michael. "By the holy saints, Eileen, I think you are right! You did just help her—for no cause of your own!"

Michael was thoroughly puzzled. He released Garry's

arm but remained alert, not knowing if both of them were playacting to test him for some reason of their own or if Garry had really been going to hit Eileen if she had continued to speak. Slowly he backed away, his eyes on Garry, but he glanced once at Eileen to see her reaction. She smiled timidly at him nodding slightly.

"What are you two up to?" Michael asked, no longer comfortable and wary of what he had gotten himself into. Last night had been bad enough, but, in a way, this seemed worse.

"You can trust him, Garry. I can tell," Eileen said, showing no fear of her burly cousin.

Garry frowned at her. "The reason you never could find a man to marry you is because you never could keep your mouth shut. You're always butting in confusing everything."

"The only reason I'm not married is that I never met a man with good sense!" Eileen snapped back.

"Oh! You are a witch, and that's the truth." Grandly he turned from Eileen to face Michael. "Sit down, Donovan. Though it hurts me deeply to have to say it in front of her, I believe the old witch is right. You are an honest man—and a decent one, too, poor soul."

Michael shook his head. "I don't know if you are serious or if you are both playing a game, but if you don't mind, I'll thank you for your hospitality and help and be on my way." He started backing toward the door slowly, cautiously, not turning his back on either of them.

Garry laughed. "Sit down, Donovan. You're in safe hands—safer than you know. And a lucky day it was for you that you picked on my cousin to help the first day you came here. What I can offer you it would take most men a year or more to come near to touching. Being new to New York, you wouldn't be knowing who you're dealing with, and that's excusable. Every sailing man up and down South Street knows Garry O'Hea, and it's to me they come when they need men for a ship to set sail. You know what I mean?"

Michael had a good idea, but he said nothing, nor did he sit. He was listening, but prepared to run at the first aggressive sign from Garry. He still didn't know if the man was serious or moonstruck.

Garry saw the look of doubt on Michael's face and, with a gesture, laughed, saying, "Ah, it doesn't matter if you know or not. I am going to take a chance on you. Money always was a better talker than any words. When you have a few dollars dulling the sound of the change in your pockets, you'll know soon enough." Then, as if he had made a terrible mistake that he didn't want Michael to take to heart, he added. "But don't you really take paper money. You can never be sure of it. You get the real thing and bite it hard to make certain."

Michael felt like he was listening to a buzzing saw. He had no idea of what the man was talking about, and the more he said, the more confusing it became. Again he started to leave.

"Come with us. I'll take you to a decent place."

"No thank you," Michael said with an air of finality. "I must be going along. I need work and a place to live. I'll just be seeing to that now."

Eileen stepped forward. "That is what Garry is going to see to, Mr. Donovan. He has no idea he is so difficult to follow. He is going to get you a place to stay and work to do, if you want it."

"What sort of work?" Michael asked.

"I will let him explain that. If you don't want such labors as Garry does, I am sure he'll help you find something else. Please don't leave. You do not know New York and neither do I, but I have been told many times that a friend is much needed here."

"I have heard it said also," Michael agreed.

"And you won't find a better friend than Garry O'Hea," Garry said.

Michael had to laugh, and Garry took advantage of the moment, walking out the door with Michael and Eileen following in his wake. As he had the night before, he led them through a rabbit's warren of streets and alleys, through back lots and past hundreds of crowded Irish all talking to each other or shouting from the windows of one tenement to another. Drunks lay in doorways and along the sides of the buildings. Michael could see great gaping holes near the foundations, and, without being told, he knew that some family had dug in so they could live beneath the stones. Some things here were no different than they had been in Ireland.

Michael had no idea where he was. He knew they were still somewhere near the waterfront. Somehow he doubted that Garry was ever far from it. They had gone up and down so many streets, twisting and turning their way, that Michael had lost his sense of direction.

Finally Garry turned into a listing frame building of five stories. He started up the stairs two at a time. Eileen and Michael followed at a more reasonable rate of speed. They climbed and climbed, stepping over the clutter of sleeping bodies and children playing on the stairs until they reached the top floor. All three of them were breathing hard when Garry stopped on the top floor and worked the lock on a door that fitted so badly Michael wondered that it didn't just fall in.

It didn't seem strange to him when he entered the flat and found it empty of other people. It was only hours later that he thought about having seen people crammed into every room and apartment except this one. He asked, "How is it that you have this place all to yourself?"

Garry raised his eyebrows and made a face at Eileen. "Now the boyo is beginning to understand! I have it because I can afford to have it, and I have a position and reputation hereabouts that warrant the respect of these people. I told you that you could not have found a better friend than me to show you the ropes. This is my town! Tomorrow I'll show you my other places."

"Other places?" Michael asked, wondering what a man would need with more than one place to live. Garry hadn't answered him then, but before the evening was over, he had learned that Garry presently rented six such flats, their locations stretching from Hanover Square up to Thirteenth Street.

By the end of the evening Garry had found out considerable about Michael as well—most importantly that he wanted to find Katie and his daughter. "I don't know so many people in the theater, but I do know all the places someone like Tully is likely to show up, and I can put a word into the right ears. If your Katie comes into my town, I'll know about it. As soon as she gets here, I can set it up so we can snatch the little girl before she knows what hit her." He laughed. "If we can pull a full-grown man right off his bar stool without so much as a whimper, one little girl will be no problem."

"Wait!" Michael said, feeling overwhelmed by the speed of which Garry jumped from one statement to anticipation of action. "I didn't say I wanted to take Keely away from Katie without her knowing."

"You want the woman too? After she ran off with that freak show man?" Garry was appalled, and Michael instantly went down a peg in his estimation.

Again Eileen interrupted. "He didn't say she had run away. He said she had left Montreal before he came out of the hospital. She probably had the devil's own time keeping life and limb together after he was taken. I suppose you would have had her starve to death in a corner waiting for him," she ended sarcastically.

"And what would you know," Garry snarled. "You who have waited for no one in all your born days."

"I want to see Katie before I do anything," Michael said quietly before the two of them got into an all-out fight over what Katie had done.

"Well, I suppose if you're really wanting her back—a man can't always account for his yens—I could get her for you."

Michael sighed and looked pleadingly at Eileen. For a moment, Eileen looked pretty, for her eyes twinkled in amused understanding as she chuckled silently. Garry was a handful, but, as Michael would come to learn, he was easily distracted, so often his wilder schemes could be postponed or made to be forgotten entirely.

What Garry was not to be distracted from was Michael himself. For in Michael he thought he had found a man to be trusted who also happened to have courage, brains, and enough brawn to survive in Garry's business. He was certain he could interest Michael in crimping as soon as he realized how much money there was to be made. Being a simple man himself, Garry could not imagine motivation any deeper or more complex than having money to buy whatever he wished. During the two weeks that followed Michael's entrance into New York, Garry took him around to all of his haunts and introduced him to the dark and stealthy world of the crimper.

As soon as it was pitch black outside, Garry got up and stretched, saying, "Well, boyo, it's time we went to work."

Without giving Michael time to think, they were out the door, scurrying through the alleys and up and down streets in the twisted manner Garry seemed to prefer. He was always looking over his shoulder and jumping wildly into intersections as if someone was going to attack him. He made Michael very nervous, and in Michael's opinion anyone who might have been watching had to think he was a crazy man. He wasn't at all sure that wasn't the case.

Garry O'Hea knew every waterfront dive in the city, and he was greeted as an old friend the moment he walked through the doors of every establishment. He was also an endless fount of information, most of which had little meaning to Michael before this night.

"You can't really be the friend to everybody, Donovan. This town is run by gangs—some good and some fit only to be shoved down the sewers. The trick is to be the enemy of none, and that, my friend, is far better than being a friend. They can hate your guts all they want and it is all right, just so long as you keep their respect and no one is calling you an enemy to be gotten rid of. Always keep that in mind—especially down here. A man's life isn't worth a whole lot. Most of us down here haven't got anything, haven't done anything to make our mark, and don't have anybody who'll miss us if we suddenly disappear."

Michael gave a snorting laugh in response to Garry, but he didn't argue.

Garry suddenly turned and began to walk in the direction they had just come. "I can see you are not taking this in the spirit I am telling you. Come along—I want you to meet a few folks. But, for God's sake, keep your head on and pay attention to what's going on around you."

Garry took him to a little place that sported a not too carefully made, hand-drawn sign. The Hole in the Wall was owned and run by Charlie Monell, Garry told Michael. "Charlie can always boast two or three murders a month, and with his help I've taken so many one-eared men out of here and put them on ships, you'd think New York would be empty of men. I just don't use Charlie's place as often as some others, because he always wants a cut of my price, and I don't trust Gallus Mag for a minute. She's likely to take a hate to her heart and all hell will break loose."

Michael started to chuckle, and he shook his head. "Wait a minute, Garry. Maybe I'm a dense Irishman, but I am not following what you are talking about . . . one-eared men . . . Gallus Mag? What does all that mean?"

Garry shoved the door open and with a broad grin said, "You'll see soon enough." He marched into the dim, smoky room. The stale odor of ale and poteen was as heavy in the air as the tobacco smoke was. He walked up to a large, muscular woman and slapped her on the shoulder. "How do you be, Mag? Got any good stories?"

The woman slapped him with gusto equal to his. "Yeah, Garry! How's it with you? Go take a look in my trophy jar. We been mighty busy of late."

Garry moved along the bar, then took a seat and indicated that Michael should squeeze in as well. As soon as he had shouted for beer, he leaned back so that Michael could see what was sitting on the bar to his left.

"What in God's name is that?" Michael asked in disgust.

"That's Mag's trophy jar," Garry said, and held up a jar about two-thirds full of bitten-off ears. "I figured this would tell you that I am telling you true when I say there are certain . . . precautions needed to be taken to survive in this town."

Michael looked at the beer that had been placed in front of him and then back at the jar of grisly contents. "I believe you," he said, and then added, "but I don't have to like it, and I don't have to drink beer here with friend or enemy." He got up and pushed his way through the crowd, heading for the front door.

Garry paid for the two beers, handed one to Gallus Mag and the other to Kate Flannery, Charlie Monell's other female bouncer. It never hurt to keep on friendly terms with those two. Then he hurried to catch up with Michael.

Michael was a quarter mile away by the time Garry ran after him—and had the devil's own time catching up. "You didn't need to run off like that," said Garry. "I'm only doing you a good turn by showing you what to watch out for and who to keep on the good side of."

"I'm sure you are, Garry, but I am sick to my death of one man preying on the misery and heartache of another."

"That's the way of the world," Garry said lightly.

"That's not the way, damn it!"

Garry laughed. "Oh, no! That's not how you have found it to be? Then tell me, Michael Donovan—where is your easy way? Why are you on the street without a place to stay or a penny in your pocket? Tell me that! Tell me why you are not all cozy and snug in your own home!"

"You know as well as I do why I am here," Michael said curtly.

"You bet I do, and that is why you will stay here. Look about you, man—we all feed on each other. By God, give me the chance to take a bite out of a bigger, richer fish, and I will not bite the poor man. But I got no chance of getting to those others who savage each other just the same way we do down here. That's what we all are anyway—every man jack of us is a savage!"

Michael stopped walking and faced him. "No, Garry, we are not all savages. The savages of whom you speak are men who are without their dignity, but not all of us have lost that. Even without a place to rest his head, or a penny in his pocket, or anyone to care if he vanishes, some men can still have dignity, and they are not savages."

"I knew it! By Jesus, Mary, and Joseph, I knew it!"

"Knew what?" Michael asked.

"That you were a bloody preacher at heart." Garry tugged at Michael's arm and they began walking again. "I suppose you'd take offense at helping out a poor ship's captain, too."

"No," Michael said after a minute's consideration. "I am not. A man might make something of himself at sea. It is better than lying drunk in a gutter here."

Garry looked at him in amazement. "You are a queer duck, Michael Donovan. I'll be damned if I know what goes on in your head."

"Now that's very funny you should say that, because I have been thinking the same of you," Michael said.

"Then shake my hand, Donovan, and for a time you and me will work together at what I know best. That will give you time to find a place to live and keep your little girl when we get her, and it will give me time to think on a few things you might want to get into."

"And what might that be you are thinking of?" Michael asked.

"You're going to be a damned do-gooder no matter how I try to teach you. In all my days I've never heard of a crimper thinking of the welfare of his sailors. By Jesus! So I was thinkin' that I might know of a man or two like yourself—always thinking of making things better for them who don't count. I'll do some looking around."

Michael shook Garry's hand.

For the next several weeks, he accompanied Garry by day to the various ships to talk with the first mates and captains, and by night they canvassed the bars and little back rooms where a man down to his last nickle was allowed to drink from a rubber tube until he passed out. When the man was found by Michael and Garry, he awakened in the hold of a ship and could count on being gone from home for several months. If he was unfortunate enough to have been taken to man the crew of a whaling ship, he might be gone for a year or two.

Michael didn't really think one way or the other about the men who were taken. He knew Garry was telling him the truth when he said that most of the men they took would end up dead in the streets. The occupation afforded him an income and a certain amount of respect. It also left most of his days free, and Michael had business of his own to see to that was far more important to him than anything else. He began his search for Katie. He walked up and down every street in Manhattan hunting for every saloon, every music hall, every back room that had performers and asking for Katie or Tyrone Tully. His first few trips rewarded him with no information whatever. He received blank stares and a reluctance to talk. The longer he was with Garry, the more loquacious men became. Very quickly he was beginning to get bits and pieces of news about Tyrone Tully, but still no one seemed to know about Katie.

One man had said, "I heard he got himself a new girl. You heard her sing? She's supposed to be something special."

Michael was discouraged and expressed doubt of ever finding her to Eileen. "It's like she doesn't want to be found," he said. "I get so angry with her—she must know I'd be looking for her."

Eileen looked at him as though he was a madman. "How? How could she know anything of what you are doing?"

"Why, I told her. I promised her we'd be together here —that I'd never leave her."

"And you broke your promise the first day you landed," Eileen said quickly. "And did you believe she was looking for you then? Did you get word to her? No! But you want a miracle from your Katie. All you men are alike!"

Michael was too unhappy to argue with her. He stared morosely at his hands, his mind blank. He didn't know where else to look, who to talk to, or what to do to find Katie, and yet he couldn't get her out of his mind. He thought of her and Keely awake and asleep. He was always restless, wanting to hunt for her and for Keely.

After a long silence, Eileen said, "You know, Garry is wrong about me. I could have gotten married, and to a good man as men go. But he was like Garry, and maybe you. He wanted all of me while giving only a bit of himself. I did not want such an unfair bargain for myself."

"I guess Katie didn't either," Michael said. "But she cannot have my daughter. I want my little girl. She belongs with me, and she was born of a woman who did give all, and she did it with a beauty that cannot be matched by all of nature. Think of that, Eileen Brennan. God's light shines from the eyes of a giving woman, so think on that."

"I will, and while I am, remember that God's light shines from the eyes of a giving man as well. You think on that, Michael Donovan," Eileen said with spirit, then her voice dropped low. "But I am thinking that maybe you are one of those who give despite all your simpleminded talk about your Katie."

Michael's eyes met hers for a moment, then he changed the subject. "Has Garry gotten you the supplies you needed?"

"Tonight," she said quietly. "That man he was going to talk with said he would be able to get them tonight."

"That's good, Eileen. When Garry comes in, tell him I've gone for a walk."

Eileen started to say that there was no use walking back along the streets they had walked earlier—Katie would not have arrived in town in the last half hour—but she thought better of it. "I'll tell him. Be on time for dinner. I'll have it ready for you by six thirty."

Michael nodded and stepped out into the moist, fresh spring air. Eileen had been correct in thinking that he wanted to look for Katie, but she was wrong about his walking the same streets over again. It was inside himself that he wanted to find Katie. He wanted to walk along the river up to Dandy's Point. It was still too cold for anyone to be swimming, but as he had expected there were several couples there sitting on the white sand, looking with longing at the East River and thinking about the time when it would be warm enough to swim. One man had his trousers rolled up to his calves and was wading, to the delight of his companion.

Michael sat down, his back against a tree. If he didn't look to his side to verify she wasn't there, he could imagine that Katie was with him, for this was the kind of place they belonged. He had promised her they would be together in a place such as this one, and he could well imagine—indeed, almost hear the conversations they would have in the darkness here by the river. For, of course, late at night this is where they would come. On days like this one, Michael would come home in the afternoon and he and Katie would bring Keely here. In the summer they would teach her to build strange and wonderful things out of the moist sand. Michael sat there dreaming until the Mechanic's Bell on Lewis Street pealed out its six-o'clock message. Reluctantly he got to his feet and headed back to Garry's flat and the dinner Eileen would have waiting for both of them.

Michael hadn't eaten so well in years, but he wondered how he was ever going to repay Garry. Obtaining money was never a problem for Garry O'Hea, but the spending of it often was. Having lived through a good portion of the famine himself, Garry had become frugal to the point of penuriousness. He hoarded his small fortune like a pack rat and dreamed of the day when he would have enough to satisfy his need for security and feel safe in moving from this area. But thus far, he had been very generous with both Michael and Eileen, saying only, "I want you to have a good start here. A good turn to good people always comes back to the giver tenfold, and you know I can never pass up a good deal."

As always, Michael didn't know how serious Garry was. Did he really expect repayment, and, if so, when and to what degree? Though Michael was grateful for a place to stay, a means of earning a living, and food placed before him, he did not want to start his life in this country deeply in debt to anyone.

One day soon, he decided, he would have to convince Garry they needed to talk seriously with none of his extravagant planning involved. For now, however, the aroma

of a stew with plenty of good meat in it came to him, and
he knew immediately that sometime today either Garry or
Eileen had rowed across the East River to Williamsburg
and gotten fresh vegetables from the gardens there. Michael smiled to himself. If it had been Eileen, then tonight's dinner would have been paid for honestly, but if it
had been Garry, most of the evening's fare would have
been filched.

Eileen was as pleased as a young girl when the two men
sat down to eat. She had outdone herself, having made not
only the stew but oat cakes and a vegetable mix of fresh
carrots, lima beans, and cabbage. She had also gotten some
preserved apples from a woman she had visited.

They had a good meal and enjoyed each other immensely that evening. Garry had brought his own surprise
home and presented them with a large bottle of beer. "German," he said. "They make the best lager a man can
drink." Garry took a long swallow of it, then saw Michael
watching him closely. "What's the matter? Am I drooling
it down my bib?"

"No. I just wanted to see what it was going to do to you.
The last time you told me you had some wonderful stuff to
drink I ended up unconscious on the floor of your shack."

The three of them laughed appreciatively and in good
harmony. Some evenings required nothing more than the
three of them to make them pleasant, and other nights, for
no apparent reason, all the talk and good cheer in the
world could not produce the companionable comfort they
had this evening.

Eileen was, for the most part, a quiet woman with bursts
of blunt outspokenness and some very strong opinions.
More than half of the women who emigrated hunted for
and got positions as servants in the houses of the well-to-
do. Eileen had vetoed this for herself from the beginning.
"I'd rather starve," she said positively when Garry told
her he knew of a couple of good places she could work.

"Are you listening to the woman, Michael?" Garry had asked, his eyebrows raised so high they nearly touched his hairline. "She'd rather starve. And what does your highness plan to do?"

"Och, Garry, don't make such a fuss. Cleaning another woman's house is not the only thing a woman can do and still be respectable. I want to sew. I am good at it and I like it," Eileen had said, then added, "You know I wouldn't be in service a week before my tongue got the better of me and I'd be out on my ear. And I would hate it and myself."

"Well, she's truthful if nothing else," Garry had said grudgingly, and that had been the end of it. All three of them knew that Garry agreed with her and would get her started.

This evening, with dinner over and the dishes nearly finished, she asked, "Have you seen the man who was to get my sewing goods for me?"

"Let me digest my meal," Garry said. "You're worse than a wife, always nagging, nagging, nagging."

"I do no such thing, and it wouldn't be hurting you to have a wife. It's past time for you to settle down and find someone to look after you."

"And are you saying I can't look after myself? I've done well these years without help from you or any other woman," Garry said. "And you—you'd starve if you didn't have me here to feed you."

Eileen spun to face him. That was the third time today he had made some mention to her about his feeding her. Enough was enough. She gave him a sour look. "If it is bothering you so much, I'll put my foot on the road this very night and close the door to your house tight behind me."

"Ha! And be writing a letter complaining to my sainted mother, too! I said I would give you a start over here, and I will do—but a little gratitude wouldn't hurt."

"Cooking your food, keeping your house, and doing your wash isn't enough thanks for you?"

Garry blushed, then got up and crossed the room to kiss her on the cheek. "It was a delicious dinner, little cousin," he said, and smiled.

Eileen accepted the performance as a sign that he had conceded that round to her. Most of the time their bickering meant nothing harmful. It was a childish habit that went back many years to when they were growing up, but it had stayed, and now even as adults they expressed their affections through this inept method.

Eileen gave him a satisfied smile, then asked again, "Have you seen the man with my materials?"

"By the blessed Lord himself, she does not stop for a minute," he said in exasperation to Michael. "Yes, woman, I have. Sit down and I'll get your goods for you."

He brought back a large bundle wrapped in newspaper and handed it to Eileen. "Does that satisfy you?"

"Oh, Garry! It's wonderful!"

"You haven't even seen it."

"But I know you would get nothing but the very best." She tore at the wrappings and exposed what looked to Michael like nothing more than piles of white cloth. Eileen was exclaiming over it, holding the sheer linens and cottons to the light, then putting them against her cheek. "Beautiful! Garry, they are wonderful! These will be the best garments in New York made of the finest materials." She then opened a smaller package that had been nestled into the larger one. In it were threads and yarns of all thicknesses and weights. Again Eileen went into another unusual display of deep pleasure. Inside the large package there was still one more square, flat packet. She looked up at Garry. "What is this?"

Garry grinned proudly. "Open it and find out."

"Silk! Oh, Garry! Gorgeous silk!" she exclaimed, tears coming to her eyes. "Only one time have I ever had silk to sew on. How did you know . . . ?" She jumped up and hugged him, then hurried back to her seat, once more going through the folded pieces of fabric.

"Have you decided what you are going to be sewing, Eileen?" Michael asked.

Eileen nodded her head. "I have. I will make the loveliest, fanciest ladies' undergarments ever seen. Of course, I'll be making other things as well—handkerchiefs and table linens and bed coverings—and I'll never want to stop doing infant clothing. But my main thing will be the undergarments."

Garry poked Michael's arm. "She'll own the whole town in a couple of years. You watch her. No one can hold an O'Hea down, and even though her name is Brennan, it's still O'Hea blood flowing in her veins." He looked at Eileen. "Of course, it is a bit diluted, and that's why she needs me to help her out at first."

Michael chuckled quietly as he listened.

Garry picked up a stack of the folded fabrics and brought them over to Michael. "Did you see this close up? I got all of this for her. The finest linen—Irish linen—the best available—and lawn—and the silk. Look at it," he said, and winked at Michael. "I got it from 'Snatchem' Leese, best river pirate around. Jack Leese knows his stuff, never takes anything but the best."

Michael nodded solemnly and felt the quality of the fabrics. "It's a credit to you, Garry. You always know the best man for the job and where to get the finest quality of anything you want."

Garry beamed with pride. Eileen took pencil and tracing paper and shears to the table preparatory to doing the delicate cutwork on a linen cloth, and Michael practiced his English by reading to them a story from a book Garry had stolen from Stewart's store.

As spring passed and the summer heat began to urge them to stay out of doors more often in the evening, Michael read more and more books, and now he had little trouble speaking or understanding any English phrase or pronunciation. Eileen and Garry both urged him to work on his writing, and, as usual, Garry was able to name several outlets for Michael's practice.

"Everybody has a cause," Garry said excitedly. "You got poor people, you got rich people looking to help poor people, and all those characters who are going to change the whole world—clean up every dirty deed in it. All of them love to talk, and then they write it all down and send out flyers and newspapers and magazines and letters. Write to them, Michael. You can talk as nutty as they can about all the wrongs in the world. You're always bending my ear."

"I can see what a deep impression I made on you."

"Yeah, you did," Garry said. "But, see, I don't care much about that kind of thing. All I want to do is nab a few guys every night and stick them on a ship and get my money. I leave all the righting of wrongs to other fellows. But I agree with you. I'll help you—like getting names of places you should write to, and I can find out who you should meet and who you should stay away from. But I don't want to do all that writing and fixing myself."

Michael, tentatively and with little expectation of any newsletter or paper printing anything he sent, began to write to some of the papers Garry named for him. For the most part, his letters were posted and never seen again, nor was anything heard about them. Then one day in mid-September a man knocked on the door to the flat and asked for Michael.

Eileen stared at the lanky red-haired man, always suspicious of who might be looking for Garry. On occasion an irate brother or father had heard rumors and come to ask Garry about the disappearance of a man. This had never happened regarding Michael. He wasn't well enough known, nor was he as avid a crimper as Garry. But Eileen believed in caution first, regret never. "What do you want with him?"

The man almost laughed. "I want to talk to him."

"What about?" Eileen said, not at all deterred by providing amusement for this man.

"He wrote a letter to a newspaper I publish. I'd like to talk to him about it."

"You have one of Michael's letters! Oh, do come in. He's not here at the moment, but I expect him to be home any minute."

"Are you Mrs. Donovan?" the man asked.

"No, I'm not. I'm a friend. Mr. Donovan and I met the first day I came here. He saved me from one of those awful men they call runners. I don't know what I would have done if Mr. Donovan hadn't come along."

"He's like that, is he? Always coming to the rescue, I mean," the man said.

"Yes, he is, Mr. . . ." Eileen said pointedly.

"Smith. I am Neil Smith, Miss . . . ," he said with equal point.

Eileen giggled. "Miss Brennan. I live here with my cousin, and we rent a space to Mr. Donovan. He writes a very nice letter, doesn't he?"

"He writes an idealistic one. I wanted to meet him." Neil Smith looked up as the door opened. He saw a well-muscled, tall man enter and quickly take stock of the scene in the room. Smith got to his feet. "You must be the cousin, or Michael Donovan," he said cheerfully, his hand extended. "I'm Neil Smith of the Pennsylvania Miners' Benevolent Association."

"I wrote a letter to you about a month ago," Michael said.

The man produced the very letter from his pocket. "I am here as a result of that letter, Mr. Donovan. I hope you are willing to spare me some time. I'd like to talk to you about our cause and what is so needed in those mines. It is my hope that I can convince you to help us."

"Eileen, see if we have anything to wet this man's whistle, and see to getting us a bite to eat." Michael pulled a chair up near to the one Smith had been sitting in. "Sit down, Mr. Smith. I am very willing to listen to what you have to say."

Neil Smith began a detailed and dry account of how several men had gotten together because of the mines that had sprouted up in eastern Pennsylvania since the 1830s. "The mines are owned by very wealthy men, and they have a control so absolute that the miners are not truly paid at all. You see, they are given a wage, but that is to be spent in the company stores and for company housing. A man has no choice, and he does not ever see a penny of his pay. It is all kept on account at the company. Once a man enters a mine, he is not likely to be leaving it except when he is put into the earth for the final time."

"But why would a man put himself into the hands of these mine owners in the first place?" Michael asked.

"Surely, having just come over from the old country yourself, you know what the agents promised for your voyage over and what you got. It is no different with the mines. The promises made give a man fresh off a boat hope. Here is work for him, and the hope of a decent wage. Few Irishmen are unwilling to give a full day's labor and more for an honest wage. But then comes the bitter truth. Before he ever has a copper in his hand, the company says, 'Sorry, Mr. O'Hara, but your family ate this week, and you owe your wage and this much more to the company store.' And what is the poor man to do? If he says anything to the company man, he is shown the door. They do not need him. There will always be another boatload of paddies to deceive."

"These are Irishmen?" Michael asked, the hair on the back of his neck bristling.

"And what were you thinking? It is no different here. Read the names of the mine owners, as English as can be, and who would they want slaving in the dark tunnels bringing out their black diamonds but we Irish?"

"How can I help you?" Michael asked without giving it further thought. "I know nothing about mines, but I am willing to do whatever I can to help the people."

The man smiled and laughed gently. "I can tell you know nothing of mines. It shows in what you write, but your letter also shows that you are a man of courage and heart. If you'd be willing to accompany me to some of the mines, I could teach you quickly what little you need to know."

"I'll accompany you, but then . . . what . . . how can I help?"

"We need money. We want to organize strikes so these men can demand fair wages and get from under the yoke of the company-run stores, but we must be able to feed them. Many will die if we cannot supply some of what will be lost by them. As I said before, the company controls everything, and they think that one man is of no special value—he can be replaced by another from the next boat, as I said. Enough of the miners must go out at one time so that it is not possible to replace them easily, and for this to happen we must have money. You can write and gather support for us, if you're willing. Too often we have tried to keep our strikes in the area of the mine—we did not venture away from the mining towns. We think that maybe we would do better if we broadened our call for help."

"So you want me to remain here in New York and write, and convince men that money is needed to back the strikes?"

"Yes—and tell others what you see in the mines. I will not tell you what is there. If you are going to help us, I want you to see for yourself. Will you come?"

"I will," Michael said.

16

MICHAEL threw himself into his new venture with the same gusto as when he searched for Katie. He commandeered the kitchen table. His papers and the lists of men he intended to write to, asking support for the labor movement, were scattered everywhere. Michael now drove himself, not allowing an hour in the day to be free. The constant work and concentration held at bay the haunting thoughts of Katie and Keely. Except for the one man who had said he had heard Tully and Katie arguing over Keely, no one else had ever mentioned seeing his daughter. Late at night, when his mind would race with questions, always would come the final one—Was Keely alive? He remembered how tiny she was and how thin. If the fever could fell a strong man like him, how could a tiny little creature like Keely remain untouched?

For some reason he did not have the same fears about Katie. He never really thought she had fallen ill. But Keely —Keely seemed so vulnerable and fragile. He tortured himself with questions. Why had no one seen her or heard her? Healthy children were rambunctious, pesky creatures. It was only the sick that could be kept quiet and hidden.

Neil Smith was more than happy to occupy some of

Michael's time. Trying to organize any kind of effective movement against the mine owners was a nearly impossible task. It was made more difficult by two other factors. The miners themselves could never be counted on to remain loyal to their own cause. They were too frightened and too dependent in their own slavery to be effective revolutionaries. And the other factor was that the miners were among the least important people in society. No one really cared about them. They were nameless, faceless men doing a job. The coal was now a needed commodity, and, as more and more factories industrialized, its importance became far greater than the importance of the men who brought it out of the earth.

The first month or so, Michael simply accompanied Neil on his rounds of bars and businesses, grog shops and groceries, listening as he talked to the owners and patrons alike, collecting what little he could from them. Another of his favorite places was the waterfront, where he spoke to sailors from every ship.

Finally Michael asked, "Why do you spend so much time with these people? Most of them haven't any more money to give than you or I do."

"But they are people who understand!" Neil said with his dark eyes blazing feverishly. "They know what it is like to be the last man counted, if he ever gets counted at all. These men are used until they no longer exist, and they understand something that a rich man never will."

"And they have little or nothing to give, and they must be fighting for their own recognition. You seem to be having those that don't count fighting for others who don't count. How are you going to get anyone who *does* count to listen?"

"They are negligible only because they have never banded together, Michael. Don't you see? Don't you understand that these men on the ships and in the factories and the mines make this country run? They are the ones who keep the rich man's pocket lined with silver. Perhaps not even the rich consider that, but, believe me, they will when these workers finally learn the value of standing as one. When they forget about the difference of working on a railroad, or a boat, in a mine, a canal, or anything else. They are workers—the backbone of this country. Without them nothing can move or happen."

Michael made a face. "That has always been the case from the beginning of civilization. Even in my village, nothing would have been done if not for us tilling the land. Did that prevent Mr. Fairmont from knocking down our houses and shipping us off to another country? No, it didn't, and it never will. Part of what the owners say is true—there will always be another boatload of hungry, desperate men who will work for nothing."

Neil had the fevered look in his eyes again and was shaking his head rapidly. "Not in this country, Michael! That's what's different about this country! The time will come when even a man right off the boat will know he cannot work for nothing. This country is too rich! And best of all, most of that wealth is uncontrolled! It's in the ground—it's even in these little grog shops. Wealth will make this kind of slavery impossible with time. Do you understand?"

Michael started to speak, but Smith's feverish eyes lit up again and he went on. "And it's in the vote! We can vote. We haven't learned the real power of that yet, but it is coming. We may be at the bottom of the heap here as we were in Ireland, but this heap is sitting on a pot of gold, and who better to extract the gold from the pot than the man on the bottom?"

"I hope you are right," Michael said.

"Oh, I know that I am right. I just hope that it happens while I am still alive to see it. I just want to see the day that a poor man lives in his own house and drives his own cart and still thinks he is poor!"

Michael scoffed.

Smith was not to be scoffed at, however. He said fervently, his hands grasping the front of Michael's shirt, "This is a poor man's land! There is no aristocracy! There is no king, nor anyone else to stop us. The doors to this land are open to all of us, and we are the majority! We hold the power. We have only to learn to use it. And we will learn! The weight of our numbers alone will overwhelm the so-called cultural elite! This will become the land of the common man. It is ours!"

Michael knew then what he had suspected for some time —Neil Smith was a half-crazed fanatic. But he also believed him. For good or ill, Michael believed that Neil saw something in the makeup of the country that others did not. Second sight often seemed to be a trait of madness. Perhaps it was the result of a fevered brain.

Neil seemed to read Michael's thoughts, but he calmed down and once more looked like the harmless, thin, pale-faced man he usually did. "You do not see, do you, Donovan? Well, it is of no matter. You can be useful anyway. Write your papers, Donovan. Call to these people in your own voice with your own view. The time will come when they are ready to hear what I have to say. Perhaps you are like John the Baptist, paving the way."

"For the Messiah," Michael murmured.

"For the Messiah," Smith hissed fervently. "He comes in many ways, Donovan. Wait until you come to the mines with me. Then you will see with different eyes."

Michael parted company with Smith that afternoon with a head full of thoughts, not all of them comforting. He could hardly believe some of the things Smith told him, and yet there was a rock-solid place inside of him that said the man was correct. For the next several days, he studiously avoided Neil Smith, and then Neil Smith seemed to forget all about him. He stopped coming to the house and Michael received none of his frequent and voluminous letters that had been coming two and three times a day to the flat. That did not stop Michael from thinking about what the man had said, however. And just as he had a place that believed in the truth of what Smith said, he also did not believe that Smith had really forgotten him or given up on him.

"Do you want me to locate him for you?" Garry asked after Michael had told him what happened.

"No," Michael said slowly, then sat forward, his arms on his thighs. "It is the strangest thing, Garry. I don't know what I want to do about Smith. I do want to do something about the miners—the workers, as he calls them —but, by God, I do not want a whole nation based on mediocrity."

"That is what Smith says he is working for?" Garry asked, eyebrows again tangling with his hairline.

"No, no, of course—he doesn't put it that way. But what else would it be? He says the weight of numbers will give the workers power, that they will be educated in public schools that are already being demanded in many communities, but that these will not teach the subjects that they once taught only the rich. They will be practical skills taught in these schools—figuring so that a man can count his money and work his own market, but not for the science of it. He will read, but not create writings that are for the rich and the elite. This, too, will be for practicality."

Garry shrugged. "If that is what he is thinking, I wouldn't worry myself about it. It has never happened before. Why would it now?"

"Smith says it is because the real wealth of this country is not controlled by anyone—it is still in the ground, and in the vast open spaces that have not even been settled yet. It is to those places he says we should go and begin a new society, one of the common man. He says once it is formed, it will have so much power and momentum, because of the numbers of people, that it will never be stopped."

"Maybe he is right, but he sounds like he is touched. Why even think about it? All you are interested in is helping some fellow Irish to earn a decent living. Do that. Let Smith froth at the mouth until someone throws a net over him and carts him off."

"Maybe," Michael said. "Even Smith admits that most of the groups he organizes fall apart. He doesn't expect this one to last either, but he says it doesn't matter. One day later he'll invent a new name and a new group is out collecting money and support for the same cause that went defunct the day before. It's endless . . . he says."

Garry laughed. "Sure it is. He has to eat like everyone else. He'll keep his cause and collect his pennies until something more lucrative comes along."

"Do you really think that is all it is with Smith?" Michael asked.

"No, not all, but a part of it—a good part."

Michael agreed, then said, "I've made up my mind that if I have not found Katie and Keely or heard something about them by the end of the month, I am going with Smith when he goes to Pennsylvania next month. Before I judge one way or the other what I really think of Neil Smith, I want to see first hand if he is telling me accurately about the conditions the men live under."

"You planning on coming back?"

"Oh, yes. I am not leaving here until I have found my daughter. This will remain my home until then. The only thing I know for a certainty about Katie is that she wanted to come here. If she is able, sooner or later she'll end up in New York, and I will be here waiting."

Garry nodded. "I'll keep an ear to the ground while you're gone. If I hear anything, I'll get word to you right away."

In the next few days Michael made another circuit of the music halls, theaters, and "gardens" that provided concerts, operas, ballets, and variety and minstrel shows. He

was told most of the road shows had left the city already
and would be back in the spring.

"Do you mean no one will be performing here?" Michael said with disbelief.

"Oh, sure," replied his informer. "They'll be in and out.
But I never heard of your Katie Ryan. I heard of Tully,
but he's not been around for a long time."

Michael was getting accustomed to short conversations
like that one. He no longer showed his dismay. He simply
left and went to the next place until there was no place left
to inquire. It took him the rest of the week to satisfy himself that for now, at least, Katie and Keely were not in
New York City.

He finally went in search of Neil Smith to tell him he
would travel to Pennsylvania with him to see the mines.

"It is a perfect time!" Smith said enthusiastically. "I
want you to see the Reynard Colliery, and then we can go
to a meeting to be held later in Pottsville." He rubbed his
hands together in excited joy. "This has worked out very
well. I knew I was right just to leave you to yourself for a
time. I had a feeling you would come round. You are one
who must be fed revolutionary ideas in small spoonfuls.
You are a cautious man."

Michael wasn't certain if he had been accurately assessed or insulted, then decided he was better off not knowing. Instead, he asked, "How long a trip will this be?"

"Who knows? We will be back when there is nothing
more to be gained by our being away. I am hoping that the
meeting in Pottsville will turn into some positive action.
One never knows. We keep stirring the pot and stirring the
pot and one day—*poof!* It all explodes, just like one of
those heathenish mines."

Michael and Smith left New York on a bright, crisp
October morning accompanied by three other men. Jack
Oakes was to travel with them until he took the road to
Mauch Chunk. Leon Wolf and Donal Farrell had the task

of visiting all the mines in Luzerne and Lackawanna counties, while Michael and Neil Smith were to go to Schuylkill County. When Michael met them as agreed that morning, he was given a horse to ride. He asked no questions about the animal. If Garry had taught him nothing else, it was to keep his mouth shut about the appearance of luxuries unless there was good cause to do otherwise. If someone gave chase to them, he would think of a way to protect himself. Otherwise he was going to ride the horse and be thankful he wasn't walking.

The four experienced organizers talked constantly, Michael noticed. For the most part, they were mentioning names and places he knew nothing about, and he quickly lost the sense of the discussion. Instead, he watched and enjoyed the scenery. It seemed a long time since he had been outside the all-encompassing city of New York, and he was enjoying it immensely. The air was fresh and scented with the toasted odors of autumn. All was a blaze of color and beauty.

The camps they made at night were modest. None of the organizers thought much of food, and again Michael was reminded of how much his life had changed since he had come to New York. Eileen had spoiled him, and he found himself wanting a well-cooked meal that would fill his belly and make him feel pleasantly sleepy as he smoked his nightly pipeful of tobacco. Less than a year ago, he would not even have dreamed of having a pipeful of tobacco. The men made a weak tea, a meatless mixture Leon Wolf laughingly called stew, and some particularly hard and tasteless biscuits Donal Farrell had fried in a pan.

Donal looked at Michael, noting the distaste with which he was eating his food. He chuckled. "We are eating like kings tonight compared to what those we will visit eat as daily fare."

Michael stared at Neil. "I have gotten spoiled in this country. I am a poor man who no longer knows what it was like to be the sort of poor I was in the old country. Neil told me that it would be thus, but until this night, I did not know what he meant."

Neil smiled. "Spoonfuls, just a spoonful of revolutionary ideas at a time for you, Donovan. Little by little you become accustomed to their taste. Soon you will hunger for more."

"Perhaps you are right, Neil, but I am not so interested in the troubles of the miners as I am in the troubles of the Irish. It is my own people about whom I care."

Jack Oakes said, "Where have you been, Donovan? Most of the miners are Irish."

"And so are those who work on the railroads, and build the canals, and the bridges, and do any other kind of back-breaking labor for little more than a thank-you and 'Move along now, Paddy'."

"Then why are you with us?" Leon asked.

"Because Neil asked me to come, and because these men are for the most part Irishmen, and because I have not found a better cause to put my energies to as yet. When I find the strongest way to defend and free my country and countrymen, I will take it. For now, Neil's cause is the best I have found."

All three men looked to Neil Smith. They weren't accustomed to such bluntness, or such a lack of fanaticism in the followers of Neil Smith. Smith gave them a crooked smile. "He is a novelty, and he speaks with the tongue of the average man. He is not like us, but he will serve us well."

Donal spit into the fire. "And what makes you think he isn't going to decide to switch sides when we get there? He could ruin everything at Pottsville. Nothing is certain as it is. He could ruin everything."

"He won't," Neil said confidently.

"Why don't you ask me?" Michael asked with some anger. "I do not even know what is to happen at Pottsville— why would I ruin anything?"

"Why should you be riding with us at all is a better question," Leon said. "Who are you anyway?"

Michael smiled. *"Is Eireannach me."*

Donal Farrell looked at Leon Wolf with a sharp laugh. "You can't argue with that, Leon."

"No, I can't argue with it. He's as Irish as Paddy's pig, but it doesn't answer my question either."

"I have no answer to your question, Leon. All I can say is that I am with Neil to learn. I will not betray you or ruin any of your plans for it is not my business yet. If it becomes my business, then I will tell you what I think. And that isn't an answer either, for I have not yet proven myself. Only time can give you the answer you seek."

Leon sat thinking for a moment, then he pulled a flat bottle from his hip pocket and offered it to all. "Well, at least you are not stupid. I'll accept what you have to say until it proves different."

"You're a hard man, Leon, and that's the truth," Jack Oakes pronounced, and lay back on his blanket, closing his eyes.

As if that were the signal they had all waited for, the rest of the men, too, went to sleep for the night.

The air in the mountains was cooler, but the colors were more vibrant. The sky was so heavy with blue, Michael thought it had come down from the heavens and surrounded him. Everywhere he looked there was the vivid, all-encompassing blue. Even the great pines and spruces looked to be tinged with blue. Pennsylvania was a grand expanse of soft mountains and inviting green valleys. Here and there he could see lush farmlands and curls of smoke coming from houses and cabins tucked in the trees or sitting near a stream. He was still awed by the vast amounts of land one ordinary man could call his own. When he thought of his father's and his patch of land at Fairmont, it was almost laughable compared to these farms. Some of the kitchen gardens here were larger than his whole potato field. For the first time Michael felt an excitement and a temptation to venture deep into this new country. He was becoming curious as to what lay on the other side of the next mountain, and then the next.

"Pretty, isn't it?" Donal asked as he brought his mare next to Michael's.

"It is what a country should be," Michael said fervently.

"This is only one face. Wait until these hills show you their underbelly. That is not so pretty."

And Donal Farrell had not lied, for the next afternoon they came upon a mine. It was not one they intended to stop at, but it showed Michael for the first time what ugliness could be dug from beauty. Shacks leaned crookedly on the sides of muddied and scarred hills. Drooping lines of wash hung from behind them, and children too numerous to count played out back of the crooked shelters.

"Those are the company houses," Neil explained. "Most often a miner isn't allowed to live anywhere but the place the owner provides, and then he pays what the owner demands for the privilege."

Michael said nothing. He thought this must be the exception and far worse than the normal. These hovels were no better than the scalpeens the Irish had dug in the hillsides at home during the famine. He turned his head away from the sight and felt a great, searing rage burn deep in his belly. In Ireland such a thing was tragic and inexcusable, but here seeing any man live as these men did was obscene.

"Another spoonful, Donovan," Neil said. "Did you like the taste of that one? Well, there will be more, my friend."

The next day, Donal, Leon, and Jack left them. Neil met with the three men privately, a short distance from where he left Michael to look after the horses. When he came back, he mounted and began to ride at a fast trot. "We will be at the Reynard Colliery before dark if we hurry a bit."

Michael had very mixed feelings about seeing the mine. As far as he was concerned, that brief glimpse of the miners' shacks had been enough for him. On the other hand, he wanted to know if all that Neil had told him was true. He had always listened to what Neil had to say with a grain of salt, thinking him to rave as much as not. Now he wondered if Neil Smith hadn't been a very accurate reporter.

Under the best of conditions, there is little that is attractive about a coal mine. The earth is scarred and the area covered with black dust and mud. The small mountains of black diamonds that were everywhere in Michael's vision had a certain beauty as they glistened in the sunlight, but it was a strange beauty that did not warm a man's heart. They had fascination for the eye, but no food for the soul.

Equipment was piled everywhere—picks and shovels, heavy roping, carts of coal, wagons, an assortment of animals, and shacks of all varieties for different functions of the mine. To Michael's eye, the shaft looked like an open door cut into the mountain, a black eye that saw into the black depths. He heard Neil say that they were going into the shaft, but he didn't move, for everything in him rebelled at the idea of entering that gaping black adit.

Neil laughed from beside Michael, but the sound seemed to come from far away. Michael didn't respond until he heard other men laughing and a bundle was shoved into his arms. He looked down and saw that the bundle was composed of stiff, soot-covered overalls, a pair of boots, and a hat.

"You'll need those, or you won't be fit to go anywhere else," Neil said with merriment dancing in his eyes. "Don't worry—the worst part is entering the mine. Once you're down in the nether world it won't bother you so much."

The men standing about laughed all the harder. Michael gave them a hot, bold stare, then began to pull the garments on over his own clothes. For a brief flashing moment, Katie jumped into his mind. How she would have hated the filth on these clothes, and all about the mine itself. Even the small houses he had seen on the way to the shaft had been covered in grimy soot. The mud here was not mud—it was a blackish mixture of coal dust and soil. He could even feel it in his mouth, gritting against his teeth, and in his nostrils, and he hadn't even entered the pit yet. He could not imagine how men who went down there every day breathed, and he knew he would never be able to do it. It was difficult enough for him to face this one time, and perhaps he would learn to bring himself to inspect a mine with greater ease as time went on, but he would never enter that pit day after day. The idea of starving and the memory of lying in the hospital day after day in pain seemed like nothing compared to being condemned to living his waking hours deep inside the earth cut off from fresh air and sunlight.

Without thinking about what he was doing, he followed Neil and the five men who led them into the dank shaft. The opening to the shaft was large, and the light followed them to the first forked tunnel, then they began to follow a seam of coal, the lead man talking and pointing to places in the black rock walls. All around him Michael could hear the sounds of picks and the rumble of iron-rimmed wheels moving unevenly. Somewhere there was the screech of metal on metal, a track, he supposed, used to bring the coal out of the pit.

The lead man turned and asked if Neil or Michael were having trouble breathing. Both men agreed that the air was pretty heavy and had a noxious odor.

"Gasses build up in here," the man said matter of factly. "Most of the fires and explosions we have are due to trapped gasses. The ventilation is bad—no place for the gasses to go."

Michael's chest tightened harshly. As it was, he was breathing in short, shallow gasps, and now he thought he'd go mad if he couldn't take a deep breath. He had already been told that the only exit from the mine was the way they had come in. His imagination went wild. It was all too easy to see how a whole shift of miners could be trapped in here. He knew that this mine had lost nearly one hundred men so far this year, and later he was to meet a group of those who had been maimed yet remained at the mine. Michael was sweating profusely, for he couldn't get the idea of a fire out of his head, and the thoughts were horrifying. Michael knew that Neil wanted the men to strike for a shorter workday, to have the hours cut from thirteen a day to ten, but he wondered that the first priority was not ventilation and a safety shaft.

Even before he had entered the mine he had asked Neil about it. Neil had answered simply, "A tired miner is a dangerous miner. In a way, he is the best safety problem of all. Wait till you go down, and tell me you wouldn't always be thinking of your safety."

They came to a narrow section of the tunnel and moved sideways, and then began to crouch. Before they had followed the seam to where the crew would be working next, all the men were crawling along on their bellies. Michael could feel the cold wetness of the walls, although he could see little. From fear of fire, his panicky mind flew to the fear of drowning. Knowing he was bouncing crazily from one anticipated disaster to another, he tried to shut out all thought. His jaws locked tight; he simply waited out the time it would take to get him out of the confining tunnel. He knew he was supposed to be listening to what the lead man was saying, but his mind was not going to do it for him. He could feel the entire weight of the mountain poised above him, just waiting for the right moment to lower itself down upon him.

They had no sooner emerged from the mine shaft than Neil Smith was hurrying after the man who was guiding them toward a big black shed. They entered a room in which there was so much racket that, had any of them shouted at the top of their lungs, they might not have heard their own voices. In a room about twenty feet square about two hundred and fifty men and boys sat at long, low, dust-encrusted benches. They had their backs to the entrance and, because of the constant din of the coal shooting from a trough above them, did not hear Michael, Neil, and the guide come in. The room was on an incline, and an open window provided some ventilation and a great deal of cold air. The boys were bundled up and wore mittens to protect their hands. Two-thirds of the way down the room was a stove that burned furiously, the skin of the metal glowing red. All heads and backs were bent, trying to keep up with the steady rackety flow of coal that poured in. The boys in the shed were six to about thirteen years old, and with them were some of the men too old or broken to continue going down in the mine. They sorted the slate from the coal and were paid one to three dollars a week for the ten hours a day they labored.

Michael tapped Neil on the shoulder and pointed to two boys and signaled that he wanted to talk with them. Neil nodded that he understood and passed the same gestured message on to the man leading them. The man grabbed the smallest boy by the scruff of the neck and hauled him to his feet. Michael could see his mouth working and tears forming in his large, almost turquoise blue eyes. The other lad, older and more accustomed to strange interruptions, complaints, or punishments, dropped the coal he had in his hands and followed doggedly after the three men.

As soon as they were out in the light, Michael whirled to look at the youngest boy. "How old are you, boy?" he asked. Before the child could answer, he had turned, scowling, to the miner. "How old is this boy?"

"I can't say I know. Answer the man, boy. How old are you?"

The child looked big-eyed from one of these tall men to

another, then a crafty look came into his eyes. "Eight. I'll be nine in a year, and very good for the mine. I am small for my age. My dad says I can get into any tight place."

The older boy snickered.

Michael looked at him. "You're laughing—why? How old are you?"

"I'm thirteen, sir," the boy answered.

"What's your name?" Michael asked quickly.

"Harry Doyle, sir."

"Why were you laughing at this lad, Harry Doyle?"

"Because he's all the time making up stories so he can go into the mine and get more pay for his daddy. He's not eight years old—he's six—but he's smart. He can make up a story faster than most men can spit."

Michael turned to the younger boy. "Is that true?"

"No!" the child shouted belligerently, then his gem blue eyes met Michael's and he hung his head, saying, "Yes, sir, it's true, but I would be good in the mine."

Michael looked at the soot-covered child. His hair was most likely blond when not covered with filth. He was a sturdily built little boy. The sight of him made Michael so deeply angry he wished that he could tear the mine, the shed, the shaft, and the foreman's shed to pieces with his bare hands. "This boy belongs in school. He's too young to be in there. How long do you work him?"

"Ten hours—like the rest," the miner said, and glanced at Neil. "Is this the first time he's been at the works?"

Neil nodded.

"Go sabhala Dia sinn!" Michael breathed, too angry to say anything else.

The child watched his every expression with fascinated admiration. Then he smiled, his eyes filled with faith. "He's going to save my daddy. He's getting better."

Michael looked down at the child, then squatted on his haunches to be on a level with him. "You asked God to save your father?"

"Yes, I did. I told the priest, and he said God was sure to listen."

Michael looked up at the miner. "His mother died a while back, didn't she, Finn?" said the man. "And his father took it hard. Now he's having trouble with his lungs." The man gave Michael a look that said much more than his words.

"Your name is Finn, and you speak Gaelic, the old tongue," Michael said softly, smiling at the boy.

"Yes, sir, my dad taught me. He says he's going back and I must know how to talk to him."

"Oh, yes, Finn, it is true that it is important to know how to talk to those you love. Finn . . . what is the rest of your name?"

"Dolan, sir. I am Finn Dolan."

"And did your dad give you that name? Did he tell you who Finn was?"

"Yes, sir. Finn fought single-handedly and saved Tara from burning so that he could get his rightful inheritance back."

Michael's smile broadened. "You may not be in a school learning as you should be, but you have a fine father, Finn Dolan. You listen to what he tells you, for there is great wisdom and many things to be learned in the ancient legends."

With reluctance Michael watched as shortly after this the two boys returned to the shed. He watched them go, the thirteen-year-old with his back bent and stooped, his shoulders rounded from too many hours for too many years bending over the coal to sort it. Finn was still a strong little boy, straight-backed and proud, but Michael knew that if he came back through this way in a few years that would no longer be true. The clear, honest, faith-filled eyes would be dulled, and his back would be unnaturally curved as Harry's was. He sighed, and repeated, *"Go sabhala Dia sinn.* God save us!"

Michael waited while Neil talked at length with the miner, then spoke to the foreman and the superintendent about the conditions of the mine and the men's complaints that there was too much gas building up in the shaft. When Neil rejoined him, Michael was still thinking about Finn and the other children in the shed. Though Keely would never have been there, for she was a girl, his sons might have been those children. He tried not to think of the sons he had lost to the famine, and most of the time he succeeded, but not when he looked into the innocent eyes of a child like Finn. Michael believed that a child was a gift from God, a touching of the man and woman by the Creator's own hand—that in their joining God reached right from heaven and made a new life from them. It was bad enough when man disregarded the well-being of other grown men, but when he had it not in his heart to see God's face in the face of a child, it was the work of the devil. Michael shook with a fury that was fueled by the memories of his own children, and the look in Finn Dolan's eyes.

Neil sensed part of what he was thinking and patted him on the shoulder. "Put the boy from your mind. There are hundreds like him. Everywhere we go you will meet a Finn Dolan. Think of them all—not just one. You cannot allow yourself to get so worked up over one boy."

"And why not? I am only one man! Do you want me to forget that inside that boy there is a soul being destroyed?"

"No, I don't, but I do want you to look beyond that and see there are hundreds of them—thousands right here in Pennsylvania alone. Hell—in this one county."

Michael didn't argue anymore, but he could not wipe Finn from his mind. He was angry about Harry Doyle, too, but he knew there was little he could do to straighten Harry's spine now, and he couldn't undo the years of ignorance that had already passed. But that wasn't the case with Finn. He was still innocent, and he was straight-backed and healthy.

The two men arranged a meeting with several of the miners in secret about four miles from the works. Michael and Neil set a small campfire and lay down their sleeping gear for anyone who might pass to see. "These men cannot be seen talking in a meeting like this, or we will have miners out of work and no benefit to be had," Neil said. "These are courageous men coming here tonight."

"Have you ever been a miner, Neil?"

"Never, and never would be," Neil answered, and placed a pot of water on the fire.

"Then why do these men come to you for leadership? Why not to one of their own?"

"There are many miners involved in organizing the movement, but there are others like me and like you. The biggest advantage someone like me—or you—has is that we are educated. We can see things from a broader view. We are free to travel from one mine to another. We do not just see what is happening at the Reynard works, but at St. Claire, and Live Oaks, and the Ravensdale Colliery. One company store that practices robbery on the miners is a crime, but it is just a symptom of the disease, not its cause. That all or most of the mine owners keep the miners no better than indebted slaves to their system—that is a cause. And men like us can see that, and talk about it, and write about it."

"I dtir na ndall is rí fear na leathshúile," Michael said.

"And what is that?" Neil asked.

"An old Irish proverb," Michael said on a sigh. "It means that in the kingdom of the blind, the one-eyed man is king."

"Appropriate, isn't it?" Neil said in satisfaction. "They are kept blind in so many ways."

Michael pulled a tin whistle from his pocket and filled the air with plaintive Irish strains. His mind was on Finn, and his heart was sad. It was the opening of a wound Michael thought he had left behind in Ireland, and now he knew it would never be left behind. He would carry his sons within himself forever, and children like Finn would call to him. As Sheila had said to him, it was Ireland calling, and her voice seemed to be everywhere. Michael played another thin, haunting melody, and wondered if Conaire Dolan would be among those men who came to talk in secret that night. He hoped so, for he wanted to meet the man who had fathered Finn.

17

IRELAND arrived that dark, overcast night wearing ten different faces. They arrived quietly, just seeming to appear out of the thick shadows. One moment Michael was sitting by the fire playing his tin whistle and watching Neil stir some pot of gruel he called soup, and the next he was surrounded by ten men.

Neil nodded solemnly at one man who stood a bit to the fore, then indicated they should all find seats around the fire.

"We will have no need of names tonight. One never knows which shadow beyond us has ears."

None of the men spoke, but they all nodded.

Michael felt a pang of disappointment. He had wanted to meet Conaire Dolan and now he would not. He looked closely at each of the men as he sat down and settled himself as close as he could to the fire or as distant from it as he felt safe. Neil quietly dished up his grayish soup, which was a concoction of potatoes, flour, a bit of chicken, a few greens he had claimed were edible, and one onion. Michael watched with interest as most of the men fell to the bowls of soup with gusto. Only two men did not. Those two exchanged glances, then put the bowls down on the ground in front of them. "We have no time for this," the one man said. "I thought we came here to talk of walking out of the mine. Every minute we are here we are risking being seen or heard."

Neil stepped forward, then folded his long legs like a bird, tucking them under him as he lowered himself to the ground. "You can talk and eat at the same time. I think we are already agreed that there must be a strike. All we need do tonight is decide which of many complaints will be the focus of the strike. We cannot gain everything we want at one time. It will be difficult enough to get the owners to grant anything."

"Decent working hours," one man said. "The shifts are too long, and mistakes are made by tired men."

"And what good will that do us?" another asked. "We'll work fewer hours, get less pay, and still be in hock to the company—only more so. If we can't break the company hold on us—get the freedom to buy where we please at fair prices or live somewhere outside of the company housing —we are always going to be taking home a bobtailed check."

Michael sat forward. "And what is a bobtailed check? I am sorry, but this is my first meeting."

The miners looked at each other, then back at Michael as if he were hardly worth bothering with if he were so ignorant. None of them answered. Neil said, "By the end of the pay period, they owe so much for rent and to the company store, their paycheck is nothing or, sometimes, an accounting of what they owe the company."

Michael scanned the group. "They work all week and end up with nothing to put in their pockets?"

"Not always. But even when we do have a packet, it is bobtailed," one man said, then gave a short bark of laughter. "We aren't going to fly anywhere."

"Too much talk," the leader said gruffly. "He can go to

school some other time. We're here to make plans—let's make them."

Neil looked at the man. "You want this man as your friend. He fights for you with his pen. If we don't receive support outside of the collieries, we will get nowhere. The forces we battle are too strong and too deeply entrenched for us to be effective without the sympathy of other powerful people."

The man looked down, then gave Michael a quick glance. "Sorry. I don't like being here like this. You never know who is listening—or even if we can trust each other." Then he looked at all his fellow miners and said strongly, "But I can tell you this. If news of this meeting gets back to the foreman or the superintendent, the next meeting we have will be attended by nine, and it will be held one half an hour after the informer is put under the earth."

Neil got the men settled again, and the talk about which cause they would strike for went on. The safety hazards of the mines were discussed at length, primarily the lack of ventilation and the buildup of noxious and potentially explosive gasses.

"If we go out on strike," said one man, "I think it ought to be over the ventilation in the pit." The man's voice ended in a whisper, and he coughed, gasping for air in between spasms.

The other men waited him out, not looking at him.

Finally, the attack ended, and with tears in his very blue eyes he looked at them. "This is what you can look forward to—every one of you."

Almost as if he had put a hex on them, several men coughed and others cleared their throats.

Michael watched the man closely. His face was dark—mostly from the dust that was so deep in the pores of his skin that they would never again be completely free of it—but his eyes were a vivid blue. Most of the spark had gone from them, but it was not difficult to imagine what he might have looked like when he was six years old. Michael guessed that Conaire Dolan wasn't much more than twenty-eight years old, but he seemed an older man. And he understood the fearful hope he had heard in young Finn's voice when he had said that God would bless them and make his daddy well. It wasn't that Michael hadn't faith, but this time he thought it would be a race for Conaire's life. Either the mine would take his life or the black dust in his lungs would.

After nearly an hour of argument and debate, the men decided they would get the most support and cooperation from the other men if they struck for shorter hours, and the agreement was made.

"You must get word to as many men as you are able and in as many mines in this area as you can," Neil said. "One colliery closed for a bit will do more harm to your cause than good. The strike must involve all of them in the district. Hundreds, thousands of men must lay down their picks and walk out of the pit resolved not to return until some concession is made on the part of the owners."

"When will this happen?" a man asked.

"For now we won't set an exact date. We'll say spring for the time being and make certain we have sufficient numbers to make the action worthwhile. If we can't get the cooperation we need, we will keep trying until we do. But there is no need to risk letting the owners be prepared for a specific date and then be able to ruin everything. You men find the support we need. I'll be in constant communication with the men we have chosen to be the spokesmen for each colliery. It isn't necessary that anyone but the man and myself know his identity. When that group of men agree the time is right and the men are loyal, then we will set the date."

"Should we all attend the meeting that's to be held in Pottsville in January?" another man asked.

"I think the more of you there, the better. While we

need not let the owners know when we plan to strike, it
will not hurt to let them know that dissatisfaction is rampant and that there are many men willing to listen to the
motion to strike against them."

"Will you be there?" another voice called.

"Yes, we will. But if we do our job well, you will not see
us there, for we will be trying to identify those likely to be
disloyal as well as convincing other men that they must
gain fair laboring practices from the mine owners."

"We'll be there," three men said almost in unison. One
of them added, "I don't like this secret meeting and I don't
like putting my family at risk, but I can't fight with your
thinking, Smith."

"No names!" someone whispered.

"Sorry, it won't happen again. But as I was saying, I
can't fight your reasoning. We must do something. We're
free labor in these mines, and our wives and children are as
captive as we are. We will never earn a decent living going
on as we are. I'm behind you, but I don't hold with violence. What are we going to do about the ones we find
disloyal? You said you'd be looking for them. What happens when they are found out?"

Neil shook his head. "We do not hold with violence per-
petrated against us, nor will we instigate it. But neither will
we stand back and refuse to defend ourselves. I don't want
anyone thinking that this battle for labor is going to be an
easy one. There will be action taken on both sides that no
decent man will like. All we can do is beg for a peaceful
solution."

After the miners had left and Neil and Michael were
breaking up the camp, Michael said, "You didn't answer
that man who asked what would happen when you found
men who were disloyal. Why not?"

"He already knows the answer, as do you, Michael. It is
nothing for you or for him to worry about, for we will

never find a man disloyal—we will only find dead men who might have been."

Michael said nothing, but a stubborn look came into his eyes, and his jaw was a hard line.

Neil chortled. "You think that we will kill them. You are wrong. They will be killed by unknown assailants, and most often those assailants will be men hired by the owners. You are still an innocent, Michael, but it won't take you long to discover how deeply depraved a dishonest man really is. He has no loyalty to anyone or anything."

It was Michael's turn to chortle. "Are you trying to tell me that none of the men on the side of fair labor practices will kill when threatened by an informer?"

"Could I?"

"No."

"Then, why would you even ask if I were trying. Of course, I'm not. But I know of no miner bent on murdering any owner or agent of the owners, do you? Have you heard any one of them speak of anything but peaceful, lawful means of attaining their desires?"

"Only you, Neil."

"And I am not a miner."

Michael continued to pack their gear and load it on the horses. As he came back for the last roll to be loaded, he asked, "Was there a man here tonight you would have thought an informer?"

Neil looked long and hard at him. Michael wasn't certain if the man was contemplating the answer or if he was wondering whether to tell Michael. Finally, he said, "One. Yes. There was one here tonight that might be an informer. He might also be a tool to be used by the miners."

"Which one was it?"

Neil laughed. "Think about it, Donovan. I am sure you can come up with the correct answer."

"I know none of those men, nor anything about them."

Neil shook his head. "But you are incorrect. You do

know about one of them—as does everyone in his presence
for more than a few minutes. One man alone here tonight
could see the end of the worldly road he travels. Only one
man knows he has little to lose and much to gain by being
paid by the owners to inform."

"Dolan," Michael murmured. "But he wouldn't, because of his son."

"Perhaps—but perhaps not. If he wants the son out of
the mines, he might think this was the way. He knows he is
not going to be alive for the boy much longer anyway."
Then Neil gave an impish look and added, "But then, by
the same means he can be made to keep quiet. It will gain
him little to be paid off for the boy's benefit if there is no
boy left to benefit."

"You will use the boy to control the father," Michael
said, but did not acknowledge how effective that might be.
Even as he stood there, he knew that if someone got a
message to him saying he could have Keely back if he
killed the owner of the Reynard Colliery, he would walk
into the man's house and shoot him at his own dinner table
if he had to. He would murder, maim, do battle with the
hounds of hell if he could get his daughter back. He knew
that Conaire Dolan, in the last months of his life, would do
whatever he was asked if he could protect Finn from harm.

Michael looked at Neil and tried to hate him, but he
couldn't. Neil was as much a tool to the mine owners as
Dolan was. The two men were simply captive for different
reasons, but both would give their lives to the labor movement, because powerful and greedy men would not or
could not see that poor men were human, too.

"That disturbs you, doesn't it, Donovan?"

"Of course, it disturbs me."

"Enough to make you want to give up what we've begun?"

"No, Neil. I am coming with you to Pottsville, and I will
learn there as I have here. But that does not mean that I

have to like all that I see or hear, and I do not like six-year-old boys being used to pressure their fathers. If there was ever a victim of the ills you are trying to right, it is Conaire Dolan—and it looks to me that his own allies are victimizing him as well. Why do you even ask if that disturbs me? Doesn't it disturb you, Neil?"

"Not nearly as much as you would like for it to, Donovan, but I have been working at this for a long time, and it is rarely a pretty business. Taking money—even a pittance —from a rich and greedy man is always a dirty business. People get hurt. Even little boys and their victimized daddies."

Michael stowed the last of their gear in the bag and put it on his horse. He waited by the animal for Neil. When the other man came, they mounted up and rode towards Pottsville in silence.

Michael spent Christmas in a field near the Ravensdale Colliery, another side trip they had taken on the way to their primary destination. It was a cold and miserable time for both men, and for those they talked to about the meeting to come after the new year and the strike next spring. With each mine he entered, he judged with a more critical eye and a more knowledgeable viewpoint. Michael often thought of the young boy who had caught his attention in the breaker room at the Reynard Colliery. At times, the child with the startlingly blue turquoise eyes even invaded his dreams, often turning them into nightmares. Sometimes Finn would appear with his innocent little boy's face on the bent and lanky body of Harry Doyle, and Michael knew that he had simply become a symbol for him of the injustices he was now seeing daily in every colliery he visited. Sooner or later, he knew, he would meet another child just as appealing and he would either replace or join Finn as a small, ghostly symbol of what one man had no right to do to another.

The meeting at Pottsville was well attended, with men

coming from all over at great personal cost and risk to themselves and their families. Michael kept a look out for Conaire Dolan but did not see him. In fact, he saw only one man he thought he had met that night in the campfire meeting at Reynard, and he wasn't certain, for he had seen him only once and in the dark.

Many speeches were given by Neil Smith and many other organizers. Public and private meetings were held until all involved were exhausted and drained. And still there was the long journey back home.

Michael and Neil prepared to leave, heading toward yet another colliery. Neil was his ever-zealous self, but Michael was thinking of returning home. A new year had begun, and he had been gone for a long time. Recently he had been thinking that perhaps Katie had finally come to New York, and he was worried that he wasn't there to look for her. Garry had said that he would get a message to him if he heard of anything, but Michael was no longer confident that a message, if it were sent, would ever reach him. Not only did they move often and quickly, but they were seldom known by name. Besides, he wasn't sure Neil would not intercept a message, to prevent Michael from receiving it. Undecided, but reluctant, he packed to go to the next colliery. All that night before they were to leave, Michael mulled over what he should do. Already he was seen as a man who was not totally dedicated to the cause as Neil was and others were, and his leaving them now would solidify that feeling about him. It might also cast suspicion on him, and he wasn't at all sure he wanted these zealots thinking he might betray them. On the other hand, his need to return home was growing, and there were many articles he wanted to write about what he had seen. All the time they had been traveling he had continued to write his letters to various organizations and newspapers, information bulletins, and anywhere else he thought it might help. There were some things, however, that he wanted to think about at greater length and depth before he wrote anything about them. But mostly he just wanted to go home.

The two men lay awake, each consumed with his own thoughts. Michael considered suggesting to Neil that they just mount their horses and go on. Neither of them was sleeping anyway.

"You still awake, Donovan?" Neil asked, startling Michael.

"I can't sleep . . . too many things on my mind."

"You remember Conaire Dolan?" Neil asked, and without waiting for an answer went on, "He's dead. They say he died when the tunnel caved in."

"Did he?" Michael asked when he was able to speak again.

"I hope so. I know I talk hard, and most of the time I don't feel much about those who die for the cause, but I try to keep them faceless. You gave Dolan a face, Donovan. I don't thank you for that."

"Maybe if all these people had faces for owners and organizers alike, the movement would do better. A tunnel caving in . . . is that likely?"

"It's likely. They happen all the time. Most mines lose several hundred men a year, and a large mine will have as many as a thousand injured. It just stuck in my craw that it happened to be Conaire Dolan. It made me wonder," Neil said.

"Where is the boy now?"

"I imagine he is right where he was when we last saw him. One of the families will take him in—he has no one else. His mother died the second year Dolan was at Reynard."

"How do you know all this?" Michael asked.

"Contrary to what you might think, I know a great deal about these men—and their families."

"I am returning to New York, Neil," Michael said in a

sudden burst of decision. "When you head west, I am returning east."

"I'm surprised you lasted this long. I've been expecting this announcement for a couple of weeks. Will you be here for the strike?"

"I don't know. I'll have to decide that when the time comes." Michael was silent for a time, then added, "I am going to stop by the Reynard works."

Michael said good-bye to Neil Smith after they had shared breakfast, then both men went their separate ways. Michael headed back over the relatively gentle mountain ranges through the mining territory he had traveled before deep in thought and in no particular hurry. It was enough to know that he was going in the direction of New York, and he had many things to think about. As he drew closer to the Reynard Colliery, he realized that he wasn't sure what he was going to do once he got there. But something inside him said he would never feel right again if he didn't see Finn Dolan once more.

It was the middle of February when Michael arrived. The breaking room was freezing at that time of year in spite of the red-hot stove. Even when his eyes had adjusted to the gloom, he could not pick Finn out from the others. All the boys were wearing several layers of raggedy coats and hand-knit sweaters, mufflers tied around their necks and lower faces. Their hands were covered with blackened, wet mittens. He shouted Finn's name several times, but the unholy din of the coal rushing into the room drowned out his words. The foreman, who had shown Michael into the room, now motioned for him to go outside. Michael threw off his restraining hand and walked deeper into the room, edging his way in front of the long, low benches where the boys sat. From time to time he reached out to raise a boy's chin so that he could look him in the face.

He finally found the boy huddled in one of the middle rows against the far wall. Even when he saw him, Michael almost passed him by, for he did not look like the same sturdy, bright-eyed little boy he had met just a couple of months before. The child's hair was matted with soot, and his grimy face was marked by the deeper circles around his eyes that bespoke his sorrow and fatigue. Michael looked at the boy, hesitant to declare him the one he was looking for, when Finn smiled tentatively at him. Michael returned the smile and held out his arms. Like a little monkey, Finn grabbed hold of this tall man's outstretched arms and crawled up into his embrace, thin arms wrapped tightly around Michael's neck.

Michael wove his way over legs and piles of coal and slate until he was back at the door. With a curt nod to the frowning foreman, he walked back outside.

As soon as they were in the weak February sunshine, the foreman said, "You let that lad get back to his task. We can't be paying him for visiting with friends."

"He's not visiting with a friend. I'm his guardian," Michael said with quick decision.

"By God, you are not! His father left him to the Flemmings, and he owes the company."

"Show me where I can find the Flemmings, and tell me what he owes you for the privilege of giving his babyhood over to you," Michael snapped.

"You wait here," the foreman said, and hurried into his hut. In ten minutes he emerged, a piece of paper in his hand. "Conaire Dolan owed sixteen dollars at his death, and the boy owes three on his own."

Michael put the boy down to stand beside him and dug into his pocket. He had little money, but he did have three dollars to pay for Finn, and it gave him a sense of power he hadn't felt since before the famine had hit his potato crops. He put the money in the foreman's hand.

"That's only three," the man said, and looked back to his paper. "I said the father owed sixteen dollars."

Michael gave him a hard, cold smile. "I am not the

father's guardian. Get that money from God." He started to walk away.

The man grabbed the sleeve of his coat and pulled him round. "Wait a minute, mister—you aren't anybody's guardian. I know that and so do you. That boy stays until his debts are paid off—all of them."

Michael shrugged free of his hand. His face was frozen into a mask of hatred and anger, his fists were doubled up, and the size of him seemed to swell in proportion to the anger that blazed within him. He moved toward the foreman, too angry to speak.

The man stepped back. "This will do you no good. You can't take the boy. If you do, we'll have the authorities after you the minute you step off Reynard land. They'll bring you back, and what will you have gained? You won't have the boy, and you'll be in jail."

Suddenly Michael laughed, gave the man a shove, and sent him sprawling. "Don't get up until you can no longer hear the hooves of my horse, because if you send someone after me, I'll get back here to you before they find me. Does that say it clearly enough for you? This is one boy whose life you aren't going to own. If I were you, I'd get smart and say he got struck by the coal and died. You don't know a thing about me—or the boy leaving."

The man started to get up and Michael planted one big foot in the middle of his stomach, pressing him back to the ground. Slowly he increased the pressure of his weight, digging in with his heel. "Don't get up," Michael said quietly. "Don't."

He took Finn by the hand and, looking back over his shoulder at the prone foreman, walked rapidly to his horse. He put the boy up on the animal, then mounted himself. He forced himself to keep the horse at a walk, but as soon as he had reached the downward slope of a hill that would block him from view, he kicked the animal's sides and urged it to a full gallop. He followed the road for several miles, then veered south, alternately keeping the horse at a gallop, then easing off.

Finally, as night fell, Michael found a wood with a stream and stopped to rest the horse and feed himself and Finn. He set the boy to gathering wood for a fire while he unpacked his gear.

"Did my daddy send you?" the boy asked as he crept close to the sputtering flames.

Michael filled a small pot with water and put it in the rock ring around the fire and added several pieces of wood, trying to build up the weak fire. Then he looked at the boy and pulled him close to him.

"I don't know who sent me, Finn. I was just riding along on my way back home, when suddenly I thought to myself, I am going to go see Finn. Maybe it was your daddy who put that thought in my head or maybe it was the Little People. All I know is that something said, 'Michael Donovan, you go see Finn Dolan,' and then it was like someone told my horse where to go, and the next thing I knew I was at the Reynard works, and now we are running away from the police. Do you think it was your daddy?"

The boy nodded his head and snuggled closer. "I *know* it was. Do you know why?"

"I could never guess," Michael said comfortably. "Tell me."

"I told him I met you the first time you came with that other man, and he said he knew just who you were. So he must have told you to come get me, 'cause he liked you."

Michael chuckled softly. "You think he liked me, do you?"

"He said he did, and Daddy never tells lies. He told me that, too."

"I'm sure he never lied," Michael answered as he took the water from the fire and mixed a little tea in it. He handed Finn a mug of weak tea, a large piece of coarse, dark bread, and a chunk of cheese. He also had an apple that he set before the boy. He set out an equal serving for himself.

"Do you want to know where we are going?"

"To another colliery," Finn said without hesitation, his eyes fixed on each bite he put into his mouth.

"You are never going to another colliery unless you choose to do so as a man."

Finn looked at him then. He had never known anything in his life but a coal mine. His experience allowed him to imagine nothing else. "Where will we go?"

"To the strangest place you'll ever see in all your life. It's called New York City, and it is very big and very noisy. It has buildings so high they almost reach the clouds. Some of them are six and seven, even eight, stories high—rooms piled one on top of the other."

"Why don't they all fall down?"

Michael laughed. "I wondered the same thing myself the first time I saw them. I think that one day they must, for men in New York keep building these places higher and higher. They like to do that, and they also like to tear buildings down so they can build new ones higher than the old ones."

"I will be scared there," Finn said. "One of those big buildings might fall on me."

"It might, but I have never met anyone who had a building fall on them."

Finn giggled, and Michael could hear the sleep creeping into his voice. Michael tucked the blanket closer around the boy and held him in the crook of his arm. It had been a long time since Michael Donovan had felt this comfortable and at peace. Finn was bigger and bulkier than Keely had been, but he did feel like his son, Tom, and that was a good feeling. It was difficult for Michael to realize that he didn't really know Finn and that he had not been with him always. It was also difficult to realize that he had just stolen a child from his rightful guardians. And equally difficult to think that at any time during the night, or tomorrow, he might be beset by some angry policemen or agents sent out after him by the colliery. He fell asleep thinking how good he felt at this moment—and how angry Neil would be when he heard what Michael had done. Certainly he would not be able to show his face at the Reynard works ever again—not if he didn't want to spend some time in jail.

For the next several days, Michael was careful to stay away from the main roads, which made travel more difficult but a little safer, in case someone was looking for them. He avoided the towns and small settlements until they had no more food and he was forced to find other people. Even then he searched for the single farmhouse rather than a settlement. He passed by several, and for one reason or another he didn't stop, not feeling comfortable. He saw another sitting deep in a valley, alone and in poor condition. "I think that is the place for us, Finn. They look like they could use a little help and probably won't care who we are."

"That's the place for us," Finn piped in imitation of Michael.

Michael dismounted and told Finn to stay where he was. "Always be ready to leave in a hurry," Michael said with a grin. "You never know what you are going to find when you open a stranger's door."

Michael rapped loudly on the front door of the log and frame house. A harried, haggard woman came to the door. On her skirts clung two small children. "Good day, ma'am. I am passing through and was hoping you might be in need of a handyman to help you out in exchange for some food for me and my boy, and perhaps a place for us to sleep a night or two."

"You don't want hard money?" the woman asked.

"No, ma'am. We'd be grateful for a good meal, a wash,

and a place to rest. I see you have uncut wood . . . and animals in the barn. The cow sounds like she needs a milking."

The woman looked down. "She does, but . . ." She peered out the door. "Where's your boy?"

"I left him with my horse, ma'am." Michael took a step back and called for Finn to join him.

The woman's eyes widened in alarm, then narrowed with suspicion as she looked from a still sooty, grimy Finn to Michael.

Finn bounded up beside Michael, grabbing hold of his hand. "Is she gonna let us stay?"

The woman's eyes were still filled with suspicion but curiosity as well. She was blunt. "He isn't afraid of you."

"He has no cause to be afraid of me," Michael said.

"My husband is laid up," she said on a sigh. "That cow you noticed needing milking kicked him three days ago. She did him so bad he can hardly get around. You come inside, and if he says you can stay, I need the help. But you said you didn't want hard money."

"That is what I said—but I would like to get this young fellow washed and cleaned up."

"How'd you let him get so filthy? That doesn't look like ordinary boy dirt—that's coal." Again she looked at Michael. "You don't look like you ever saw the inside of a mine."

Michael was ushered into the presence of Jeb Wilson, who sat not six feet inside the door with a musket across his lap. He introduced himself, and learned that the woman's name was Flora. Finn stood quietly by Michael's side as the two men sized each other up and agreed that Michael should work for his and Finn's keep until such time that Michael moved on or Jeb no longer wanted his presence.

Michael and Finn went back outside, Michael with the ax in his hand, Finn to collect the wood Michael was to cut into stove-sized pieces and then to stack them. Michael worked with an easy rhythm. It wasn't quite the same as cutting squares of peat from the bog, but neither was it so different that his inexperience slowed him down much. He had soon discarded his coat and was singing as he swung the ax at the wedge time after time.

Finn sat on the growing stack watching Michael, his arms wrapped around his legs, a small crumpled, smiling sprite. Every time Michael sang a song that Finn's mother or father had taught him, he joined in, his high, thin voice blending with the deep strong voice of the man.

Flora Wilson watched and listened to the two of them from her kitchen window. She turned to her husband and shrugged. "They are a strange pair, but I think we did right. We need the help, and I don't think they mean us any harm."

Jeb nodded his agreement, but said, "I think I'll keep this near me for a time longer." He patted the musket. "They got some story to tell or I'm not Jeb Wilson. Before I put this down, I want to hear it."

Michael didn't stop working until Flora opened the door and called to him to come into the house to get ready for supper.

"You and the boy can wash in the back room. You got fresh clothes for him?"

"I don't," Michael said. "I thought I might be able to wash his clothes out tonight so they'd be clean and dry by morning."

She handed him a pair of pants and a shirt. "This might be a tad small—my boy isn't as big as him—but they'll do till we can get his freshed up."

Finn squealed and protested violently as Michael scrubbed his hair and ears. When he had finished, he saw the boy uncovered with soot for the first time. He was a very handsome youngster with a thick shock of unruly, wavy blond hair. He was also feeling too well scrubbed and had a pout.

"Better stick your lower lip in or Mrs. Wilson will mistake it for the table and set it for dinner."

Finn tried to maintain the pout, but couldn't. He burst into loud laughter. "She won't! You made that up."

Michael drew a cross over his heart and raised his right hand. "Never! She told me herself she is looking for a new table."

Finn squealed again and jumped onto Michael's flexed arm. They came back into the kitchen with Finn dangling from Michael's arm and looking as bright and shiny as a new penny.

"Well!" Flora said. "I wondered what kind of boy was under all that dirt! You're right nice-looking, young Finn."

"Are you going to set the table on my lip?" Finn asked.

Flora frowned and looked at Michael questioningly.

Michael grinned and said with a shrug, "He was pouting, and I said you might use that stuck-out lip for a table."

"Oh," Flora said. "And well I might. We like smiles in this house."

Finn smiled.

By the end of the first evening, Michael knew that he liked the Wilsons, but he didn't confide in them yet. He and Finn slept in the stable on the fresh straw. As soon as the cock crowed, Michael was up and in the farm yard. He finished what little was left of the wood chopping, milked the cow, saw to the hens, gathering eggs and feeding them, fixed a loose rail on the hog pen, got Finn up, and was inside before Flora had breakfast finished cooking.

"My word, if you work like this, we won't have anything to do in a few days."

"Wouldn't it be nice if that were so," Michael said.

"I expect it would be nice for only a few days," Flora said on a sigh. "It sure would be nice to have a few days to sit back and do nothing but watch the clouds, and listen to the sounds, but then I am thinking I'd be wondering what I could do, and if there was nothing needing me I'd be feeling pretty low."

Michael stayed with the Wilsons until Jeb was up and about again. As soon as Jeb was outside on a regular basis and helping with the chores, Michael declared his intention to move on. The last night he was there, he told Jeb how he happened to have stopped and how he had gotten Finn.

"You did right," Jeb said firmly. "And now I got to do right by you. I know we agreed no hard money, but you kept my place going for me and I know you would have been on your way days ago if I could have done my own work. I want to pay you."

"I don't want any pay other than what I have had—and a parcel to take with us."

After several minutes of argument, they compromised, and Michael and Finn left the Wilsons' house with a large bag full of provisions and one dollar in Michael's pocket.

For the next several days they traveled steadily and slowly toward New York. Michael figured they would enter the city at the end of March. For the first time he told Finn about Keely and how he had lost her. The little boy listened with avid interest, then, with his small jaw set and his mouth screwed up in determination, he said in manly tones, "We have to find her."

"Yes, we do have to find her," Michael agreed. "And we will."

18

"THAT little scamp has been on the streets begging!" Eileen said as Michael came into the kitchen to see what the commotion was about. "Talk to him, Michael. You and Garry provide more than enough for us, and I won't have this child out on the street like some kind of urchin! I won't stand for it! Mrs. Murphy is already giving me fish eyes like we can't take care of our own."

Michael looked at Finn, who was standing in the corner, his head hung low, the toe of one shoe rubbing slowly and steadily at the other foot.

"I'll take care of young Finn, Eileen. You needn't worry yourself about it any longer," Michael said solemnly. He looked at Finn and reached out, pulling the boy after him by one arm. "Come with me, young man, we have some correcting to do."

"And about time," Eileen said, hands on hips. That Finn was a handful. He had been here less than a month and had been in some kind of trouble every day of it. Then she let her face relax into a smile. He was a smart little urchin, though, and had all the charm he'd ever need to keep on getting into trouble for the rest of his life. Suddenly she was sorry she had made such a big fuss of it to

Michael. He would probably punish the boy harshly. Men were like that—always thinking that they had to make a big show of being in command every time a woman complained. She could almost hear in her head the tears and regret that would be forced from young Finn. Eileen's heart twisted, and she vowed she would never tell on him again. She would take care of his misbehavior in her own way, because he really was a good boy. He was as affectionate as a small puppy and filled with high spirits. Now all she could remember were the exuberant hugs he gave her whenever she baked cookies or a cake for them, and how he always made a special thing of saying goodnight to her, kissing her and wanting her to sing to him after Michael had tucked him in and heard his prayers. Eileen was almost in tears as she stood in the doorway to the kitchen looking down the hall at the closed door to Michael's room. What awful things were happening behind that closed door?

Michael pulled Finn inside and closed the door. He sat down on the bed and stood Finn in front of him. "You were out begging again? Why?"

Finn kept his eyes down. He shrugged.

"Come on. You can do better than that, Finn."

Finn looked at him, his blue eyes huge and filled with contradictory thoughts. He said, "All the kids here do that. And Jack Murphy does it! He's the best beggar of all, and I'm going to beat him. I almost did yesterday. All I needed was thirteen cents and I would be the best—but he outdid me." He paused and looked again at Michael. "Why can't Aunt Eileen give fish eyes to Mrs. Murphy?"

"Maybe she can. How much did you get?" Michael asked. He put his hands under Finn's arms, lifted him, and rocked back on the bed until Finn was sprawled on his chest. "Come on—tell me how much you got."

Finn squirmed, trying to get up. "I'll show you," he said, his face already rosy-cheeked with excitement.

"Tell me. I'll see your loot later."

"I gotta show you!" Finn cried.

"Tell me," Michael insisted, tickling the boy.

Squealing with laughter, the boy screamed, "I can't count that high! I gotta show you!"

"Ha!" Michael scoffed. "You told me all you needed was thirteen more cents to beat him. How could you know that if you can't count that high?"

"Teddy told me!" Finn cried with another burst of laughter. "He counted for me."

"Teddy Wright?"

"Yes!"

"Don't tell your Uncle Garry you let someone else count for you, or you'll really get a paddling. He'll say you got cheated 'cause you didn't know how to take care of your own money." Michael released Finn and sat up again. "Go get your treasure, and let's see what you really have been up to."

Finn dived under the bed and struggled out with a small wooden box. Inside it he had a cloth bag that Eileen had unwittingly made for him to use in his begging. He grunted as he picked up the box, his eyes, shining with pride, fixed on Michael. "It's heavy, 'cause it's a very big treasure. Very big."

Michael was half smiling, half frowning, not expecting a box, nor Finn's pride. He took the box from Finn's hands, and it was heavy. "What all have you got in here?"

"My treasure," Finn said, as if Michael were simple-minded.

Michael started to open the bag, but Finn jumped forward. "I want to do it." Realizing he had been rude, he looked sweetly at Michael and added, "Please."

Michael nodded, and Finn dumped his whole treasure out onto the bed. Coins spewed everywhere, and Michael was agog at the pile of money. By the time he had finished counting, he saw that Finn had slightly over six dollars. He knew men who got little more than that in a week for six full days of labor. "You got all this begging?" he asked.

"Yes. It's a lot, isn't it?" Finn beamed.

"It's a lot, and don't you dare tell your Aunt Eileen how much it is either. It takes her a long time to earn this much money."

"Oh, she doesn't need to work. I'll give her my treasure and she can make cookies for me. She'd like that, wouldn't she?"

Michael hugged him and laughed, then quite suddenly he stilled his mirth, remembering how angry Aislinn used to get at him for just this sort of thing. She would cry at him that he spoiled the children and was worse than they in promoting bad behavior. He held Finn at arm's length and said seriously, "No, your Aunt Eileen would not like that, and neither would I. And Uncle Garry probably wouldn't either. We don't want you out on the streets begging. Only little children who do not have families beg. You have people to take care of you, and your job is to help us. Maybe Aunt Eileen can teach you to cut pieces of cloth for her, or sort thread."

"But I don't . . ."

"Or perhaps I can teach you to build some useful things you could peddle. But you cannot beg in the streets, Finn."

"But I was going to be the best!" Finn howled.

"You'll have to be the best at something else. You started school. Are you the best there?"

"I don't like school. I like it better when you or Uncle Garry teach me. Why can't you always teach me?"

Michael sighed. He didn't like all these questions, and to make it worse, for the most part he agreed with Finn. Why couldn't he be taught at home all the time? He learned much faster and better here. Michael had seen it time and time again. The very subjects he hated to learn in school he learned with gusto at home.

After a bit he focused again on the small boy. "Finn,

there are some things we must do in this life just because
they must be done a certain way. You go to school, and
you learn in an orderly manner. You are with other children who are learning the same way you are." He paused,
trying to think what Aislinn might have said if it had been
she sitting here rather than him. He couldn't think of anything. "You just have to go, and that is all there is to that.
And since you have to do it, be the best at it."

"Yes, sir," Finn said dispiritedly, and Michael could
hear what was being said in the boy's mind as clearly as if
he had said it aloud: "But I won't like it—ever!"

Michael gave him a listless pat on the rear end. "Look
sad or your Aunt Eileen will know I didn't paddle you.
You could try for a tear or two."

Finn said nothing, his small shoulders slumped.

"You are disappointed in me," Michael said.

Finn stared at him for a long moment, then threw himself in Michael's arms, but he still did not deny that he was
disappointed in Michael.

Both of them came back into the kitchen, and Eileen
saw immediately that neither was happy. She felt wretched
and was certain that it was because Michael had been
overly harsh regarding the begging. She had thought the
sounds she had heard coming from the room were laughter, but now she could see she had been wrong. Finn was
miserable, and so was Michael. Eileen didn't know what to
say. This was all her fault. She was still trying to think of a
way to make it up to Michael and Finn when Garry burst
in through the door, his cheeks bright red from the cold,
windy March day, and his eyes glowing with a peculiar
excitement that always meant he was on to a new and
better money-making scheme.

"Have you been out today?" he asked before greeting
them, and then didn't waste any time. "You should see the
docks—full of gold hunters trying to get to California."

"Where's California?" Eileen asked.

"I don't know—west. Way west, on the other coast somewhere," Garry said impatiently. "But listen—we can make a quick fortune."

"Quick fortune!" Eileen scoffed. "Easy come, easy go. I don't want to hear about your schemes."

"Then don't!" Garry shouted with instant anger. "It's no business of a woman anyway! Go do your knitting or clean the house."

Eileen smacked him with her stirring spoon. "Don't talk ill of those labors that keep you clean, well fed, and in comfort!"

Garry pounded his fist on the table in frustration. "Damn! I am a man with news! Shut up for a minute, woman, and let me tell my tale!"

Grudgingly Eileen calmed down and indicated a chair. She turned and gathered cups and saucers. Less than two minutes later, they were all amicably seated, drinking coffee and hearing of Garry's new scheme as if no tempers had flared at all.

"All right, Garry—what is this great venture that is going to make your fortune?" Eileen asked, still not willing to let him have it all his own way.

"There is news of a great gold find in California. It is in all the newspapers. Men from all over are trying to get out there. They know no more about hunting for gold than you or I do, but they all want equipment—the latest, best equipment money can buy." He stopped and with sparkling eyes looked from Eileen to Michael. "So do you know what I did?" He waited, wanting them to guess.

Michael started to chuckle softly, his head down. "You bought up every pick and pan in the town, and we are going to make up gold hunting kits."

"And make a fortune! And fast! This won't last long, but while the fever is high we can sell hundreds of the kits."

Michael looked at Eileen and shrugged. "It might be

that he has something this time. Even I have heard about the gold fever."

On a sigh, Eileen admitted, "So have I. At least half a dozen women I sew for have men who have already left. They are already spending it like they were going to be able to bathe in gold."

"And most of them will come back penniless most likely," Michael said, "And then what will happen?"

"That's the beauty of this scheme," Garry said. "It doesn't matter to us if they are successful or not. All this equipment is bought before they find anything or come home broke. We can't lose with this, I tell you. We will be out of this hellhole of a slum in no time at all, and I already have my eye on a nice place large enough for all of us and a yard we can call our own and that you can plant, Eileen."

"I can plant?" Eileen said haughtily, immediately rising to his bait. "And what is wrong with you? Can you not handle a shovel as well as I?"

"Woman's work," Garry said, then burst out laughing as Eileen turned red in the face and began to sputter angrily. He reached out and took her hand. "Och! Eileen Brennan, were you not my cousin, I'd make you my wife, and that's the God's truth."

"And what makes you think I would want to be your wife? Are you such a prize that even a *distant* cousin would want you? Or is it that only a relative, no matter how far removed, would be willing to put up with your awful ways?"

Michael grinned, tapped Finn on the shoulder, and the two of them quietly disappeared. They put on their coats and left the tenement.

As soon as Garry had mentioned having his eye on a place out of the Five Points slum, he knew that he had meant the Drydock area near the east end of Fourteenth Street. He and Garry had spoken of this area before, but only in vague, someday terms. For some reason Michael had faith in this latest get-rich-quick scheme of Garry's. He and Finn walked along, and Michael pointed out those houses and tenements that had vacancies.

Michael asked Finn what he would think of living around this place. The boy looked critically at the houses and the neatly tended patches of green yard, the few trees, and the street that was very quiet compared to what he had been used to. "I don't think the boys here would like to beg," he said. "I bet they don't take things from the fruit stand either." He kept looking from one thing to another. "I guess it would be all right."

"That's what I was thinking, too," Michael agreed. "If we lived on a street like this we would be like any other family, Finn. You and Keely could play in front of our house. It would be nice."

When they returned to the tenement, Michael told Garry he would like to join him in selling the gold hunter's equipment. In the evenings Finn, Michael, Eileen, and Garry made up the packets that were called gold hunter's outfits. The package was comprised of a pan, a flat sieve, a pick, shovel, and a bright red flannel shirt. They were able to sell as many packages as they were able to make up, and sometimes Garry sold the pieces individually. Later he heard about a devise called a rocker, and Michael built several of these, for which they charged the exorbitant price of fifteen dollars—and got it. Gold fever had driven men wild, and enough men had returned from the gold fields to fetch their families that the tales of great riches could be believed.

Neither Michael nor Garry said much about the gold fields or those who were going to dig in California, but they each had their own thoughts. Had they shared their thinking they would have been surprised at how similar their ideas were. Michael had thought often of packing up his belongings and heading west with Finn. It was only his desire and determination to find Keely that held him back. He would not leave the east until he had gotten his daughter safely back with him.

Garry had everything he could do to hold himself back. Though he seemed to be a headstrong, independent man, he was actually sensitive to the constant criticism of his harebrained money schemes. He wasn't at all certain that going to California wasn't the most harebrained of all. But he wanted to go. The idea of such a win-all or lose-all venture appealed to him. The idea of being in a wild, untamed place as he had heard California to be was also appealing. It all sounded like an adventure like those he sometimes had dreamed, when he was the only hero.

Even Eileen had thoughts about the gold diggings, but she would never have dared mention it to Garry or Michael. Not only would they tell her it was not a woman's place, but both men would have teased her to her death. She also kept her thoughts to herself, and counted herself lucky, as did Michael and Garry, that they were making so much money selling supplies to those who were going. That was the sensible way to make money from the Gold Rush—everyone said so.

All through April they sold their packages and counted the windfall that came to them. It was a good feeling. And even though Michael still had not heard a single word more about Tully's troupe, he felt closer to finding Keely than ever before.

Lately Michael had longed for her so deeply that even Garry noticed something was not right with his friend and commented on it to Eileen.

Eileen had given him one of her "why-are-you-so-stupid" looks and said, "He's pining for his daughter."

Garry growled at her, "Why don't you talk some sense into him? He listens to you. Make him see he's never going to get that little girl back. He should be happy. Didn't the good Lord give him a boy to take the place of the girl he lost?"

Eileen folded her hands as if in prayer and rolled her eyes heavenward. "Och, Garry O'Hea, you know nothing of men and love—or women either."

"And isn't that the biggest fib you've ever told, Eileen!" He stuck his face close to hers. "I know Donovan wants his daughter. That I do know. But he can't have her. The girl is gone, and that's the last word on it."

"Then time will tell him better than I can," she said.

"But he won't leave here until he finds her—you know that! And a stubborn man he is."

Eileen laughed. "Now we come to the truth. You have something up your sleeve and you want Michael to cooperate, only he won't because he wants to find Keely. Is that it?"

Garry said nothing, but looked away. "It's none of your business. It's man's work."

"It's too bad for you, Garry. Whatever you have in mind you will have to do without him, or you could try to find his daughter for him."

"I have tried," he grumbled, and got up, stalking out the door without a backward glance.

Garry hurried off to talk to every person he knew that had any connection with or knowledge of theater people. He got no information about Katie, for everyone was in a frenzy about some slight that had been made to Edwin Forrest, the American actor, when he had appeared in London. Now, it seemed, the English were sending their best man to this country to appear at the Astor Place Opera House. William Niblo and J. H. Hackett had taken a lease on the theater with the intent of bringing William Charles Macready over to perform *Macbeth*. The originally scheduled opening was to be May 7, however he was booed off the stage. Several prominent New Yorkers encouraged Macready to appear again, and promised him attention. The new performance was to occur on May 10. Adherents of Forrest were livid over the treatment of the American in England and vowed trouble if Macready appeared in New York.

Garry scratched his head. "Why so much ado over two actors?"

"Ado over actors!" the stage manager he was talking with screamed. "It has gone far beyond that. Every red-blooded American will stand up and say his piece the night Macready tries to take the stage. This is no different than any other English invasion. We don't want the English here! We rule America."

Garry still thought the whole thing strange and nonsensical. He failed to see the connection between an English invasion and an actor appearing on a stage, but he didn't admit that to the stage manager. Whatever he didn't understand about the affair, he did sense that there was something real and very big happening, and Garry O'Hea couldn't stand the idea of being an outsider to excitement. He would keep his ears and eyes open until he could make better sense of all this.

He hadn't long to keep awake, for on the very next street corner he saw a poster stating:

> Workingmen, shall Americans or English rule in this city? The crew of the British steamer have threatened all Americans who shall dare to express their opinion this night of the ENGLISH AUTOCRATIC Opera House! We advocate no violence, but a free expression of opinion to all public men. WASHINGTON forever! Stand by your Lawful Rights!

> American Committee.

"Och! and won't it be a jolly night at that!" he said aloud to himself. He still hadn't the slightest idea why two actors should cause such a furor, nor did any of it make good sense, but he no longer cared. The May night of Macready's performance promised to be a night no one would soon forget, regardless of sense and nonsense.

He raced back to the tenement with his news. As usual, his boisterous excitement was infectious. He had all of them laughing as he told of the very serious men he had heard ranting and raving about patriotism and upholding the rights of all Americans to free opinions. "And, by heaven, they have a whole shipload of British in the fracas. We will go that night. Oh, what a night it will be!"

KATIE had begun to think that Tully was deliberately avoiding New York. It was the only place she had ever expressed a desire to visit. Of all cities, New York was the most noted for its theaters and the public support of them. She was not the only one who had commented on it either. Amory told her that never before had they stayed away from New York for so long a time, and Max had verified it. Joe Dawson had gone so far as to hint that she was the cause.

"And why would I be the cause of Tully refusing to go to New York City? I've begged him to take us there. He knows there is no place I'd rather be."

Joe exchanged glances with Angela, but he did not look at Katie. "I can't speak for Tully, but it is a bit odd that we performed in New York about three times a year until you joined the troupe, and now we haven't been near the place in over a year."

Katie stared at Joe, then looked to Angela. "Is that true —the troupe was there three times a year?"

Angela's expression was sympathetic. "It is, Katie. None of us understands Tully's reasons, but it does seem like you're somehow the cause of it. Before you came we always considered New York our home base. No matter where we went or how long a tour we started, we knew that we would take time off in New York and would perform there for a good part of each year."

Katie was baffled. She put her hands out helplessly. "But why? Why would it involve me, when he knows there is no other place I'd rather be?"

Joe shrugged. "Maybe that in itself is the answer. Maybe he has his own reasons for wanting to keep you from New York."

Katie started to talk, then shook her head. "No! You must be wrong. Tully wouldn't do that—he can have no cause." Perplexed and upset, Katie hurried in search of Tully.

Katie did not see him until that evening at supper, when the rest of the troupe was present. It was all she could do to eat her food and not blurt out what was on her mind. Tully was in an expansive mood, laughing and joking with everyone at the table. He paid no particular attention to Katie. His gaiety was brittle, and the tension in the room crackled electrically. As the dishes were being cleared from the table, Katie asked Daisy if she would take Keely upstairs and put her to bed this evening. Then, before Tully was successful in disappearing from the gathering, she walked up to him. "I would like to speak with you privately, Tully. May we go to the parlor?"

Tully caressed her cheek. "Not tonight, my dear—I have pressing plans on the other side of town." The look in his eye told her his plans had something to do with a woman.

"I won't take much of your time, Tully, but I really must speak to you," Katie insisted.

Condescendingly, Tully again caressed her cheek, his mouth puckered in appreciation of her smooth skin. "And you shall, my dear one, you shall—first thing tomorrow morning. First thing, that is, after I am able to face tomorrow." He stepped back from her and straightened his waistcoat and cravat. Turning slightly, he posed, then asked, "How do I look?"

Katie was seething. She wanted to slap the posturing ass! He always carried on like this when he was displeased with her.

He bent over and stuck his face into hers. "What's the matter, Kitty Ryan? Jealous?"

"You can be so crude," Katie said through clenched teeth.

"And right you are. But you, Kitty Ryan, are pure class, aren't you? Pure Irish class right out of the bogs and dung heaps of a little shanty village."

Katie slapped him so hard his ears rang, and before he could touch her, Katie had turned on her heel to walk away and Amory had grabbed Tully's arm.

"As your friend, I must tell you that you deserved that and more, Tully," Amory said. "Don't harm her or you will find yourself with a troupe filled with enemies, not friends."

Tully shook free of Amory and glared at him. "And a fine thing it is when you turn on me! Where would you be if it were not for me? I ask you that, Amory. We've been together for a long time—near to ten years—and you stand here and tell me I haven't your loyalty! That little trollop has it!"

Amory cleared his throat. "She isn't a trollop, Tully. That is the whole problem. If she would lie on her back and spread her legs for you, we would not be at each other's throats."

"You presume too much, Amory. If I were to start tonight, I could not sleep in all the beds available to me."

"Yes, I know, Tully—but none of those beds would be hers."

With a snarl deep in his throat, Tully swung away from Amory and raced up the stairs two at a time. He slammed the heel of his hand against Katie's door, making it pop open.

Katie turned around, but showed no surprise when Tully burst in. She had her satchel out and a valise she had bought in Boston and all of her own and Keely's clothes strewn about the room.

Tully took several menacing steps toward Katie, then noticed the disarray. He dropped his hands to his sides. "What's all this?" Then he whirled back to Katie. "What the hell are you doing?"

"I'm packing," Katie said curtly. She would not look at Tully.

He came to her and turned her to face him, holding her by the arm. "By heaven, I'm getting a bellyful of you, woman. You said you wanted to talk to me, so talk."

"I don't need to talk to you anymore, Tully. Go on about your business."

He made a sweeping gesture. "Is this what you wanted to talk about? You're leaving?"

"Yes, I am leaving, but I hadn't thought of going when I asked to speak to you." She looked him squarely in the eye. "Let me go, please, Tully. All that needs to be said has been said. Let each of us get on with what we must do."

Tully's eyes flashed with anger. He shook his head. "You may be a woman, but, by God, you've got brass balls. Who do you think you are? I decide when this troupe moves on and when it doesn't. Over my dead body will some little jealous bitch dictate to me."

"I'm not dictating to you, Tully. The troupe is not going anywhere—just me and Keely."

"Just like that? Not a word of explanation to me? Nothing but 'Good-bye, Tully. See you in hell, old man'?"

Katie slumped down to sit on the edge of the bed, one of Keely's small petticoats clutched in her hand. "Oh, Tully —why are you belaboring this? You know as well as I that

it will be better if I leave. You and I are the cause of some
awful feelings in the troupe lately."

"And whose fault is that?"

"It's mine, Tully, but I can't help it. I can't force myself
to love you. I like you, and I have admired you, but I don't
love you."

"I didn't ask for love."

Katie sighed. "It doesn't matter. I need love. I can't give
you what you ask." She looked up at him, her eyes pleading. "Please, Tully—just let it rest. Let me go without a big
scene."

Tully hesitated, then made an impatient gesture. "Even
if I did, what do you think you're going to do? Have you so
quickly forgotten how it was in Montreal? Don't you remember begging money from a poor priest?"

"I remember," Katie said softly. "I'll never forget. But it
doesn't change anything. I'm leaving."

"You're going to New York," Tully stated. There was a
sound of despairing resignation in his voice.

Katie looked up at him and for a moment felt great
sorrow for him. "What is it about New York, Tully? Some
of the members of the troupe told me that you have always
spent a good deal of time there, yet since I joined the company over a year ago, we've never gone near it. They say
that is because of me. Is it? That is the only place I have
ever said that I wanted to go."

Tully gave a sharp, harsh laugh.

"Is it true, Tully? Did you keep us out of New York
because of me?"

He walked over to the window and looked out at the
darkness. "We don't need New York. There's plenty of
work without ever going near the place. I thought we'd
head west. They say there is gold to be picked up off the
streets out there. We could all make our fortunes, and the
men out there are starved for the sight of a pretty woman.
If we go to the gold towns, Kitty, we could make your

name one of the biggest. You could be San Francisco's darling."

"You haven't answered me, Tully."

He turned and came to the bed to sit beside her. The anger was washed away now, and Tully seemed tired and saddened. "I kept you out of New York." He took her hands in his and looked deep into her eyes. "If you had just agreed to let me court you, it would have been different, Kitty. That's all I was waiting for. Just give me a sign that you will consider my suit and I'll book us into New York."

Katie frowned in puzzlement. "Tully . . . why? What has one to do with the other?"

He smiled, embarrassed. Shrugging his shoulders, he said, "Call it superstition—or premonition. I've always known I would lose you if we ever went to New York. I had always hoped to take you there as my wife. It would have been all right then."

"Oh, Tully," Katie crooned, her head hung low. "Being in New York wouldn't have made a difference. I haven't wanted to go to New York for a reason—it was just a dream. When I was in Ireland it was all I knew of this country."

Tully laughed sadly and shook his head. "I would have lost you. I know it . . . I can feel it."

"But why? How? I would have been as close to you there as I am here or in any of the other places we have gone."

Tully looked at her. "You don't understand, do you? You don't know what I mean."

Katie stared at him for a moment, then her heart started beating wildly. She whispered, "Michael? Is Michael alive? Do you know that, Tully?"

Tully quickly shook his head and grabbed her hands tighter. "No. No, I know nothing of Donovan. But I have always known that if he is alive, he would search for you in New York."

A rush of conflicting emotions flooded over Katie. Her chest was so constricted, she could barely talk. "Tully . . . even if you knew Michael was there . . . why would you do that to me? If you love me—as you say—why would you keep me from what I most want and need? Tully, can't you understand that without Michael I am as arid as a desert hungering for water? I am like the dead leaves that have fallen from its tree. I can't be yours, Tully, for I have nothing to give you. You are not my springtime, nor my life-giving rain. I gave myself to Michael long ago, and it wasn't just my body, Tully—it was my soul. All that is left for me to give belongs to his daughter. I have nothing else."

"You love him that much?" Tully asked in amazement.

"Yes, Tully. I've tried to tell you so many times."

Tully sat quietly. He released her hands. "I don't suppose there is anything else to say, is there? That he is likely dead doesn't make a difference?"

"It may someday, but not now." Katie looked down. "I know I have had time, and I should have been able to accept his death by now—but I haven't been able to. I'm trying, and maybe someday I will."

"What will you do in New York?"

She shrugged. "I don't know. Go around to the theaters probably, try to be accepted into another company. If I can't, or I am not good enough, I can always find a position as a house girl. People aren't as afraid of the Irish as they were when I came. I'll be all right—I'll find something."

"I can give you the names of some people to see . . . and a letter to introduce you." He reached into his pocket and pulled out a wad of bills. He peeled off twenty dollars and handed it to her.

Katie pushed his hand away. "I can't take that, Tully.

You've already paid me—that belongs to you—or the troupe."

"Don't be such a saint, Kitty. I've never paid you what you were worth. If it hadn't been for people wanting to hear you sing, there was a time the troupe would have folded. You've earned this and more. Take it." He laid the money in her lap.

Katie stared at the money, then covered her face with her hands and began to cry.

Tully wanted to gather her into his arms and comfort her, but he held himself back, standing in front of her, but not touching her. Softly, he asked, "Are you sure this is what you want to do, Kitty?"

Katie nodded her head, sniffed, and with tear-stained face, red nose, and watery eyes looked at him. "I'm sure, Tully. I'm just frightened—and I'll miss all of you. And Keely will too. Max is her favorite playmate and Amory— well, Amory seems like he is part of our family. And you have taken care of us for so long. It was all right while I was angry, but now . . ." She began to cry again, then, blowing her nose, she said, "I am just frightened."

"You'll be fine, Kitty. Once you get to New York and get settled, you'll do just fine. And if you don't, you can always get in touch with me." He smiled at her and gave her an apologetic little cock of the head. "I always have been a sucker for a pretty face—especially one who can sing."

Katie hopped up from the bed and threw her arms around his neck. "Oh, Tully, I wish I were in love with you. I do! What is wrong with me? Why can't I . . ."

Tully removed her arms and pushed her to arm's length. "Don't do this, Kitty. Don't start looking back now. You finish your packing, and I'll have Max take you to the boat. Look ahead to New York, Kitty Ryan, because if you look back to me one more time, I am going to take you and I will never let you go."

She stared at him, doubt and confusion still shining in her moist green eyes. Almost imperceptibly, she nodded.

Tully puffed out his chest, took his watch from his pocket, and smiled. "Well, I've been keeping a very lovely lady waiting for almost half an hour. Good luck to you, Kitty."

Katie sank back down to the bed, staring at the empty doorway. She could hear Tully going down the stairs. His step sounded jaunty. She felt empty and unsure. What was she doing? She sat there staring at nothing for a long time before she could force herself to get up and complete the packing. With everything put into the two cases, Katie undressed and got into bed. For a long time Katie lay staring into the blackness of her dark room, tears rolling down the sides of her face. She couldn't stay here and, as Tully had said, she couldn't go back to him now, unless she wanted to be his wife. But she was terrified at going on alone. New York seemed like a big, scary, lonely place to her tonight.

The next morning, when Katie got up and dressed herself and Keely, Tully was nowhere to be found. She and Keely came into the dining room to find the rest of the troupe gathered dispiritedly around the table for breakfast.

Angela got up as soon as Katie entered and came over to her. "You are doing this because of what Joe and I said, aren't you, Kitty? We didn't mean we wanted you to leave. Please—we feel awful."

"It isn't because of you or Joe, Angela. I should have done this a while ago, I think." She smiled at all the sorrowed faces looking at her. "I am going to miss all of you terribly. You will write to me?"

Amory pulled a chair out for her to sit in, then stole Keely away to sit by him. "Of course we will write—and we'll come to see you as well."

No one had much of an appetite, but they all kept pushing the food around their plates, for neither did anyone want to get up from the table and thus hasten the moment when Katie and Keely would leave.

Finally Katie couldn't stand it any longer. She looked over at Max and said, "Whenever you are ready, Max, Keely and I are ready to leave."

Amory said, "If it is all right with you, Kitty, I'd like to ride with you to the boat."

"Oh, Amory, I'd be so appreciative," Katie said.

There was another round of tearful good-byes and hugs with the rest of the troupe. Everyone promised to write faithfully and to see her in the future, but all of them knew that Katie was most likely going out of their lives for good.

Once they were settled in the coach, with Max on the box driving and Amory sandwiched in between Katie and Keely on the seat, Amory patted her hand. "You are doing the right thing, Kitty. Tully will get over this. You were never meant for him."

Katie smiled at him. "I know, Amory, but it is so hard."

He sniffed, his long face seeming to grow longer. "For us, too."

Max hugged her good-bye as he put her on the Albany-to-New York City steamer. "I'll visit when I get to New York. Don't forget to write and tell me where you are staying, though."

"Will you really visit, Max?"

"I think you have given me courage, Kitty. I've been threatening to leave the group for a long time, but I could never quite bring myself to do it. Now I think I can. Eugenia has waited for a long time. If I am ever going to marry her, it seems like it should be soon."

Katie broke into a broad smile and leaned forward to kiss him on the cheek. "Max, I'm so happy for you! And I'm proud of you. I love to sing, and I love to hear the audience applauding me and cheering me. But you will find a far deeper, more abiding love in Eugenia's arms than any that comes across the footlights. God's blessing on you

and Eugenia, Max, and may he grant you a houseful of
children to make the music of your home."

Max hugged her again. "Good-bye, Kitty." Then he
squatted down and took Keely's hands. "And you my lit-
tlest and best love. You take care of your mama."

Keely watched him, knowing something was wrong.
Leaving one place to go to another had little meaning to
her—she had done it so often. She knew this was different
and everybody was saying good-bye, but she hadn't yet
comprehended that she wouldn't be coming back or that
these people she had learned to love wouldn't be with her
sometime later. She hugged Max as she always did. Then
she kissed him on the cheek. "Will you take me to the park
when we get back?"

Max squeezed his eyes shut, then he opened them and
rubbed his nose against her small one. Keely giggled and
rubbed her nose. "I'll take you to the park as soon as I
can," Max said. Then he stood and lifted her to his shoulder. Keely perched there, her arm outstretched, one small
leg out straight with her toe pointed. "Got your balance?"
Max asked.

"I'm ready," Keely said in a high-pitched, excited voice.

"Let's go! Come along, Kitty, or you'll miss the boat."

Max got the two of them and their luggage on board,
then, as the final whistle blew, he leaped back down the
gangplank, doing a handspring for Keely's benefit. Katie
and Keely stood on the deck waving to him until they
finally could see him no more.

Katie took Keely by the hand and walked the full length
of the steamer, threading her way through the knots of
other passengers who had remained on the sunny deck.
They stood at the bow of the ship looking down the Hudson. Katie blinked a couple of times, then she smiled.
"Down there, Keely—far down this river—is New York
City. That's where we are going to live."

"Is Uncle Max going to live there too?" Keely asked.

"No, but that is where your Daddy and I always planned to live when we came to this country. I think that is where he would want us to be, and so that is where we are going."

20

MICHAEL was bent over the kitchen table, papers scattered all around him, as he wrote, rewrote, and revised one essay after another to be sent to Neil Smith and used in the labor cause as he saw fit. Garry sat on the other side of the table, his fingers drumming impatiently as he stared at Michael.

"You're wasting your efforts, I tell you, Donovan. The strike in January didn't do a thing for the miners in Pottsville, and now the man wants you more deeply involved than ever. He's going to get you killed, because he won't be happy until he has you right there in the midst of one of those fracases."

"You're a fine one to talk, Garry. I'm more likely to be killed one of these nights when you and I are out grabbing men out of the saloons to be put on a ship," Michael said with a chuckle.

"It's true—there's a bit of a risk in crimping. But the labor movement is getting dirtier by the day, and there's spies looking for nothing but to get a troublemaker—like you. Up in those mountains it's too damned easy to erase a man and hide the evidence. Hell, what does it matter? The mine owners have the courts in their back pockets anyway.

Even if one of their agents is caught at his dirty work, he's going to come out looking like a hero."

"Wait until I am finished with this, Garry. I can't think when you are talking at me like a runaway horse."

"What I've got to say to you is more important than what you are doing, Donovan, so—damn it, man—listen to me!"

"Give me fifteen minutes—that is all that I need," Michael said, without looking up from what he was doing. "If you want me to go with you to that theater tonight, I've got to get this done." He finally glanced up. "I can post this on the way."

Garry went back to drumming his fingers. In a minute he pulled his watch out. Patience was not his strong suit, and fifteen minutes of sitting quietly and waiting loomed as long as a month to him. He shifted his weight in his chair, drummed his fingers some more, got up and got a cup of tea, drank it down in one long swallow, looked out the window, then triumphantly pulled his watch out again. Only five minutes had passed. He looked at Michael. He was still writing furiously.

Finally Michael gathered up his papers, folded the ones to be sent to Neil Smith, and put them into a large envelope. He got up and poured himself a cup of tea, then sat down and looked at Garry.

Garry frowned. "It's been so long, I can't remember what I wanted to say."

Michael laughed and started to get up.

"Sit down—I didn't mean it."

"Look, Garry, I know you and Eileen are worried about what is happening in the collieries, but I must do something. Those men are no different than I am, except that they didn't meet Garry O'Hea their first day in New York. They need help, and if I can give it, I can't turn my back on them."

"That's what I wanted to talk to you about!" Garry said,

and sat forward, leaning far over the table. "Let me ask you something. Why do you write those tracts?"

Michael gave him a blank look. "You know as well as I do—to raise money and support for the miners."

"And who are you trying to get to listen to you?"

"What is this, Garry? This is more of a game than . . ."

"Indulge me, Donovan. Just do me the favor and answer my question."

Michael sighed, mildly annoyed. "Wealthy men—influential men, men who can balance the power of the mine owners."

"And who is the more important—you or the man with the influence and wealth?"

"He is, of course. All I have to give is paper with a bunch of words on it. Look, what are you getting at? I've had enough of this . . ."

"What I'm getting at is that you are choosing to take the lesser role when the opportunity is here for you to be one of those men of wealth and influence. Damn it, man— wake up and see this is your time!"

"If you are talking about going west, forget it, Garry. I am not leaving New York."

"Why not?" Garry shouted, all but tearing his hair out.

Michael shouted back, "Because, damn it, I won't leave here without my daughter!"

"Your daughter? You've been looking for your daughter for over a year! When are you going to face the fact that you are never going to find her? If she's alive, which is unlikely, if what you said about Katie is true, she is far from here. You might think of giving up what the good Lord doesn't want you to have and be thankful for the boy he gave you to take Keely's place."

Michael's voice dropped very low and deceptively soft. "Finn has his own place, and it is not Keely's. The good Lord has not taken my daughter. I would know." He touched his chest. "I will find my little girl, Garry. There is no wealth or influence, nor even a cause, that is worth losing her."

"You have a rock for a head!" Garry said in disgust. "Well, let me tell you. Eileen and I want you to come with us, but we are not staying here so you can walk up and down the streets hunting for a little girl who isn't even here."

"I've never asked you to wait for me. Finn and I will be fine."

"Sure you'll be fine, and will you be taking the boy with you on these jaunts to the coal fields? Are you going to expose him to all the dangers you expose yourself to, or will you leave him here to take to the streets again?"

"I can easily get someone to stay with him. We'll be needing a housekeeper."

"And when one of those mine owners' agents' bullets get you, will you find Finn another man to take your place? The poor wee boy has already lost one daddy to the mines."

Michael clenched his jaw tight and stared out the window. He didn't need Garry reminding him of all this. He had thought of it often enough on his own, and he didn't have any answers.

"Would you at least admit that, if it weren't for your daughter, you'd go to San Francisco with us?"

"I've never denied that," Michael said. He played with the edge of the envelope. "I know you think I am a madman, Garry, and sometimes I think the same, but I can't give her up—not yet. My head tells me that if I haven't found Keely by now, I never will—she was such a frail little thing—but in here, in my heart, I still feel her like it was just yesterday I held her in my arms and rocked her to sleep, and it will be no more than tomorrow until I will do it again."

Garry looked away. He was not comfortable with such

naked longing being expressed openly. He fidgeted, then said, "Eileen and I have decided we'll get married."

Michael smiled, then put his hand out to shake Garry's. "Congratulations on finally coming to your senses."

Garry made a face and, cocking his head, said, "Well, it made good sense. It makes travel easier, and we were going out there together anyway. It will make my mother happy. She's always wanted me to get married."

Michael laughed. "It might make you happy, too."

"Yes—well, Eileen's a good woman—when she's not talking."

"Have you told her yet?"

"She agreed," Garry said in a choked voice. He began to squirm, getting uncomfortable with this conversation as he had the last.

Michael looked with affectionate amusement at his friend. Garry would never grow up, and would probably never learn how to express what he felt with any grace. It was a blessing Eileen was willing to put up with him.

Michael stood up. "I promised Finn we'd go over to the river and fish a little bit before we went to the theater tonight."

"You won't be late coming back?"

"No, but I still don't see why you want to go to hear a gang of British sailors and the American Committee hurl insults at each other."

"Have you no patriotism?" Garry yelled, rising to Michael's bait.

Michael laughed. "I'll bring you back a fish."

Katie had come into New York three days before, and with the help of the letters Tully had given her and some names that Max and Amory had given her, she had had to spend only one night in a hotel. The very next afternoon she and Keely had moved into a nice three-room apartment on the edge of a pleasant German neighborhood. Katie stood in the middle of the barren parlor, her arms stretched wide. Keely stood two feet away in imitation. The tall, slender figure and the petite small one began to move slowly, then faster, as Katie led them in a dance around the room. They whirled faster and faster until both of them were in a heap on the floor, a tangle of skirts and laughter.

Katie lay back on the floor, her arms stretched over her head. "We've done it, Keely. We really have our first home in New York City."

"We will stay here?" Keely asked.

Katie sat up and touched Keely's rosy cheek. "We will stay here, and you will have your fifth birthday right here. We will count it as your first—then you will always stay young."

"No-o-o," Keely said, then burst into laughter. "I don't want to be a baby again."

"And maybe we will even have a party for you," Katie said, then fell deep into thought. "I wonder if any of these people whose names Tully and Max and Amory gave me have children your age? Wouldn't it be fun to have them here for a party?"

Keely looked around. "Where would we sit?"

Katie laughed. "Tomorrow we will remedy that, little one. You won't know this place after I get a few things in here—and curtains at the window—pretty lace curtains like my grandma had. Only she made her own. I will have to teach you to sew. I think you would like that. Oh, Keely, we have so many things to do while you are growing up!"

They just sat there in the middle of the floor for a time, enjoying the feeling and the sounds of their new home, then Katie got up and pulled Keely to her feet. "If we are going to eat tonight, we'd better go shopping for some food."

"And a table and chairs," Keely added.

"You are really worried about those chairs, aren't you?
What about a bed? You didn't say anything about that."

"Well, we could sleep on the floor. We have lots of cover-
lets."

Katie smiled. "I see. Well, we know what things you
consider important, now, don't we?"

Katie had often done shopping for the troupe and had
learned where to find bargains and how to make her
money stretch until it was so thin she could see through it.
By the time they returned home late that afternoon—tired
but successful—the first cart man was waiting in front of
their building waiting to take up their table and chairs.

"Look, Keely—the most important things came first."

"He was the nicest man, too."

Katie directed traffic, instructing the man where she
wanted the furniture placed. She hadn't finished with one
before the other cart men had arrived with her bed, and a
sofa, and an assortment of things she needed in the kitchen
and for the windows.

Katie worked until late in the night to have her home
looking the way she wanted it to before Keely would
awaken the next morning. She couldn't have said why, but
it seemed terribly important to her to establish what she
considered a normal home right away. Perhaps it was a
craving for stability and security now that she had left
Tully and was once more on her own, though very unsure
of her ability to support them. Whatever the cause, Katie
knew that, for the next several days, she and Keely were
going to have a good time and enjoy this new place before
she had to get down to the weightier things such as earning
a living. She would sorely miss Max and Amory's constant
help with taking care of the girl. She had never had to
worry when she went to rehearsals or performed, because
there was always someone free to keep an eye on Keely—
to feed her and make certain she was bathed and put to bed
at a decent time. She would no longer have that luxury,

and she almost laughed when she thought of herself hiring a housekeeper for Keely when she was thinking of hiring herself out as a maid. But she could laugh for a while, for she had managed to save quite a bit from her earnings, thanks to Tully, for he had bought all her gowns and costumes for her, and he had given her a bit extra from time to time, and the twenty dollars on their parting. It would keep them for some time—plenty of time for her to visit the theaters and use her letters of introduction. Then, if that failed, she would seek a position in a house as a maid just as she had in Canada. But New York would be different. Here she would find what she needed. She had been able to tell that just upon entering the busy city. This was different from all other places. Change was the order of the day. People came and went like spring rains, and even buildings seemed to be knocked down as quickly as they were built up.

During the next few days, Katie met several of the people whose names Max and Amory had given her. Unfortunately none of these had children Keely's age. She finally realized that, while a birthday party was a grand idea for Keely, it was totally impractical this year. She set her sights on something else—something that in her opinion was grander.

"I am going to take you to the theater to see William Macready. He is one of the finest actors to ever come from England. Of course, we don't much like the fact that he is English, but nonetheless he is *the* actor of his time."

"Does he do somersaults like Uncle Max does?"

Katie laughed, her mind running rampant with pictures of the dignified and elderly Macready somersaulting across the stage. "No, he is a very proper gentleman."

"Oh," Keely said, with a noticeable lack of enthusiasm.

"Don't worry," Katie said, tweaking her cheek. "You'll have a wonderful time—I promise you." Then she frowned. Macready wasn't performing until May 10, and that was after Keely's birthday. Then she brightened. "Do you know what, Keely? We will celebrate your birthday twice. Once on the day, and the other when we go to the theater."

"Will that make me six?" Keely asked.

"No, you will be just five, but with two celebrations."

Katie had some difficulty in getting the tickets for the performance and was a little perplexed, for all she heard wherever she went was talk of the performance, but it was all mixed up with politics, and patriotism—things that made no sense to her in connection with the performance of *Macbeth*. She had even read strange posters around town with messages of American rights and all manner of peculiar things that to her should have no relationship to a theater performance. She had never seen anything like it before, but then she had never seen a city like this either. The city itself was a mixture of oddities, so she had no intention of letting the unusual furor about Macready's performance interfere with her enjoyment of his talent as an actor. Seeing him was the chance of a lifetime.

Katie was in a flurry of excited activity as she cut and sewed a new dress for Keely to wear on the night of Macready's performance. Keely was cross and restive, having been stuck with pins too many times to count. But even she considered it worth it when finally Katie told her it was time to try the dress on.

Katie had chosen a soft lavender-blue silk to enhance the deep blue violet shade of Keely's eyes and her dark, curly hair. Her pantalettes were a rosy lavender, and her kid shoes had been dyed the same shade as her dress. Keely turned in front of the pier glass that Katie had insisted was not an extravagance but a necessity.

Keely beamed, her vivid eyes gleaming with pleasure at the sight of herself. "I look beautiful, Mama," the child said in awe.

Katie knelt beside her and smiled into the mirror. "You

are beautiful, Keely. The dress can only help, but it is you who are beautiful."

Keely turned quickly and hugged her.

For herself Katie had chosen a sea-foam green silk that did the same wonderful things for her green eyes and auburn hair that Keely's lavender did for her. The gown was cut off her shoulders, displaying Katie's flawless milk-white skin. The bodice fit tight and was accentuated with rich creamy ecru piping, which then formed panels down the full, flowing skirt. Her slippers were ecru, as were her kid-and-lace gloves. She wore her hair in a waterfall, covering it only with a circlet of creamy roses just above the nape of her neck. A choker of pearls given to her by Tully in one of his frequent moments of generosity nestled at the base of her neck. Both she and Keely wore shawls of cream velvet. They spent nearly half an hour admiring each other and themselves before they stepped out onto the street. They began to walk toward Astor Place, when Katie stopped, a devilish look on her face.

"Shall we be very naughty and extravagant, Keely?"

The little girl giggled and nodded.

"Good! We'll take a cab," she said, and darted near to the street to hail one.

They arrived at the theater amid scores of shiny black carriages, hacks, and a variety of elaborate vehicles. Katie looked over the women and their finery with a critical eye. "Well," she thought to herself, "No one was going to mistake her and Keely for wealthy theatergoers, but neither were they going to be thought of as hoi polloi." She held Keely's hand tight, for she could see the little girl was both excited and a bit frightened.

Katie herself was a little uncomfortable. She had been told to be sure to get there early, and it was only quarter to seven, but already there seemed an unusual number of people around—far more than could ever get into the theater. She prayed they would be among the lucky ones.

"Mr. Macready must be the most popular actor in the world," she whispered to Keely, who was staring wide-eyed at the masses of people.

"Are all these people going where we are, Mama?" Keely asked.

"Some of them are—but not all. The theater won't hold that many. Maybe they are people who are hoping to get tickets after the show begins—sometimes there are empty seats or people pay just to stand in the aisles."

"I don't like them," Keely said. "I want to go inside. All those men look angry."

"We'll be inside in just a minute," Katie said. But she agreed with Keely. The people around the theater did look angry; yelling and gesturing at those going inside. She heard Macready's name several times, and garbled phrases about rights and patriotism. She gave a slight shudder, and gratefully approached the doors of the Astor Place Opera House. However, she was not at all grateful for the manner in which she was propelled through the entrance. At the strike of seven, a huge surge in the crowd came as the doors opened. Katie and Keely were carried into the theater, upon a human tidal wave of people determined to get inside.

Katie's shawl was falling off one shoulder and she had all she could do to keep Keely by her side. She was flustered and angry by the time they were in the lobby of the theater. She turned to a man standing next to them, straightening his own disarrayed clothes. "Is it always such a hazardous adventure to go to the theater here?"

The man looked crossly back toward the doors. "No—it is that mob out there. The police should disperse them. They want nothing but trouble."

"Why should they care about a theater performance?" Katie asked.

The man looked at her in surprise. "You must not be from the city, or you would know that this performance has been made into quite a controversy, being extended to parallel the battles between this country and Britain. It is all quite ridiculous, but then most of the causes that catch the ear of the mob are ridiculous."

Katie looked worried and disappointed. "Oh, I so wanted this to be a special evening for my daughter. It was to be her birthday celebration. But perhaps we should go home with all this going on."

"Oh, no, don't let them dismay you. I am certain the police will be here at any moment and clear these ruffians away. You will see an outstanding performance tonight. Enjoy it, and forget what is going on outside. I can assure you that I am going to."

Katie glanced at the doors. She could hear the shouting outside and some people were pounding on the theater. Surely the man was correct. The city authorities would not permit that to continue. And she wasn't at all certain she wanted to risk leaving the theater and having to get through that mob to return home. Keely was clinging to her, and Katie gave the child a reassuring squeeze. Deciding the police would take care of what was happening outside, she moved forward to be guided to their seats. Once they were seated, the magic of the theater and of all the elegantly dressed people reestablished itself. The theater was beautiful, and Keely was fascinated by its impressive dome. The sounds from outside could barely be heard from where they sat. The other patrons seemed oblivious to the mob outside, and were chatting happily, some debating the comparative talents of the much touted Macready and the equally touted American Edwin Forrest, who had been booed in London.

Katie turned to Keely and smiled. "New York is a very different kind of place, I think, Keely. We will have to get used to it. But I like it, don't you?"

"It's awfully noisy," she said, then lost interest as she pointed, then remembered it was impolite to point, at a

woman in a white satin gown standing farther down the
aisle.

Katie looked at the woman and felt a sharp pang of loss.
For so long she had worn nothing but white. She had come
to think of it as her own color. She felt the sharp sting of
jealousy as she looked at the woman.

"She looks like you, Mama," Keely said.

"Do you think so?" Katie asked weakly.

"You're prettier," Keely added.

Katie squeezed her hand, and then she saw the first of
the policemen and she began to relax. Apparently the man
she had spoken to knew what he was talking about. She
wasn't certain what was happening outside, but at least the
police were here to quell anything that might have happened. Soon she saw others and realized they were stationed throughout the house.

"It won't be long now," she said, and as the time for the
curtain to rise came nearer, her own excitement rose.

When the house lights dimmed and the curtain finally
did rise, she was as alarmed as she had been upon entering
the theater. Macready wasn't on the stage, and not due
until the third scene, but the audience went mad. Many of
them jumped up out of the seats and the whole theater
vibrated with hisses and hoots, stamping feet, cheers, and
groans. As the din continued, the police moved in along
the aisles, taking several of the shouters and pulling them
to an apartment situated underneath the boxes.

Bravely, Mr. Clarke, appearing as Malcolm, came on
stage. The audience shouted and cheered again. However,
this time it was a positive response, and Katie nervously
and almost timidly clapped her own approval.

The rioters were still having their say, however, and little could be heard of what was going on on the stage.
Keely was terrified and clutching frantically to Katie's
sleeve.

"I want to go home, Mama," she whispered in Katie's ear, her voice quivering with fright. "Can we go home?"

Katie didn't know what to do. It seemed that everyone who moved from their seats was being taken away by the police, but, on the other hand, she didn't know how to find out if it was safe to venture out of the theater other than by asking a policeman.

The actors on stage were doing a remarkable job, going on with the performance as if the audience were as quiet and attentive as ever. At least, it seemed to Katie they were. She could see their actions, but for all she knew they were speaking gibberish—nothing could be heard over the racket the tormentors kept up.

In the third scene, Macready, playing Macbeth to Mrs. Coleman Pope's Lady Macbeth, came out on stage to a storm of cheers and hisses. Most of the audience seemed to be friendly to Macready, cheering or waving hats and handkerchiefs in the air. Those who had come to start trouble, however caused a tremendous uproar that was truly frightening.

Keely was now crying and Katie immobilized with indecision and fear. She didn't dare try to leave their seats now. She had no idea of what might happen. Nearly everybody in the theater was on his feet, but Katie and Keely remained seated, huddled together against the noise and disturbance.

The tumultuous disorder lasted minute after minute until it seemed hours rather than the fifteen minutes it went on. No one knew quite what to do until finally a man brought a sign on the stage on which was written: "The friends of order will remain quiet."

Amazingly most of those in the theater responded to the sign and sat down quietly. Only those bent on disrupting any performance given by Macready continued the din.

Katie took advantage of the curtain coming down after the first act and quickly moved into the aisle, with Keely trailing behind. She sought out the first policeman she saw. "My little girl is terrified, sir, and so am I. Is it safe for us to leave the theater?"

"There's a riot out there, missus. You go back to your seat and stay there."

"Is there no one who could escort us out of the theater and to safety?" Katie asked, not willing to be put off.

The man fixed angry eyes on her. "I said, there is a riot out there. We need every man and more to handle what we have now. We have no one to escort ladies and their little girls anywhere. Now sit down, before I take it in my mind to let you sit with the other rioters in the room over there."

Katie's temper sizzled, but she knew better than to antagonize him further. She took Keely's hand and they returned to their seats.

Michael and Finn had returned from their fishing excursion to Dandy Point at quarter past six, and Garry was hopping with impatience. Even Eileen seemed anxious for their arrival.

Garry said, "Hurry up. We are going to be the last ones there. We'll miss out on everything."

"Don't you want to see our catch?" Finn said.

"Oh, yes, I do, Finn, but not just now," Eileen said, uncharacteristically curt. She always had time for Finn's triumphs. "Just now I want you to wash your face and put on a clean shirt. You look like a little street ruffian." She gave him a pat on his back and sent him off, pouting a bit and looking over his shoulder to Michael.

"He's very proud of the fish he caught," Michael said.

"The fish will wait, Michael. You did put them in water?" Eileen asked, then went on. "Do hurry and wash up. I don't want to miss seeing the arrival of the carriages. I wouldn't be at all surprised if I saw some of my own handiwork on those fine ladies."

"Why don't you and Garry go on ahead. Finn and I will catch up later."

"No, you don't," Garry said. "I know you—you won't come. And we are going to celebrate tonight. We're all going to see the doings at the theater and then eat in a fine restaurant. It isn't that long before Eileen and I will be leaving, and we are going to have our last grand night in this grand city."

Michael spread his arms in a gesture of helplessness. He grinned at Eileen, saying, "If you are going to put it to me that way, how can I help myself. I wouldn't miss that kind of celebration for all the world."

It was nearly eight o'clock by the time they walked from Bowery to Astor Place, but they could hear the mob long before they saw it.

Michael looked at Garry. "What is this supposed to be, Garry? It sounds like a riot. I thought you said there were going to be speeches."

Garry began to walk faster, dragging Eileen by the hand at his long strided pace. Finn was excited and hopped alongside of the men, dancing out in front of them from time to time.

"Did you know it was going to be like this?" Michael asked again as they came in view of the throng of shouting people. The lower level of the theater could not even be seen for the mass of people assaulting it.

"Something must have happened," Garry said. "I thought it was just to be a gathering so folks could air their views about British rule and a few other things."

"The police are in good supply . . . but they don't look very effective, do they? What do you suppose caused all this?" Michael said.

"I don't know, but I'm sure going to find out." Garry plunged into the rear line of onlookers and pushed his way nearer to the theater, Eileen was forced to follow, and Michael and Finn trailed behind.

For the most part, it was rather a jovial crowd. Most people were having a good time venting their anger and frustration against all that the British represented to them by pounding on the doors of the theater where Britain's finest actor was performing. It would have been quite benign, and perhaps amusing, Michael thought, if there had not been so many of them. But he had seen too many bottles being passed among the revelers and too many were high spirited enough to cause real trouble—at least in the eyes of the police.

The crowd pushed them over to the edge of the street, where there were piles of paving stones and an excavation where a sewer line was being put in. Michael flexed his arm and Finn grabbed hold, to be swung lightly over the pile of stones. He loved it when Michael transported him in that manner and was always begging him to do it again.

Michael stilled Finn as he listened to a group of police standing together with one man shouting for order and for the crowd to disperse. Even Michael giving it all of his attention could not hear all that was said, and he doubted that more than a hundred or so had paid any attention. The crowd did not disperse. They ignored the directive with the same diligence with which they had been ignoring the police all evening. One of the policemen detached himself from the group and raced off on foot down the street in the direction of City Hall. He was probably to give a report, which would most likely result in still more policemen being sent to Astor Place. Michael chuckled. Before this was over, there would be as many blue uniforms in the crowd as there were citizens. But in the back of his mind there was a small corner of reservation, for not only were the police at City Hall, it was from there the state militia and the national guard could be dispatched. He didn't really expect that. Even though the mob was large and very loud, they were not particularly disorderly unless pounding on the doors and sides of the theater building was considered a threat. He supposed it could be.

He stood tall, craning to see over the heads of those around him as he tried to locate Garry. It wasn't long before he saw him eight or nine people in front of where he and Finn were, his fists in the air, shouting for all he was worth. Michael pushed and shoved and excused himself until once more the four of them were together.

Garry was having a wonderful time. "Ever see anything like it?" he asked, grinning at Michael. "Old Macready will go back to England with a bee up his rump for sure. This is one night he'll never forget."

"He probably isn't aware of it. I doubt they can hear this inside."

"We've got people inside too," Garry said, having taken on the American Committee's cause as though it was his own even if he didn't understand what importance it might have.

"Well, it's my suggestion we go get something to eat, and if you want we can come back past here when the theater is letting out. If anything is going on we can join them then, when Macready is likely to realize what is happening out here."

"Oh, that performance is never going to be completed," Garry said. "I've heard that such a din is going to be raised in the theater that Macready will give up. And then you know they will try to sneak him out the back. That could happen at any time. We can't miss that."

Michael agreed that he didn't want to miss that.

Finn thought the whole thing wonderful. He could shout and yell with the best of them, and no one told him to be quiet. And when he wasn't yelling there were all the nicely shaped stones on the street to pick up, examine, and collect. His pockets were bulging and heavy with the stones and rocks already.

It was near ten o'clock when Garry whirled to face in

the direction of Broadway. He put his hand on Michael's shoulder to quiet him. "What's that I hear? Do you hear it? I wish these people would be quiet for just a minute."

As if they had heard him, the crowd did become considerably more quiet, the outer edges moving toward those in the very front.

With the noise lessened, the sound of horses coming up Broadway was unmistakable, and the message: "It's the cavalry. My God, they're sending in the First Division!"

But instead of striking fear and misgiving into the mob, it stirred their determination and sense of their right to be there.

"If they're going to run somebody out of here, let it be Macready!" someone behind Michael shouted.

"Run out the Brit!" became a chant that caught on with one segment of the mob.

Michael felt excitement crackling through the mob, an electricity that hadn't been there before the cavalry had been heard. He watched as he saw over the heads of others in front of him as a troop of horses turned from Broadway into Astor Place. They came at a steady pace, moving toward the crowd. Michael herded Finn, Garry, and Eileen nearer to the theater building and away from the path of the mounted troops. As the horsemen reached the edge of the crowd, and it was clear that they were going to ride straight through it regardless of who was in the road, the people picked up the paving stones that Finn had been playing with all night. The soldiers kept coming, but the stones rained down on them like a hail storm. From their bodies and their horses the stones ricocheted and bounced back to the road to be picked up and hurled again.

Finn watched openmouthed for a moment, then, when he saw Garry bend down and pick up a rock and heave it, he began to empty his pocket of his collection. With childish cries of joy, he heaved the rocks indiscriminately over the heads of those in front in the general direction of the cavalry.

A few minutes later the mob realized that the National Guard were present as well. Their mounted troops tried vainly to force a passage through the crushing mob to the theater. The enraged mob began to hiss, catcall, and hoot their derision. This was their town, their country, and their right to be here. The Guard should be after the Britisher, not them. They had a right to be there. Resentment and anger sparked all about and the stones were being hurled in earnest. Some of the missiles were far too large to be called stones now. The attack was so vehement, the troops were thrown into disarray. Breaking rank and having trouble with their mounts, they hastened back to Broadway in whatever fashion, and by whatever route they could.

At Broadway, they rallied and reformed ranks and made another futile attempt to reach the theater. Disgusted at being used as human battering rams without the right to defend themselves, the officer in command informed the sheriff, who was directing the operation, that if the Guard were not given leave to fire their weapons, they were going to leave the streets to the mob. "I'm not sending my men in there again to be stoned."

The sheriff hesitated. But when he saw that the commander meant exactly what he said, the idea of being left to handle this mob without the Guard forced his decision. "You may fire—but over their heads."

The order was quickly passed to the troops to fire the round over the heads of the crowd. Immediately, the fired muskets sounded sharp and thunderous over the shouting mob. The show of force did not still or cow the crowd at all. They heaved the paving stones at the troops with even greater fury, moving like a huge wave of enraged humanity toward the theater, and another block of them toward the troops.

Major General Sandford was rapidly becoming as irate

and heatedly righteous as the mob. He issued the order that the troops should fire into the crowd. Most of the men did not aim for anyone in the mass of people, but some did, and two men fell. One was shot in the arm and the other shot through his right cheek. People scurried to the aid of the fallen and got the man shot in the arm out of the mob and on his way to the hospital. The other man was dead.

Michael could hear moans from other parts of the crowd, but he saw no one fall. He wondered how many other than the two known had been hit. The crowd was milling and moving away from the immediate area of the theater a bit. The crush was so great that Michael, Finn, Eileen, and Garry could move only as far and fast as the mob allowed. Just as suddenly as the shots had come, the crowd changed direction and surged back toward the theater and the troops, carrying Michael and the others with them.

Urging each other to take up arms, shouts and whispers could be heard in every quarter of the mass of people. Another volley of shots were aimed into the crowd, and again Michael heard cries of pain and anger. He could see where several bent down, forming a depression in the sea of heads, and knew that at least one person had been shot, if not more.

He grabbed Garry's arm, pulling him close so that he could shout in his ear to be heard over the noise. "Do you know a way out of here?"

The National Guard and the First Division had blocked the street both at the Broadway side and the Bowery side. Behind them was the theater and in front of him was the mob—as well as all around them.

Garry shook his head. "We'd better just keep down and as distant as we can from those guns."

Major General Sandford issued orders for more troops to be brought to the scene and for two brass pieces loaded with grapeshot to be brought immediately. The troops succeeded in placing themselves in front of the theater. When the pieces were brought shortly, they, too, were placed in front of the theater aimed at the crowd. Major General Sandford was taking no more chances, for he had heard that the crowd was going to arm itself.

21

THE performance of *Macbeth* ended close to one o'clock in the morning, and those inside the theater were told that everything was being brought under control outside. A man came out on the stage and called for order and attention. "Everything is calming now, the National Guard is in control, so sit back and enjoy our afterpiece." He smiled broadly, and with a little bow he skipped, then slowed to a walk offstage.

Keely had her face buried in Katie's shawl as she had had for the past hour. Katie turned back a corner of the shawl and exposed one frightened blue eye. "We will be able to go home pretty soon, Keely. I think you can come out of hiding now—you might like the little play that is about to begin."

Still hanging on to the shawl, Keely turned her head toward the stage, one eye peeking over the soft material. Slowly she let the material drop to the level of her mouth with both eyes open as she began to be interested in the easily followed piece.

Moments later the audience was electrified as it sounded like the theater had been ripped open. A heavy round of musket fire was heard throughout the theater. At the same time, a man in the audience cried out, "The house is going to be blown up! They're blowing up the house! Run!"

Katie grabbed Keely and got to her feet as did all the other patrons. All were clambering and pushing to get into the aisles and out of the theater.

A well-dressed, important-looking man made his way to the stage. He stood there calling for attention. "Remain in your seats! Remain in your seats! There is no danger! There is no danger to the house!" He paused for a moment, then repeated the message. Calmly and with great authority, he kept reassuring those in the theater that there was no danger."

Slowly many of the people began to respond. The panic had gone, and some had even taken their seats, already talking about the troublemaker who dared shout such a thing in a crowded theater.

Order had barely begun to be restored when another voice cried out, "A man has been shot!"

The performance came to a standstill. No one could continue on this frightening night, and the audience was again pushing and shoving in a mad rush to get out of the theater. No one could gain their attention or cooperation this time. Katie clung to Keely, then, fearing she would be torn from her grasp, she picked the child up and carried her. She hadn't gone more than a dozen steps before she knew carrying Keely was not practical. Keely was too heavy for Katie to move surely with her in her arms. She was going to be knocked down by the crush of people.

"You have to walk, Keely, but hang on tight to my skirt, and I will hold your other hand. Remember, Keely! Don't let go. We can't be separated."

"Carry me! Mama!"

People in front of Katie screamed as a shower of rocks shattered one of the remaining windows in the front of the theater. Now she could see that the other windows had not only been knocked out, but while they had been watching the play and listening to reassurances, the police had been boarding the windows and doors against the conflict going on outside.

Bricks and paving stones crashed in and bounced on the lobby floor. People turned back in confusion, smashing into the ones coming after and then turning to run like geese in another direction. Katie and Keely were buffeted and pushed first one way then another, Katie merely trying to keep her balance and not lose her hold on Keely. Police and workmen were frantically replacing boards in windows, until the lobby looked like a fortress, and it did indeed feel as though they were under siege.

Keely was screaming in one long continuous howl by this time, and Katie was frantic, tears running down her own face, for she didn't know what to do or which way to go.

She tried to make her way back to the parquet. The crowd was not so heavy there for everyone was trying to get out, and slowly the pack was thinning. She looked up at the stage in time to see Macready in disguise with some of his friends coming over the stage to mingle with the audience and find their way out. She asked one of the men with Macready if the stage door was blocked.

"They won't let you pass," he said. "If they won't let him through"—he indicated Macready—"you aren't going to get through."

"But I have to get to safety—I have this child to think of."

"Lady, there is nothing anyone can do for you. That's bedlam out there, and you'll have to take your chances like everyone else. But I wouldn't stay in here. You never know when one of those hotheads will take it in his head to really blow this place up. They want Macready's blood, and God knows what they'll try."

"Come on, now—hurry up!" One of his companions called. The man quickly left Katie and ran to catch up with Macready and the others. He called back. "Get out of here, lady—you're better off taking your chances."

Katie shivered. The idea of going back into that rock-throwing, howling mob made her sick with fear. She looked around her and the parquet was empty. With the hideous sounds of the mob all around, the comparative empty silence was eerie and equally frightening. She began to imagine all sorts of furtive noises. Certain someone was hiding in there, probably to blow it up, she was propelled into action. With a sobbing Keely in tow, she ran back up the aisles and plunged into the crowd, once more being shoved and pushed toward one of the exits.

Once outside, the confusion was worse, for there were the citizen's mob and the people from the theater, the National Guard, and the militia pushing through everywhere in an effort to break up the crowd. Musket fire would energize a group of people and start them running, carrying with them anyone in their path. A shot from the other direction would bring another wave of people coming back into the swell of the first wave. People fell to the pavement wounded or simply toppled, to be trampled or scramble back to their feet and run again.

Katie decided she had to gain some kind of control over what was happening to her or she would never get out of the mob. She glanced toward the Bowery and the mass of people and troops looked impenetrable. The Broadway side looked nearly as bad, but she was a bit closer and decided it was her best chance of finally getting free of the crush of people. She yelled at Keely, but had no idea if the child heard or understood what was being said to her. Keely looked like a wide-eyed, terrorized urchin. She was no longer screaming or crying. She was no more than a rag doll being dragged along by Katie. Once more, she bent to pick the little girl up to try to carry her again. Her shawl was torn from her shoulders and she let it fall. A woman pushed past them, and Katie staggered forward, falling

into a man and catching her balance only because he had
held her up long enough for her to regain her footing.

Katie tramped along a few more yards with Keely in her
arms, her eyes fixed on the intersection of Broadway and
Astor Place. Her dress was torn and her hair was hanging
down in her eyes. Her chest was like fire, she was so out of
breath and labored from carrying Keely. But she staggered
on, determined to get them out of the mad, constantly
moving crowds. Muskets cracked around her and she
heard someone scream. With a suddenness and a force that
stunned her, a block of people turned and ran back toward
the theater from Broadway, with five cavalrymen after
them, their horses butting into the people and shoving
them out of the way.

Katie didn't have a chance to turn or run to the side.
She was pushed one way, then the other. Without even
knowing what had happened to her, she was face down on
the stone-strewn street, Keely torn from her arms. She
tried to get up, and each time she was bumped to the
ground. A horseman came so near to her head she could
see the sparks the horse's hooves made on the paving
stone. She didn't move, her hands covering her head.
When the horseman had passed, she got to her feet and
looked around for Keely. She couldn't see her. Certain that
the child had been thrown to the ground and was perhaps
injured, Katie shoved people aside like a madwoman,
shouting, "Keely! Keely! Answer me! Keely!"

Michael, Garry, Eileen, and Finn had managed to stay
close together through all the confusion, but they had not
gotten out of the riot. They began to move slowly and
cautiously toward Broadway, which seemed to offer the
greatest promise of an escape route. They had just gotten
to a point where they thought they could move more rapidly, when Michael noticed a tightly drawn gathering of
forty or so people standing near the side of the road. By

their feet was a pile of rocks and not twenty feet from them were five cavalrymen. Without explaining his action, Michael pushed Garry, Eileen, and Finn to the opposite side of the road as close to the buildings as he could get.

Garry gave him a shove back. "What in the hell are you doing?" he grumbled.

Michael pointed at the group of people and the rocks now being hurled at the horsemen. As they stood there and watched, the cavalrymen charged forward, pushing into the crowd. From behind the troublemakers a large mass of people were coming from the theater toward Broadway. Unaware of what was happening ahead of them, they moved right into the line the cavalrymen were taking in order to break up the group of rock hurlers.

Before Michael knew what was happening, Finn broke away from his grasp and scampered across the road through the crush of screaming people and horses. Though Michael tried to follow him and keep him in sight, he was quickly lost from view. Michael pushed and shoved, throwing people to the side without bothering to think of consequences. He shouted Finn's name, his attention still focused on the last spot he had seen Finn. Anger and fright mingled as he cursed himself for letting the boy go. Why had he run off, he wondered? All night long he had stayed right with them. Why would he do such a foolhardy thing?

As people scattered and the crowd thinned a bit, Michael heard a piping voice yelling, "Donovan! Donovan!"

"Finn?" Michael called, and tried to head in the direction of the sound. Crouched down by the pile of rocks the people had been throwing, Michael saw a small huddled form that was Finn. With him was an even smaller form. Without questioning or pausing, Michael swept both children into his arms and raced back across the street to where Garry and Eileen waited. Taking advantage of the confusion and the movement of people away from them, the five of them raced for Broadway and safety from the mob.

Michael didn't even consider that he might be taking the child Finn had found away from her parents. All he had on his mind was being clear of the danger. Once the noise and the riot were behind them, they headed back to the apartment. Eileen all but fell through the door. She had a gash on her face from where a rock had hit her, and her dress was in tatters, the hem covered with filth and smelling like something out of a dung heap. She hurried to her room and changed, as did the others. Only Finn remained with the little girl. The two of them sat side by side on straight-backed chairs, exhausted and staring. Neither spoke a word. The little girl's hands were in her lap. She moved one of them slightly. Finn watched from the corner of his eye, then he reached over and took it in his equally dirty hand. They continued to sit in silence, not looking at each other.

Eileen was the first to come back into the kitchen. She looked at the two children and wrinkled her nose against the terrible street odor that hung about them. "Go with Donovan and see what he can do about getting the slime off of you," she said to Finn. "I'll see what I can do for your little friend."

"She's scared," Finn said. "I think I better stay with her."

"You get! Go! Right now to Donovan."

The little girl's eyes followed Eileen as she moved about the room taking water from a pail and setting it on the warm stove. She said nothing.

Eileen turned to see Finn standing stubbornly next to the little girl. "Young man, if you don't get yourself into that room in the next minute you are going to feel my wooden spoon on your backside! You can sit with her all you want just as soon as you get that stink off you and some clean clothes on."

Finn looked at the little girl. "I'll be right back, I promise," he said, his face only inches from hers.

She blinked beautiful blue violet eyes at him twice, slowly, but in no way did she otherwise indicate that it mattered to her or that she knew what he had said.

Katie screamed Keely's name until she had no voice left. Frantically she ran up and down the street looking for the child. The area was now rapidly clearing of people, the only ones remaining being the troops of the National Guard and the militia. Katie walked up one side of each of the three streets, Broadway, Astor Place, and the Bowery, hunting and calling for Keely. Even among the small clusters of people moving slowly because they were aiding injured, she could not find Keely.

She finally went to one of the Guardsmen, explaining that she and her daughter had been in the theater and caught by the riot when they had come out. "She was torn from my grasp, and now I can't find her," Katie said in little more than a rasping whisper. "Have you found any children? Would your men take her to safety?"

"We have found no children, missus. I suggest you go home and get off the streets. Tomorrow you can ask at the hospital or the orphanage."

"I must find her tonight! She's only five years old. She's terrified."

The man frowned at her. No one had patience left on this night. "What did you bring her into a thing like this for?"

Katie looked at him, then turned away to continue her wandering. She stopped before another Guardsman and asked him the same question. He knew nothing of a child being found. He suggested she get off the streets and go home. Over and over Katie asked for help and got the same unhelpful responses.

Finally even the Guards and the militia abandoned the

streets. No one was left but Katie, wandering up one street and down the other calling Keely's name. Dawn was beginning to lighten the sky before she gave up in exhaustion, knowing that Keely was not anywhere in the vicinity of the theater. There was not a street nor a building, nor alley, nor yard through which she had not searched.

Michael got Finn into reasonably clean condition. He gathered all the clothes each of them had worn that night and threw them into the garbage out back. The garments were so badly torn and stained that they were past saving. He returned to the kitchen to see Finn sitting on the chair next to the little girl again, her hand in his. He glanced over at Eileen.

"He's taking care of her," she said quietly. "I tried to clean her up a bit, but that gown is hopeless. You don't suppose she could put one of Finn's shirts and a pair of pants on, do you? She's so tiny, I don't think I can even cut something of mine down to fit her."

"I'll get something for her," he said in a strangely distracted voice. The little girl was haunting. Had she not been so healthy and well fed, she would have reminded him of Keely. "Has she said who she is . . . or where she lives?"

"No, but that dress is a good one. Someone is going to be looking for her—you can count on that—and I just hope they are grateful to us for saving her and not thinking that we stole her."

"Has she said who she is?" Michael repeated.

Eileen looked at the child. "She hasn't said a word. She just sits there and stares. I'm not sure she can talk. Maybe something is wrong with her."

Michael's heart twisted. He wanted the child to be Keely. Why couldn't she be? He quickly figured how old his daughter would be now and was surprised when he came up with five. When he had last seen her she had just turned three, and she had been so starved and wizened, she had seemed little more than an infant. But she hadn't been able to talk either, and she had had such beautiful eyes as this child had. From time to time he felt her eyes on him, but as soon as he would look at her, she would look away or lower her eyes.

He walked from the room and went to the bedroom to root through Finn's cast-off clothing, hunting for something small enough for the girl. He sighed. If the child didn't talk soon, it was going to be near impossible to find her parents. He hardly knew where to begin, except that he could tell by her clothes that it wasn't likely she lived in Five Points or any of the other tenement districts of the newcomers. This child was well fed and well dressed—well cared for. He wondered what would happen if he couldn't find her family and then was ashamed at the joy that thought gave him. He was beginning to think he wanted Keely with such a desperation that he was beginning to steal other people's children. When he thought about it, what had he done with Finn? He had never even talked to the Flemmings about taking the child. He had just done it —and no one had cared enough about the boy to come after him. Now he was wishing that this little girl's family could not be found. Eileen had said she hoped that they didn't think the child had been stolen rather than rescued. He wondered if she realized how strong a possibility his stealing this child was? But Eileen didn't know Keely—she couldn't possibly realize how much this child made him think of his daughter and how much she stirred his imagination. Keely might have looked like this child if she had not been starved by the famine and all the terrible things that had come after.

He returned to the kitchen with the clothing and handed it to Eileen.

Eileen took them in her hand, but cocked her head toward the children. "You were a bit slow. We won't be needing these. I'll bundle her up in one of my night-dresses."

The little girl and Finn were slumped against each other, sound asleep on the chairs.

Michael picked the child up, and as if she were accustomed to being carried in her sleep, she wrapped her small arms around his neck. Michael felt tears prickling behind his eyelids. He took her into Eileen's bedroom and laid her on the bed. Quickly he brushed away the tears before Eileen could see and returned to the kitchen to get Finn. He carried the sleeping boy into his own room and placed him on the small cot they had gotten for him. In his mind, however, there was the picture of the little girl. Perhaps she was Keely. Perhaps Katie had lost her or something had happened to Katie. The child might have been put in an orphanage and then adopted. He thought of the distance between New York and Canada and then pushed logic out of his mind. He wanted her to be Keely. He wanted his search to be over. Around his neck he could still feel the impression of her warm child's arms. He could still feel the feathery softness of her breath against his cheek.

He sat by the window, staring out at the darkness as it was slowly being conquered by the dawn. Occasionally he would hear the sound of a human voice. The lonely sounds of people yelling or crying in the nearly deserted streets were almost as desolate as Michael felt. Michael's spine tingled as he heard a piercing scream from inside the apartment. He crossed the room in two lunging strides. Without thinking, he threw open Eileen's bedroom door and saw the little girl sitting straight up in bed, her eyes wide in terror, screaming in great sobbing gasps. He wasn't even aware of Eileen as he shoved her aside and took the child in his arms. He held her close, rocking her back and forth. With his mind back in Ireland before a peat fire on the hearth in the West Room, he began to sing in a low soft voice.

After a few minutes, Eileen came and touched him on the shoulder. "She's asleep, Michael. She wasn't really awake to begin with. The child is exhausted. You can put her down now."

Reluctantly, Michael did as she asked and left the room, stopping at the door to take a last look at the little girl.

Eileen hugged herself as he closed the door behind him. She had always known he longed for his daughter, but never had she known how deeply he missed her. She had never seen a man so tender with a child before as Michael was with the girl. He was good with Finn, but this was different. She promised herself she would talk to Garry in the morning. They had to convince Michael to go west with them. He couldn't stay in New York, tearing himself apart hunting for a daughter he was never going to find. The sooner Michael accepted the idea that Keely was never coming back, the sooner he would begin healing the wound her loss had made. She lay down again, but she couldn't sleep, tired as she was. She could not forget the look on Donovan's face as he had sung to that child. It both warmed her and chilled her, for it had been such a raw and untamed love she had seen blazing from him.

She thought of her own father and wondered if there had ever been a time when he had felt about her the way Donovan did about his daughter. She thought not, but how she wished it had been so. A daughter's image in her father's eyes is a treasure beyond all value. She was annoyed at herself as tears slipped down the sides of her face. What use was it to cry now?

22

MICHAEL did not sleep all that night. Before anyone
else had arisen the next morning, he was up and out of the
apartment. He went straight to City Hall and waited for
someone to arrive so that he could get a message to Major
General Sandford. His best hope for finding the parents of
the little girl was to have someone inform the militia that a
child had been lost.

He had frightened himself last night with the strength of
his emotions, and he knew that the sooner he took the little
girl to her rightful guardians, the better off both he and the
child would be. He also realized he was going to have to do
something about finding Keely soon, or do as Garry had
been suggesting for months and accept the fact that she
was either dead or lost to him. He sat on the steps to the
building waiting and thinking and hoping that someone
would be able to tell him where the child should be taken.

Eileen awakened later than she could ever remember.
When she had finally drifted off, she had known the sleep
of the dead. Still feeling tired and disinclined to begin the
day, she rolled to her side and looked at the little girl. The
child had awakened twice more with nightmares, but Mi-

chael had not repeated his strange impassioned performance. She seemed to be sleeping peacefully enough now. Eileen debated with herself between wakening her and giving her something to eat before trying to find out who she was and letting her rest for as long as possible. She decided on the latter. For some reason she didn't really want to face the task of finding the child's parents—at least, not until she could talk to Garry about what had happened last night.

Finally she got up and dressed herself, and went to the kitchen just as Garry came in yawning and stretching.

She looked down the hall, then asked, "Is Michael up yet?"

"I haven't heard him, but I just woke up."

"Go look in his room. I want to talk to you about something that happened last night, but I want to be certain he is not going to overhear us."

He gave her a strange look, but he did as he was asked without questions. He came right back. "He's not even here. He must have gone out early this morning. I suppose he's after the little girl's family."

Eileen put her hand to her heart. "Oh, dear Lord, I hope so!" she said on a long expelled breath. "Sit down while I fix your breakfast, then listen to what I have to say." Hurriedly, she completed cooking fried eggs and a slab of ham, which she set out on two dishes. As soon as she sat down, she began telling Garry in detail all that had happened the night before.

"How did the child react to him?" Garry asked.

"Och! The child was never really awake. She was caught in a nightmare. It is himself I am worried about. We must find out who that child is and return her to her rightful place as quickly as possible. It's no good for him to have her around here." Eileen sat deep in thought, then said, "And then we must make Michael see that he must leave here. He cannot go on like this, Garry. I never realized before last night how much he yearns for that daughter of his."

"I have been telling you all along that we must convince Donovan to come to San Francisco with us. There is nothing here for him."

"I know. But you didn't realize this . . . did you?"

He gave her a knowing look, then glanced down at his eggs. "Not exactly, but what does that matter? I have always said that he should not stay behind after we leave. Now, tell me I haven't always said that!"

"I cannot," Eileen said. "You always have, and I'll be the first to give you credit. But what am I to do with the child?"

"Wake her up," Garry said simply. "Ask her what her name is."

"I asked her last night. She didn't say one word. I'm not certain she can speak."

"Well, you never will know if you sit here all day jawing at me. She's slept enough, and so has that little lazy bones Finn. Get those two out here, fill their bellies, and ask the child who she is. Then, if she still can't talk, we'll figure something else out."

Eileen got up and started toward the bedroom. Garry called after her. "It would be a blessed thing if we could get the little girl back in her rightful place before Donovan comes back. Then it would be over and he never need know who the child is. We could say that the parents came here."

Eileen nodded, then disappeared inside the bedroom. For a moment, she stood just inside the room watching the child. She was a beautiful little girl, and she wondered if she really did resemble Donovan's daughter. She walked over to the bed and sat down. Gently she shook the child's shoulder. With a start, the little girl's deep blue violet eyes flew open, and immediately Eileen read the confusion and fear there.

"It's all right," Eileen said quietly. "We are going to find your mama and your daddy today. You'll be home soon."

The child just stared at her.

"Can you say something to me, dear?" Eileen ran her finger along the side of her cheek. "Are you able to talk?"

The little girl watched her for a long time, then very slowly she nodded.

Eileen smiled. "Well, that is something. At least I know you understand. That is very good. Can you say your name for me?"

Again the little girl nodded, but she didn't speak.

Eileen laughed softly. "Is this a game we are playing? Shall I guess your name?"

She shook her head.

"Then you must say it for me. If you won't tell me who you are, then I can't find your mama and daddy. Will you please tell me?"

"Keely," she said.

The blood drained from Eileen's face and she felt light-headed. "Keely," she repeated in a thin voice. "Your name is Keely?" Her mind was racing. It had to be a coincidence. It was not possible that this was his child—not after all this time and not to be found on a night like last night. Eileen's voice was quivering when she asked, "What is your last name, Keely?"

"I am Keely Donovan," she said.

Eileen couldn't stand it. She got up off the bed and backed away from the child as though she were poison, then she ran from the room. "Garry! It's her! Garry!"

Garry had been outside the flat in the hall. He came running back inside. When he saw her disarray and the sheet whiteness of her face, he took her by the arms and sat her down. "What happened?"

"It's her. Holy Saints, bless us—it's Donovan's daughter herself. I asked her name and she says pretty as you please,

'Keely.' Keely what, I am asking, and the child says, 'I am Keely Donovan.' "

"She must have heard us say the name," Garry said. "It can't be."

"That's what I thought, but no child that young is going to be lying—even if she did hear the name. She can't be more than four or five."

"How old would Donovan's daughter be?"

"Five, I think. I'm not certain—maybe four."

Garry touched Eileen's shoulder, then walked to the bedroom. "What is your mother's name, little girl? Is it Katie?"

Keely nodded her head, but she wasn't speaking—she wasn't sure of Garry. He talked gruff, and she didn't know if he liked her or not. She wished the big tall man with the name like hers would come back.

Garry went back to the kitchen. "Get her dressed and give her some breakfast. She's probably hungry."

"What are we going to do? Do you think she really is his daughter?"

"I don't know. I have to think on this."

"It's the Lord's hand in this if it's her, Garry," Eileen said reverently.

Garry looked at her, but he said nothing. He walked to the door. "I'll be back in half an hour. I am going to walk for a spell by the river."

Eileen sat where she was. She still felt stunned.

Keely climbed out of the big bed and, holding great handfuls of Eileen's voluminous nightdress away from her feet, she padded out to the kitchen. "Is Mama here?" she asked.

Eileen started, then smiled as she saw the ludicrous figure of the tiny girl in the massive gown. "No, not yet, dear. Come along and sit while I make something good for you to eat. Are you hungry?"

"Yes, please. But I want to see my mama now, please."

"First some oatmeal, and then I want you to tell me just a little bit more. Do you know what street you live on?"

"We have a new home," Keely said brightly, and set to eating her oatmeal.

After a couple of interesting but uninformative answers, Eileen gathered that Keely and Katie had recently come to the city and that Keely did not know where her new home with the beautiful chairs was exactly. She sighed, then laughed softly. "We are going to have our work cut out for us. I bet your mama is real unhappy not knowing where you are."

"She fell down," Keely said with tears coming to her eyes. "Those big horses knocked her down and I got lost."

"I know, dear, I know. It was an awful time last night, but don't you think about that. We'll make it right, and we'll hunt and hunt until we find your mama. Don't you worry."

As Eileen said this last, the door to the flat opened and Michael walked in. His eyes immediately fell on the little girl, but then he looked away and thought to protect himself.

Keely looked up at him, her face animated, though still marked by circles of tiredness under her eyes. "Did you find my mama?" she asked.

Eileen looked from one of them to the other. "Michael, I think you had better sit down. It is important that you talk to . . . the child."

"Has she been able to tell you anything about herself yet?" he asked.

Eileen felt like she was choking. She knew that she should tell him, and she didn't know why she couldn't, but she was unable to. She got up and started from the room. She turned back. "Ask her to tell you her name." Before he could question her odd behavior, she was gone.

He stared after her, a perplexed frown on his face, but then he put it aside and smiled at the little girl. "Well, can you tell me your name. It is about time we got you back to where you belong."

She smiled at him. She liked this man. She remembered him picking her up last night, and she remembered him singing. She had liked that and it was very comfortable to her—something that made her feel good and warm. "I am Keely Donovan," she said clearly and proudly so that he would understand her, just as Katie had taught her to speak. Suddenly she felt frightened. Something was wrong with the man. Maybe he didn't like her name. His hands were shaking, and he was crying. Keely squirmed back in her chair, moving away from him.

Michael fought for control. He could see that he was frightening her, and he hardly dared believe what he had heard. How could this healthy, normal child be his Keely. He brought forth a picture in his mind of her as she had looked when he had last seen her. There was so little resemblance, except for her remarkable eyes and a certain familiarity he had credited to his own longing for her.

Finally able to speak without his voice breaking, he asked, "Do you remember your daddy, Keely?"

She shook her head, and after finishing a mouthful of oatmeal, she said matter-of-factly, "He got lost, just like I did. Mama looked and looked for him, but he is gone. Maybe he is in heaven now."

"What would you think if I told you he isn't in heaven?"

She shrugged her shoulders. "We can't find him. Mama looked and looked. She told me he isn't anywhere to be found. Tully wanted to be my daddy, but Mama said no."

Michael could barely stand sitting still talking to her in so casual a fashion. He wanted to grab her and hug her to him and tell her he was her father, but he dared not. He knew it was ridiculous to expect her to know him. She had only been two and a half years old when she had seen him last, and she had been ill and near starvation. It was a miracle that she was the healthy child he now saw before him. He dared not even contemplate the miracle that had brought her to this place. She thought she was lost, and only he knew she had been found.

"Would you like to find your daddy?"

She looked at him through thick dark lashes. "I really would like to find my mama," she said in very adult fashion. Then her eyes grew moist and teary, but she went on. "I am not permitted to be out by myself, you know, and Mama will be very worried . . . and I am very lonely." With that her face crumpled, and she began to cry hard.

Michael felt like someone had put his heart in a vise and had begun to squeeze. He reached out and took Keely's hand in his. "I think what we had better do is go find your mama right now. What do you think?"

She sniffed, and turned the deepest blue violet rays of trust on him that he had ever seen. She couldn't stop crying, so all she did was nod her head, then turn her face up to him as he wiped away her tears and helped her blow her nose.

Almost as if she had been eavesdropping, Eileen bustled back into the room bearing a pink cotton skirt. "You are going to find"—she looked at Michael almost with trepidation, for she wondered if he would ever forgive her for being so cowardly that she had not prepared him—"her mother?"

"We are," Michael said, but he was too filled with his own raging emotions to have given thought to anything Eileen might or might not have done.

"She will be needing this. It isn't much, but at least it will keep her decent. She can wear Finn's old pants for pantalettes . . . I didn't have time to make any of those . . . and she can wear one of his shirts for a blouse."

"Is Finn still asleep?" Michael asked.

"Yes, he has barely stirred. Do you think I should awaken him?"

"No, no, let him sleep. Last night was . . ." Michael

halted in confusion. He had been going to say it had been a horror, and yet it had brought his daughter back to him. He thought of Katie for the first time. And again he was barely able to contain the wave of emotion that shook him. She had to be terrified, and frantic. Keely had said she had looked and looked for him, and now Keely was missing, too. He stood up and said, "Get her dressed right away. We have no time to waste. Katie will be frightened."

Keely looked sharply at him. Eileen took her by the arm and began to lift her from the chair. Keely didn't want to leave the man. She pushed at Eileen's hands. "No! I want to stay."

Michael took her into his arms, and she clung to him like a small vine, Eileen's huge nightgown dragging about her and covering her hands. "I will dress her, Eileen."

Eileen looked shocked. "You'll do no such thing! It isn't decent!"

Michael's eyes blazed. "It isn't what? Who better than I?"

"But she doesn't know . . ."

"She knows! She just hasn't put it all together, but she knows!"

Eileen backed away from him in confusion. All of this was so very strange. She handed him the clothing she had been going to put on Keely, then retreated to her room. She wished Garry would return. She didn't know this Michael—this man was a stranger to her. His intensity was frightening.

Keely, however, wasn't afraid of him. She liked him, and she felt safe with him just like she did with Mama. She wished that he would sing to her, for she had liked that best of all. It gave her nice feelings and dreams like she had had a long time ago someplace else.

Michael's brain was racing as he tried to think how he would find Katie. He had tried to often before and always he had failed. He asked Keely about where she lived and got the same vague answers Eileen had. Apparently Katie and Keely had come to New York just a few days ago, and Keely did not know the name of their street. "It's a number street," she said. "A big number."

He wondered what a big number meant to her. He asked, "Is thirteen a big number?"

Her nose wrinkled as she thought about it. "Does thirteen come after eleven?"

Michael chuckled. "No, it comes after twelve."

"That's a big number," she said positively. "I can count to ten," she added.

They lived above tenth street, Michael thought. That left a lot of city. "What do you like best about your home, Keely?"

"Oh, our chairs!" she said happily.

Michael stifled his laughter this time. Those chairs were important. "What is the worst thing?"

Again she wrinkled up her nose and thought. "I can't understand what the lady next door says. She talks funny. Mama says she doesn't speak our language. But she gives me cookies sometimes."

This bit of information meant more to Michael than anything else Keely had said. It was just like Katie. She was still trying to rid herself of her Irishness and to avoid the pitfalls that brought with it. She had chosen a home where there were no Irish, even if the people were immigrants.

Finally he had her washed and dressed. She looked a bit peculiar with Finn's outgrown trousers peeking out from beneath her makeshift skirt, and the shirt that was too large for her as a blouse, but as Eileen had said, she was at least decent.

"Eileen, will you please tell Finn where I have gone when he awakens? I'll be back later this afternoon—after we've found Keely's Mama."

Eileen stared at him. "You haven't told her. Aren't you going to tell her?"

"When the time is right, I'll tell her."

Keely said nothing and did not even seem interested in what they were saying to each other, but when she and Michael were out on the street walking uptown, she asked, "Do you have a secret?"

He smiled down at her. "I have a secret."

"I am very good at keeping secrets," she said, but did not go so far as to ask him to tell her.

A little later, she asked, "Are we going to find Mama now?"

"We are going to try. You tell me when you see someplace you have seen before." Michael was trying to think of all the neighborhoods that were comprised of immigrants that were not Irish, a place where Katie would feel comfortable.

"Is she lost, too?" Keely asked.

"A little bit, but we will find her."

"Maybe we won't ever find her," Keely said, and looked up at him.

"Like your daddy?" he asked.

She nodded.

"What would you say if I told you we could find your daddy and your mama?"

She didn't say anything, but stared at him. "Are you my daddy?" she asked finally.

Michael smiled. "I am your daddy."

Keely smiled back and put her hand in his. With that small gesture, she accepted her father as her own just as though he had never been lost to her. Now she knew she was going to find Mama, too.

23

MICHAEL racked his brain, but came up with no clear idea of where to look for Keely's home. He had resigned himself to having to walk up and down every numbered street in the city until she saw something she recognized, when he thought of one other alternative. Questioning himself as to what he would do if it had been him who had lost Keely in the riot, he knew that he would haunt the area where he had last seen her. No matter how little sense it made, he knew he would go back over and over again wishing he could relive that moment and change it.

He turned from Broadway toward Astor Place. At first he thought he had been foolish to come here. Few people were around, and the street was covered with rubble and reminders of the night before. Keely didn't seem frightened, but he decided it had been a very bad idea bringing her here. He began walking faster, then picked Keely up so that he could get away from the theater as fast as he could. He was walking toward Bowery, when he heard a man shout, "Get away from here!" and poke at a rag woman with his walking stick. The woman staggered into the side of the building, then caught her balance. She was mud stained and her hair was hanging in her face. Then she looked at the man and asked in a hoarse, rasping voice, "Have you seen my little girl? Have you seen Keely?"

Keely's head whipped around and she cried, "Mama!"

Michael broke into a run, calling, "Katie! Katie!"

Katie's eyes were barely focused. She had not been asleep since the night before she had lost Keely. She had wandered through the streets ever since then searching for the little girl. She put her arms out to the child, then her eyes shifted to Michael. Her mouth formed the sound of the letter *M*, but she could go no further. Her eyes rolled up into her head and she slumped to the ground.

Keely cried, "Mama, Mama," over and over, pushing at Katie's shoulder as Michael knelt in the street, patting at her cheeks and chafing her wrists.

People walked around them, giving them a wide berth, some with unpleasant comments about the drunken Irish. All Michael could think was that he wanted to take her away as quickly as possible before someone called for a policeman. With both Keely and Katie, he wasn't entirely sure what to do. He comforted Keely first and got her to stop crying. "Mama is just asleep. She's very tired—she's been looking for you for a long time. We're going to take her home. Can you hold on to my hand while I carry Mama? I don't want you getting lost again."

Keely sniffed, then said she would hold on tight.

Michael fished in his pocket and counted the money he had with him. He would have enough for a cab, if he could find one willing to give passage to such an odd assortment of humanity as he and Katie and Keely. He prayed that he would find one, for it was a long walk home for a little girl and he knew he could not carry both of them. He started in the direction of the flat. He hailed five cabs before the sixth one agreed to take them, provided Michael show him money first.

Inside the cab, Michael once again tried to awaken Katie. She opened her eyes once for no more than a fraction of a second and fainted again. The driver stopped, demanding the rest of his money, and left as soon as Michael managed to get Katie out of the cab. He had told the man to stop three blocks away from the flat, for he was certain the cabbie was going to report to the police that Michael was running around the streets carrying a dead body. Katie certainly looked dead, and badly mauled. He put her over his shoulder again and, with Keely in tow, walked to the flat. He was breathing hard from the effort when he finally opened the door to the kitchen.

Eileen was busy over the stove when he entered, and, for a moment, he thought she was going to faint, too. Her soup pot clattered to the floor spewing hot broth all over. She put her hands to her face. "Sacred Heart of Jesus! Blessed Mary, Mother Virgin!" She swayed, then righted herself. "Katie?" she said.

"Help me," Michael said.

Finn came running into the kitchen. He took one look at Katie and yelled. "It's her! That's the lady who fell down!"

"That's my mama!" Keely yelled back at him.

"Is she dead?" Finn asked.

"Go outside and play!" Eileen shrieked, her head pounding with tension. "And don't beg! Stay there until I call you. Take her with you." As soon as the children moved to obey, Eileen changed her mind and grabbed Finn's arm. "Wait—where's Garry? Get Garry, and tell him to buy you ices."

Garry had been taking a nap and now grouchily stuck his head into the hallway to see why everyone was shouting. He saw Eileen going in six directions at once and Michael standing like a poleaxed dolt with a woman slung over his shoulder. Keely and Finn were chasing back and forth in wild confusion. "What the hell is going on here? Who's that?"

"Do something!" Eileen yelled. "Get the children ices."

"All right, all right! Is she dead?"

"No!" Eileen yelled—she didn't seem to be able to do anything else. She turned her frightened anger on Michael. "Don't just stand there—take her into the bedroom!"

Michael moved toward his own bedroom and Eileen shouted, "No, not there. Put her in my bedroom."

Michael stopped and looked at her for a moment, then he said, "No. This is where she belongs—this is where she will be."

That was more than Eileen could take. She walked back to the kitchen and knelt down in her spilled soup and began to scrub the floor.

Michael took Katie into the bedroom and laid her on his bed. He washed the grime from her face and hands, then undressed her. He picked up the nightgown of Eileen's that Keely had worn the night before and began to put it on her, then decided not to. He put her under the coverlet just as she was, then brushed her hair free of dirt and tangles. Katie was as limp as a rag, showing no sign of awakening. Only her regular breathing and the pulse at her neck told Michael she was alive. She was colorless, and the bruises of exhaustion marked her face.

With her hand in his he sat beside her on the bed and remembered how it had been with them, and all the promises they had made to one another. He no longer knew if those promises could be kept or if Katie would want them kept now. He touched the curve of her cheek and let his finger trace across the firm roundness of her lips. She moved slightly, and for a moment he thought he had seen the whisper of a smile. But it really didn't matter if the smile had been there or not, for just to have her near him was enough.

He had been sitting beside Katie for hours, marveling over what had happened to him. His daughter was with him again, and so was Katie. He had no deep thoughts for he was too filled with awe to do anything but feel and float on the joy of it.

It was dark when Eileen opened the door and peeked in. "The children are fed, Michael, and it's time they were in bed—they are very tired."

Michael just looked at her.

"What should I do?"

"Bring them to me, and we'll put them to bed."

"Both of them?"

"Of course, both of them."

Eileen pressed her lips together, but she didn't argue. She had known he was going to say that. She brought the two children into the room, Keely again swathed in one of her nightgowns—her only other one, and she hadn't dared to think of what she was going to sleep in that night. Finn hopped up onto his cot, and Keely stood waiting. She walked over to Katie and touched her face, then she looked at Michael.

"She's sleeping, Keely, but she is all right."

"Will she wake up in the morning?"

"I don't know. We'll have to wait and see. She will wake up when she isn't tired anymore."

He picked her up and put her at the other end of Finn's cot.

Eileen rolled her eyes heavenward. She still couldn't get it in her head that these four were a family. It seemed to her as though two strangers had just come in, and Michael kept putting more and more people in his bedroom. It didn't seem decent, but then she couldn't think where else they all belonged. Keely was his daughter, and if Katie wasn't his wife, she didn't know what a wife was. Michael settled the children, telling them a story, and then he sat back and in a low voice sang as he had sung to Keely when she was just a tiny child.

Keely's eyes were heavy and her mouth was turned up in a smile. She couldn't look at Michael and see Daddy, for she had never really known him when she was old enough or well enough to know him. But this voice singing in the

darkness behind her closed eyes—that was her Daddy—
and every part of her knew that man and that love.

Michael looked at the three people in this room whom
he loved. All were sleeping, and all were safe. He looked
long at Katie and wondered if she would awaken. He
thought she would not, so he undressed and got into the
bed beside her. Her skin was warm and silky next to his.
He wanted to run his hands over her, to awaken her with
kisses, and speak to her of all the feelings he thought had
died in his heart almost two years ago. But they hadn't
died. None of the longings or the desires had died, they
had only been waiting for the time of their spring. Michael
now knew that no matter how long or how hard were the
winters of the heart, there was always a spring, for that
was God's way.

It was a long time before he could bring himself to sleep,
his mind churning with thoughts of Katie. His body ached
to touch her, but he would not until he saw in her eyes that
she still wanted the promises they had made to be kept.

Gray dawn was just beginning to shred the night when
Katie opened her eyes. She was completely disoriented, not
being able to sort dream from reality. She knew she did not
recognize the room she was in, but then she thought she
was with the troupe and they were in another hotel in
some nameless city. Then she thought about the riot, but
she wasn't certain that hadn't been a nightmare. Had she
really lost Keely? As she tried to think she fell asleep
again, moving closer to the warmth of the man beside her.
She thought nothing of his closeness, just that it made her
feel safe. She awakened about fifteen minutes later. She had
lost Keely! She was caught in a riot! With a panicky feeling
coursing through her she got out of the bed. Two things
happened at once. She realized she was naked, and she saw
Keely asleep in the cot beside her—and there was another
child with her. She staggered, and fell back on the bed, and
touched the man. She jumped away from him, and then

nearly fainted again. He was Michael! He certainly looked like Michael. She was shaking like a leaf in a gale. Her teeth were clenched tight and still they were chattering so hard they hurt. She was afraid to move. She could not grasp what was happening. Maybe they were all dead, or maybe this was all a dream. She dared not touch Keely, because she might not really be there, and she couldn't touch Michael, because she *knew* he couldn't be there, and she had no idea who the other child was.

She sat back on her spine, her knees drawn up, and her arms wrapped tightly around them. She was cold and cramped and everything ached, but she wouldn't move.

Michael moved and rolled over in his sleep. His arm flung across the spot where Katie had been sleeping. She watched in petrified fascination. He moved again and then he frowned. She tried to shut her eyes, but they stayed wide open and staring. This was the cruelest of all the things that had happened to her. She knew he couldn't be real, yet she could not rid herself of the ghost. She was going mad. She knew that, and she couldn't help herself. All she could do was sit there and hold on to her knees and watch the tantalizing apparition of Michael.

He moved again, and then he opened his eyes. Katie stopped breathing. She stared at him glassy-eyed, holding her breath.

"Katie," he whispered.

Katie didn't move. Involuntarily she was forced to take a breath, and it sounded like a hiccoughing sob.

Michael propped himself up on one elbow. He put his hand out to touch her and Katie's eyes grew wider than ever. He touched her and his touch was warm. Katie's eyes closed, and she rolled over to the side, unconscious again.

Michael sat up and grabbed her before she rolled off the bed. This time he was not content to let her sleep. He pulled her to him. Her head lolled back, and he put one large hand under her head and brought her up against him.

He called her name and patted at her cheek until he had made her skin pink beneath his hand. "Damn it, Katie— you're going to wake up!"

Katie did not make a move or show any signs of listening to him. Michael tried to think what could penetrate whatever place she had gone to hide herself. He got up, pulled on his trousers, and left the room. Barefoot and shirtless, he walked out of the house and down the street to the greengrocer. Without a thought, he threw a brick through the window, climbed in, and stole half a dozen limes. He ran all the way back to the flat, raced up the two flights and into the kitchen. He poured water into the basin, sliced the limes and squeezed them into the water. He raced back to his bedroom, pulled the coverlet from Katie, and began to bathe her in the warm fragrant water. Quickly the whole apartment smelled of limes. Michael bathed her over and over, saying to her, *"Ta se ina shamhradh."* He no longer held back, kissing her face as he reminded her of their promise of everlasting summer of love. *"Ta se ina shamhradh,* Katie."

Katie awakened, but she didn't open her eyes. Now she knew she was dead. She was back on the ship, sheltered behind the tattered blanket, and the stolen limes were filling the air. At least death was nice. She liked having Michael kiss her again. She remained motionless for a moment, then she began to return his kisses, and her arms just seemed naturally to find their way around his neck. Katie stayed still for what seemed to her a long time, then she whispered, "Michael? Are you alive?"

He buried his face in her neck for a moment, then he said, "I'm alive, Katie. So are you, and so is Keely. We're all here—we're all at home again."

Katie trembled in his arms. He could feel her tears. He kissed them away. "Am I awake?" she asked.

"You are," Michael said.

"Hold me."

"I am holding you," he said, amusement lightening his voice. Then he added, "After you have rested, we have many things to talk about."

"I am afraid to sleep. You won't be here when I awaken. I know you'll be gone again, and I won't be able to find you."

"But I am here, Katie, and here it is I will stay, if it is what you want. I have been searching for you, too."

"Were you in that hospital in Montreal?" she asked.

"For a long time," Michael answered.

Katie let her eyes close for a moment, and her voice was heavy with sleep. "I knew you were. I kept telling them I could find you if they would just let me in, but no one would."

"Let go of it, Katie. Go to sleep. I will be here when you awaken, and so will Keely."

"She wasn't hurt?"

"No, not at all. A couple of scratches and a bruise or two, but she is fine and well."

"Isn't she beautiful, Michael?" Katie slurred.

Michael kissed her eyes again. "Go to sleep, Katie—go to sleep so that we will have tomorrow for ourselves. We have so many things to do—and a long, long line of days to do them in."

Katie wiggled closer to him and finally closed her eyes and fell asleep. Michael soon followed suit. It had been a brutal two days for all of them, and exhaustion rode them like spent horses.

Eileen was awake and up early. She had done very little sleeping last night. Her mind would not rest as she tried to sort out all the peculiar events that had happened in the last two days. She shook her head in disbelief as she reviewed it once more as she dressed. She had been in a riot, and a child had been found, Michael's daughter, and then Katie had come into their lives. It was as if a hurricane had passed through their lives and blown everything up into the air. But, she reflected with an amazing lift of spirits, it had not been destructive, for it had blown everything back the way it was supposed to be. She thought of all the hours Michael had spent walking the streets and talking to anyone who might have had any knowledge of Katie and Keely. He had never found out a single thing that was of any help. And then, in that one frightening night, a night when twenty-two people had died and an unknown number had been wounded or injured, they were all back together again.

Michael and Katie would have much sorting of information and feelings ahead of them, but Eileen knew, even if they were not aware of it yet, that nothing would ever part them again. Their love for Keely would never allow it. Where Keely was, Michael would be, and where Keely was, Katie would be. And she had watched Finn as well. He, too, was captivated by Keely. A little child, she thought, such a little child. She was still shaking her head in wonderment when she went into the kitchen. She stopped at the doorway and looked openmouthed into the room.

"What in heaven's name?" She bent down and picked up the peel of a lime. Then she saw another and another. They were scattered everywhere. "I thought I was dreaming . . ." she murmured as she recalled awakening in the night to what she thought was the smell of limes. She began to laugh. "What are they up to now?" she asked herself. For some reason the oddity of this was making her feel better. She was beginning to think of these peculiar things as normal, and she had the idea that with Katie and Michael they *were* normal. And then, with laughter bubbling from her, she realized one more thing. She and Garry were just as tied to this Donovan family as they were to each other. They would be together for a long, long time, and the thought made her very happy.